Say It's Forever

NEW YORK TIMES BESTSELLING AUTHOR

A.L. JACKSON

First Edition

A.L. Jackson
www.aljacksonauthor.com

Cover Design by RBA Designs
Image by Michelle Lancaster Photography
Editing by Stylistic Editing
Proofreading by Julia Griffis, The Romance Bibliophile
Formatting by Champagne Book Design

Print ISBN: 978-1-946420-57-2

More from

A.L. Jackson

NEW YORK TIMES BESTSELLING AUTHOR

Redemption Hills

Give Me a Reason

Say It's Forever

Never Look Back – coming 2022

Promise Me Always – coming 2023

The Falling Stars Series

Kiss the Stars

Catch Me When I Fall

Falling into You

Beneath the Stars

Confessions of the Heart

More of You

All of Me

Pieces of Us

Fight for Me

Show Me the Way

Follow Me Back

Lead Me Home

Hold on to Hope

Bleeding Stars

A Stone in the Sea

Drowning to Breathe

Where Lightning Strikes

Wait

Stay

Stand

The Regret Series

Lost to You

Take This Regret

If Forever Comes

The Closer to You Series

Come to Me Quietly

Come to Me Softly

Come to Me Recklessly

Stand-Alone Novels

Pulled

When We Collide

Hollywood Chronicles, a collaboration with *USA Today* Bestselling Author, Rebecca Shea

One Wild Night

One Wild Ride

Say It's Forever

Chapter One

Jud

IT WAS JUST BEFORE TEN WHEN I SLOWED MY BIKE AND MADE a right onto Dawson.

Darkness had long descended on the small, mountain city, but a storm had rolled in, and the sky pounded its fury on Redemption Hills, California.

"Shit," I grumbled under my breath when I saw the red blinking lights up ahead. The last thing I wanted was to play savior right then. I was soaked through, and I was itching to get back so I could peel the drenched clothes from my body, hit a hot shower, and maybe kick back a beer or two considering I'd picked a really fuckin' bad night for a joyride.

But the storm had hit from out of nowhere, and I'd been halfway back to my place before I'd realized I was about to get slammed.

I slowed my Harley, barely moving as I passed the car, hoping it had been abandoned for better weather.

No such luck. The hood was open and…shit…there was a woman leaned over the front peering down at the engine.

I groaned out a sigh and eased to a stop about fifty feet in front of the car.

I could keep on going, but that would be a dick move. On this side of town, it was industrial, most every shop closed and locked up tight, and I knew full well the only ones out prowling at this time of night were hunting for trouble. Out looking for targets to unleash their sickness and depravity.

I figured the pile of sins I was paying for was high enough not to add leaving some chick stranded in the rain to the top.

Besides, it wasn't like metal and oil weren't in my blood. It was what I did.

Kicking the stand, I killed the engine and swung off the bike. I dug into the saddle bag, pulled out a flashlight, and clicked it on. The beam glittered through the flood pouring from the sky. My boots were heavy, sloshing through the river that ran the curb as I strode that way.

The woman whirled around, and I was squinting to see her where she had her back pressed to the front of the car, clutching her damned keys between her fingers with the tips facing out.

Could feel the energy.

Her fear rushing the air.

Shit.

I didn't want to freak her out, but what the hell was I supposed to do? Leave her there? Fuck no. I might have been a monster, but my mother had at least taught me better than that.

She slowly came into focus the closer I got.

Well, fuck me.

Would peg her at about twenty-four or twenty-five.

The girl as drenched as me. Long, black hair was matted to her face. She wore a thin t-shirt, jeans, and sky-high heels, the fabric sticking to every inch of her lush body.

The scattering rays of light caught on her eyes.

Thunderbolt eyes.

Blue strikes of lightning that raged.

Turbulent.

Tumultuous.

Her face was a clash of soft and hard, her brow and chin and jaw sharp, but her cheeks and mouth were full and plump.

So damned pretty I almost stumbled in my tracks.

With my approach, terror ridged her expression, but she clenched those keys tighter. It was clear if I became a threat, she wouldn't go down without a fight.

A wild animal backed into a corner.

Feral.

Fierce.

"Hey there, darlin'. You look like you're having some trouble." Basically had to shout to be heard over the driving rain that pounded against the pavement.

Her chin lifted, and I could see her attention darting all around while she still focused on me, the girl calculating her escape route, her flight if she needed it.

I stepped closer.

Carefully.

A roll of energy trembled the ground.

"I'm just fine." Her voice was this deep, sultry, wicked thing.

"You sure about that?"

Ferocity flared in her features, and shit, that was the wrong thing to say.

I lifted my hands out to the sides, light blinking off to the side. "I'm not here to mess with you. I saw you were in trouble, and it looked to me like you could use some help. Not like I want to be standing out here in the rain, either."

A little of the edge drained from her shoulders, but she watched me, refusing to let her guard down, not that I could blame her.

There were some twisted motherfuckers in this world. Figured I'd known half of them by name.

"Not out here to hurt you," I told her, words gruff.

She scoffed out a dismissive sound, shooting me daggers as she did. "That's what they all say, isn't it?"

A slight chuckle rumbled out.

Little wildcat.

Hoping to put her at ease, I angled my head toward the engine. "Do you have any idea what the problem might be?"

She huffed out her frustration and gestured wildly at it, all that soaked hair sticking to her gorgeous face.

It was really damned distracting, if I was being honest.

"It just died. I was barely able to coast to the side of the road."

Warily, I peeked at her as I moved closer because I was pretty sure she wouldn't hesitate to chop off my dick if I made the wrong move. I leaned over the engine, jiggling a few hoses and wires to see if it was something simple that I could fix right there.

"Hopefully it's just the alternator or battery," I mumbled as I poked around.

"And how much is that?" An edge of hysteria slipped into her voice, like she was going to lose it if one more thing went wrong.

My chest squeezed tight as I peered her way through the rain.

Could see it written all over her, this desperation that lined her being. Padded her in steel and severity.

"Not sure. If it's the battery or alternator, it won't be a biggie. If your engine seized—that could get dicey. Will have to get it into the shop and take a look before we can know for sure."

"Shop?"

Our voices were raised over the drone of crashing rain.

"Have one, right up here around the corner. Iron Ride."

So okay. Iron Ride was a custom bike shop. A spot for a restoration was highly coveted and didn't come cheap. Our specialty was motorcycles, but every now and again, we brought in a collectible car that we rebuilt from the bones. Didn't need to tell her my mechanics were going to have a field day when they found out I'd hauled in a '99 family sedan.

Her eyes narrowed in contemplation before she suddenly stepped back and shook her head. She looked like she was the one commanding the raging storm.

This dark chaos that thrashed in the night.

"What are you doing out here by yourself, anyway?" I asked, swiping the deluge pummeling my face.

"You know what? It's fine. I'm fine. Just…I'll figure something out. I'll call for a ride. You can go."

She flung her hand at my bike sitting in the distance, totally ignoring my question.

Through the rain, I looked at her, studied her face that shimmered in the glow of hazy light. Her teeth were clenched, and my gaze locked on the long, jagged scar that ran the side of her left jaw that the grinding somehow accentuated.

I had the urge to reach out and touch it. Run my fingertips along the flesh.

That was some serious fuckery. This reaction she evoked. Like I suddenly couldn't move.

As stranded as she was.

My hand curled into a fist to stop myself from doing something stupid.

Like she felt the attention there, her teeth ground harder, but instead of dipping her chin and hiding it, she lifted it in some kind of challenge.

Lust jumped into my guts.

Yup.

I was losing it. Mind traipsing into things that could set this freezing cold rain to boiling.

I was there to help and that was that.

But this girl was seriously hot and seriously savage, and my dick didn't seem to get the memo that we were going to help her out and send her on her way.

Thing was, I thought she could cast a spell with a glance.

Hypnotize and mesmerize.

Could feel it—some kind of magic that floated in the air.

Enchantress.

It wound with the storm and beat into the ground.

A bolt of lightning lit the sky around us.

One second later, thunder cracked.

The hairs lifted on my arms.

I inhaled a steadying breath and shoved the crazy shock of attraction down. I angled my head. "Do you really think I'm just going to leave you out here in this storm?"

Defiantly, she crossed her arms over her chest. "I said I was fine. You can go."

Another bolt of lightning. I saw her flinch.

"Go? That's not gonna happen. Come on, we need to get out of this rain."

"That would be great...you know...if my freaking car was running."

I almost laughed. She was a fiery thing.

"Grab your purse."

Her brow curled as a river of mascara ran down her cheeks. "What?"

"Let's go." I pointed at my bike.

She huffed and stomped her foot like I was crazy. "I don't even know you."

"Name's Jud. Jud Lawson. Like I told you before, my shop is around the corner. We can take shelter there until the storm passes. And guess what, don't know you, either, darlin', yet I'm out here trying to get my ass electrocuted to help you. So how about we get the hell out of here before we both end up on tomorrow's news, yeah?"

Distrust filtered through her expression, gaze narrowed before she huffed and threw up her hands. "Fine."

She strode on those sexy-as-fuck heels over to the driver's-side door. She dipped in and grabbed her purse and slung it over her shoulder before she stormed back my way like a tempest.

I closed her hood and reached for her hand.

She glared at it like it was poison.

A rough chuckle flooded the air around us as I dropped my hand. "Not gonna bite."

That wicked gaze narrowed.

Damn. This girl could slay me with a look.

I moved for my bike, and she kept her distance as we went. I swung my leg over and pressed the ignition button. The loud roar filled the night, mixed with the rhythm of the rain.

The woman hesitated at my side, warring, looking back at her car that sat like a heap of disappointment behind us.

I stretched out my hand again. "Get on. That thing's going nowhere tonight."

Thunderbolt eyes pierced me, as sharp as a blade. "Touch me, and I stab you."

Deep laughter rolled. "Have no doubt about that, darlin'. No doubt at all."

Finally, she gave and put her hand in mine.

A shockwave streaked my flesh.

A clash of that severity that blistered in the air and coalesced with her touch.

What the motherfuck?

Sucking it down, I steadied her as she swung a long leg over my bike and tucked her body close to mine.

She curled her arms around my waist, her breath hot on my neck.

I felt her all around. Heat and flames and ferocity.

Need went stampeding through my veins.

I silently scolded my cock like it was a thirteen-year-old boy who'd cut class to get high.

Make bad choices and you're gonna end up no place good.

I knocked my bike into gear and took back to the road that was turning into a river.

A flood of water streamed down, and the tires of my bike cut through and created a wave.

I took the next left, ignoring the way I could feel the hammer of her heart beating into my back, like that thunder could sink right in and take over.

The way her arms curled tighter and tighter. Clinging to me like I could be her refuge.

To the left was Absolution, the club my brother Trent ran and owned, though I had a piece of it since I'd invested in it when we'd come to build new lives here in Redemption Hills.

Blue neon lights glowed through the storm like a mirage. A sanctuary sitting in the middle of factories and shops.

It didn't matter that the sky was dumping, the place was packed as always, the club set in an old warehouse that we'd taken from the rubble and built a new dream.

Where we'd taken the worth of our depravity and done our best to pour it into something better.

Where we'd left behind the crimes and misdeeds and tried to come clean.

But where Absolution was Trent's baby, mine was on the lot at the back.

I took the two short lefts that wound around the club to where Iron Ride sat on a four-acre lot behind Absolution.

The building was massive. Two soaring stories. The customer lobby and entrance were through big glass doors that were on the right, and a row of huge garage doors ran to the left.

I could feel half the woman's tension drain away when she saw the building with the glowing sign.

Slowing to a crawl, I pushed the button mounted on my bike that made the farthest garage door crawl open. Lights flashed on inside. They glinted against the shiny black epoxy floors of the shop.

I eased my bike in, pulling it alongside my truck, ushering us out of the rain and into safety.

My boots came out to plant on the ground to balance the bike as I turned off the engine and kicked the stand.

In an instant, quiet surrounded us. The pounding of the rain that echoed on the metal roof had become a steady drone that covered us.

A hazy, mesmerizing dream.

The girl's arms tightened around my waist like she didn't know what to do with herself from there, and I could feel her reservations return full force.

"This is it," I rumbled low.

Warily, she eased back to inspect the shop.

Iron Ride was ten-thousand-square-feet of pure bliss.

A sanctuary.

Where I found my joy. Where I found new *purpose*. Where I created beauty when my past life had created devastation.

It was all thick, brick walls, gleaming black floors, and massive steel bay doors.

Bikes in varying states of renovation were in different bays and workspaces. A few classic cars were situated about, too.

You knew when you brought your baby into Iron Ride that you were getting first class. The equipment was state-of-the-art, place ultra-clean and ultra-modern.

Still, it remained authentic.

"Wow." She breathed it.

Slowly, I shifted, taking her hand to help her off.

She stumbled back onto her heels to the side of my bike.

My damned breath hitched in my throat.

Bright lights glowed from where they were hung from the rafters, and for the first time, I got a good look at her.

The girl was devastation wrapped in a black, seductive bow.

Ebony hair and eyes the color of a toiling sea. The darkest, deepest blue. An abyss where it'd be so easy to get lost. That soaked white tee stuck to the contours of her curvy, pin-up body.

She wasn't exactly tall, but with those heels, she looked like a force.

A motherfuckin' knockout.

A fantasy.

A dream.

My dick twitched, and my mouth went dry.

Her eyes were doing the same thing to me. Taking me in. Something flaring in the depths and radiating out.

It was the same feeling that had erupted when she'd touched me before.

Yanking her attention from me, she looked around. She huffed out a sarcastic sound as she flung out both arms. "Awesome."

My eyebrow quirked. "Yeah?"

Because it didn't sound like she was impressed.

Once again, her arms were crossed over her chest, and I was doing my damned best not to notice the way it pushed up her perfect tits.

"Do you think I can afford this? I mean, what is this place?" Her accusation jerked my focus back to her eyes.

"Told you…it's my shop."

"Um, yeah, and it looks like you should be on one of those TV shows where you have wars to see which shop can make the showiest bike, and I'm pretty sure I can't afford that."

"We can talk about that tomorrow."

Her head shook. "No, we can't. When I say I can't afford it, I mean it."

She dug into her purse and pulled out her phone. She dialed a number and pressed it to her ear before she began to frantically pace in a five-foot radius. "Come on, come on, come on."

She curdled a frustrated scream in her throat and held her phone out in front of her, eyeing it like it was single-handedly responsible for her predicament. "Why the hell isn't it going through?" she grumbled.

I climbed from my bike. "Storms always throw the service."

"Shit," she hissed, glaring at her phone like it'd grown horns. She swung her attention back to me. "I need to get home."

I tossed a glance at the open garage door where the skies continued to dump. "Don't think that's going to happen right now, darlin'."

Her mouth pinched in worry, and something that looked like dread twisted through her being.

My head angled as I took her in, trying to keep from spitting the words. "You have a man waitin' on you?"

She choked a pained sound. "No."

She looked like she wanted to kick herself for admitting it, while relief flooded through me, as deep as the rain.

Idiot.

Couldn't stop it, though.

"You're safe here. Promise you."

She stilled, and our gazes tangled.

Thunderbolt eyes sparked in the light.

Deep and dark.

Ghosts welled from their depths.

Felt them tugging at my heart.

Compelling me to look closer.

Drawn.

Like I should recognize something in this girl that just wasn't there.

Magic.

I blinked to break me out of the stupor.

"We're just going to have to wait it out," I added.

In exasperation, she glanced down at her soaked clothes.

"Let's go upstairs. I'll find you something dry to change into."

Her brows shot for the ceiling. "Excuse me?"

A rough chuckle tumbled from my chest, and I took two steps her direction. "I live upstairs."

Disbelieving laughter rolled from her throat. "You're serious?"

"Yup."

"And you want me just to follow you up there?"

"Do you have a better idea?"

She waved an erratic hand. "For my car to actually work. That would be a great idea."

A smile tweaked at the corner of my mouth. "That's called a dream, baby, not an idea."

Her eyes narrowed.

A tease of a laugh left my lips before everything softened when I saw a shiver race across her body. "Come on, let's get you dried off. You're freezing, and the only thing I want right now is a shower and a beer, and I'm guessing you're feeling about the same."

"This is insane."

"Insane is standing here freezing our asses off when we could be getting warm."

I didn't think it prudent to mention all the ways I could conjure warming her up.

Maybe she saw them play out in my mind, anyway, because she glowered at me as she gave. "Touch me and I stab you."

Could feel the grin split my face. "You've made that much clear, darlin'." Unable to stop myself, I edged closer, voice soft when I murmured close to her ear, "And who said I wanted to touch you?"

Oh, I did, but I kinda wanted to mess with the little wildcat, too.

Trembles rocked her.

Energy lashed.

Attraction so fierce I was itching on my feet.

"Just so we're clear," she gritted.

My grin turned into a full-fledged smirk. "Crystal."

Her spine straightened in all that rigid defiance, her hair smelling like toasted coconut, sex radiating from her skin.

Intoxicating.

"Good." The word was hard as she hissed it between her lips.

"Good," I rumbled back, hitting the button to close the garage door and striding for the metal stairway that ran the far back wall and led to my loft above.

I could hear her heels clacking along behind me.

Her presence was potent.

Overpowering as I bounded upstairs.

Girl followed me step for step.

At the landing at the top, I punched in the code at the door and swiveled around to face her. The breath hitched in my lungs all over again at the look on her face.

The dread and the relief.

My heart fisted while my head spun.

Enchantress.

"What's your name, darlin'?"

She hesitated a beat before she whispered, "Salem."

A disbelieving chuckle got loose without my permission.

Yeah.

Black-fuckin'-magic.

Chapter Two

Salem

"Come on in, darlin'. Don't be shy. Make yourself at home." The man's voice was basically sandpaper, rough and raw, though it somehow carried an undertone of casualness.

My heart thudded. A wild stampede that beat out ahead of me as I inched toward the door Jud Lawson left open.

I had to have lost my mind.

Following this stranger into his apartment.

Giving him my name like it didn't matter.

Hell, getting on his bike in the first place.

Like he could command any truth out of me, and I had no power to control it, even when I knew better than giving him anything.

But I'd called my brother about fifteen times while I'd been stranded out in the rain in the middle of nowhere. Each call had gone without an answer.

My spirit had sunk deeper into hopelessness with each attempt.

It's funny how I'd prayed for help, then I'd wanted to turn around and refuse it when the single headlight had come spearing through the storm.

As if he were some kind of wicked savior, the man had emerged through the hazy darkness.

Bearded and muscled and covered in tattoos.

An imposing force.

A liberator or a conqueror, I couldn't be sure.

The only thing I'd known was my knees had knocked and my stomach had flipped and every ounce of self-preservation I possessed had flared in warning at my recklessness.

But when you were desperate? You were left with few options, and the ones you were given you had little choice but to take.

Which was precisely the reason why I warily stepped through the door at the top of the stairwell and into his loft.

My eyes raced to take it in. It was just as massive and over-the-top as his *shop* downstairs. Everything was matte black, burnt metal, and expensive leather.

Rugged and rough and jaw-dropping.

Just like the man.

Jud Lawson moved ahead of me. Each step of his boots across the black bamboo floors sent a shockwave of heat blistering through the cool air.

I fought for conviction. To remain unaffected and aloof.

Not to be the fool that melted on the floor in a puddle of need at his feet.

Accomplishing it would be a feat of nature because the man was outrageously gorgeous.

Forbiddingly so.

So ridiculously tall and wide he had to double me in size.

Intimidating and raw.

Nothing but a beast of a man with this sexy, devilish smile.

And somehow, he seemed soft at the same time, rippling with this charm that tweaked the edges of his plush, sexy mouth and sent a skitter fumbling through my chest.

The hardest part was the way he kept looking at me with these obsidian eyes that were darker than the night. That gaze left no question that if I gave him the chance, he would devour me.

Sucking in a deep breath, I stepped into the loft on shaky legs. I was soaked through, dripping, unsure of what to do.

I wrung my fingers.

The man felt my pause, and he shifted to look back at me with mischief playing across his handsome face.

My stomach twisted in a show of want.

Crap.

I knew better, I knew better.

But attraction was something you couldn't control.

It was instant.

Unstoppable.

Awakened in a beat before you even knew what was happening.

So, I'd deal with it. Not act on it.

Lifting my chin, I gestured at myself.

I shouldn't have.

Because those eyes swept over me, head to toe.

Energy lashed.

A crackle in the air.

A whip of lust.

"I'm wet." I said it like a challenge.

His tongue darted out like he was suddenly thirsty.

Shit.

I took a slippery step back, realizing what I'd said. Where his mind had gone. My thighs pressed together because with the way he kept looking at me, it was the truth.

But seriously, he just wanted me to go parading into this ridiculous luxury that he called a house? It looked like a friggin' showroom for pretentious masculinity.

Except the man—the man didn't look so uptight.

A rough chuckle scraped from his throat, and I was wishing it didn't sound so nice.

"As am I, darlin.'"

He gestured at the giant wet footprints he'd left in his wake.

My throat tremored and my tongue swept my dried lips.

Double crap.

He chuckled more, the deep sound mixing with the pour of the rain on the roof. It was a low whirr that whispered and cast a hazy tone over the space. Lightning flashed at the windows and thunder rumbled through the heavens.

"Wait right there."

He turned and hulked away, across the living area that took up the right side of the open-concept loft, through the kitchen, and toward the set of double doors at the far back wall.

The man was nothing but bristling, thick muscle, arms and legs bound in overbearing strength.

The exposed skin on his arms was covered in a labyrinth of ink.

His stride was long and purposed, easy, but still, there was a hint of harshness in his stance. I knew in that confidence the man was no stranger to hazard and jeopardy. He would strike in the face of danger, and his opponent was unlikely to make it out unscathed on the other side.

He disappeared through the double doors.

My pulse thudded and beat while I stood there waiting like a fool. I glanced at my phone again, cringing when I saw I still hadn't received a word.

They'd be worried.

Hell, I was worried.

But if my calls weren't going through, neither would theirs.

A minute later, Jud came striding back out, though he'd ditched his boots, and his feet were bare. He carried a stack of clothes and a towel.

"Not much, but at least you can grab a shower and get into something dry until the storm blows over. We'll get your clothes into the dryer."

A soft smile hitched his mouth as he moved my way.

My spirit flailed.

Sweet and intense and intimidating.

That combo promised he might be the most dangerous man I'd ever met.

This flirty charm that radiated from his being, sure to wrap every unsuspecting female around his fingers. Salivating for a taste of what he had to offer.

That shock of pitch-black hair on his head was wet, longer on top, sticking to the stony angles of his face.

His thick beard was the same color as his hair. A beard I had to fight the sudden urge to run my fingers through when he offered me the pile of fresh clothes.

The man was nothing but a tease and a trap.

"There you go." He tipped his head toward the row of three doors on the opposite side of the room. "Guest room is third door on the left. Get yourself a shower."

Our fingers touched when he passed me the stack. Shivers raced, a flashfire across my flesh.

He angled in, his voice so low and rough, "You need to get warmed up, darlin'. You're cold."

A fingertip trailed my wrist where a rash of chills lifted.

He eased back, those obsidian eyes sparking with mirth.

Jerk.

He knew exactly what he was doing to me. Still, I mumbled, "Thank you."

"My pleasure, gorgeous. Like I said, make yourself at home. I'm going to grab a shower, too."

I leaned down and twisted the stupid heels off my feet so I didn't leave a trail of pockmarks on his floors. I dangled them from my fingers and clutched the pile of clothes in the other hand. I padded as quickly as I could across the floor in the direction of the door he had pointed to, feeling the warmth of his gaze on me the whole time.

This was insane, but truth be told, I was freezing, the trembling starting from deep within.

It didn't help when the AC came on and started to pump cold air into the space.

At the doorway, I paused to peer back. The man remained across the room.

His stare intent. His being profound.

There was something about him that was so big and overwhelming, and it didn't have a thing to do with his size.

No doubt, I should fear it, so I figured it was a big, big problem that I suddenly felt comfort under his watch. Safety in his refuge. Damned stupid.

I knew better than to trust anyone, and here I was in this stranger's house, and not a soul knew where I was.

I tore myself from the hook of who he was and rushed the rest of the way into the bedroom. It was dark inside, and I shut the door, quick to lock it. I turned and rested against the door, struggling for a breath. To get myself under control. To shake myself out of whatever fantasy I felt like I might be falling into.

But there was something about tonight that made it feel like none of this was real.

Outside reality.

Because I didn't do things like this. Was never so reckless. The last four years had been lived in complete caution. One foot moving and one eye over my shoulder. No room for mistakes or missteps.

But my brother had convinced me it was safe to come to this small town where he'd brought our grandmother to live three months ago.

Years had passed.

Years of running.

Years of barely existing.

He'd insisted it was time, and we couldn't keep on the way we had.

My chest clutched, and I rocked my head back against the wood of the door.

God, I had to believe him. Had to cling to the hope of that truth.

Laughing off the confusion of it, I pushed from the door and moved to the en suite bathroom.

I flipped on the light.

It was every bit as ostentatious as the rest of the loft.

Exposed white brick walls with reclaimed wood floating counters that had been stained black. The fixtures were roughened gold, and the floors and the entire back wall behind the shower were a matrix of white and black. The shower was clear glass, open on one side with a rain shower hanging from the ceiling.

Well then.

I set the clean clothes on the counter and rushed to turn the faucet all the way to hot. I peeled off my drenched clothes and left them in a wet heap on the floor as steam began to fill the bathroom.

I stepped into the heated spray, and a moan whimpered free at the feel of the water hitting my skin.

At the chills that raced from the contrast of hot and cold.

I blew out a relieved sigh.

Suddenly…thankful.

So extremely thankful.

I always expected the worst in people, and in the luxury of this shower, I couldn't help the thought that this guy might actually be nice.

Genuine and good.

I steeled myself against it.

Trusting only made you vulnerable. Put you in a position where you could be hurt.

And I didn't have the time or space for that.

Besides, I was pretty sure it didn't take much for that boy outside this room to have girls falling at his feet, and I was even more certain my heart wasn't up for a fling or even a one-night stand.

But damn, would an orgasm I didn't give myself feel nice.

Visions flash-fired at that.

Those big, big hands and that flirty mouth and that massive body.

Squeezing my eyes closed, I tried not to imagine him in the next room over, naked and beneath the heated spray.

Nope. Nope. Nope. Do not go there, Salem.

Get clean, get dry, get out.

That was my goal tonight.

But still, I stayed under that relaxing cascade for probably a little too long and let my mind drift a little too far.

But could you blame a girl?

This place was like a fantasy.

The man a fantasy, too.

A wicked fantasy where it'd be so easy to get lost.

Finally, I shut off the shower. I stepped out onto the plush white mat, and I grabbed the fluffy towel. It completely engulfed me when I wrapped it around my body, and there was nothing I could do but take one end and push it to my face and inhale the scent—the same scent that had taken me over when I'd slipped onto his bike and found my nose at the back of his neck.

Citrus and cinnamon and spice.

It smelled like he'd washed his clothes in a late fall night.

I inhaled a little too deeply, committing it to memory, though I doubted much that I'd forget, anyway.

Okay creeper, stop fantasizing about a man who is just trying to be nice.

The internal pep talk worked for all of five seconds, because the moment I pulled his giant shirt over my head, I was sucked right back down into that delusion.

It was warm and scented and god, I felt like I was wrapped by the man. Then I was giggling when I pulled on the giant pair of boxers and looked in the mirror.

I looked ridiculous.

Swamped in fabric that was ten times too big.

Fighting the smile, I rolled the boxers down to my hips, praying they wouldn't slip off, then I wrapped the towel around my hair, swooped up my wet pile of clothes, and moved back out to the bedroom. The room was only illuminated by the light from the bathroom, though it was clear the two rooms matched.

Nothing but dark, masculine luxury.

A king-sized bed with lavish linens.

I shook my head and forced myself to move, though I slowed in caution when I unlocked the door and peeked out. When I was hit with silence, I tiptoed out into the main space.

The open loft was dark save for the lights under the kitchen cabinets, but what my attention locked on were some paintings hanging on the far wall of the living area that were cast in muted spotlights.

I hadn't noticed them when I'd first come in, but in the quiet, they seemed like they were the only thing I could see. My feet involuntarily moved that direction.

The images a lure that hooked my heart and mind.

They ran on four big canvases, floor to soaring ceiling. Two were situated on either side of the massive TV sitting on a stand along the wall. The paintings were raw and candid, and my chest clenched around my thudding heart as I stared and tried to make sense of what they represented. I got the unsettled sense I was peering directly into the artist's soul, right to where his demons thrashed and thrived.

Depictions of ghosts that screamed and howled. Demons that climbed from fiery flames to crawl and ravage the Earth. Vague, obscured faces were woven in, as if they were hidden in the scene, prisoners that didn't belong but were stuck there, anyway.

Others were stark, haunting beauty. Stars and eternity and lost hope.

Each was breathtakingly tragic.

Earth-shatteringly inspired.

I leaned closer to them.

Enthralled.

Enraptured.

Like I had become a piece of the torment written in the bold strokes of paint.

In the agony weaved in the canvas.

The air thickened and locked in my lungs, and the fine hairs prickled at the nape of my neck.

I froze, somehow trapped. Unable to look or move or act as I felt him approach like a wraith. Like one of the paintings had come to life and closed in from behind.

It covered me whole and caressed me in shadows.

I was right. This man was definitely, definitely dangerous.

His breath hit me on the shoulder where his shirt draped wide. "Did you get warmed up?"

Such an innocuous question, though the rough scrape of his words moved through me like seduction.

"Yes, thank you."

I found I could barely speak, the severity of the paintings stealing my voice and my sanity. "These are..." I couldn't even form a coherent thought.

His tone tightened to a grumble. "Just something to fill the empty space."

A frown filled my brow at his indifference, at the way he shrugged it off, and I wanted to ask him more but was distracted by the slow chuckle that suddenly brushed across my flesh and sent chills racing again. "You look..."

Finally, I found the strength to peek back at him from over my shoulder. Only when I did, my eyes were filled with a wide chest that was...bare and tattooed and oh my god.

I thought I might pass out right there.

I attempted to look away, but his hair that was much longer on top and short on the sides was wet from his shower, and he was wearing this grin on his face that twisted me into a knot of desire.

Not to mention the heat that radiated from his body.

A stroke of that severity thrashed.

I was pretty sure it short-circuited my logic.

"Ridiculous," he seemed to finally settle on, sitting back on his heels and crossing his arms over his wide, wide chest.

What?

His words knocked me out of the trance.

What a jerk.

I mean, I'd thought so, too, but he didn't need to bring attention to it.

Gulping, I stumbled away, my chin jerking for the sky, every defense set to high. "I didn't have a lot of other options, now, did I, unless you wanted me to drip all over your *ridiculous* floors?"

That smirk edged his mouth.

Damn him.

"Didn't say I was complainin', now did I, sweetness?"

I glared at him. What was with this guy?

Really, what was with *me*? Why was I all hot and bothered by a man I didn't know other than the fact he had really great taste in interior decorating, and I'd give my left boob for his guest shower?

Well, that and he'd stopped to help a stranger in a torrential downpour despite clearly being loaded.

I couldn't tell if he was an asshole toying with me or if he was genuinely kind.

From the flaring in his eyes and that teasing at his sexy mouth?

There was a part of him that was definitely toying with me.

"Besides, you're still dripping all over my *ridiculous* floors," he grumbled with that rough, low voice.

On a gasp, I jerked back to see the wad of clothes I clutched were indeed dripping onto his floor, and a small puddle had gathered at my toes.

"Shit."

The asshole laughed and stepped forward. "Give me your clothes."

I held them closer like he was a common thief. A plunderer of sound judgement.

Obsidian eyes glinted and danced, and his laughter floated out of his mouth and surrounded me like a dream. The man leaned forward to whisper in my ear, the words coming from his mouth temptation and a tease. "You're lucky I'm not asking you for the ones you're wearing. Stand there a minute longer, and I just might."

My eyes narrowed as I angled back. "I'll stab you."

That time, his laughter boomed. Like I was the *ridiculous* one.

Reaching out, he snatched the dripping wet ball from my hands. He held it to his chest, and the man waltzed away like doing it was the most normal thing in the world.

"Come on, Wildcat, laundry room is this way."

Um…what?

"Excuse me?" I scrambled along behind him.

He just chuckled as he moved through the kitchen to a door on the left of it. He opened it and stepped into a laundry room that was as big as the kitchen back at our house.

I froze at the doorway because there was no chance in hell I was getting that close, and he was grinning as he tossed my clothes into the dryer and punched some buttons.

It beeped and spun to life.

"See, now that wasn't so hard, was it?"

That mischief played, the man eyeing me up and down as he edged me out of the laundry room.

Huffing, I crossed my arms tight over my chest.

"What is it, darlin'?"

His voice had gone soft. Like he didn't have the first clue he had me spun up.

"You don't think this is a little bit weird?" I waved an erratic hand over my head.

He grinned. "I like weird, if I'm being honest."

He reached out and gently brushed his fingertips over the scar on my jaw.

It happened so fast that I didn't realize what he was doing before his hand was already there. As if it were second nature. As if he did it all the time. As if he had the right.

Fire streaked my flesh.

Horror and fear and the fight.

Worse was the flash of comfort that came along with it.

Aghast, I ripped myself back.

"What do you think you're doing?" I wheezed, the words haggard and pained. Panic raced my veins and nearly sent me screaming out the door.

Screw the rain and the storm.

But I forced myself to remain standing.

I wasn't weak.

I wasn't weak.

I lifted my chin defiantly like I was daring him to do it again because if he did it this time, I was going to teach him a lesson.

He actually had the nerve to look apologetic, and he shoved his hands into the pockets of his low-slung jeans that showed off an expanse of chiseled abs, his hip bones peeking out over the top. The packed, rippled flesh was covered in those designs there, too. Ones that I refused to study even though I was itching to reach out and touch them the same way as he had done to my scar.

Like it was natural.

Right.

God, I kind of hated this man. Hated that he stirred something in me that I couldn't afford to feel.

"Sorry. That was rude." It sounded like he meant it.

"I don't even know you."

He dragged a hand from his pocket and uneasily roughed it through the longer pieces of his hair. "Know it."

He hesitated, then added, "But there's something about you, isn't there, Salem?" That gaze narrowed and his head pitched to the side, the man studying me as if I were a riddle he was trying to decipher.

Energy shivered and flashed. A blanket of lightning flickered at the windows. A current of it ran the dense air.

The way his eyes caressed my face, it might as well have been his hands. "Is it wrong if I want to get to know you?"

Attraction billowed and boiled. Held in the bare space that seethed between us. A snare to hold me back.

Gravity.

I scrambled around in my brain for the last vestiges of my common sense.

"I have no interest in that." The words were bitchy and a straight-up lie. "I just want to go home."

The blunt of the rejection struck across his face before he dropped his gaze to look at the floor.

"Right, okay," he mumbled, his head bouncing in affront as he stared at his bare feet with his teeth gritting.

Thunder cracked.

With it, the rain intensified to become a violent pounding at the roof.

He looked up at me, and every angle of his face hardened with the promise. "Told you my purpose tonight was gettin' you to safety."

I was pretty sure it was *here* that wasn't safe. Not with the way my pulse battered and my stomach coiled and this needy interest was taking me over. I swallowed hard. "What does that mean?"

"Means you're stuck with me tonight. I'll get you home first thing in the morning."

"You expect me to stay here? With you?" It was a shriek of disbelief.

"Didn't mean in my bed, darlin'." He angled forward again, his breath caressing my skin, sex and seduction rising to the surface. "But that sure would be fun, wouldn't it?"

The air locked in my lungs, and he was chuckling low and looking at me like he knew the flush of desire he elicited in me. Then the man so casually strode away, overpowering his kitchen, so sexy when he dipped into the black metal refrigerator and grabbed a beer. He twisted the cap and took a long pull, then he lifted it in the air, facing me as he backed away. "Goodnight, Wildcat. Guest room is all yours. Make yourself at home. I'll see you in the morning."

My mouth dropped open as he disappeared back through the same double doors, catty-corner to the room where I'd taken a shower.

The room with that giant, luxurious bed where he expected me to sleep.

I stood there in the dark for at least ten minutes, wondering what the hell I was supposed to do, because this was crazy, while the heavens continued to dump and pour and deluge.

Finally, I accepted that I was stuck there tonight and reluctantly crept to the guest bedroom where I shut the door and locked it.

I slipped under the covers and sank into the plush comfort.

I typed out one last message on my phone and prayed at least someone would receive it.

> Me: I still can't get through to anyone. My car broke down, but I ran into a friend who offered me a place to stay for the night. I'll be home first thing. Please don't worry, I'll be fine.

A friend was stretching it.

But they didn't need to worry even more than they already would be.

Then I relaxed into the warmth beneath the heavy comforter as the exhaustion from the day pulled me under. Lulling me into a dream. Sleep taking me down to the darkest depths of consciousness.

Where everything faded and drifted and took old shape.

Where dreams possessed and nightmares haunted.

Where the here and now and the past intertwined. Where they merged and crossed and slayed.

Where grief whispered and crawled and sucked the life from the air.

Where I had no idea what time it was when I jolted awake. When I heard the muted roar. A roar of pain. A cry of agony.

And I wasn't sure if it was his or if it was mine.

Chapter Three

Jud

It didn't matter that it wasn't even eight in the morning, heavy metal blared from the speakers that hung at each corner of the soaring ceiling of Iron Ride.

Had slept like shit last night, tossing and turning with the thought of Salem in the room right next to me, that fiery wildcat who could so easily get under my skin.

Apparently, the only thing it took was a hot-as-hades stranger standing wet in my living room to make me lose my mind. My rationale. My sense and reason.

My purpose.

So, I'd gone and done something so *ridiculous* as tell her I wanted to get to know her.

Seriously fucked up.

A chuckle of disbelief rolled up my throat as I studied the piece of metal on the worktable.

What did I think? She was going to get to know me and be cool with who I was? And why the fuck had I even suggested it? Thought for a second that I wanted it?

I knew firsthand it didn't go down like that. The second I'd let it slip from my mouth, I'd known I was setting myself a trap. That it ran contrary to everything I knew. Everything I was striving for.

But still, it'd been there, tangled in my guts—interest—and not just in that tight little body.

At least the girl'd had a little sense and shot that shit down, but still, it'd left me rattled, my dick hard and my brain mottled as I'd slunk away to my room, hoping by shutting myself behind my bedroom door, I might be able to shut off thoughts of her.

Hardly.

I'd finally given up when the sun breaking at the horizon had snatched the darkness from my room. I'd pulled on some clothes and made my way down to the shop.

Had plenty to do, anyway, so it didn't hurt to get a jump start on my day.

Besides, Iron Ride was where I found my peace. Where I created beauty when my past life had created devastation.

It was where I welded and sanded and painted and rebuilt. Brought back to life the worn and run-down. The dilapidated and decayed. Priceless gems left to rot in backyards and in forgotten lots. Cars and bikes that I would take back to bare bones, then restore them to a newfound glory.

Art manifested of my hands.

Dirty hands that I was doing my best to make clean.

I got lost in it. Entranced in it.

Ears full of the pounding, thrashing beat, I watched through my protective mask as fire scored through metal. Sparks flew and spit as I made the precision cut.

I was hyper-focused, though somehow enthralled by the movements, like my soul had jumped in on the revelry.

I heaved out the breath I'd been holding when the metal for the bike fender finally cut apart, the tension bound in my muscles draining away. I shut off the torch so I could study my handiwork. My finger covered by a leather glove glided over the cut.

Ensuring perfection.

Nothing less was tolerated in my shop.

The only thing going out these doors was going to be spectacular.

Awe-inspiring.

I mean, fuck, I'd made old bikers weep when they'd come to claim their ride. If a man shed a tear or two when he saw his beast for the first time? That shit was a win.

When I heard the rumble of a truck come into the lot, I tossed off my gloves and moved for the open bay where Brock eased in the tow. He pulled horizontal to the building before he put it into reverse and backed it in. He left the engine idling when he hopped out the driver's door and came striding my way. "Yo, boss. This it?"

His voice was pure speculation. Like I hadn't given a specific description of the car and directions to where it was sitting.

"That's it."

He shook his shaved blond head, a grin spreading to his face as he pushed the button to lower the lift.

Brock had been the first mechanic I'd brought onto my team. Dude was quick with a wrench and possessed this natural instinct with diagnosing issues. Swore the asshole could get an engine that had been rusting for twenty years out in a deserted field to spark.

He also ran his mouth twenty-four seven.

"This a joke? A test? Or is business runnin' dry and you're getting desperate? Thought we were booked solid for a year?"

Considering it was Saturday and we were all working double-time to keep up with the workload, the answer to that was obvious.

"Helping out a friend," I said, giving him a look that told him the reason the car was there was none of his concern.

"She pretty?" he cracked.

"That required to do something nice?" I growled. Had to restrain myself from punching the scrawny punk in his smug face. But that would probably lay him out for the week, and I needed him on a '63 Ford pickup that was set to roll next month.

He shrugged. "Hey, man, I just know what it takes to get a spot here, and you have me rollin' up with an old sedan? You must be getting something out of it."

I ignored him, and instead, I turned my attention to watch as Darius made a left into the lot in his black pickup truck.

Darius had only been with us for the last month. Guy was the opposite of Brock. Quiet and intense. Tatted and hard and nearly as big as me. Lost in thought most of the time, though he got the job done. He was a basic technician that'd come from one of the dealerships, but he was hungry to learn, and I was desperate for help.

Like Brock had said, we were booked a solid year, and I was turning away clients left and right.

Brock was moving to unlatch the chains on Salem's car when Darius came to a stop and jumped out of his truck. "What's going on?"

He stormed across the lot, his attention locked on the sedan.

Awesome.

I was gonna get shit from him, too.

Then I was stilling, tingles rushing my flesh as a shock of energy came blasting through the shop. As fierce as the storm from last night. I eased around to find Salem coming down the stairs from my loft above.

The breath knocked from my lungs.

Fuck me.

This girl was even prettier than I'd remembered from last night.

Crazy hot.

Wicked sexy.

Back in her clothes she'd been wearing last night, though her face was bare, and all that black hair was piled in a crazy knot on her head.

Nothing but a perfect fantasy floating down from my loft.

Figured it'd been the storm that had left that feeling zinging in the air, and it would have disappeared this morning.

This connection that made me want to explore something I knew damned well I shouldn't explore.

Couldn't explore.

But it was there, pulling through the atmosphere, vibrating along this invisible band that had us tied.

Neither of us could look away.

Thunderbolt eyes speared me from across the space, piercing me through and holding me hostage.

Wondered if anyone else noticed, the way we just fuckin' stared.

Tangled in a beat.

Held in a moment.

Something powerful lit in my veins.

Need.

Possession.

Girl was nothing but an enchantress.

Black-fuckin'-magic.

Because what she had me feeling wasn't possible.

"Ah, she's pretty, all right." Brock spewing his bullshit broke me out of the spell. "Knew you had to be gettin' something out of it, and that something is fine as hell."

Fuck the Ford.

I started to go for him except Darius had me grinding on the brakes when he charged Salem's direction, his footsteps enraged. He stopped halfway to her, right in the middle of us.

His hands were clenched into fists as his attention darted between me and the girl.

Swore, he had murder written in his expression.

Knew that look well.

He turned that venom on her. "Salem, the fuck are you doing here?"

Well shit.

She told me she didn't have a man waiting on her, and I had a feeling that things had just gotten messy and fast.

Had the urge to yank him back, stand between them, especially considering she'd come walking down like she'd been properly fucked when, unfortunately, that wasn't even close to the way things had gone down.

Except Salem rolled her eyes in annoyance as she hit the landing and strode our way. All fierce fire and stormy conviction. "I called you fifteen times and texted you more. My car broke down."

Darius' eyes swept back to take in her car.

Brock was standing beside it, dude grinning like the fuckin' Joker, laughing under his breath as he took in the scene. No doubt, he was eating up the tension.

The way Darius looked back at me like he was envisioning peeling the flesh from my bones.

"Tried calling you this morning," Darius grated, though he was still glaring at me when he said it.

"My phone died, and I was asleep and safe because some nice guy stopped to help me in the middle of a downpour. That was it."

"I bet he helped her," Brock needled.

I spun and pointed at him, the threat whipping from my tongue. "One more, Brock, and I end you."

He laughed like it was hysterical.

"Was about to lose my mind, Salem," Darius grated, swiveling his focus to the girl.

"Did my texts from last night come through this morning? The ones where I told you what happened and that I was fine?" Her voice was a challenge.

"Yeah." He seemed reluctant to admit it.

She crossed her arms over her chest. "So, you knew I was okay?"

He roughed a hand over his head. "Yeah."

"Then I'm pretty sure this anger is misplaced."

Coming to the quick decision of where to *place* it, Darius turned to glare at me.

I pushed a placating hand toward him since the dude looked like he was about to snap. "Hey, man, had taken a ride and got caught in the storm. On my way back, I came upon her car over on Dawson. Shady as shit over there, you know that, and I wasn't about to leave her by herself."

Didn't really need to explain myself because I hadn't done a thing wrong. His anger wasn't on me. I'd had no clue Salem was with someone. On top of it, she hadn't done anything wrong, either. She'd let someone help her. There was no crime in that.

Wasn't like she was betraying her man by seeking refuge under my roof.

The fact the idea of her having a man coiled my guts in some kind of twisted, pissed off jealousy?

Yeah.

That one was on me.

Except Salem was scoffing and cocking her head in offended disbelief.

Wildcat claws coming out.

Salem was fuckin' hot in all that ferocity.

"You don't need to explain to *my brother* why you stopped to help me, Jud. We didn't do anything wrong, and he has no right to act like we did."

She emphasized *brother*, and shit, was that a breath of relief that punched from my lungs?

Why, yes. Yes, it was.

Darius glared harder.

Fuck.

I scrubbed a palm over my face.

He shifted back to her, voice full of condescension. "I'm sorry if I'm concerned that I roll up to work and my sister comes waltzing out of my boss' apartment."

He was back to shooting daggers at me.

Brock howled and rocked his hips. "Friend...just how friendly are you, Jud?"

"One more word." My finger was back to jabbing in his direction.

Apparently, none of us were going to make it out alive because Salem was tossing her hand in the air, her outrage shifting to me. "And why is my car here?"

Surprise lifted my brows. "Uh...because it's broken down?"

She lifted that scarred chin, and fuck, I was itching to reach out and touch it again. "I told you I can't afford that."

"Didn't ask you to. I'll handle it."

She and Darius scoffed at the same time. Maybe I should have recognized the resemblance from the get-go. "I don't think so," they both said.

Lord help me.

I roughed both palms over my face. "I'm just trying to help out over here."

"Help—"

The second Brock opened his mouth, I picked up a wrench and threw it at him before he could get it out. It hit him square in the chest and dropped him to his knees. Dude started rolling around on the shiny black concrete.

Crying and laughing like the fool he was.

He was lucky he was good.

I turned back to Salem who looked like she was about to freak out right about then. She glanced at her brother. "Do you have time to give me a ride home?"

He gave her a tight nod. "Yup. Just give me a second to take my things to my station." He lifted the bag he'd dumped to the ground in front of him. "That is, if it's okay with the boss?"

There was a challenge in that, and hell, I thought I'd learned more about the guy in the last two minutes than I had since he started working here.

I jutted my chin. "No problem."

"Good." Salem spat it, then stormed on those heels out the open bay door and toward Darius' truck.

"Hey," I called from behind her, unable to do anything but follow.

Girl this gravity that I couldn't shake.

I needed to completely cut off this bullshit.

But there I was, chasing her out into the bright light of the coming day, the ground damp and the air humid from last night's storm.

"What the hell?" I demanded when she refused to look back at me. "Salem. Wait."

I nearly stumbled when she whirled on me like a hurricane. "I'm not a charity case."

"Didn't imply that you are."

She gestured wildly at the front of her car visible through the bay door. "Do you expect to get paid for that?"

I rocked back on my heels and scratched the back of my neck, unsure of what the right answer was supposed to be here. "Uh, no."

Her head cocked to the side, voice hard. "Charity case. I told you last night that this place was going to be too much, and you hauled my car in, anyway?"

"Everyone needs a little help every once in a while, Salem. Not a thing wrong with that. And if this is about what happened with your brother, he has to know you weren't doing a walk of shame, that you—"

She flew into my face.

The words died on my tongue as that severity cracked.

A whip.

In a heartbeat, my guts were tangled in those thunderbolt eyes.

She poked me in the chest. "Walk of shame? If I fucked you, it'd be because I wanted to, and I wouldn't feel an ounce of shame, so you and my brother can both kiss my ass."

Uh…wow.

I didn't know if I should be turned on or offended.

Visions hit me like a backhand of lust.

Okay, fine.

Definitely turned on, so there I went, easing in, my words rumbled near her ear. "Might like that. Don't tempt me, enchantress."

Screeching, she tossed her hands up and stomped the rest of the way to Darius' truck before she swung back to face me as she opened the door. "Fine, fix my car, Jud, but I will figure out a way to pay for it. I refuse to owe you anything."

She hopped in and slammed it shut, and I just stood there staring as Darius passed by, the dude eyeing me with outright distrust as he went.

He climbed into the driver's side and started the truck and whipped out of the lot, the loud engine roaring as he disappeared down the street.

While I stood there wondering what the fuck had just happened.

Laughter ripped from behind. "Whelp, there went your balls, boss."

I strode back into the shop, not bothering to tell Brock where to shove it.

Not when I had the sinking feeling the motherfucker was right.

Chapter Four

Salem

CRAP. CRAP. CRAP.

I peered back at the huge industrial shop as Darius floored the accelerator out of the lot and sped down the road. The hulking man stood where I'd left him, his mouth gaping open in shock and a bit of hurt and something else that slipped beneath my skin like the kindling of flames.

An old-seeded fire that had long died out that threatened to burst back to life.

My stomach was in knots and my pulse thundered like an out-of-control freight train that blew into town. A coming disaster that I wasn't sure I could derail. Because falling prey to what that man had to offer would likely destroy the bare semblance of any control I possessed.

It was a promise of the type of recklessness I could not afford.

Not to mention the fact that Darius was seething in his seat beside me. He white-knuckled the steering wheel as harsh breaths panted from his nose.

"What the fuck, Salem?" he hissed as the building disappeared from view.

My brow curled as I shifted my head to look at him. "Excuse me? I already told you that my car broke down and he stopped to help me. Do you have a problem with that?"

I couldn't keep the pissiness from my voice. He didn't get to do this.

His words were shards. "I was worried about you."

Uneasily, I readjusted my bag on my lap. "I tried to call you a bunch of times, Darius. Service was out for everyone. I was coming downstairs to ask him if I could borrow his phone to call you."

A grunt left him, and he pitched me a hard glance. "He's my boss."

"Which I didn't know, considering I just got here last week, and you never told me where you're working. I thought you were still at the dealership?"

He released a strained sigh, a wash of bashfulness softening his formidable features. "Didn't say anything because I wasn't sure if it was going to work out. Not exactly qualified to be working there."

Tenderness pulled at my chest. "Of course, you are. Who wouldn't want you working for them? I thought we didn't keep secrets from each other?"

He cut me a glance. "Don't we?"

There was an accusation there.

"Darius." Frustration laced his name.

He shook his head. "Doesn't matter, he's my boss and he's—"

"He's what?" I challenged, defensiveness making a rebound.

No, I might not know the guy, but the one thing I knew was he'd been kind.

The thousand emotions I'd felt last night scattered through my consciousness.

The cornerstone of a man I couldn't quite put my finger on.

Hard and cocky. Sweet and flirty. Overbearing and...dark. I

guessed it was that layer hidden beneath that sexy smirk that held the power to knock me from my feet.

It billowed through me then. The memory in the night. The feeling of not being alone when the torment came. Like the man could give me comfort in the storm that hit me night after night.

I shook my head out of the stupor. God knew, those thoughts were dangerous.

I couldn't go there.

But if I were being honest, I had to admit there was something about him.

Something that compelled me to look closer. To touch and explore and feel. A piece that ached to come alive under those massive hands.

Yeah. Definitely dangerous.

Still, regret fluttered, shame at the way I'd reacted.

Instead of thanking him, I'd blown up in his face.

Darius seemed to war, peeking at me every couple of seconds as he flew down the street, his words controlled as he bit them out. "He's my boss, Salem, and you need to stay away from him. Simple as that."

But it was the way my brother looked like he was about to snap the steering wheel from the dash that made me think it wasn't so simple.

The way his jaw locked, and rigidness took to his spine.

His anxiety ripped through the air and banged through the cab.

Slowing, he made a right into an old neighborhood. Here, the houses were quaint and modest, fronted by lawns and ancient, towering trees.

Darius' breaths filled the air.

Anguish tightened my chest, but still, granite filled the words. "I took care of myself for four years, Darius. You can't tell me who I can and cannot see."

Not with Jud. Not with anyone else.

"And I barely got you back, Salem. You think I didn't worry about you every second of every day? Do you think I wasn't terrified? Do you think I didn't know you were out there, fuckin' scared and hiding for all that time?"

He blanched with the admission. "Spent years not sleeping through the night. Not knowing how you were or where you were. Desperate for the rare calls you made to let us know you were safe. Having no way to change it or make it better. And now that we brought this family back together? I will do anything—absolutely anything—to make sure you two are safe."

Sadness swept through my being. "It's not your responsibility, Darius."

Foreboding whispered through my consciousness. A warning that I'd been a fool, agreeing to come here. That maybe Darius was wrong. That it would never be time, and it would never be safe, and thinking it would only destroy us in the end.

But there was no question Darius was right on one account. We would never find a normal life if we were running forever. Would never find peace or safety or stability.

I owed her that. Wanted it more than anything.

I had to take the chance.

For her.

Years had passed without a word or a trace, and I had to pray it was enough.

Darius' brow pinched as he made a left into the single drive of the house he'd been renting for the last three months. "It *is* my responsibility," he countered, blowing out a sigh as he put his truck into park and shut off the engine.

But he didn't make a move to get out. Instead, he shifted, reached out, and set his hand on my arm. His voice tightened with the plea. "I need you to know that I will do anything to keep you safe, Salem. For you to have a good life. No matter the cost. It's time."

Tears filled my eyes. Love filled me up to overflowing.

It spilled free with the rush of moisture that slipped down my cheeks.

Marked and true.

I touched his face. My big brother who I had always looked up to, adored, and revered. The one who was taking the chance, too.

"I know you would, Darius, and there is no way to express my gratefulness for that. For what you've done. For what you're sacrificing. And I'm terrified the only thing I'm doing is putting you and Mimi in danger. That I might be responsible for—"

A swell of sorrow crested. My breath caught on the snare of it.

Tight and hot.

A hole so deep it would never be filled.

It was my fault.

It was my fault.

I nearly buckled with the grief.

"You're not putting us in any danger," he insisted. "We're safe. Promise you."

I swallowed the torment, my thickened tongue rushing over my lips so I could get this out.

"What happened…it's going to hurt…haunt me forever…"

No, there were no actual words. No way to verbally express what this kind of loss felt like. The empty pit that festered.

I forced myself to continue. "You convinced me to come here. To start a new life. That it was time. And because of that, I'm looking forward for the first time in years. For the first time, I'm not just surviving, I'm living. And I'm so thankful for you. So thankful you love us so much that you would stand in front of anything to protect us. Thankful you moved here to create a safe place for us. But you also can't stand in the way. I know I've made a million mistakes and I'm sure I'll make a million more, but I have to do this, Darius, and you can't freak out every time I step out the door. Not if I'm actually going to live."

His expression twisted in grief. "I know, and that's all I want for you—for you to live. Free. Without fear. Without ever havin' to look over your shoulder."

Affection pulled a soggy smile to my mouth. "I know you do, and I want that, too, but none of that is your responsibility."

"The hell, it isn't," he grumbled.

He was such a protector, too.

I forced some lightness into my voice. "Thank you for the ride, Darius. I'll figure the car out. Don't worry about it. Now, you'd better get to work. Your boss seems like he might be the type to get grumpy."

Darius didn't laugh.

His lips pinched, and he swallowed hard as I unlatched the door and started to slide out. Before I made it to standing, he reached out and took me by the hand to stop me. His words were razors. "Just… stay away from Jud, Salem. He's not the kind of guy you can trust."

Sadness slipped beneath my skin. "Don't worry, Darius. I don't trust anyone."

Only this tiny family.

I stepped from the truck just as the front door banged open and Juniper came bounding out. She jumped off the single step and raced down the sidewalk to meet me.

"Mommy! There you are finally! Jeez louise, doncha know we got the worries about you? Where did you go? I thought you got lost all the way in the rain and floated all the way down to the ocean and you had to live with the dolphins."

Love squeezed my ribs in a fist.

Crushing.

So intense it nearly dropped me to my knees as my little girl came flying my direction.

Juniper was nothing but giggles and smiles and black, messy hair that had been twisted into two wild buns on the sides of her head.

Pink, chubby cheeks and the tiniest, sweetest mouth.

She threw herself into my arms, already knowing I would catch her, that I would sweep her off her feet and swing her around before I brought her to my chest and hugged her tight.

Our cheeks were pressed together as I inhaled her sweet plum scent. "Get lost and live with the dolphins? Not a chance. I will always find you."

Behind us, I caught sight of Darius pulling away. His eyes were on us. Staunch protectiveness in his gaze.

And I got it…got that he'd felt helpless for all those years, and now that we were here, he would do anything for us.

But he had no idea what I'd been through. I guessed in the end, I had to respect that. For years, he'd wanted to fight and, now that he had the chance, he couldn't do anything but come alongside me.

Another giggle slipped from Juniper's lips, her little nose scrunched as she edged back enough to see my face. Her dark, dark eyes were the same blue as mine.

But hers?

They burned with innocence. With the hope and belief I wanted to give her.

"Because I'm your world, right, Mommy?"

I held my five-year-old close.

My life.

My source.

My purpose to get up each morning for the last four years and fight. My purpose to go on.

"That's right, Juni Bee, no matter where you go, I will always find you."

I spun her around. She squeezed her little arms over her chest as she laughed and squirmed in my arms.

Devotion erupted from that crater.

The one that would forever be carved inside me.

"Even if I'm all the way up high in the sky?" Her tinkling voice danced around my ears and seeped into my soul.

It was all a tease. The game we played. How far would I go to find her? To protect her?

Little did she know, there was no distance because I would go to the very, very end.

"That's right. Even if you're up all the way high in the sky."

"Even to Mars?" She flung herself back at that, her arms outstretched, her face lifted toward the cloudless sky.

I could feel her bright, bright spirit burn in my arms.

A precious treasure I held in my hands.

"Even to Mars."

She swung herself up to grab onto my shoulders. She wore a gigantic grin. "That's because you love me all the way to the stars."

"That's right…all the way to the stars."

To the moon.

To the sun.

My guiding light.

My one purpose.

I felt the movement at the doorway, and I looked up to find Mimi standing there. Her weathered face was full of worry and relief.

My grandmother was eighty-seven, short and heavyset, and the strongest woman I knew.

The years might have blurred the edges of her youth, but they hadn't robbed her of her vitality.

"Well, there you are, young lady," she said. With the tone of it, I was pretty sure I was in trouble with her, too.

I held Juniper close as I trudged that way. "I hope you got my messages. I hated that I couldn't make it home."

"When my phone started working, I saw the text that your car broke down and you were with a *friend*."

She said friend like an accusation.

We both knew I didn't have any of those.

"Didn't mean I wasn't worried about you." She quirked a concerned brow.

"I know. I'm sorry. My car just died." I waved a flustered hand in the air, another bolt of distress lighting me through. The last thing I'd needed was another issue.

"Told you that thing was about to go kaput."

"You weren't wrong."

She leaned against the doorway and crossed her arms over her chest. "Which is why I didn't want you out gallivanting by yourself last night. Told you a storm was a'comin'. My poor aching bones are at least good for something."

Gallivanting?

Not even close.

I'd somehow convinced my grandmother and brother I was

meeting the neighbor lady I'd met across the street for drinks downtown.

Unbelievable?

Absolutely.

But I guessed all of us had become complacent.

Easing into normalcy which was the goal.

Our claim.

What we were desperate for.

She didn't need to know I was hawking the last piece of jewelry I still owned of my mother's.

Mimi's eyes narrowed in speculation. "So, who was this friend?"

Uneasily, I took the last step up to the front door, my gaze dropping to my feet for a second before I met Mimi's eyes. I thought to lie, but then I figured the woman could see right through me, anyway.

She'd raised me, after all.

"I guess you could say he just became my friend last night."

Juni clapped, her voice full of a thrill. "You got a new friend, Mommy? That's so, so good! Meeting new people is really important."

"That's right, Juni Bee," I told her, though my attention was still locked on my grandmother who eyed me up and down.

"He a looker?" she asked, her brow rising in what appeared glee.

"Mimi," I chastised as I stepped into the old house. The main room was small, the carpet worn, and the furniture old. But Mimi had taken to making it a home. Every nook and cranny was filled with the same knickknacks from her house growing up, and she'd covered the walls in family pictures.

Juni and I were staying in the main living room since there were only two bedrooms, and I wasn't about to oust Darius and Mimi from their beds. Darius had tried to argue, but I'd insisted. He was paying for this place, and like I'd told Jud, I was no charity case.

I'd managed to scrape by doing odd jobs for the last four years, and that wasn't going to change.

Mimi laughed as she followed us inside. "Oh, I was young once, missy. Don't even be givin' me that. It's about time you had yourself a little fun."

"I'm not anywhere near being in the position to entertain the idea of *fun*, Mimi," I told her, setting Juni on her feet. Juni scampered over to the dolls she had set up by the window, singing under her breath when she climbed down onto her knees to play.

A light in the shadows. My beacon in the dark. Where my heart would always follow.

I realized I must have been staring at my daughter because Mimi's expression had gone soft when I finally looked back at her.

"The heart usually decides when you're ready, Salem, not the head."

A doubtful chuckle rippled out. "Honestly, it was nothing, Mimi. Just a nice guy who stopped to help me in the rain. A guy who just so happened to turn out to be Darius' boss. There was nothing there, so you just forget whatever scandalous ideas you have spinning in your brain right now."

"I live for scandalous ideas."

"Mimi." I huffed.

Laughing, she started to shuffle toward the kitchen. "I might be old, but I'm not dead, girl, so don't pretend like I didn't just see that blush light up your cheeks. Nothing there, my ass."

"I am not blushing, Mimi," I hollered behind her.

The second she disappeared through the doorway, I touched my cheek, feeling the heat on my fingertips.

Crap.

"And while you're at it, you might as well fess up about whatever you were up to last night because I sure know it wasn't meeting up with a *friend*, but I sure like the idea of you making some new ones." Her voice carried from the kitchen.

Double crap.

"Mimi, *ass* is bad words." Juni said it so casually, like she'd been a part of the entire conversation. "You're the one who'd better be fessing it up, young lady, before you get in troubles and have to go to timeout all the way in Antarctica."

"Time out in Antarctica? Well, we don't want that now, do we?

How about I trade you a popsicle, instead, angel girl?" Mimi all but sang.

Juni hopped to her feet and raced for the kitchen.

The child was nothing but pink bows and bright, blinding life.

"Deal!"

"Ugh, Mimi, you are going to spoil her rotten."

"That's what mimis are for, sweet child."

"And you're my greatest mimi, right?" Juni asked, standing at her side with all that hope shining on her adorable face.

I'd followed them to the entryway, light laughter rolling from my throat. Juni kept smiling up at her great grandmother. Mimi touched her chin. "That's right, Juni Bee. The greatest, and don't you ever forget it."

My chest squeezed tight.

I nearly hit the ceiling when the doorbell rang five times in a row. Carefully, I inched that way, forever on edge. I peered out the drape and the dread that had bottled fizzled in a flash. I worked through the lock, calling, "I think you have a visitor, Juni Bee."

She was already at my side by the time I got the door open to the little neighbor boy and his dad's girlfriend, Eden.

You know, the one I'd supposedly gone out with last night.

We'd met them yesterday when they'd been out playing in front of their house. The child's hand was wrapped up in Eden's as he anxiously jumped at her side. "Hi, hi, hi! Do you remember me? I live right there."

In excitement, he pointed at the house directly across the street.

Juni giggled and squirmed, and I was pretty sure she was blushing, too. "'Course, I remembers you! You're my new best friend Gage, you silly willies. I seens you yesterday with your brand-new red bike."

The little boy laughed like what she'd said was hysterical, all dimples and brown eyes. "It's the coolest bike in the whole wide world. I'm gonna ride it to the highest mountain. You wanna try it today? My Miss Murphy said I was allowed to ask you. Right, Miss Murphy, right?"

The words rambled from his mouth in a slew of excitement.

"That's right, Gage."

Eden's smile was adoring as she looked between the two of them, knowing as she glanced at me in small wonder. As if she couldn't believe she was experiencing it herself. I didn't really know her, but it was clear she'd taken up a role in the child's life that had changed everything in hers.

Adoration stark.

Love fierce.

Devotion whole.

Eden was tall and slender and blonde. Wearing a modest floral dress and sandals. Everything about her was soft, gracious, and kind. "I hope we're not imposing. Gage woke up this morning and the only thing he could talk about was getting over here to ask if Juni could play."

My chest pressed with hope and twitched with nerves. "You're not imposing at all."

Eden smiled, pure affection rolling from her tongue. "Okay, good. We can be a lot to handle."

"You wanna try it?" Gage asked Juni.

"Yes! Oh, please, yes!"

The second we'd come in after meeting them yesterday, Juni had begged for a bike so she could play with him.

And I was trying…trying so hard to give her everything she deserved.

Which was the precise reason I was out at nine at night in the middle of a storm trying to scrimp something together.

Stupid?

Maybe.

But I couldn't ask Darius for anything else, couldn't put another burden on his shoulders, not when he was paying for Mimi's medications and this house, so I'd slipped out when he'd gone to hang out with the girl he'd been seeing for the last few months and had headed straight to a pawn shop.

A piece of me felt guilty for parting with the last ring I had of hers. But my mom? I had to imagine she would have done the same.

We'd lost her so young, when I'd been four and Darius eight. A heart condition she'd never even known she'd had. Gone in a failed beat.

Since our father had never been in the picture, Mimi had stepped up to raise us.

Gage turned his attention to me, all dimples and cuteness and manners for days. "Miss Salem, is it okay if Juni can come play with me because you know I live just right across the street, and she's got to be my best friend forever?"

"I think that would be really nice," I whispered.

Suddenly overcome.

Overwhelmed.

Because Juni and I had never stayed in one place for longer than a couple months.

This was what I dreamed of for her.

Wanted for her.

More than I could say. More than I could express.

A friend.

A safe place where she knew the people would care for her. Look out for her. *Love her*.

A *home* she could always go back to.

Emotion gathered at the back of my eyes. The hope blinding and terrifying at the same time. I had to blink the moisture back, to hold myself together so I didn't crumble.

Eden reached out and gently touched my arm, her voice so soft, held so it was just for me as the two children began to jump around on the stoop. "We're so glad you're here."

"Thank you." The words wobbled.

She smiled. "And also, I don't want to be forward, but I'm teaching a beginning ballet class for five and six-year-olds this summer after school ends. It starts next week. Three days a week. It's free at the school where I work. We'd love to have Juni join us."

"Ballet? Oh, Mommy, Mommy, please!!!" Of course, Juni had heard it, her little eagle ears in tune, her fingers threaded together in a prayer. "I want the ballet shoes so bad, and maybe I will get to go to Russia and do the dances!"

Affection pulling tight, I glanced at Eden.

Those dreams right there.

The ones that'd been unthinkable for so long, and now? Maybe... maybe they were within reach.

"That would be wonderful."

How I was going to get those ballet shoes, I had no idea, but I would figure it out.

Eden's smile spread. "Great. I knew these two would be a good fit. I think you and I will be, too."

She gently touched my wrist again. Like she saw everything written in me. Every secret. Every fear.

Like she was silently offering to come alongside me.

A friend.

I hadn't had one in so long.

My throat grew thick. "I do, too."

"Come over and chat with me while the kids play in the front?"

"Sure." I leaned back into the house and called, "We'll be out front, Mimi."

"Have fun," she hollered.

I stepped out and shut the door behind us.

Hand-in-hand, Juni and Gage started to run down the sidewalk.

"Wait at the curb," Eden called, and the children skidded to a stop. We flanked them as we crossed, and we walked up the sidewalk to the house that was basically the same as the one we were renting, though it'd obviously received a little more care and updates through the years.

I nearly stumbled when a man came sauntering out the front door. Tall with a shock of black hair, tattoos covering every inch of exposed flesh.

He was pure intimidation.

Menacing.

Extremely so, in a way that set me on edge.

Bad was written all over him in bold streaks and hard lines.

But this sweet, sweet woman all but floated over to him and let him wrap his arms around her.

So opposite it was like they slipped into the other to form a whole.

They whispered below their breaths, their words only meant for the other.

Something familiar pushed at my consciousness when he looked at me with the darkest eyes from over her shoulder.

The way they pierced and flayed.

My pulse thudded.

Eden spun around with her hand wrapped in his. "Salem, I'd like you to meet my boyfriend, Trent. Gage's dad." Her voice deepened with devotion. "Trent, this is the new neighbor I was telling you about, Salem, Darius' sister."

The man looked me up and down, cautious, but still, he stretched out his hand to shake mine. "Nice to meet you, Salem. I didn't even realize Darius had a sister. He works for my brother at his shop."

I froze as I realized the familiarity.

The resemblance.

The way those sharp eyes held the power to slice me in two.

Jud Lawson was his brother.

The man in the rain. The man who sparked something inside me that I hardly recognized in myself anymore.

A want that had sizzled across my flesh. A need I'd all but forgotten.

A fire in my guts.

But it was the fire that burned.

The flames that ruined.

And I knew I needed to stay far, far away from the blaze.

Chapter Five

Jud

"Do we have an issue?" I stood behind Darius where he worked to install the gas tank to a 70s chopper that I'd finished painting last week. Thing was pure beauty, if I didn't say so myself.

Turquoise and black.

Like someone's eyes that I was having a damned hard time getting off my mind.

Same eyes responsible for the tension that had bound the shop for the entire day. Animosity fierce in the stone set of Darius' spine.

Dude hadn't even looked at me when he'd returned, but that didn't mean I didn't feel the malice radiating from him for the last four hours.

He barely cranked a glance at me from over his shoulder. But I saw it there. This fierce protectiveness that kinda pissed me off. He went back to working a screw while he mumbled under his breath, "Not if you stay away from my sister, we don't."

A low, hard chuckle rumbled out. "You have a problem with me stopping to help a woman stranded in the rain?"

"Have no problem except for the one where Salem came waltzing out of your apartment this morning." He grunted that. The tattoos on his forearms writhed over his muscles that flexed with the words. "She seems like a big girl to me."

A fierce, hypnotic, gorgeous girl who'd kept me tossing through the night.

Didn't think I'd point that out.

Before I could make sense of it, Darius flew to his feet, wheeling around with a threat in his stance and venom in his voice. "Stay the fuck away from my sister. She doesn't need any more shit in her life than she's already been dealt."

My chest tightened with the confirmation, the sense I'd gotten that the girl might've only had a purse, but she'd been carting around a shitton of baggage.

At the same time, a disbelieving smirk kicked at the edge of my mouth. "I don't think I appreciate the implication."

His dark eyes flashed, and he leaned in closer, his voice grit, "You think I don't know you? Kind of man you are?"

Unease gusted, blistered and blew through the scorched wasteland of who I'd been. Where my soul had gone dry.

My hands fisted. "I'm not sure who you think you are, Darius..." I bit out his name through clenched teeth. "But I'd suggest you watch what you say. Took a chance on you. Don't make me regret it."

I wasn't one to fly off the handle. Had learned to play it cool. To keep the old demon that thrashed inside chained.

But this?

I was half inclined to toss him from my shop. The other part knew we both were overreacting. He was only doing what he thought was right.

Standing up for his sister before she got herself hurt.

I mean, fuck, could I blame him?

I took a step back, trying to put some space between us. Wasn't like a thing had gone down between his sister and me, anyway, so every bit of this was misplaced.

Darius winced, finally catching up to the fact that he was out of line. He scrubbed a palm over his face, and he dropped his gaze to the ground. "I'm sorry, Sir." He might have been apologizing, but his voice was hard.

"She's been hurt, and I'm not sure I could stand aside and watch it happen again," he admitted low.

"Not necessary, man. Just…chill. All's good. I got her to safety to ride out the storm. She slept in my guest room. It started and ended at that."

Left out the part where I'd felt chained.

Spellbound.

Truth be told, if the girl had wanted one of those wild nights that caught you unaware? Nothing but pleasure without any of the aftermath? I'd have gladly peeled her out of those drenched clothes.

But that possibility had sailed the second I'd realized she was related to Darius. I sure as shit didn't need that kind of complication. Think more than that, though, was the fact there was something about her that felt like *more*.

Pain lanced. A dull moan from that vacant space.

A knife in my chest where my heart had gone missing.

And in the middle of that void, there was no space for *more*. I forced a smile. "Are we good, man?"

Nodding, Darius lifted his gaze. "Yeah. Sorry. That was uncalled for. Get a little crazy when it comes to my family. Want you to know I appreciate this job. Need it, and I know you hired me when I wasn't exactly qualified."

I let a huff of a laugh leave my nose, and I reached out and squeezed his shoulder. "Don't sweat it. Something is wrong with us if we don't go a little crazy when it comes to protecting our family."

Truth that family should mean everything.

"Just watch how you do it next time, yeah?" The warning dropped from my mouth as I backed away. I might get it, but I wasn't about to take any shit, either.

I started to walk before I punted out the words, hard and direct, "And I've got her car covered. Gonna need her number. Text it to me before you leave."

For a beat, he hesitated, clearly wanting to argue, but he finally dipped his head in surrender and turned around to get back to work, grumbling, "Whatever you say, boss."

I spun around, only to catch Brock grinning like a smug prick from where he stood next to the engine he was rebuilding, asshole rocking his hips and wagging his brows.

Boob shots, he mouthed with an overexaggerated nod and a wink.

I roughed a hand over my face.

Fuck my life.

Ignoring him, I strode back to the bones of the bike I was slowly rebuilding. I cranked the music back up, pulled on my welding mask, and got lost in the work. Got lost in the feel of the metal beneath my hands.

The peace in it.

Guessed it reminded me I still had something to offer.

That the darkness could create beauty.

That the condemned could whisper grace.

That I had something good to show for my life.

A purpose.

Hours must have passed, I didn't know, I was so lost in thought, sound banging through my ears and vibrating through my body, that I nearly jumped out of my skin when a hand landed on my shoulder. I ripped off my mask as I whipped around, ready to floor a motherfucker.

Old habits died hard.

I blew out the strained breath when I saw it was my youngest brother, Logan.

Asshole cracked up, stumbling backward and shouting over the music, "Bro, you jumped like fifteen feet in the air. If the whole restoration thing doesn't pan out, think you have promise. Olympic hopeful."

He lifted his hands out like he was catching a dream.

Fucker.

I tossed my mask to the table and wiped the sweat from my brow with my sleeve. "Yeah, and you're lucky you're not *fifteen* under. Don't sneak up on a man like that unless you wanna get cut."

Logan laughed like it wasn't our reality.

I rolled my eyes as my attention drifted to our older brother, Trent, who was smirking behind him.

And there was Trent's son, Gage, jumping at his father's side, all kinds of hope and light and every-fucking-thing that was right in this world.

Took a beat just to take in this messed up, beautiful family.

Our scars went deep.

Were ugly and brutal.

But here we were, forever fighting for the other.

"You're gonna give him a one, two, three, kapow, right, Uncle Jud, right?!" Gage tossed his little fist forward and gave a good kick, giggling the whole time. My sweet nephew who nearly slayed me every time I looked at his adorable face. Kid too much. Had so much love for him, it hurt.

"That's right, Gage in the Cage," I told him, and the kid came barreling my way the second I said it.

Affection pushed hard at my ribs. Didn't matter how many times I met him this way, the loss still screamed.

Begging to be filled.

I caught him just as he was throwing himself at me, and I tossed him onto my back the way I always did. I spun him around, pretending like we were in the ring.

"What? You think you're gonna pile drive me! I won't even let you, Uncle." My favorite little wrestler scrambled around, locking his tiny arms around my neck like he was going to choke me out. "You might be big as a monster, Uncle, but I'm as wily as a coyote. You won't even know what hit you."

I was holding my laughter, and Trent rested back against the worktable, his arms crossed over his chest and his booted feet crossed at the ankles.

A chuckle rode from his mouth. "Pains me to admit it, but for once, Logan is right. We've been standing back here waiting on you for the last ten minutes. You didn't even notice we were here. Now that is the shit that's not safe."

I glanced at the huge clock mounted on the wall while Gage kept trying to take me down.

"Sorry, lost track of time." Honestly, I'd forgotten we'd planned a family meeting this afternoon. Had to blame it on my thoughts getting tied up on things they shouldn't.

"No shit." Trent grinned.

Gage slowed his attack, staring over at his father.

"Sheesh, Dad, doncha know you're gonna get in trouble saying those kinda words? And trouble is really bad. Have you learned nothin' yet? We have to get all the A's and you keep gettin' the F's." Could feel Gage shaking his head in stark disappointment.

Laughing, I flipped Gage off my back, kid squealing like mad as I set him onto his feet.

I straightened to Logan tossing me one of his smirks. "Think it's your uncle Jud here who is getting the F's, oh young Gage."

Asshole widened his eyes at me like he was vexed.

"Here I was, just rolling in to remind him of our meeting, and he goes threatening me. Why so violent?" Logan blinked, his head barely shaking.

Dude was a nut.

Constantly goofing and throwing barbs.

Arrogant as fuck.

Still, he was good, through and through. It was the only reason I let him get away with that shit.

His hair was as black as the night, same as mine and Trent's, but where Trent and I had eyes that were so dark they were basically coal, his were these sparkling emeralds that forever glinted with a tease.

My heart tweaked at the sight.

He favored our mom so much that sometimes it stung to look at him.

Dude stuck out in both the club and the shop considering the asshole might as well have been an Armani model, wearing his tailored suits and driving his flashy car.

A scoff rolled up my throat. "If I wanted to hurt you, you'd be hurt."

"Can you believe this guy?" Logan hooked a thumb at me while talking to Gage. "Grizzly, I tell you."

Gage cracked up. "Like a bear? He sure has enough hair."

Sound that left me was close to a growl.

"Did you hear that, Gage? Proof. Right there." Logan pointed at me.

I smacked his finger out of my face. "You point that finger at me again, and you're going to lose it." Warned it like he was a little kid, but hell, since he acted like one half the time, that's what he got. Funny, considering he ran stocks and was fuckin' flush. Smarts for days yet as heedless as they came.

Dude was a walking, talking mindfuck.

"Jud, man, come on. Lighten up. I'm just playing with you. And here I thought this one over here was the funsucker." He tossed a mocking jab to Trent's upper arm. "All thanks to pretty little Eden. Remind me I owe her."

"Oh, oh, now that he's gettin' some, he doesn't have to be such a d-i-c-k anymore, right, Uncle Logan, right?"

Little Gage was grinning way too big, and I was shaking my head. We were going to have to watch it. Kid was getting way too clever, and I was pretty sure one day he was going to surprise us by knowing exactly what we were talking about.

Leave it to Logan to egg him on.

"That's right, Gage. We finally got a little mercy from the beast. Thank the Lord." All kinds of dramatic, he pressed his hands together in a prayer and lifted his face toward the sky.

A chuckle got free of my throat just as Trent was throwing a punch back at him, only a little harder than the one Logan had landed on him.

Logan jumped back, holding onto his arm. "Ow, a-hole, that hurt."

We might give Logan shit for being smaller than the two of us, but I was pretty sure if push came to shove, dude could hold his own. He was as easygoing as they came, but there was something there, running below the surface.

Lawson blood. And that blood ran thick and dark.

Pussy, Trent mouthed over Gage's head.

"Wow, Trent, wow." Logan touched his chest, mocking injury. "Two of you are dangerous to a man's ego."

"Believe me, a little depletion to your ego would not be a bad thing," Trent grumbled.

I grabbed a hand towel and ran it over my face and hair to soak up the sweat.

"Are we ready to do this thing?" Logan asked, smacking his hands together. His entire demeanor shifted when he got down to business.

"Yup."

"We got work to do!" Gage hollered, grinning at his dad as he ran to his side and took his hand again.

I followed them out of the stall where I'd been working and into the main shop.

Doubted anyone but me noticed the skeptical glance Darius shot as we passed.

We filed into my office made of glass walls that was tucked at the far-right corner.

I clicked the door shut.

Logan spun around, lifting his arms out to the sides. Cockiness streamed from him in waves.

"Now, now, I know we all know how brilliant your baby brother is but prepare for me to take it to the next level."

He dug into the bag he was carrying and pulled out his laptop. Setting it on my desk, he faced it out, lifted the lid, and punched in a few things to populate the charts he updated us with quarterly.

He waved a dramatic hand at the screen as he sank into one of the chairs in front of the desk.

All kinds of smug.

But in this case?

It was warranted.

"Read 'em and weep, boys."

"I'm not weepin'," Trent mumbled in shock when he looked at our skyrocketing numbers.

Logan laughed. "Happy tears, brother, they're good for the soul. Let's see them."

"Seriously, Logan, you some kinda wizard? Because this shit can't be legal." Disbelief filled my voice.

The smile dropped from Logan's face, his expression morphing in sincerity. "You know I'd never gamble with your money like that. You're my brothers. You wanted it aggressive, I did it aggressive, and it paid off big. Simple as that."

Trent roughed a tattooed hand over his mouth. "Don't even know what to say."

A smirk took to Logan's face. "Hmmm…let's see…pretty sure it goes something like, *Forgive me, oh, amazing one, I underestimated you. Big time. You're definitely the smartest and best looking of us Lawson bros. Where would I be without you? And just because you're so awesome and handsome and basically the coolest guy I know, I solemnly swear to never punch you again. Not even when you're checking out my smokin' hot woman.*"

His smirk widened as he pressed his hand over his heart in a mock oath. "A little somethin' like that will do."

That was two seconds before he got punched again.

"You even look at Eden, and I gouge your eyes out," Trent growled.

Gage giggled wildly. "You better watch it, Uncle. Everyone's comin' for you, and even I won't be able to save you."

"Never, Gage. These ogres love me."

That time, the tease drained from Logan's tone as he looked between us.

"Of course, we do. Doesn't give you the clear to check out Eden, though." Trent almost smiled when he said it.

Miracles did come true.

Was pretty sure that miracle came in the form of a sweet little blonde who'd changed Trent's world.

Logan lifted both his hands in surrender. "Fine, fine. You know I'm just messing with you. Happy for you, brother. Honestly. Love that you found someone as awesome and *hot* as Eden."

The ribbing was back on the last as he tapped his fist on Trent's knee.

Trent grunted. "Know it. Still feels like a dream. Never thought I'd get so lucky. Speaking of…there's a reason Gage is here with me today. We have news."

He tipped his gaze down to Gage who beamed up at him.

My chest stretched tight.

Was hard witnessing something so perfect.

"You want to tell 'em, buddy?" Trent urged.

The whole room lit up with the force of Gage's smile, and he started jumping on his toes, all that caramel hair bouncing around his face. "We're gonna ask Miss Murphy if she wants to get married!"

Excitement poured from his mouth. Almost as fierce as the hope and worry that blazed from Trent's spirit.

I saw it roil in his eyes. Old wounds that would never let him go fighting against the truth that he deserved happiness. Dude would give it all for us. It was about damned time he got it in return.

"We even got rings and everything and Miss Murphy is gonna be the happiest in the whole wide world. All the way to the highest mountain." He stretched his arms over his head. "And that's where we're gonna love her forever and ever. Right, Dad, right?"

"That's right, buddy, that's what we're hoping."

"Hoping?" My brow arched. "That girl's mad for you, brother. You don't have a thing to worry about."

"Jud's spot on," Logan said, slouched back in the chair. "Eden is amazing. You two might be opposites, but you're perfect for each other."

Gage squeezed his dad's hand tight, belief stretched across his face.

"Dad, see, you don't got nothin' to worry about. *She loves us.*" His little voice twisted in emphasis.

Adoration came riding out with Trent's. "I know it, buddy. Sometimes it's just hard for me to realize it."

"Realize it, already, sheesh."

On a chuckle, Trent blew some of the tension from between his lips, and he glanced between me and Logan. "I want to do it on the last day of school this Friday. As soon as school lets out. Figure one ending can be our new beginning. Was hoping to set up a surprise. Have everyone we care about there to witness it."

"I'm there," I promised.

"Like you could keep me away," Logan added.

Trent grinned down at his kid. Joy lit against the darkest places in his being.

I felt it spark, too.

Satisfied in the truth that my older brother was happy.

That this family was finally safe.

That we'd truly left the crimes and misdeeds and corruption in the past.

My attention drifted out the bank of windows that sectioned off my office from the rest of the shop, landing on the sedan sitting on the car lift on the opposite side.

Something shifted through me.

The draw.

The attraction.

The fire.

The force of that woman hit me like an avalanche.

A rumble knocking me from my feet.

Black-fuckin'-magic.

Needed to ignore it.

But then I figured it was some kinda cosmic shit when my phone beeped in my pocket at the exact same time, and it was a text from Darius with Salem's phone number.

A grin slid to my mouth.

And I was pretty sure that grin made me a damned fool.

Chapter Six

Salem

"WHAT ARE YOU GIGGLING ABOUT OVER THERE, Juni Bee?" Drying my hands, I leaned against the kitchen archway and looked at my daughter who was propped on her knees in front of the living room window, her hands plastered to the glass.

She giggled more and pressed her face to the pane.

Amusement rippled through me as I moved that way so I could peer out into the night at what she was staring at across the street.

Or rather, who.

Little Gage was in the exact same position, blowing his lips against the glass and making his cheeks puff out.

The lights were on in both the rooms, and the two of them were lit up in their own personal fishbowls.

Juni howled with laughter. "Mommy, look! My new best friend is the funniest in the whole world, and did you knows he even likes the stars, too?" Her voice lifted in excitement. "He said he's gots the whole solar system hanging in his room."

She looked back at me with her blue eyes wide with delight. "Even Mars!"

"Even Mars? No way."

"Yes, ways!"

Soft laughter slipped from my mouth, and I moved to stand behind her, brushing my fingers through the long tresses of her black hair that was still damp from her bath. Gage waved like mad when he saw me.

Another laugh slipped free, and I waved back.

A grunt sounded from behind us. I glanced back to find Darius standing at the end of the hall. "What's going on in here?"

"Apparently, our Juni here found a new way to tell her best friend goodnight."

"Like this, Uncle D!" She leaned up higher and copied the blowing that Gage had been doing, but she didn't get her mouth fully on the glass, so she just ended up spluttering air and slobbering all over the window.

It only made her laugh harder.

Darius grunted again. "Still think you and Juni should take my room. More privacy that way."

I smiled back at him. "She clearly doesn't mind."

"Nope, not at all. Not one little bits."

His head shook, all that overprotectiveness pouring out. A frown took to my brow, my heart hurting that he felt this way. Fear and sorrow the thief of his joy. The thief of belief.

"They're harmless, Darius." My voice was a whispered plea.

He moved to the front door. He paused with his hand on the knob, contemplating before he swiveled to look at me. "Thought we didn't trust anyone?"

Sadness bound my spirit. "Maybe it's time we did."

Dread tightened his expression. "Trying so hard to give you a life, Salem. A real life. One where none of us have to be afraid."

A wistful smile pulled to my mouth. "Is it wrong it's finally starting to feel that way?"

His lips thinned as he contemplated. "No," he finally said.

Juni grabbed her favorite doll and pressed it to the window, the same as Gage was pressing a teddy bear to his. Darius watched her, his love pouring out. He returned his gaze to me. "I'm going to Carly's. Just...be careful, okay?"

"I am."

I'd been *careful* for years. I'd basically perfected it.

Darius slipped out the door and into the night, and I leaned down and kissed my daughter on the top of the head. "Come on, Juni Bee, you need to finish getting ready for bed."

"Oh, man, do I have to? Looks it right there. Gage still wants to play, and Molly is finallys getting to say hi to him." She held her doll out to me like she was a person.

Light laughter tumbled from my mouth, though I kept my voice firm. "Tell her to tell him goodnight."

She poked out her bottom lip. She turned her sad face to Gage. He pouted right back.

The two of them were wrapped up in their own little language, so sweet, especially when he drew a little heart on the window.

It panged in mine.

Juni giggled and blushed and brought her shoulders up to her cheeks. "I loves him the mostest, Mommy!"

"It looks like he loves you, too."

I sent a wave to the little boy then shut the curtains. Cutting off her view was the only thing that finally coaxed Juni to her feet.

We moved into the short hall where the second bathroom was across from Mimi's room. We could hear her snoring from behind her door.

Juni scrunched up her nose and held her laughter, her words a secreted whisper, "Mimi is a snorin' up a morin'."

"A morin', huh?" I quirked a brow.

Juniper nodded with a blink. "The worst kind."

I touched her chin. Affection pulsed at my chest.

Powerful.

Unending.

A gift that'd made it out of the ash.

My one purpose.

"It's time for you to get to snorin'," I told her.

"Oh, fine, okay," she grumbled.

She went to the sink and brushed her teeth, and then she was running back for the living room. "Story times!"

She dove onto the makeshift bed we'd made on the floor, and I climbed down beside her as she grabbed the book we'd been reading together, the first in The Boxcar Children. Sitting on the mat, I pulled her onto my lap where she sat facing out. Her little heartbeats thumped against my chest as I went to the page we had marked.

I began to read.

Soft and slow.

Changing my voice the way Juni demanded I do.

She rocked her head back to look up at me, those eyes full of their belief. "I'd live in a boxcar with you and goes on every adventure you wants to take, Mommy, but I likes it here the best."

My spirit squeezed in sorrow.

Each time we'd moved from one place to another, I'd amped it up, told her we were going on a great adventure, and tried to make it seem as if it were exciting rather than a horrible reality of our lives.

I leaned down and pressed my lips to her forehead. Inhaled her sweet scent. The truth that the last four years of our lives had affected her in a way that I doubted I could fully understand. Prohibited her from planting roots. From feeling stable and safe.

I whispered at her skin, "I like it here best, too, Juni Bee, so much."

"But we'll be just fine just as long as we're togethers, right? Wherever we go?"

"Wherever we go," I promised.

A playful grin stole over her lips. "Even Antarctica?"

I tickled her. "Even Antarctica."

She squealed and laughed, and I nuzzled my face into her cheek. Loved and made a million silent promises.

Wherever we go.

Wherever we go.

Resolution pulsed through my chest. I was determined it would never again come to that.

I would never let paranoia take me over.

I would never again frantically pack the empty suitcase that now sat against the wall.

We'd never again drive away in the middle of the night from a place that had barely become home.

Twenty minutes later, Juniper was sound asleep, and she had her cheek pressed to her pillow and her black hair was spread around her precious, cherub face. I'd dimmed the lights so she could sleep, and night danced and played across the walls as I brushed my fingers through her hair.

Softly.

Methodically.

Quietly giving her the peace that we'd lacked.

Praying it would stand.

That we no longer had to be afraid.

A frown took hold when my phone vibrated from where I'd left it on the couch. Precisely three people had my number.

Mimi, Darius, and now Eden.

I dipped in and pressed a gentle kiss to Juni's temple before I stood, my eyes narrowing as I picked up my phone and read the words that had come through on a text.

Strike that.

Four.

Unknown: I have good news and I have bad news, darlin'.

My heart fluttered in my chest. Way too light and excited when I saw the words, though I read them like I was hearing the deep scrape of his voice. Kind of the way I changed the tone for Juni when I read to her. But the really reckless part of me didn't want this story to end quite so innocently.

Crawling onto the couch and crisscrossing my legs, I tapped out a message.

Me: Who is this?

I pressed send. Of course, I knew who it was. Don't judge a girl for playing coy. I didn't know how he'd bribed Darius for my number, but I was sure this bad boy had his ways.

Jud: What, you don't recognize me? Your knight in shining armor?

I was gnawing at my lip and fighting a grin when I typed out a response.

Me: Except he doesn't ride in on a horse and he's dressed all in black?

Jud: That'd be him.

Me: I don't know about knight...he seemed awful...dangerous.

Why I was playing this game, I didn't know. All I knew was my heart felt like it was on an unexpected joyride as my fingers flew across the screen. Hungry for his response.

Jud: You have no idea.

Shivers raced across my skin. I should take them as a warning. Not as a slow slide of need that slipped like silk into my bloodstream. I forced myself to get it together before I let this go in a direction I couldn't let it.

Me: How bad is it?

Jud: Timing belt. There was some engine damage.

Shit. I glanced at Juni where she slept. Worry fisted in my chest. I went back to my phone.

Me: And the good news?

I wondered if he could hear the sarcasm in my question. If he could feel the edge of hysteria that infiltrated my consciousness. Because I was pretty sure there wasn't anything *good* about this news.

Jud: Didn't take out the engine block so it saves the big bucks. And you've got me.

I warred, not knowing how to respond, how to tell him I basically had nothing. That even if it was saving the big bucks, I had *no* bucks.

The only thing currently in my wallet was a hundred-dollar bill I'd gotten for a ring that should have been worth at least a thousand. One I had no intention of going back to claim because I was set on saving to buy a bike with training wheels for my daughter.

A little voice called in the back of my head, *Make good choices.*

My attention was back on my daughter. How was that not her? Besides, there was no way that hundred bucks would make a dent in covering the car.

I guessed I'd been stewing for too long because another message buzzed through, and I wondered if he'd been contemplating, too, because I could feel the shift. The change in his tenor.

Jud: I have you, Salem.

My ribs clamped around my aching heart.

Okay, this didn't feel so *careful*. The way this man made me want to slip out from behind the walls I'd built. Where it was fortified and guarded and safe.

Knowing I couldn't go there, I forced myself to respond.

Me: I'm not your responsibility.

Jud: Isn't that what friends are for?

My brow curled.

Me: Is that what we are? Friends?

Jud: If that's the only way you'll have me.

Me: You don't even know me. And who said I was going to have you?

There I went, digging myself in. Deeper and deeper. But I didn't know how to stop the attraction that pulled and begged.

He wasn't even here, and my heart was beating out of time. A frenzy lighting in my veins, hands shaking as I sat there waiting for his next message to come through.

Jud: See, there's this thing where strangers who meet get to know each other…

I rolled my eyes and fought an affected laugh, caught up in the tease that pinged in his text.

Me: Is that so?

Jud: Uh-huh. Was thinking you and I might do a bit of that.

Giddiness swept through my being. Lifting high then sweeping low. A beat of exhilaration before I had to come back down to reality.

Me: I don't think that's a good idea, Jud. My brother works for you.

And this man didn't want my mess, and I couldn't afford to form any attachments. Couldn't afford to care.

My heart clutched in dread.

What if we had to pack up and leave again?

My gaze was back on my sleeping Juni Bee. On her precious, precious form.

Agony slayed me at the thought.

Yes, I wanted to stay. Prayed we could. But I needed to do it one step at a time.

On top of that? Jud didn't know the first thing about me. Didn't know my responsibilities. My greatest, most beautiful obligation.

Nor did he know my deepest, darkest pain.

Jud: That's right. Your brother works for me.

I felt the ferocity in his tone. The fact he didn't give a crap. This man took what he wanted, and he made no apologies.

And there I was, the fool who wanted to tell him I wanted it, too. To explore this attraction. An attraction so intense it couldn't be faked.

But I couldn't.

I couldn't.

I forced myself to type out a reasonable response.

Me: I don't have the money to fix my car right now. I'll see if Darius can have it towed back to the house.

He must have felt my blow off because it took him a minute to respond.

Jud: Already told you, I have you. Already ordered the parts.

Crap. I needed to argue. Tell him it wasn't his duty. Stop this from going any farther than it already had. Still, a bout of worry climbed through my mind, digging holes in my refusal.

While I didn't want to be in debt to him, I needed a car.

Me: I can't believe I'm saying this, but okay. I really need a car. I will find a way to pay you back.

Jud: Not necessary.

I warred with what I wanted to say before I let my fingers fly free.

Me: Thank you, Jud, for being my savior.

My wicked, gorgeous savior.

Jud: My pleasure, darlin'.

I could almost see his smirk from across the space. That intimidating, hulking body standing in his kitchen. Barefooted and bare chested.

My breath hitched.

The memory inundating. The way it felt beneath that decadent stare. So sexy, he'd made my knees weak.

Jud: How about a pic of that gorgeous face to save with your number?

Disbelief slid into my grin. This guy was something.

Me: I don't think that's a good idea.

Jud: I think it's a great idea. I'll even return the favor.

Could feel the mischief woven in the words. Temptation and a trap.

Shit. This man was trying to do me in. I hesitated, my tongue stroking my suddenly dried lips. In an instant, I was parched. I glanced around the darkened room like I was doing something criminal, then I tapped out the message and pushed send before I could think better of it.

Me: Fine. But if you send a dick pic, I will stab you.

My eyes nearly bugged out of my head when I saw his response.

> Jud: Don't worry, darlin'. You see my cock for the first time? It's going to be face-to-face.

Desire blistered through my body. Flames lapping at my flesh as I thought of what that might be like. I swore, I was burning up.

I blamed it on going without for so long.

Blamed it on my fear of being seen.

On my fear of being touched.

And right then? In the sanctuary of the words of this man?

It was the only thing I wanted.

To be touched.

To be seen.

To feel *real*.

I was wearing a light-blue satin pajama set. The bottoms were shorts and the top was a short-sleeved button up. I opened my phone camera and saw my face in the reflection. My eyes were dilated, and my cheeks were flushed.

All bad news.

Still, like a fool, I leaned back against the arm of the couch, let my hair fall around my shoulders, unbuttoned the first button of my sleep shirt, and lifted the camera high.

I snapped a shot that captured my face, my shoulders, the skin of my chest, the barest brush of cleavage showing through.

In the shadows, it appeared…sexy.

Or maybe it was just the way Jud Lawson made me feel.

Real since the moment my spirit had gone dim.

With trembling hands, I pressed send before I thought better of it. Before I let myself contemplate the dangerous game I was playing.

> Jud: Fuckin' gorgeous. Thought I had to be dreaming when I saw you in the rain.

Another message came in right behind the last.

Jud: Tell me one thing, darlin'. Did you feel it? Did you feel it last night?

He didn't even have to clarify what *it* was. Not when it'd been so vibrant and bold. The crash of energy. The crackle of attraction.

The shaking in my hands intensified, and I knew I should lie, tell him goodbye, that I couldn't keep up with whatever we were doing.

It was only going to hurt in the end.

But what did I do? I typed out the confession on a needy breath.

Me: Yes.

A second later, a picture popped through.

And that needy breath was punching from my lungs. Jud was there as promised, lying back in this massive bed fit for a king.

Black hair long on top and cropped at the sides, a thick black beard, those eyes piercing me in the night. Every rugged edge of his face was on display, those plush lips curved into a smirk.

He'd sent the same angle as I'd sent him.

Just enough of his chest showed to make lust fist in my stomach. It overflowed like the rush of hot lava where it tingled my thighs and pulsed my center.

My teeth clenched, my eyes devouring every inch. There wasn't enough light to make out the obscured tattoos that covered him whole, though I could tell the images were as mysterious as the man. Certainly drawn by the same artist who'd painted the pictures on his walls.

A dichotomy of demonic and angelic.

A war of dark and light.

A clash of evil and hope.

A fresh rush of desire streaked through my veins when another text buzzed through.

Jud: What I wouldn't do to that tight little body…

And that was it, all I could take. I was on my feet and tiptoeing to that little bathroom. I shut the door and locked it behind me. Gasping, I leaned against the wood.

Darius was right.

I didn't have enough privacy.

Not when I was feeling things I hadn't felt in four long years.

Well, probably in ever.

It was something the trauma had turned sour, ugly and vile, that now boiled like bliss in my blood.

I set the phone on the counter and pressed my hands on either side of it, dropped my head as I tried to get a cleansing breath.

But I might as well have been breathing him in with the way I was assaulted with the memory of the man.

His aura filled my senses.

Citrus and cinnamon and spice.

I raised my gaze and saw my reflection through the shadows in the mirror. The room dark except for the nightlight plugged into the wall to the side of the sink.

My pupils were wide, my skin flushed, my tongue dried.

I wavered, teetered, torn between refusing the visions and giving into the fantasy.

To this feeling that lapped and burned and begged.

I spread my hand over my trembling belly, no longer recognizing myself.

Jud had ignited something long gone.

Flames and sparks and fire.

I should run from them. Fear them.

I slipped lower, whimpering when my hand slid beneath my underwear, where I found myself wet and throbbing. My fingertips brushed over my clit.

That fire spread.

I bit my lip to suppress a moan, and I squeezed my eyes closed and welcomed the visions of the man.

His scent.

His eyes.

That body.

That mouth.

I pretended it was him kneeling in front of me when I pressed my fingers into my pussy. Pretended it was his tongue that stroked. His mouth that whispered and sent my entire body quaking in ecstasy.

I gasped as I came, shocked, stunned, the ground slipping out from under me.

My eyes flew open when my phone buzzed on the counter and another message blipped through.

Jud: You touching yourself, Sweet Enchantress? Because you can be sure that I am.

Chapter Seven

Salem

Thirteen Years Old

"OH MY GOD, SALEM, HE IS THE HOTTEST EVER." TALIA whispered the scandal as she hugged the heart-shaped pink pillow to her chest. Salem and her best friend sat facing each other with their legs crisscrossed on Salem's bed, their voices hushed, the hour late.

Scandalous, was right.

Furtively, Salem's gaze darted toward her closed door as if *he* might be right there with his ear pressed to her door, listening to their conversation.

Salem's heart thudded at the idea, and her stomach tangled in a knot. She couldn't tell if it was in a good or bad way.

"Shh." Salem leaned forward with the secret. "Someone's gonna hear you. They're right in the next room."

About twenty minutes ago, Darius had stumbled in after a party with his friend Carlo.

Talia grinned and widened her eyes. "Um, hello. That's the goal."

Salem poked Talia's knee, her words held low as they squeezed from between her lips. "He is way too old for you…and he's my brother's best friend."

"Even better. Older men are more experienced."

Salem's nose curled. "Gross. And he's…"

She didn't know how to frame the words. The unsettled feeling that swept through her each time Carlo was around.

"A Greek God? An Italian Adonis? Do you need me to go on?"

Salem rolled her eyes. "That was sufficient, thank you."

Giggling, Talia scooted off the edge of the bed and shimmied over to the dressing table mirror, checking herself out as she swept a tube of shimmery gloss over her lips. She smacked them before she looked at Salem from over her shoulder. "And who cares how old he is. I mean, I look way older, don't I?"

Through the dim twinkle lights strung along the edges of Salem's ceiling, she nodded. They both did.

But Salem knew better. For years, Darius had chased her off, warning her to stay away from him and his friends.

She knew better than letting her thoughts traipse that direction.

Not that she wanted them to go there, anyway.

Right?

Deep laughter echoed through the walls.

Her stomach did that tilting thing again.

Talia held a squeal and beelined back to her, jumping onto her bed and landing on her knees. "Did you hear that? Even his laugh is hot." Her eyes nearly rolled back in her head before she flopped dramatically onto her back. "Too bad he's already in love with you."

Salem's chest tightened, and she rushed to say, "Stop being stupid."

Talia pushed on Salem's arm with her toe. "Only when you stop being blind."

Talia had passed out in the middle of a sentence ten minutes before, just like she did almost every time she spent the night.

Mimi always joked that her best friend had an on and off switch. Come six a.m., she'd pop right back up at full speed.

Salem had slinked out without waking her to use the bathroom, brushed her teeth, then twisted her hair into the braid she wore to sleep.

Flicking off the bathroom light, Salem slipped out the door and back into the darkened hall, her bare feet quieted as she tiptoed for her door.

She stilled with the presence that fell over her from behind.

Close. Close. Closer.

The hairs at her nape shivered and lifted, and she gulped, gathering herself to turn around.

Carlo stood right behind her.

Talia was right. He was hot. Tall and thin but strong. Mostly a man. He'd stopped going to school two months ago, which she'd heard Mimi lecturing Darius about just yesterday.

Carlo was a bad influence.

Trouble, she'd said.

And Mimi didn't want Darius hanging around him as much as he used to. Obviously, Darius wasn't quick to listen, but it was hard to blame him when Carlo had been his best friend since they'd moved in with Mimi all those years ago.

Carlo's short black hair was wavy, and even in the middle of the night, it appeared styled. His clothes and car expensive and flashy. His eyes as sharp as his jaw.

With a wry smile, he leaned against the wall. "What are you doing out here, sneaking around in the middle of the night?"

Salem's heart thundered like crazy, but she managed to send him a scowl. "I could ask the same about you."

He laughed a low, rolling sound that vibrated on the dense air. "Ah, bambola, it's my job to sneak around. And yours is to be sweet."

He grinned when he said it, a joke she didn't understand.

Salem suddenly felt trapped, though she let her voice fill with defiance as she lifted her chin. "This is my house. I'm no concern of yours."

He reached out and ran his fingertips along her jaw. "That is where you are wrong."

Trembles rocked through her. She was pretty sure they weren't the good kind.

"Carlo."

Salem jolted when she heard the voice, and she stumbled back far enough that she could see Mimi at the head of the hall.

"I think your momma is probably wondering where you are. You should go home." Mimi's voice was harder than she'd ever heard it.

Carlo roughed a chuckle, so casual, like he didn't care at all about the cut of bitterness in her words. He just angled forward, whispered, "One day, pupa…one day," before he turned and eased down the hall, dipping his head in a faked pleasantry at her mimi as he passed.

The door opened and rattled shut behind him.

Mimi's face was red. "Stay away from him, Salem. As far away as you can."

Frantic, Salem nodded. "Okay, Mimi. I will. I promise."

Chapter Eight

Jud

It was early Monday morning when I was down in the lobby searching for some paperwork that probably didn't exist.

The place was a fuckin' disaster, stacks of forms and receipts and shit piled for days.

Okay.

Months.

It was no secret I'd let this shit get out of hand.

Suffice it to say I wasn't paying much mind when the black pickup truck rolled into the lot. It was early, yeah. Just after seven. But I figured Darius was getting a jump on his day.

Except it pulled into a spot on the opposite side of the lot from where he normally parked, the truck facing away, and it was a hot second before the driver's door finally opened.

A very hot second.

Because it wasn't Darius climbing out.

It was Salem.

That girl straight devastation.

A gift wrapped in a black, seductive bow.

I froze, watching her through the bank of dark-tinted windows that fronted the lobby.

That ebony hair was curled into these fat waves that danced all over her shoulders, and there was no missing the way nerves scattered around her as she hesitated for a beat. She glanced around like she was hoping this little visit was covert, girl inhaling deep before she seemed to get it together and started walking across the parking lot toward the building.

"Fuck me."

Today she was wearing these fitted black dress pants that hit her just above the ankles, the waist high with a silky, baby blue blouse tucked into it. Sky-high heels and red lipstick and fuck…my dick stirred, guts tangling at the sight.

This girl was a motherfuckin' knockout.

A fantasy.

A dream.

Everything that I knew better than to want but was thirsting for, anyway.

Wanting her went directly against every commitment I'd made for myself.

Went against the grain of what I was striving for.

Against everything Darius had asked of me.

But I couldn't seem to find it in myself to give a shit about either of those things.

Definitely problematic.

Figured she was there to argue about her car, which kind of sucked, but she was just going to have to accept I wanted to do the favor.

Didn't mean she owed me.

It just meant I was offering something easy. Something that wasn't going to hurt me a bit but clearly would give her a leg up.

Searching, she lifted her face to the building. Her lips puckered in confusion as she changed directions. She started toward the row of bays that ran the opposite side that were currently all locked up tight.

When she disappeared from view of the lobby windows, I pushed out from behind the counter and moved for the main door. Pushing it open, I stepped out into the warmth of the breaking day.

I looked to the right in the direction she'd gone, and the girl was strutting in those heels down the row of garage doors.

"You lost?" I leaned an arm against the wall, grinning that way as she whirled around on a sharp gasp, her face curdled in surprise before she blew out in relief.

Thunderbolt eyes narrowed.

"Didn't anyone ever tell you not to sneak up on someone like that?" Her voice was doing that low, seductive thing, and need was grappling around for a place to take root in my belly.

Growling for a fill.

Rough laughter scraped free. "Sneak up on you? I'm fifty feet away. Would hardly call that sneaking up. I saw you out here rambling around and figured I'd come put you out of your misery."

"I was looking for your door." She waved a flustered hand at the massive building.

I quirked a brow. "To my loft?"

Reluctantly, she nodded, like standing there she was rethinking her purpose. "Yeah."

I angled my head. "Around to the side of the building. There's a separate exterior entrance. For next time."

I let the smirk take hold, as clear as the suggestion.

She huffed with a slight tug at the edges of her delicious mouth, and she started my way. "Right. Okay."

She moved closer.

Each step sent a shockwave of that electricity vibrating the ground.

Zinging my flesh and stoking my senses.

"Listen, I know it's early, and I figured you'd still be upstairs which was why I was looking for another door, and I'm sorry I showed up here without an appointment so long before opening, but I needed to use Darius' truck before he needs it for work and I—"

She clipped off the avalanche of words that had started rolling from her mouth, her lips thinning as if she'd just realized she'd been rambling faster than one of those old-school auctioneers.

Could feel the amusement twitching through my expression, and she stumbled to a stop ten feet away.

She blew out a sigh, then turned her phone to me with a hint of desperation tinting her voice. "Is this you?"

I pushed from the wall, squinting as I took a step forward to see what was on her screen.

An ad.

An ad that I'd been running but had been ignoring the calls for interviews for over the last four weeks because I just didn't have time to see it through. Not exactly the most prudent of business decisions, but it was what it was.

"Yeah?" I answered it like a question.

Her head bounced at the confirmation, and she was looking out to the forest that hugged the lot before she was returning that gorgeous face to me. "Let me help…temporarily…until I pay off the car."

Could feel the frown curling my brow. "Told you not to worry about it."

"And I told you I would find a way to pay you back."

Tension stretched between us.

Taut and tight.

"Please, Jud. I can't just accept a handout from you."

Air wheezed from my nose.

This girl definitely didn't want to accept help.

Truth was, her car was so old, it was hardly worth fixing.

Thing was a pile.

Unsafe and unreliable.

What she needed was a new one. But I doubted much that was an option considering she was standing there begging me to let her work to pay off the repairs.

"Are you asking me for an interview, Salem?"

Her brows spiked. "You want me to interview?"

"You wanna work here…temporarily…?" I let the question hang.

"Ugh." She pressed the heel of her hand to her forehead, peeking at me around it. "Fine."

A low chuckle flooded the air, and I shifted so I could open the lobby door. "Come on in, darlin'."

Salem blew out the strain, and she straightened her shoulders and waltzed that fine ass past me and through the door.

It wasn't like I was going to turn her away. Hell, I didn't need her to repay me at all, but since she was insisting, figured I at least needed to know what she could do. Truth be told, I needed the help.

It didn't hurt that I kind of relished the idea of her strutting around here in those heels all day long, either.

I stepped in behind her, and she stood there in the foyer of my lobby.

A storm.

Sweet, sweet ferocity.

There was something about her that was so compelling.

The girl was a fucking cocktail of toasted coconut and sultry sin.

Wanted to take a long, satisfying drink.

A smirk kept tugging at the corner of my mouth as I edged by her and rounded the counter. I started shuffling through paperwork again.

"So, tell me, gorgeous," I mumbled as I foraged around, "why do you want to work here?"

From where she stood five feet away, she sighed out in defiance. "To repay a debt, Mr. Lawson. Obviously. And I'm pretty sure you should probably stop calling me gorgeous if I'm going to work here."

I tossed a glance at her from over the high counter. "Impossible. Not when it's true."

Thunderbolt eyes struck.

A lash of lust.

A stroke of greed.

I slowed, pressed my hands to the counter as I looked her up and down.

I should lock it up.

Stop this fall before I hit rock bottom.

But there I went, tossing my ass right over the side. "You didn't text me back."

Her cheeks flamed.

Yup.

The girl was affected.

Could feel it thicken the atmosphere.

Tighten the cord.

The connection keened in the space between us.

Air suddenly shot from her nose, a burst of reservation and determination. "Because that would be inappropriate."

"If you think that's inappropriate, I think we should rethink our boundaries."

Her head shook. "This can't happen."

"What's that?"

She frantically gestured between us. "This."

Her rebuttal didn't even feel like an obstacle to hold us back. Not when it was clear she wanted it every bit as much as me.

I let the feigned confusion climb into the twist of my brow, unable to stop from teasing her. Not when she was so damned hot when she got all feisty. "This?"

"This," she hissed in frustration.

A roll of low laughter tumbled out, and I was leaning closer. "You're going to have to be clearer, darlin'."

Frustration shot from her mouth, and the girl sauntered the rest of the way over to me.

The ripple of her hitched the air in my throat.

"Don't toy with me, Jud. You know exactly what I'm talking about. I get it. I'm sure you're more than accustomed to getting what you want, and I'm sure women jump into your bed whenever you flash them that smile. You're charming and handsome and—" She bit down on the word she was about to let go. "But I'm here because I want to do what's right, not because I find you attractive. When I saw the listing, it felt like a sign…a way to repay a debt. So please, if I can help, let me help."

Damn.

This woman.

This fierce little wildcat who didn't hesitate to put me in my place.

"Not tryin' to disrespect you, Salem. I'm only making it clear how you make me feel."

For a minute, she stared, two of us tied, before she shook herself out of it. "I don't think it would be a good idea for either of us to explore that."

She was right. The problem was how fuckin' bad I was aching for her to be wrong.

She dropped her gaze, inhaling before she peered over at me. She tied me up all over again with the way that striking face deepened with loss and hope. "But I think we could try that friend thing."

Something fluttered through my chest. Something hard and soft squeezing at my heart. "Okay, then, darlin', but I'm not going to pretend like I haven't been imagining more."

Heat flamed, a rush of red to her skin, and it was clear she'd been imagining it, too.

I blew out the strain and went for a little of that pretending I'd just promised her I couldn't do, while I searched around for the form I was looking for. "So, have you ever worked as a receptionist before?"

"I worked at the front desk of a dental office for a while."

"Perfect. Honestly, if you can just answer the phone, that would take a huge burden off my shoulders."

I felt her frown. "I'm pretty sure I'm capable of handling more."

"Well, this office is a fuckin' mess. Not gonna lie. My last office manager left five months ago for maternity leave and never came back. Not that I can blame her."

Salem popped onto her toes and peered over the counter at the disaster hidden on the other side.

Horror filled her gasp.

"Having second thoughts?" I asked, quirking a brow.

So yeah, there were five months of incomplete contracts and receipts and shit piled everywhere.

You couldn't see the desk with the stacks of files and papers covering it, so many that I'd taken to piling them on the floor.

"You can't run a business like this." Her tone filled with disbelief.

I snorted an incredulous sound. "Obviously."

I finally found the folder I was looking for, and I lifted it victoriously. "Ah. Here it is."

I pulled out an application and passed it across the counter in her direction.

If she wanted a job, figured I'd give her one. Clearly, the woman needed some cash, and I needed the help. Seemed like a win-win.

She fingered the paper, her breaths coming short, dread swelling and coming off her in waves.

"What is it, darlin'?"

She dropped her head, but not far enough that I couldn't see that she was chewing on her lip in worried contemplation. Finally, she lifted her gaze, that chin lifted high, but there was no missing the tremble in her voice. "This can't be on the books."

I thought her dread must have burst and jumped directly into my veins.

All while she remained there, fierce and hard and determined. A challenge on her face.

I'd lived a seedy enough life to know people did things under the table for one of two reasons—they were either crooked or they were hiding.

I would bet my ass it was the latter.

There was nothing I could do. My rationale was smashed to dust. Particles that no longer existed.

Every wall she kept trying to toss between us obliterated in that single confession.

Or maybe it was just that my conscience had decided to scale right over the top of them.

Because protectiveness swelled.

Brutal.

Severe.

Violent.

Somehow, I managed to keep my hand steady when I reached out and set my palm on her cheek. My thumb went to stroking the scar on her jaw.

Just fuckin' knowing.

Seeing the trauma written there.

Her body rocked like an earthquake, and her hands came out to support herself on the counter, her breath gone and her eyes squeezing tight.

I wanted to demand a thousand things, but a name and an address would do. That demon screamed, thrashed and wailed from the darkest place where I kept him chained.

But I reined it.

I knew that wasn't what this girl needed right then, and I gave her what I was sure she'd been missing.

This time, when I uttered the words, they were a promise. "I have you, Salem."

She remained there for the longest time, her breaths shallow, barely contained panic vibrating through her body, though she leaned deeper into my touch.

"I have you," I reiterated, words coarse and raw.

Finally, she opened those eyes, their depths a tormented sea that I recognized too clearly.

Understanding burned between us.

She'd just offered me something she didn't offer many.

A tiny spec of her trust.

Stepping back, she broke the bubble that'd held us, adjusting her shirt and her breaths and the beat of her heart.

She gestured to the door. "I should get Darius' truck back to him before he notices I'm gone."

A surprised bolt of laughter ripped from me. "Sweet Enchantress, you are somethin', aren't you?"

She almost smiled as she backed away. "I'll be back with him, and I'll start getting this place in order."

I rested back on the filing cabinet behind me, arms over my chest as I gazed at the girl who got lit in the streak of sunlight blazing through the window.

Black hair and gorgeous body and this spirit that was hard to ignore. "Thank you for saving me."

A grin spread to her mouth. "I'm pretty sure it's the other way around."

She opened the door, then hesitated before she looked back. "Darius is going to be pissed."

Anger curled in my chest. Apparently, he hadn't just had words with me.

I hiked an indifferent shoulder. "I can handle it if you can."

"I can."

"Good."

Her expression softened. This fierce, unrelenting girl going sweet.

"I'll see you in a bit," I told her.

"Thank you, Jud."

Every part of me turned tender. "It's my pleasure, darlin'."

My fuckin' pleasure.

Chapter Nine

Jud

"YOU WILL ALWAYS BE MY SWEET BOY. NEVER LET anyone convince you of anything different." His mommy whispered the words before she swept her lips over the top of his head. Her eyes were so green, like emeralds in the night. She looked at him like it was the truth when she tucked him into his bed.

He was safe.

Safe.

But the world canted as the years passed. The ground disappeared below him and he was gobbled by the abyss.

He fell and tumbled as darkness rained.

Bullets fired.

Blood.

So much blood.

His mom was gone.

"You belong to me." His father hissed it into his ear as he wept. As

the man forced him from his knees and onto his feet. He pressed the gun into his hands. "You or them."

Shots rang.

Echoed in his ears for eternity.

His soul shattered as the demon raged.

Nothing mattered.

No right or wrong.

But the wrong glared too bright.

He rocked in the corner. Tore at his hair. Begged to be different. Screamed for peace. For forgiveness. For it to go away.

He crawled from the rubble.

Built walls. A solid ground.

Hope.

"Dada." He held the child. Loved her to the moon.

He wanted to be good. Everything for her.

But the flames leapt, climbing the walls and licking at the ceiling.

Smoke billowed. A heavy darkness that filled the air and choked out hope.

Consuming.

Disorienting.

A black plague that annihilated everything in its path.

Still, he rushed, searched, fumbled through the disorder from one room to the next.

Nothing.

Nothing.

Fear crushed, as suffocating as the smoke that filled his lungs. He pulled his shirt over his face, his eyes wide and unseeing, the world a blur of fire and white-hot pain.

It didn't matter.

He pressed on.

Pushed.

Forever passed.

A second.

A moment.

Misery the time that ticked on the clock.

A roar rose from the depths of him. "Where are you? Please. Fuck. Can you hear me?"

The whooshing of the flames screamed back.

He was on his knees. Blind as he searched.

Torment wailed.

As loud as the sirens he heard coming in the distance.

Tears blurred, burning against his charred flesh.

No. Please. No.

I jolted to upright on a choked gasp.

A rasp of pain.

Fevered, my eyes darted around to take in my surroundings. My senses were shocked to find I was no longer tumbling through the years that tormented me, but rather my ass was in the comfort of my own fucking bed.

Pale ribbons of pink streamed in through my bedroom window, a slow dance of warmth, while I felt like I was being burned alive.

Sweat soaked my flesh and my sheets while my heart raged with grief.

The scars on my back screamed like they were still red and raw.

Those? I could handle.

It was the ones written on my conscience, on my heart, embedded in my blackened soul that made me feel like I was getting torn apart.

I sucked for air. To draw oxygen into my lungs when they felt like they'd been charred and singed and scorched all over again. Like I was back in that day that had turned to the darkest night.

It was the moment my mind always returned to. Where the dreams lured me into a nightmare that'd been real.

It was when I'd lost my soul. My purpose. My right.

My head dropped forward, and I focused on trying to slow the rampage in my heart, the chaos that raged.

I deserved it, though, so what the hell did I expect?

Yet, still, I tried. Tried to be better. To pay a penance for the sins that could never be made right.

I'd wait—wait for the day when maybe it would be enough.

Lumbering to standing, I started for the shower. I knew I was fucked when in an instant a face infiltrated my mind.

The face of a girl who had spun me into a thousand mangled knots.

The one who'd be downstairs in the office when I got there.

The one I couldn't seem to scrape from my thoughts.

There was something about this Salem. Something dangerous. Something I should avoid. And I was the masochist who wanted to find out.

Chapter Ten

Salem

I'D BEEN WORKING AT IRON RIDE FOR THE LAST THREE DAYS.

I'd been right.

Darius had been pissed.

But even though he'd been all surly and grumbly and annoyed, there was enough work to make him forget why he was upset at me in the first place.

Hell, there was enough work to keep us all distracted for the next five years.

After the interaction with Jud on Monday morning that had left me completely rattled? That was precisely what I'd done. I'd thrown myself into getting the office whipped into shape and tried to pay as little attention to the man who rocked my whole world every time he got into my space.

Stoically trying to pretend like each smile wasn't driving me mad.

Like each smirk wasn't making me contemplate things I had no business contemplating.

So, I dove into the stacks of receipts and contracts and unpaid invoices, doing my best to organize them, to make sense of them, inputting them into the accounting software and trying to get it to balance since there had been no less than fifteen unanswered emails asking for that information from Jud's accountant.

Not to mention the number of late notices I'd sent out on Iron Ride's behalf to customer accounts that had never been paid.

My spirit had both lifted and sank with the amount it was adding up to, and I'd barely made a dent.

It only made the man who owned these floors like a hunter more mysterious. His life beat clearly found in the pulse of the motorcycles and cars he restored. I peered through the glass door that separated the lobby from the shop to where he was at the far, opposite side.

He was knelt over, his big body this force as he worked the metal.

My stomach tightened.

I guessed I recognized it, why it would be so easy for this part of his business to slide.

He was an artist.

A sculptor.

A crafter.

His care wrapped up in the rugged, fierce beauty he had to offer.

He shifted, and his shirt stretched over the wide, wide expanse of his muscled back.

My mouth went dry.

Before I stared so long drool would drip onto the desk, I forced myself to return my attention to the computer where I was inputting his positives.

None of this mess appeared to be hurting him, anyway.

His accounts were plentiful. Enough that it'd taken me a moment to process the balances.

It was weird, he'd just given me access to it all, his trust so easy.

That was something I didn't come close to understanding.

How to just…give.

Because giving was dangerous.

I forced myself to focus on the task at hand. Slowly but surely,

I made my way through a box of receipts that had been stuffed in the corner. Lost in the work. In using my hands. In being a part of something that felt like it mattered. As if I were making a difference for someone else.

Someone who was making a *difference* for me.

Only I stilled when a sense whispered across my flesh.

An aura.

An innuendo.

It was close to chills lifting on my skin, though not quite as intense.

It was just this disquiet that gusted through the muted intensity of my focus.

Slowly, I pushed from the stool where I'd been sitting at the desk that ran off to the side of the main high counter. I eased closer so I could peer over the top and out through the windows that I knew were a shimmery pitch from the outside.

Because of it, there was no chance a soul could see through the tint.

Still, my heart thugged like lead when I saw a car sitting on the far side of the curb. It wasn't directly across the street, but a bit farther to the left, mostly concealed by the thick foliage of shrubbery and trees.

But I saw it—the tail-end of the same black car I could have sworn I'd seen outside our house earlier this morning.

Again, up the street.

I'd barely acknowledged it then, where it'd sat up the road like any other.

But this?

Alarm sparked in the place where I would forever be on edge, and it sent a tremor rocking through my being.

A warning that blared.

My being buzzed, jumpstarting the fight or flight reaction it always did.

But me?

It was always flight.

I had to get out of here.

I had to get out of here.

Run. Run. Run.

I stumbled back from the counter as panic seized the air in my lungs.

In an instant, I felt as if I were suffocating.

The world spinning. The floor trembling.

It was the only thing I could do—*flee.*

Frantically, my attention darted for an escape route, only to scream when a hand landed on my shoulder.

I whirled around in shock, in fear, in a tiny bit of that *fight*, ready to battle through to the end.

"Salem."

That rumbly voice broke into the frenzied paranoia.

"Salem, look at me, darlin'. It's just me."

I gasped and blinked and tried to reorient myself.

I realized I was pressed against a row of black file cabinets that ran the left wall behind the counter. There was a small wall that jutted out to keep them hidden from the lobby.

It left me out of view of anyone who would walk through the doors.

But Jud saw me.

Watched me carefully.

That obsidian gaze fired and flared and rushed over me in his own bid of panic.

"Not gonna hurt you, darlin'." Those big, big hands were held out in front of him in a calming fashion, and I squeezed my eyes closed and attempted to swallow over the jagged rock that had lodged itself in my throat.

My lungs panged and my heart hammered and God…this was so embarrassing.

"Are you okay?"

My nod was tight.

"What's going on? What freaked you out?"

My head shook and my body shivered. "Nothing."

"Not nothing if it's got you spun up like this." The words cracked like venom.

Manic laughter tumbled from my tongue, and I waved a crazed hand toward the window, unable to stop the flow of words.

"I just…there's a car out there sitting on the street, and I swore I saw the same one sitting across the street in our neighborhood this morning. It's probably nothing."

What was I doing? Giving this to him?

But a spec of that trust was there, offered into the air. Into his hands. Into his big, beating heart that battered at his chest.

His attention darted to the windows. I saw the moment he saw it, too. The way every bulky muscle in his body flexed in a bid of aggression.

"It's nothing," I reiterated, mostly trying to calm myself down.

Only Jud didn't seem to think it was *nothing* because he grunted, "Wait right there."

Then he turned on his heavy motorcycle boots, his giant body hulking around the counter and across the lobby, the man casting me a harsh glance as he slipped out the door.

He didn't slow.

He strode like menace across the lot.

I watched in abject horror and awe as he slipped his hand around to his backside and under his shirt and pulled a gun from the waistband of his jeans.

His muscles vibrated with hostility.

With violence.

I'd known there was something about the man that whispered of his darkness.

Of danger.

Of bloodshed and barbarity.

But I'd never been so sure of it until then.

He was about three-quarters of the way across the lot when the black car suddenly peeled out, flying from its perch with a squeal of tires and a billow of dust.

Running from the monster set on savagery that clumped that way.

I saw it there, when he turned around.

The expression on his face.

A gnarl of wickedness.

A disorder of malice.

My stomach twisted.

My pulse flew.

I could feel the tumult blister through the air when he looked back at the spot where the car had disappeared. When it seemed clear, he reluctantly turned, stuffed his gun back into his waistband, and marched back across the lot.

My heart thundered, a careening stampede.

It hammered harder and harder with each step that he took.

Tremors rocked the ground.

Shockwaves of animosity and duty.

I didn't know how to stand.

Didn't know how to do anything when he tossed the door open and strode through, rays of bright sunlight streaking over him as he entered, lighting him up like some kind of unrighteous god.

Intensity cracked.

Snapped in the room.

An imposing force.

The man a wicked, wicked savior.

I was back to pressing myself against the cool metal of the file cabinet, unable to breathe, unable to process the thousand thoughts that spiraled through my mind.

I never should have come.

I never should have thought I could stay.

I never should have allowed myself to start to feel safe.

And most of all, I never, ever should have started to think of this place as home.

Jud edged forward, the colossal, beast of a man coming closer and closer.

Black hair and black beard and black eyes that I could have sworn fired red.

My chest squeezed tighter with each step.

My pulse thudded like a snare with each powerful stride that he took.

Though those steps were slowed.

Cautioned.

I fought for ground. To remain unaffected.

Not to whimper when the forbidding man suddenly towered over me with those eyes pinning me to the spot.

"They're gone." The words scraped like barbs from his tongue. His anger barely contained. "Probably a drug deal or some shit. Not exactly the best side of town over here."

I gulped around the rock that pressed like razors to my throat. Warily, I tried to gather the fear and the panic, to be reasonable and not jump to the first horrible conclusion, the way I always did.

It was hard not to do that when I'd spent years running. When every sound and whisper and intonation had made me terrified someone was coming for us.

The worst part was knowing it wasn't illogical. I had the holes carved out inside me to prove it.

The truth that I would be a fool to take the chance.

On a jittery nod, I faked a smile. "Probably."

Jud's brow pinched, and those eyes raced over my face like they could see through to the very depths of who I was.

To every secret.

To every fear.

He leaned closer, and his warm breath whispered across my skin. "But that's not what you were thinkin', was it, darlin'?"

This.

This was why I'd been diverting. Why I'd been trying to distract and pretend and ignore that I'd revealed a piece of myself I shouldn't have at the beginning of the week.

"Who are you running from?" I could have sworn his words were underlined with murder.

My head shook, and my eyes found the intensity in his. "Please, don't ask that of me."

I didn't know him.

Couldn't trust him.

Fury flashed through his features.

He took my hands and threaded our fingers together.

Vibrations zapped through the connection.

Palpable and real.

His growl was menace. "Want to destroy whoever hurt you. Just need a name."

A gasp ripped up my throat when he suddenly lifted my arms above my head and pinned them against the cabinet.

"Just a name." It sounded of sex and coercion.

My eyes squeezed closed. "I can't."

His big hands slipped down my quivering limbs, as if he were gathering up every ounce of terror that I possessed. Taking it into his hold. Caressing away the panic.

"I have you, Salem." He grumbled it, and those eyes never left mine as he ran his hands all the way back up my arms to my hands and then down again.

Though that time, he didn't stop.

He ran them over my shoulders and down to my sides.

My lungs squeezed tight, and our hearts raged in the bare space that separated us.

Need spiked in the dense air.

His wide, wide chest jutted and heaved, and every muscle in his body strained.

I knew we were concealed behind the wall, but there was something about this that made me feel exposed.

As if there was an audience watching as I slipped into recklessness.

As I tiptoed into sin.

My stomach twisted in want, and my nipples hardened beneath his stare.

Jud groaned as if he felt the desire ravaging my flesh, and his hands were splaying wider at my ribs, so big they nearly wrapped all the way around.

Harsh air puffed from his nose when he brushed his thumbs over the rock-hard peaks of my breasts.

A whimper fled from my lips. "Oh, god."

"Beautiful. Losing my fuckin' mind over you, Salem." He rubbed harder, watching me like he wanted to devour me as he stoked that long dimmed flame.

He seemed to war, his body rocking in indecision, lost to his own battle before he snapped.

In a flash, the last bit of oxygen remaining in my lungs was gone.

Because his mouth crushed against mine.

As if any barrier between us had been floored.

I couldn't do anything but give. No control but to open to the demanding ferocity of his kiss.

Desperate to feel anything different than the constant fear that raged.

To feel supported.

Seen.

Held.

Real.

For just a moment, to touch on something that might feel like hope.

It was wrong. So wrong. But I couldn't stop.

I wrapped my arms around his neck in a desperate play to feel.

I opened to his kiss.

Surrendered.

Gave.

His tongue stroked out and swept over mine.

Hot and warm and sending a crash of lust blistering through my blood.

A moan got free, his or mine, I wasn't sure.

He pressed closer, that giant body eclipsing me.

Every inch of him was hard.

The muscles that bunched his arms.

The crash of the beating in his chest.

His huge cock that begged at my stomach.

Sounds climbed my throat. Needy and wild.

Our breaths turned ragged as our mouths clashed and demanded and fought for possession.

Reckless.

So reckless.

Jud took more with every lick of his tongue. Raw, rough rumblings rose from his soul. "Sweet. So sweet. What are you doing to me? Blowin' my mind."

Desire consumed.

Blinding.

I ached in a way I wasn't sure I ever had.

Like maybe if I let myself fall deeper into him, things might not hurt so bad.

But I knew better.

Knew better.

I tried for resolve, for clarity, for restraint.

I made a vain attempt at slowing the kiss, but the man just licked down to kiss along the scar on my jaw.

He moaned before he ran his nose along the mangled flesh.

The gentlest caress.

God.

If I let him, he could do me in.

Then he was lobbing for a breath, like I'd somehow affected him the same way he'd affected me.

He eased back when I finally found the strength to roll my head against the metal to stop this madness. That smile tweaked beneath his beard, his sexy lips red and wet, his words a rough scrape that rumbled my spirit. "Black-fuckin'-magic."

He was right.

It had to be.

This spell that curled and whipped and bound us together.

I blinked through the stupor and tried to push at his chest. "Jud, we can't do this."

I might as well have been pushing against a boulder.

"Yeah, and why's that?"

"Because I work for you."

"Huh. Weird. Didn't see you on the payroll."

A frown pinched my expression, regret coming in fast. "That's not fair."

He softened, and he ran his thumb across my scar.

A tremble rocked me through.

That wasn't fair, either.

His touch.

His charm.

His charisma.

This tenderness that butted up against all his bad.

This *call* that made me feel like I was where I was supposed to be, when I knew letting my guard down was the most foolish thing I could do.

He stared down at me, searching.

Looking for the answer to this unspoken question that ravaged between us. I figured after everything, I at least owed him a little bit of truth.

"I'm in no position to fall in love, Jud."

His hand was still spread across my face, the thumb caressing along my jaw doing that thing that twisted through me like agonized comfort.

"Who said anything about love, Salem?"

His response might have stabbed if I didn't see the stark, gutting pain slash across his face.

The way those obsidian eyes went dim with grief.

My heart panged.

And I wondered if it were possible that he might be as broken as me.

That was a big, big problem.

The truth that it only made me like him more.

This rough, sweet man who could so easily rip me apart.

"Then what are you—" My words clipped off when a door slammed. We jumped apart, Jud flying back to the opposite counter while I hopped away from the file cabinets deeper into the recesses of the lobby office space.

Anxiously, Jud roughed his fingers through the longer pieces of his hair, doing his best not to look my direction when Brock sauntered in, all smirking grins and salacious smiles.

His gaze darted between the two of us. Glee lit on his face. "Well, hell. I was just comin' in to see if Salem here would like to grab a drink after work, but it appears I'm a few minutes too late."

Jud actually growled.

Massive hands curled into fists, and I was a little scared he might actually rip a limb or two from Brock's body.

Brock just cracked up, no care in the world, his voice packed with suggestion as he pushed his hands out in surrender. "Down boy. No need to get up in arms. A man knows when he's been outbid."

He backed away with a smirk dancing over his face.

"Not sure what you think you're talkin' about, Brock, but I suggest you get your ass back to work and don't come sniffing around in here again. Hear me?"

Brock swung his attention to me, and his eyes raked down my body.

Jud's lie hung in the air.

The falsity of it was clear in my mussed hair and disheveled clothes, my blouse untucked on one side of my dress pants.

Crap.

I tried to inconspicuously readjust things.

Apparently, that made things worse because Brock's smile only grew. He looked back at Jud. "Loud and clear, boss, loud and clear."

He dipped back out through the door, and Jud was coming my way again, and I was pushing out my hands like I could protect myself from the impact of him. "No, Jud. I don't think I can do this."

He was in my face, dipping down, a heated whisper at my ear. "I'm taking you home tonight. Want to make sure you get there safe."

I could feel the refusal curl between my eyes, every reason we shouldn't do this pouring out. "I ride with Darius, and you know it's a bad idea, anyway. I think we should just leave it at that. You don't know me and I don't know you and—"

Jud leaned in and softly smoothed the wrinkle out, cutting off my refusal. "Don't get those pretty panties in a twist. It's just a ride."

Then he started to saunter away, only to pause at the organized stacks I'd made, his index finger jabbing at the papers. He looked back at me. "And for the record, you've already earned me far more than the cost of your car. You're off the hook, darlin', but I sure as fuck hope you'll stay."

Then he strode out, tossing open the single door that led to the shop, leaving me there gasping in his wake.

Chapter Eleven

Jud

IT WAS JUST AFTER FIVE-THIRTY WHEN I FELT THE SHIFT IN the air. One where shivers went racing along my spine and my stomach thought it fit to tighten in a fist.

I swiveled around from where I was kneeling in front of the chopper I was working on to find Salem strutting out.

She wore that silky blouse, painted-on black pants, and those sky-high heels that were trampling all over my good sense.

Poking holes in the commitment that seemed to get hazier and hazier with each moment that passed.

It blurred over the edges since the sight of her caused every cell in my body to go haywire.

Short-circuiting.

My senses on overload because fuck…I wanted her.

Wanted to fist my hands in those tresses of black. Get lost in the turbulence of those blue eyes. Drown on that vixen mouth.

I wanted her in a way that wasn't right. In a way that slanted dangerous. In a way that was at odds with every damned thing I'd been living for.

Remnants of earlier in the lobby still buzzed in my nerves.

The way I wouldn't have thought twice about fighting for her when I'd gone for the blacked-out BMW parked on the opposite side of the street.

The way the demon inside had gone to thrashing and jerking and tearing at the chains in a bid to get free.

The way I'd wanted to hop on my bike and hunt the motherfucker down when the pussy had jumped from the curb and fled.

Truth was, everything about whoever had been sitting out there was sketch as fuck.

Knew it in a moment.

In a heartbeat.

The *instinct* that had kept me alive for all those years when I'd been living in the dregs of society.

I'd been set on ripping the asshole from the car and demanding to know what he was doing creeping around my lot.

The problem was, that rage hadn't dissipated when the threat had gone, it'd only shifted.

Changed.

Taken new shape.

It had grown into a beast that wanted to fight for her all the harder when I'd come back in and found this fierce, ferocious girl pale and shaking, like she'd come face-to-face with a ghost she couldn't outrun.

I'd only meant to comfort her.

Promise her it would be fine.

Then I'd touched her, and all bets were off.

This girl who with one kiss had knocked me senseless.

"Hey there, darlin'," I called.

She normally strode in here all kinds of confident, but this time, those eyes darted around, landing on every single thing except for me.

Finally, she exhaled the strain and lifted that chin as she sauntered my way. "Are you ready?"

A grin cracked my face as I pushed to standing and tossed the wrench to the worktable. "You in a rush?"

Suggestion rode out with the words, no holding it back.

Not when just her walking into my shop knocked the breath right out of my lungs.

Her tone turned almost defiant. "I am, actually."

I hooked my hip on the table and crossed my arms over my chest. "Yeah, and why's that?"

She heaved out a breath and shook her head. She looked around again, not answering my question but giving me one of her own. "Where's Darius?"

"Cut both him and Brock loose early. Figured they deserved an early night to unwind considering the hours they've been putting in this week."

Salem quirked a brow. "And Darius didn't argue?"

"Told him to go on. That I had you." I shrugged. "And I'm the boss."

Amusement played at that pretty face, and she crept nearer, like she was testing out just how deep she could get before she went under.

Before that lure would be too intense.

But it was already there.

Baiting and tugging and pulling.

Drawing us closer.

Gravity.

"Wow, you really like using that to your advantage, don't you?" A tease wound its way into her voice.

Fighting a smirk, I shrugged again. "Only when I really have to."

"And this was one of those instances?"

Salem's heels clicked on the hard floor. Each one sent a reverberation across the ground that vibrated my boots and climbed my legs.

Girl invading.

Sweet, sweet enchantress casting her spell.

Wrapping me around those fingers that I'd really like wrapped around my dick.

I edged her way, loving how her breaths went shallow when I moved to stand over her.

Woman this tiny, curvy thing with a big-ass presence that overflowed the room.

Thunderbolt eyes struck in the middle of it.

Motherfucking thunder.

Deep and dark and seductive.

Her plush lips parted like she was getting lost in the memory of that kiss, too.

Yeah, that wasn't helping things, either.

My fingers twitched, urging me to reach out and take what I was itching to make mine.

Then she seemed to think better of it, and she took a step back. She toyed with the end of a lock of her hair, looking away for a beat as she pondered what to say. "Listen, Jud—"

"Let's get out of here."

Salem's attention whipped back to me, a solemn line denting her brow. "I think we should talk."

Yeah, and I knew what that talk was going to be. Could feel her reservations flying.

Spiky barbs of rejection.

I leaned in close, scent of the girl infiltrating my nose.

Toasted coconut and sultry sin.

I swept my fingertips along the length of her chin. "How about we get you on the back of my bike, instead? Right where you belong."

Shock edged her back an inch.

Yeah, sweetheart, you keep shocking the shit out of me, too.

The way I couldn't control my reaction.

The need that made me think I just might be losing my mind.

One second later, a playful scowl scrunched her forehead as she crossed her arms over her chest. "You want me on your bike? That's what this was all about?"

All?

Not even close.

But it was a damned good start.

The truth was, I didn't want to let her out of my sight.

Still, I played along, kept the words light. "Might be the only way I get those legs wrapped around me."

She bit down on her bottom lip, though a slight giggle rippled free. "You're unbelievable. Some savior you are."

A grin took hold. "Have you looked in a mirror, gorgeous? You can't blame a man."

She glared at me, but there was laughter in her expression, and some of the edge I'd been fighting the entire day drained away.

"Fine. Since you already sent my ride home, I guess I don't have any better options, do I?" she goaded as she turned and strutted to where my bike was parked in my personal bay.

Her hips and ass swaying across the shop.

Damn.

"You really, really can't blame a man," I mumbled under my breath. I grabbed my phone from the table and followed her. "Front locked up?"

"Yes, everything is ready."

"Thank you, sweetheart."

"It's my job," she tossed back.

I moved to press the button for the garage.

Warm, evening light tumbled in.

Bright, golden rays that lit up the girl and my bike.

My fingers itched with the urge to paint. To create something beautiful. Hope in the rubble.

I grabbed a helmet, situated it on her head, my fingers quick as I fastened the strap.

Whole time, my attention was trapped on that face, not a chance I could look away.

Not when I swung my leg over my bike, hit the starter, and stretched out my hand.

In a beat of contemplation, she dropped her gaze before she accepted it.

It damned near sent me spiraling again.

The way something that was a cross of desire and devotion went zapping through my veins.

The way I wanted to wrap her up and never let her go.

I fought that thought.

Knew it was stupid.

That my heart was pushing against a line that couldn't be uncrossed.

What I needed to focus on was the task of getting her home.

To escort her across this small mountain city, drop her at her door, and ensure she was safe.

Leave it at that.

Except Salem wrapped her arms around my waist and exhaled at the sensitive flesh on my neck. Right about the time she was pressing those ample tits that I was dying to get my hands on again against my back.

Need crashed.

Lust spiraled.

I forced myself to ease out of the garage bay. I closed it behind us before I carefully took to the road and headed in the direction of her house.

Rays of sunlight danced and drizzled over the soaring trees that hugged the road like a hedge of protection. They sent glittering orbs slanting through the branches and dappling through the leaves.

The road was lit up in golden glitter.

My body lit up, too.

Salem kept tightening her hold.

Her heart thundered at my back, a drumbeat of confusion that pounded through her spirit.

Want.

Fear.

This uttering of hope that pulsed through her being and whispered in my ear.

I should ignore it.

Hell, I never should have even pushed for this, but I was the fool who was taking a left when I should have been taking a right.

I could feel her perplexity, the disquiet in the flinch of her arms, but before either of us could think better of it, I'd taken two more turns that led just out of town.

Slowing, I eased onto the familiar, earthy path that cut through a row of towering trees.

I came to a stop in the middle of the secluded meadow.

Its bed was covered in wild grasses and flowers. Purples and whites and pinks. The floor a bright, misty green. The scene was cast in an entrancing glow as those shimmery rays of receding light burned through the space.

I cut the engine. The only sound was our battering hearts and the babbling of the creek that flowed through.

"What is this place?" Salem whispered. Awe in her voice. Then it was twisting again. "What are we doing here?"

"I come here sometimes when I need to clear my head." The admission rumbled out on the peaceful quiet. It was the truth, though I doubted much coming here was going to rid this girl from my thoughts.

With my boots planted on either side to keep us balanced, I glanced back at her. "You said we should talk, so let's talk."

Unsure, Salem blinked. "Jud, I—"

She yelped when I suddenly turned and took her by the waist. I pulled her around onto my lap so her legs were wrapped around me.

You know, all *friendly* like.

Just couldn't fuckin' help myself.

Surprised pants jutted from her mouth, and those eyes were doing wicked things as I unfastened her helmet and let it drop to the ground. Her hands curled into my shoulders. "Jud. What the hell?"

A grin quirked my mouth. "Sorry."

She rolled her eyes. "You are clearly not sorry at all."

She wiggled on my lap like she was gonna get free.

My dick stirred.

Salem bit down on her bottom lip and stilled and fuck...I wanted to kiss her all over again.

"I told you I needed to go home."

There was some kind of pain lacing those whispered words, and a war went down inside me as I stared at her stunning face. I took her chin between my thumb and forefinger. "I know it, and we will, but I need to know one thing, Salem. Need to know if you're in trouble? If you're safe?"

I already was sure of the answer, but I needed her to confide it in me.

A million things played through her expression.

Fear.

Dread.

Grief.

Then she pasted on a sexy smile. A valiant attempt at a distraction. "I'm just fine."

My brow dented. "Wish you wouldn't lie to me, darlin'."

Her smile slipped, and she shifted her attention out over the beauty of the meadow.

Locks of thick, black hair whipped around her face.

My chest tightened, and I forced myself to keep my hands at her waist, my thumbs barely caressing her stomach, like I could coax her into giving me her truth.

Wishing she'd understand that she didn't have to be alone.

She peeked back at me. "And I already told you not to ask that of me."

She blinked through the emotion that writhed, lashes of her spirit flailing in the air.

She inhaled, then seemed to steel herself for whatever she was about to say. "I appreciate everything you've done for me, Jud. Since the second I met you, you've been nothing but kind. I honestly don't know what I would have done if you hadn't shown up during that storm. But my life?"

For a moment, she slowed, gathering herself before her head barely shook and the pained words burned free. "It's been a mess for a long time. More than a mess. It's basic survival, and I'm barely holding it together."

Torment swirled in the abyss of her eyes.

"Then let me hold some of it for you."

"Jud..." It was a breath.

"Not sure I can turn a blind eye to whatever is goin' on with you, Salem. Besides, that's what friends are for, isn't it?" With that, I let a grin spread to my mouth.

Salem wiggled again. "Friends, huh?"

I choked as she rubbed herself on my cock, then on a surprised chuckle, I was letting my arms curl around her so I could wrap her up in a hug.

I pressed my lips close to her ear. "Not gonna lie, Salem. Want to fuck you. Peel these clothes from this hot little body and lay you down in this meadow. Show you how insane you've been making me. Show you how beautiful you are. Show you how fuckin' bad I want you. Make you come again and again."

Shivers wracked her body, and her nails sank deeper into my shoulders. "Jud."

"But I'm not sure that's what you need right now," I continued.

Peeling herself back, Salem met my eye. "You're right, Jud. But the problem is, I don't know what that is. What I need or what I want or if I can hope for it once I figure it out. I don't even know if I'm staying or how long I'm going to be here."

My guts revolted at that.

I forced down the riot of possession, the part of me that wanted to demand that she stay. I reached out and set my palm on her cheek.

"All I'm saying is I think I should be a part of whatever that is for however long I can be. I'm right here, darlin'. All of us need someone on our side. Someone to lean on when times get tough."

Her brow quirked. "As friends?"

I bucked my hips just a bit. "Is that all you're gonna let me be?"

There I went.

Pushing.

Crossing those lines that kept getting blurred.

But I wasn't sure there was a thing either of us could do to stop this attraction.

A tiny whimper left those gorgeous lips, and this fierce girl dipped her eyes again like she didn't know what to say. Finally, she looked back at me, a mystery in her gaze. "You make me feel something I'm not sure I've ever felt before, Jud, and honestly, that terrifies me. That you make me feel something I can't have."

Rage burned.

A boil in my blood.

I wanted to hunt down whoever had put this look on her face and show them what it was like to really be afraid.

Draw it out.

Make it hurt.

Do what I'd promised myself I'd never do again.

Maybe that was the most dangerous part of all.

"Seems you make me feel something I haven't in a long time, either, darlin', and that scares me, too."

Light laughter left her, and she looked at me with this expression that cut me in two.

With hope and hopelessness.

With faith and despair.

"We're a mess, aren't we?"

My fingers threaded through the hair at the side of her head, thumb tracing the angle of her jaw. "Yeah, gorgeous. A beautiful fuckin' mess."

For a minute, we sat there smiling at each other like cheesy saps. Like we were meeting in some place that neither of us knew existed.

"I really should go," she finally whispered.

"Okay, darlin'."

She hesitated, then asked, "I can trust you, right?"

My chest squeezed tight.

How did I answer that when I didn't trust myself?

Still, I rumbled, "Of course."

"Then there's something you should know about me, Jud. If we're going to be friends."

I kept brushing my fingers through her hair. "Yeah? What's that, gorgeous?"

"I have a child." Salem's blue eyes deepened with sincerity. "She's my world. My entire world."

I didn't mean to flinch, but fuck, I did.

A knife driven right into my soul.

I tried to hide it. The impact of what she'd admitted. Of what she was trying to trust me with. I was getting the sense she didn't show that card often, and that was unsettling, too.

But she felt it. Felt it different than I meant it.

She took the gutting pain for rejection.

Rigid defiance took over her demeanor, and that hypnotic gaze grew sharp and hard, the wildcat showing its claws.

Her love for her kid stark and gutting.

And I was getting it then, the vehemence that lined her bones.

Respected the fuck out of it.

Still, every single thing I wanted to say got locked in my throat when she slipped off my lap.

Every confession.

Every reason.

The purpose that screamed and clawed and made me feel like I was coming out of my skin.

After I sat there like a mute for God knew how long, Salem shook her head in disappointment, snatched the helmet from the ground, put it on, then climbed on behind me.

She curled her arms around me, though they were rigid. Like a canyon had broken open between us and a sea had risen up through the middle of it to push us farther apart.

Heart in my throat, I pushed the button for the ignition and the heavy engine rumbled to life. I turned it around in the meadow and slowly rode back through the trees and onto the road.

It wasn't that I didn't like kids.

I fuckin' loved kids.

My guts clenched. My spirit moaned.

That was the problem, wasn't it?

Could feel the bitter venom fill my mouth as we rode, as I took the turns just as carefully as we'd come, but somehow the glittering rays streaking through the branches on the trees and onto the road felt different.

A light going dim.

I fought it.

The agony that wanted to lift.

To take hold.

Suck me under.

Where I'd drown in that darkness that would forever possess.

When I made the last turn into Salem's neighborhood, I pinned a fucking smile on my face so I could give it to her when I dropped her off.

Let her know I wasn't a total dick.

I pulled up in front of their house.

My guts were in turmoil, torn between wanting to turn around, take her into my arms, tell her it was awesome—that kids gave a whole new meaning for breathing—that I'd protect that too if she'd let me—all while wanting to run.

Fuck.

I was getting in too deep.

Too deep.

I managed to kick the stand and cut the engine, and I helped Salem to stand. She kept watching me warily as I climbed off, too, as I took two steps up her walkway, following her, searching for a way to apologize.

To give her something when I knew full well there was no chance of a sound making it up my throat.

Not when the front screen door of their house banged open.

The air punched from my lungs.

A kick to the stomach.

I stumbled back.

A little girl about five came blazing out.

All grins and smiles and pitch-black hair worn in pigtails.

I stumbled like an oaf.

A fuckin' meathead without words.

"Mommy! You made it back from doing all the works and oh my gosh you rodes on a motorcycle?"

Her little voice was a screech of excitement. A squeal of joy.

Salem breathed out, love pouring free, though I could still see her reservations when she tossed a confused glance at me before she turned back to her daughter. Her voice twisted in faked enthusiasm. "I sure did!"

The little thing kept running until she threw herself into Salem's arms. Salem swept her up and hugged her close.

Nausea clawed at my insides.

Thought I was going to puke right there.

"Did it go so fasts? Like a thousand miles in one hour? I bet you could rides it so fast we could make it all the way to China by the time we gets to eat dinner. What do you think?"

The child grinned at me when she asked it.

The most brittle smile took to my mouth. "That's awful far."

"That's what the adventures are for. You gotta go all over to the places that you've never beens before so you can experience new things even if you don't wanna go at first. That's what me and my mommy do."

I scraped a hand over the top of my head, that smile faltering. Part of me wanted to ask more. Wanted details. Wanted to know.

To invade.

To step forward and succumb to this.

This pull.

This lure.

This want that made me consider saying fuck it all.

Loyalty shorn in the glance of a woman in the storm.

Black-fuckin'-magic.

The other part knew I had to resist. Had to end this right then.

To remember.

I looked back at my bike, contemplating my escape.

Only my attention snagged on the car that was coming to a stop on the opposite side of the road.

Tessa, Eden's best friend, hopped out, all smiling and eager.

Awesome.

Liked her, but the girl was a handful, and I sure as shit couldn't deal with her right then.

Not when I could see the hurt splitting Salem's expression.

Her single treasure held in her arms that I was rejecting.

"I'm gonna go." My words were bricks that toppled to the ground.

Energy whipped. A tempest.

Screaming in the air like Salem's spirit was physically clawing its way to me, hooking in and refusing to let go.

Or maybe the real problem was that it was mine.

This piece that had already toppled out and landed at her feet that wanted to beg for whatever she would give me.

Salem lifted that defiant, scarred chin, brandishing a look that promised she'd been to Hell and was prepared to fight with her last breath to claw the rest of the way out.

Ferocity surrounded her, and she bit the words from her tongue. "Yeah, I think you should."

Chapter Twelve

Salem

WHAT THE HELL WAS THAT?

I hugged my daughter closely while I watched the backside of Jud as he rode away. The sound of that heavy motor rumbled as his big body disappeared over the dip and into the falling night.

"Wow, Mommy, he really hads to go so fast. I bet he decided he had to get to China fast because it's already almost dinner. Did you know Mimi's been cooking for already almost the whole day? And guess what! It smells *deeeeeelicious*!" Juni turned her sweet little face up to me with that grin.

Then her voice dropped like a secret. "Do you think he got the anxious flies in his stomach to go on the new adventure?"

My arms curled tighter around her, wishing I knew, that I understood, that I wasn't the fool who'd already gone to the place where it hurt.

Where I expected something different.

Something better.

I pressed a kiss to her temple. "I think so, Juni Bee."

Right.

So anxious he couldn't even stick around long enough to learn her name.

My chest tightened as the disappointment raged. Hurt bottled in the middle of it.

What a coward.

I mean, come on, we were just supposed to be friends and he freaked out because I had a child?

But I think we both knew better than that, didn't we?

That kiss this afternoon had felt like an awakening.

Like I'd been touched for the first time in my life.

Truly seen.

Then the way he'd treated me out in the meadow? With unbridled care? With that raw, untamed gentleness?

We were fools if we thought it wasn't more.

Maybe it was for the best. I couldn't get complacent. Couldn't start to rely on someone else. Couldn't trust that they would stand, fight, and advocate.

Couldn't invite someone into the places they couldn't go.

Worst?

My stomach twisted.

I doubted much that we could stay and losing another part of myself was not something I could entertain.

It was better that he left before this went any farther—with his tail tucked between his legs and that expression on his face. One that rejected the single gift I had offered.

For him to know this part of me.

My one, single purpose.

I inhaled Juni's hair, and she giggled and squirmed. "Mommy, let me go. It's not the snuggles time. You gotta wait for the story times to get those."

Affectionate laughter managed to work its way through the sting as I set her onto her feet.

"Is that so?" I whispered, my fingers caressing down the side of her chubby cheek.

Then I stilled when I heard a squeal coming from across the street. I was half inclined to pick Juni back up and run into the house.

Hide her away.

"Oh my gosh, you *have* to be Salem."

I'd gotten so wrapped up in Jud's reaction that I hadn't noticed someone was there.

Awesome.

Another strike against me.

This carelessness was becoming too much.

I swiveled to watch a woman shut her car door and start to walk across the street like she knew me. She was tall and rail thin with the palest skin and freckles covering the entirety of her face. Shiny, undoubtedly natural red hair was caught up in a ponytail that swished around her shoulders.

"It is so nice to finally meet you!" Her voice was lifted in welcome as she stepped onto the sidewalk. She didn't pause, didn't slow, just threw her arms around me in a giant, overbearing hug.

My spine went rigid.

Trust no one.

But I was pretty sure she knocked the chip right off my shoulder when she started rocking me back and forth and making these happy sounds. She pulled back and held onto me from the outside of the arms.

"Seriously, Eden told me you are gorgeous, but on all things holy, woman, you are about to start a fire."

I could feel the force of my frown, the confusion winding tight.

"Oh sorry. I'm Tessa, Eden's BFF and partner in crime." She gave me a little shake. "She has been going on about a new friend who was living across the street, and I couldn't wait to meet you. We are going to be the best of friends. I just know it. Get ready for it—the three amigos."

I bit down on my bottom lip as she issued them toward the sky.

This woman was crazy. And I kind of loved her.

That was a bad sign, too.

Warily, I looked around, trying to think of an excuse to get out of there before I got wound any deeper, only my attention got lost on the empty road where Jud had just disappeared.

My heart sank like a stone.

What a jerk.

And why did I care? What did I expect? I already knew not to get involved. This is what it got you—or way, way worse.

"And my god, Jud Lawson?" Tessa fanned herself.

Her words knocked me back into reality.

The frown that'd curled my brow slipped into nonchalance. "He's my new boss, and he gave me a ride home because my car is broken down."

There.

It was truth enough.

Glee filled her freckled face, and her blue eyes danced with the scandal. "Friends? If that's what you call friends, I need to rethink the definition. I thought I was legit going to catch fire, walkin' over here on the two of you. Spark, crackle, boom."

Her hands moved just as quickly as her mouth.

"Oh, no, it was nothing like that."

She smirked. "Sure, sure. And hot lava isn't *hot,* and believe me, that volcano was about to erupt."

"Volcano?" Juniper's little voice broke into our conversation. "I want to go to a volcano! Did you know they make islands and mountains and all the mostest beautiful things? One day my mommy and me are gonna go on an adventure to the Hawaiis."

I ran my fingers through her hair. Thank God for my little thing redirecting the exchange.

"Oh, yes, I'm sure your mommy would love to climb that volcano."

The woman sent me an overexaggerated wink.

Oh my god.

Redness flushed, and I wasn't even shy.

"I bet so! They're so, so big!" Juni hopped her way.

"Oh, yeah, definitely big." Tessa sent me a smirk when she said that before she bent at the waist and leaned toward my daughter. "And you must be the one and only Juni that Gage cannot stop talking about. He told me he has a brand-new best friend and she is pure awesomesauce." She tapped Juni's nose.

Juni scrunched it up and giggled. "He did?"

"Yep, he sure did…and let me tell you, he is one happy little boy that he has someone as cool as you living across the street."

Exasperated laughter tumbled out, and I took a step forward, setting my hand on Juni's shoulder, still in protector mode even though I was pretty sure the only danger this woman posed was killing you with kindness. "Tessa, this is Juniper, my daughter."

Juni stretched out her hand. "Pleased to meet you, ma'am."

Tessa cracked up. "Oh, the manners…but I'm way too young for someone to call me ma'am." She said that out of the side of her mouth, whispering it to Juni with a tease slipping from her tongue.

"How olds are you, anyway?"

That time, a straight shot of laughter ripped from me. Scrambling forward, I put my hand over my daughter's mouth and hauled her back. "We are actually still working on that manners thing."

Tessa cracked up. "Oh, don't even apologize. I love her."

The woman smiled at me. "Seriously, I'm really glad you're here. I need a little backup on my side since loverboy over there came and stole all my BFF time with my Eden."

With an exaggerated pout, she hooked her thumb in the direction of Eden's house. "She's always over there after all that cake."

My mind raced to keep up with her.

Cake?

"I mean, I can't blame the poor girl, the man is h-o-t," she rambled on, "kinda like his brother, if you know what I'm sayin'."

She checked me on the shoulder with hers, words all kinds of suggestion.

Wow.

"Okay, I better bolt. It was so nice to meet you both."

My head spun.

Before she made it a step backward, her face lit up. "Oh my gosh, wait."

Her voice dropped with whatever epiphany she'd had, and she took me by both hands, as if we'd been friends forever, a secret on her breath when she buzzed, "Guess what?"

"Um...?"

Her voice dipped into an excited hush, the words barely breathed as she mouthed, *"Trent is proposing on Friday."*

My heart panged, and I looked to the house where the woman who lived there had been so kind. One who'd welcomed us without question and apparently told her wild friend about us, too.

Home.

It whispered at the back of my mind. I shook it off before it took root.

"That's wonderful," I forced out.

She squeezed my hands. "Yes, we have this surprise planned for her at the school where we work. Both their families are going to be there, and oh my god, it's going to be so romantic. Then Jud is going to take Gage camping that night, but we're doing a big surprise celebration dinner for them on Saturday. You and Juni have to come."

"Oh, I don't—"

She cut off my refusal before I got the chance to get it out. "Um, you do. Eden already claimed you, which means I claim you, and apparently Jud has, too, so..."

She let that hang.

"Jud hasn't..." I couldn't even form the words.

A salacious grin took to her mouth. "Um, that bad boy is nothing but charm and charisma and cockiness, never missing a beat, and here you had him stumbling around like he didn't know his feet from his ass. I'm pretty sure he *has*."

A frown pinched.

"He did leave really super-fast, Mommy. Like he had ants in his pants. I'm pretty sure he has the nervous about his new adventure." Juni beamed up at me, like the child had it all figured out.

Tessa laughed. "Oh, yeah, he's definitely nervous about his new adventure." She went to winking again then she reached out and tapped Juni's nose. "I like you, sweet one."

Juni beamed. "I like you, too."

Tessa returned her attention to me. "Okay, I really have to run."

She rushed in and squeezed me tight, shocking me again. But this time…this time…I hugged her back.

A fool.

A fool.

She backed away, talking as she did. "I'm going to swindle your number from Eden's phone, and I'll text you the details. Be there, baby. I won't take no for an answer. Your *presences* are expected. And shhh…"

She made an exaggerated sound with her finger pressed to her lips.

"I can keep all the secrets, Miss Tessa, don't you worry, not even a little bits," Juni promised.

"I'm counting on you," Tessa said before she spun and went darting back across the road and up Eden's walkway.

A little hand took mine, Juni almost tsking, so matter of fact. "Whew…that one's a whirlwinds, Mommy."

And that was exactly what I felt.

Like I'd just gotten swept up in a whirlwind.

My gaze slid back to where Jud had disappeared.

And I didn't know how to get off.

Chapter Thirteen

Jud

So, I wasn't one to buck a family celebration, but shit, Tessa was taking this thing to a whole new level.

When me and my brothers celebrated?

It usually entailed knocking back a few beers while tucked in our booth at Absolution.

But this girl was flitting about the private room like a frantic bird pecking around her babies.

The private room in the upscale restaurant where clearly a hot-pink bomb had exploded.

Decorations spewed everywhere.

Streamers were strung from the ceiling, black and hot pink balloons everywhere, matching flower arrangements sitting on every surface, and a custom sign that hung from the back wall.

"Would you calm down?" I grumbled. "Eden already said yes. Pretty sure that's the only thing that matters to the two of them."

For the third time, Tessa had started rearranging this over-the-top display of cupcakes that were decorated with candy playing cards. All of them were aces, whatever the shit that was about.

She sent me a scowl.

"You shut it. I want it perfect. This is my BFF's engagement party. When she walks through those doors to her surprise…" She waved a hand at the double doors that sectioned off the upscale room. "She needs to be wowed, shocked, her breath literally stolen from her lungs when she sees what we put together for her."

She pressed her hand to her chest like she couldn't believe I would think otherwise.

Girl was a nutter.

But she loved Eden like mad, so that was what counted.

Still, I couldn't help but give her shit. Considering Eden was about the least pretentious chick I'd ever met, I was pretty sure she wouldn't care if we were throwing together a barbeque with hot dogs and a few cold brews.

But whatever.

Place was nice and the food smelled like heaven, so I wasn't going to complain too much.

"Besides, you don't exactly look like a party planner to me. Your opinion on these matters doesn't count." Tessa needled that from the side, shooting me a mocking glare.

"Yet you don't have a problem with me footing the bill." My brow arched in challenge from where I was leaned against the long banquet tables where the servers were setting up. Four of them were scurrying around about as quickly as Tessa, bringing out these giant, silver chafing dishes and setting them over burners.

A full prime-rib, lasagna, chicken piccata, and a vegetarian entrée, plus a bunch of different sides and shit, too.

Other trays were filled with fruits, cheeses, and meats.

Not to mention this dessert fiasco Tessa was in up to her wrists.

"Only the best for Eden."

"That's right! Only the best for my dad and my new mom

because they are the specialist in the whole world, and we love them all the way to the highest mountain. Right, Auntie, right?"

Gage had come skipping over, all eager smiles and delight as he pushed up on his toes to get a better look at the cupcakes. "Yummy!"

"That's right, Gage," she said, poking out her lips like I was some kind of common criminal.

It wasn't that far from the truth.

"Right, Uncle?" Gage pressed, angling his head, little peacemaker that he was.

"Yeah. That's right, Gage in the Cage. Only the best for your mom and dad."

"Now you got to find a nice wife who's so pretty like my new mom who makes the best pigs in the blanket ever and reads me stories every night."

Affection tightened my chest, all mixed up with a knot of agony.

I patted his head and tried to keep the anxiety out. "That'd be nice."

The words were brittle and a total lie, but I couldn't help but agree, considering the kid was so damned sweet.

He had dropped to his knee with Trent yesterday, Trent asking Eden to be his wife while Gage had asked her to be his mom.

Think everyone had just about lost it with how adorable it was—mostly my big brother who'd been completely rocked again, like somehow in his head he'd thought there was a chance that Eden wasn't going to say yes.

Preparing himself for another blow.

Not a chance. He'd found the best girl around. Someone who knew his demons and loved him in spite of them. Saw beyond the scars to what was underneath. The two of them coming together to make each other better.

Old pain cut me to the core.

A dull blade slowly driven through my chest.

Fuck.

Had to beat it back. Wasn't about to be jealous of my brother. He deserved it.

What didn't help was the wash of guilt that came rushing in behind it. The kind that wanted to consume.

My mind kept traipsing back to Wednesday evening when I'd dropped Salem at her house.

I'd acted like a total prick.

And did that stop me?

Nope.

I'd just continued to basically ignore her for the rest of the work week. Problem was, I didn't know what to say. Didn't know how to explain. Had no way to break through the grief that got bottled in my throat every time she and I were alone.

It would only amplify it when she'd cast those dark blue eyes on me like she'd expected something different.

Something better.

When the only thing I'd felt was shame.

Even when she'd looked at me with disappointment, the draw we both were trying to ignore still had raged.

It was like her spirit was surrounded by a brick wall. Only that wall had a fuckin' crater gaping open in the middle of it, and there was a part of her silently begging me to find my way through it.

Thing was, we both knew that weak spot shouldn't have been compromised to begin with.

Thursday had been plain painful, nothing but feigned pleasantries and barely clipped conversations.

Tiptoeing.

Pretending.

At least the whole proposal bit had provided a distraction. I'd cut out of work at noon on Friday to make sure I was at the school in plenty of time for the proposal, then Logan and I had taken Gage camping last night so Eden and Trent could spend the night alone together.

Eden thought we were camping tonight, too, and believed

Trent was taking her out for an intimate dinner for the two of them to celebrate.

Little did she know *intimate* meant about every single person she knew.

"They're gonna be so surprised that they get to have the best party in ever and ever."

"That's right. No thanks to your uncle Jud here. You know, since he never knows what's right in front of his face." Tessa sent me a saucy grin filled with some kind of implication.

My brow furrowed. "And what's that supposed to mean?"

She shrugged. "I'm just sayin'."

"Just sayin' what?"

She gave me a confused look that was just a little bit sketchy. "What do you mean?"

That frown deepened. Girl was talking in circles.

I didn't get to press her, though, because Logan came striding in carrying a present and a grin on his arrogant face.

"The party is here. We may begin."

Tessa rolled her eyes. "Um…the party begins when Eden and Trent get here, dorkface. Now get your butt over here and help. You were supposed to be here forty-five minutes ago to help set up."

"I was having a bad hair day that turned into an awesome hair day." Fucker looked at himself in the mirror above the mantle, touching the poof that he'd probably spent two hours perfecting. He made a bunch of ridiculous faces at his reflection before he turned, tossing out guns with his free hand. "Killin' it."

A grunt sprung from my chest. "I'll show you killin' it."

He cracked a smirk. "My, my, testy. Seems to me someone here is in need of some lovin'. Too bad all the ladies come running to his baby brother instead. Damn shame."

"Dream on."

"Oh, I'm dreaming all right. Living it."

I shook my head, holding back the laughter that wanted to rumble out.

Dude was ridiculous.

He set his present on the gift table before he waltzed our way as he took in the opulent room. He let out a low whistle. "I know who's *not* paying tonight."

Luckily, he was close enough that all I had to do was reach out to smack him on the back of the head.

"Dude. What the heck? Why so violent?" Logan spat it like I was in the wrong, that mischief playing around his mouth.

"Manners, man."

With a roguish smile, he waggled his brows. "Only time I'm willing to spend this much money on dinner is when I'm getting something out of it."

"Well, you're not gettin' dead, so there's that," I shot back.

Gage giggled like crazy. "Oh, you better watch it, Uncle Logan, Uncle Jud is about to Take. You. Dowwwwn."

"That's right, Gage in the Cage. Uncle Logan is about to go down." I cocked my head at my crazy-ass brother.

"Pssh. You wish."

"No wishin' to it," I grunted. "I speak facts."

"Would you two knock it off? We have work to do," Tessa scolded. "Logan, you put out the favors at each spot at the table. Jud, you set out the name cards. I have them in order, starting at the head of the table with Trent and Eden and working around the right."

She shoved the stack at me.

"You serious?"

She had a freaking seating chart?

"Dead serious." She sent me a glare.

Right. Of course.

Fuckin' Pinterest.

In exasperation, I shook my head, but I figured I wasn't going to win this one. I moved to the table set for twenty and placed the cards for Eden and Trent at the head of the table. Then I worked my way down the long side to their right, Logan, Gage, then me. Next to me on that side was a few of our employees from

Absolution who'd become more like family. I rounded the opposite end then started up the other side where Tessa had sat some of Eden's teacher friends, herself, Eden's dad, and then…

What the ever lovin' fuck?

I froze at the name written on the card.

Salem.

It was set up so she was sitting directly across from me.

My stomach sank and tightened, and then the world shifted. Felt every hair on my body stand at attention, and fuck me, my dick did the same when that energy struck the air.

I looked back just in time to see her standing in the double doorway.

Her hands were latched on the shoulders of the same little girl who'd nearly dropped me to my knees on Wednesday. She seemed unsure, wary to take a step forward because she might just be treading into a field of landmines.

"Juni Bee! My bestest friend in the whole wide world! You came to have a party with us?!" Gage screeched it as he went racing that way.

"Yes!" she squealed. "Miss Tessa said we hads to come because you and your daddy are getting married!"

My chest fucking fisted.

"And look at my pretty party dress! My mommy sewed it up because we gots it at the special store for the seconds and now it fits and now I'm a princess!"

That fist tightened in a death grip.

Had to rip myself from the snare of the sweet little thing.

Only it had me jerking up to meet the ferocity in Salem's eyes.

Thunderbolt eyes.

They seared through me and sent every sane thought I possessed scattering.

Mindfucked.

She was nothing but hot-as-hell body. Lush curves and tempting shape.

She wore this slinky, cream-colored blouse that had my hands desperate to sink right in. A black, flowy skirt with another pair of those heels, and shit, my heart was doing that stupid, wayward thing.

Emotions ran rampant.

Wild as they tugged and pulled.

Want.

Shame.

Relief.

Regret.

Most foolish one of all?

This feeling that everything that'd gone bad for the last three days had just been made right.

Chapter Fourteen

Salem

I FROZE IN THE DOUBLE DOORWAY THAT LED INTO THE PRIVATE party room.

I should have known better than coming here. I'd rethought it at least fifteen times as I'd gotten ready. I'd finally decided to forget the whole thing since stepping out this way was clearly a horrible idea.

Then I'd received a text from Tessa.

An SOS asking if I could do her a favor and pick up some black ribbon on my way so she could focus on getting set up.

No doubt, that was exactly what this was.

A set up.

Because Tessa shifted to look at me from over her shoulder.

In an instant, I saw the smirk curve her mouth as her attention darted between me and the man who stood stock-still by the table.

A torrent of energy sucked the oxygen from the room and overflowed it with his presence.

Jud stood by the table, blinking like he thought I was a hallucination.

His jaw clenched tight though something soft filtered through his expression. Something that threatened to make my knees go weak.

Curling my hands protectively on Juni's shoulders, I lifted my chin.

I wanted to refuse any of his attention because he clearly didn't deserve any of ours.

He'd made me feel safe. Protected.

But the second I'd opened up a fraction, gave him just a little, he'd crushed it under his feet.

I deserved better—Juni deserved better—and maybe being here in Redemption Hills had helped me realize it was okay to dream of something better.

But I was the fool who'd let my mind think that *better* might be Jud Lawson.

Gage and Juni jumped around at my feet, hugging each other as if they hadn't seen each other in years when it had just been yesterday morning.

"Come on, you gotta see the cupcakes!" Gage threaded his fingers through Juni's, and the two of them scampered across the room.

The second Juni was gone, I felt exposed, standing there fidgeting like the outsider I was.

While Jud stared.

Heat blazed and severity throbbed.

I swallowed against the impact of it and forced myself to smile when Tessa moved my way. "Oh, thank god, you're here! I have no idea what I would have done without that ribbon. My cupcake display is a disaster."

My eyes narrowed as delight whipped through her features. I handed her the bag with the black fabric ribbon. By the looks of the decorations, she was doing just fine.

"It's the least I could do." Sarcasm wound into my voice.

Feigned innocence lined her expression. "Um, I have no idea what you're implying. You straight-up saved this party. Could you imagine

Eden walking in here and there was no matching ribbon on the dessert display?"

"The tragedy."

Laughing, she wrapped me in a massive hug.

"Seriously, I am so happy you're here, and you can so be mad at me, but I could tell you were thinking about not coming, and we really can't have that happen. We're best friends now, remember?"

My spirit danced and emotion climbed into my throat. Squeezing my eyes closed, I hugged her back.

But I couldn't escape the heat of the man.

My eyes peeled open to find his gaze slaying me through.

I really hated how good he looked wearing fitted, dark gray dress pants and a light gray button-down, sleeves rolled up his forearms to expose the ink on his flesh.

I hated more how my stomach dipped. The way my thoughts went streaking back to the feel of his hands and mouth on me.

My thighs trembled.

I tore my attention from him when Tessa peeled herself back, and she held onto my upper arms the same way as she'd done when I'd met her. Her gaze swept over me. "Damn girl."

I reached out and held her the same. "Ha...have you seen you?"

Tessa was wearing this shiny electric blue dress—the same color as her eyes. It was a halter-top, fitted and ruched, and dipped low between her breasts. Her red hair was pressed into giant curls that bounced over her bare shoulders.

She shimmied and winked. "Not too bad for the class nerd, huh?"

"Not bad at all."

"Okay, I need to finish setting up. The rest of the guests should start arriving soon, and Eden and Trent should be here in fifteen."

"What can I do?"

"Can you take a peek at the buffet and make sure it looks like they've put out everything we need?"

"Sure thing."

I moved over to the long row of tables where the food was being set out. Chills skated down my spine because with each step, I could feel those eyes hooked on me.

Conflicting and confusing.

I had the urge to peek back. I stopped myself before I slipped into that recklessness.

Jud had already shown his hand, hadn't he? His knee-jerk reaction had been clear enough. I needed to remember it.

But he never let me go of that connection.

A force came to tower over me from behind. It stole my breath and sent a rash of shivers racing across my flesh.

Citrus and cinnamon and spice.

A warm fall night.

I forced myself to remain turned away because I wasn't sure I could handle him face-to-face.

"You're here," that deep voice rumbled.

I guarded myself against the pull of it, putting up every defense I possessed.

"I was invited." It came out snippy.

Jud had the audacity to reach out and grip the two outside fingers of my right hand.

Heat zinged up my arm.

"I'm not saying I'm complaining."

That resolve cracked, but it was fire that came out through the fracture. I whirled on him, and my voice dropped to a hiss. "I don't think you have the right to say anything, Jud, so why don't we leave it at that?"

Every rugged, handsome line on his face twisted, and those black eyes flashed.

Flames and seduction.

"Think we need to talk about that."

A scoff shot from my tongue, and I crossed my arms over my chest to put some space between us. "I tried to talk to you, Jud, to open up, and the second I did, you reminded me of why I can't. So, like I said, let's leave it at that."

Searching for a safer place for my attention, I turned to look to the far side of the room where Gage and Juni were on the floor, sifting through the stash of toys Gage had brought in his backpack.

Giggles rippled from her, her joy so easy and right.

Emotion welled at the base of my throat.

Jud's attention drifted there, too, and there was no missing the way his hands curled into fists and every muscle in his being tightened.

Was he serious?

I swallowed around the disbelief, around the anger, around what I'd thought had been genuine care that he'd shown me in his office Wednesday when the panic had nearly consumed me.

When he'd promised he would be there.

When he'd kissed me.

Giggles fell from Juni's mouth, and I shivered with the hope they elicited.

It's what I wanted most—to give my daughter a normal life.

A good life.

One filled with happiness and safety and friends.

A *home.*

Jud's jaw clenched, but there was something beneath it that looked like—*sorrow.*

I blinked against it, against the care that wanted to press free of my ribs, against the urge I had to reach out and hold a part of that sorrow for him.

A bunch of new guests piled in, and Tessa's voice lifted over the disorder. "Trent texted, and he and Eden just parked. Get ready, it's party time people."

Juni popped up from her perch on the floor and came bounding my way. I reached out to take her hand.

"It's party time, Mommy!" Then her smile grew. "Look it, Mommy, it's your motorcycle friend. Did you go so fasts all the way to China?" she asked Jud when she took my hand.

I wanted to wrap her up. Cover her and protect her from the pain of rejection.

Only a rough chuckle slipped from Jud's mouth, and his expression went soft as he looked down at her.

My ribs clamped around my aching heart, and I swore, in an instant, my entire being went to war.

A battle of intention.

One side that urged me to grab Juni and run, leave this place because I never should have put either of us in this position, and the other that begged for surrender. For a place to belong.

"Yeah, I had to go fast." Regret filled his voice as he returned his attention to me. "But I came back."

My throat tingled, and my skin felt sticky, and I tightened my hold on my daughter.

Before this could get any harder, I whispered, "Excuse me."

I wound around him and led Juni away.

Away from the connection I could feel pulling taut behind me.

A lure I knew better than to heed.

The pull that was making me question my sanity.

Juni pranced along beside me, so adorable in her princess dress. "We are gonna haves the bestest time, Mommy."

"Is that so?"

"Yep! Did you smells the food? And there are so many kinds, and my belly is rumbling and I'm gonna eat it all gone so I can have a cupcake because Gage said they're super extra special all the way to the sky."

She hopped three times when she said that, yanking me to a stop.

Um wow.

Someone was excited.

Realization settled over me.

What tonight meant to my daughter.

Juniper had never experienced anything like this.

Our celebrations had always been just the two of us. Our *adventures* ours, even when neither of us had wanted to take them.

Reliant on the other.

Apprehension mixed with the hope. With these building dreams that I tried not to allow to terrify me.

Juni squeezed my hand like she felt my reservations. A calm slipped through my blood.

"Wow. Those must be some cupcakes," I finally managed to say.

"I think they gots diamonds in the frosting." Juni whispered it, even though she dipped her chin in an emphatic nod.

"Diamonds?" I gasped our secret.

"Um…did you see the sparkles? They gots to be."

Amusement tugged at my mouth. "It sounds like we'd better get to our spots so we can have the best party ever."

I led Juni over to the table where the rest of the guests gathered.

A silent groan clamored in my chest when I saw Jud was seated directly across from me.

I glanced to the left at Tessa who tried to hide her smile as she started passing out hand-painted signs that had different sayings of congratulations on them.

Definitely a set up.

I peeked back at Jud.

Without shame, those darkened eyes raked over me. Hot coals that flashed with greed and something else I'd be a fool to diagnose.

Because that tension pulled and yanked and tumbled through my rattled spirit.

It felt as if it called out to the broken pieces. The pieces that had come to life under his touch—under his care—pieces I refused to let him shatter.

Dinner was amazing.

The table was full of Eden and Trent's friends and family who were there to share their joy.

Eden had been shocked, tears springing to her eyes when she'd come in to her surprise.

Her new fiancé continually pressed kisses to her cheek, her temple, her knuckles, her mouth.

Love poured from them.

I was thankful to be a part of it, but I couldn't stop the waves of unease that kept rustling through.

I didn't do this.

I hid.

I lurked and concealed.

I existed along the fringes.

I didn't step out to become a part of something big and beautiful this way, but I was having a harder and harder time pretending like I didn't want to be there.

Eden's father, Gary, sat to the right of me, the man so warm and genuine as he'd chatted with me throughout the meal and made me feel as if my daughter and I were a part of this tightly knit crowd.

The entire time, Jud kept peering at me from over the table. Watching me as if I mattered. As if something inside him had shifted and taken new shape during the two hours that had passed.

When I looked up and he pinned me with the severity of that gaze again, I set my napkin next to my empty plate, pushed my chair back, and stood. "Excuse me for a moment."

Gary looked up at me in worry. "Everything okay?"

I sent him a feigned smile. "I just need to get another drink."

He grinned and winked toward Juni. "I'll hold the fort down while you're away."

Gratefulness spread through my veins, and I gave him a little nod as I moved to the bar set up on the far side of the room. I ordered another glass of champagne. I was going to need it to make it through the night.

Because I felt myself getting closer to an invisible barrier my heart kept trying to break through.

I accepted the flute then jumped when I felt the hand on my elbow. I whipped around to Eden who stood there wearing one of her soft smiles.

"Eden. Hi."

"Hey, Salem. I had to sneak over here so I could tell you how happy I am that you're here. That you and Juni came to share this night with us."

An unsure breath crept free. "I wasn't sure we should come."

Her smile deepened. "I hope there's no question now…that you belong here."

My chest pressed full, and I thought to deny it, to act as if this little family across the street hadn't already marked themselves on my heart, but the confession bled out. "And you have no idea what that means to me."

"I think I might."

Tears burned in my eyes, and I stepped forward and pulled her into a hug. "I realize I don't know you that well, but I do know you and Trent belong together, and I'm so grateful to get to witness it."

"I still can't believe it. I feel like I'm floating. I feel like the luckiest woman alive," she admitted when I stepped back.

"I think you might be."

She gazed at me with the gentle smile she always wore, though her attention kept peeking over my shoulder to the force I suddenly felt pressing in from behind.

Commanding and potent.

She squeezed my hand again, and her voice dropped to a whisper. "I think sometimes we stumble upon it when we least expect it."

She angled her head toward Jud and moved his way, and I swiveled just in time to see the emotion crest on Jud's face. She wrapped her arms around his waist, and he curled his arms around her shoulders, holding her head against his chest.

I was sure it was meant only for her, but I could hear him mumble the words, "Thank you for seeing him for who he is and not what he's done."

She mumbled into his chest, "I couldn't have seen anything else."

Energy pulsed through the air. I tried to look away, tried to remind myself it was none of my business, that Jud and Eden were sharing a private moment, but I felt like I was snared.

Held as he looked at me in remorse from over her shoulder. I fumbled back, only I bumped into another body. I whirled around and another set of big hands shot out to catch me.

"Logan. Hi."

I'd quickly been introduced by Tessa to the third Lawson brother before the party had started. He was as handsome as his two brothers, but different, as if he held all his intimidation in the lines of his arrogance.

He smiled down at me with these sparking emerald eyes, a tease and something wicked in their depths. "We didn't get a chance to talk, so I thought I'd come over here and remedy that."

Jud suddenly was at his side, smacking Logan on the back of the head.

Logan rubbed at the spot, laughing and glaring at Jud. "What the hell, man? Why always so violent?"

Jud grunted, staring his brother down while somehow glancing at me. "Don't."

Logan's brow lifted, and there was a grin playing around his mouth as he looked between Jud and me.

"Don't...what?" A tease was woven into the words, a ribbing that made the muscles in Jud's arm bulge.

"Just...don't." Jud's words were hard, and that lump in my throat grew tighter.

Because Jud kept looking at me in a way he shouldn't.

Possessively.

Indulgently.

Intensity lapped.

Lifting and burning and wrapping me into this confusion that I couldn't afford to feel.

"Ahh." Logan smirked. "I see how it is."

"Not in the mood, Logan." The rough warning scraped from Jud's mouth.

"Well then," Logan said.

Jud grunted again, though he tipped his chin at Logan.

The two of them shared a silent conversation.

I shifted on my feet when they both looked at me.

"It was nice to meet you, Salem," Logan said as he backed away, amusement playing across his features as he did.

"You, too." I forced the strangled words from my throat, then I turned and darted for the hall so I could escape.

I needed a breath. To clear my head. To rid myself of the mayhem the man incited.

Only it grew as his heavy footfalls echoed behind me.

Out in the desolate hall, I whipped around and lifted my chin. "I don't know what it is you want from me."

Jud stepped forward and backed me against the wall. My heart ravaged in my chest. I should be afraid, and I knew I had a problem when it had the opposite effect. When I wanted to sink forward and press my nose to his shirt.

"I'm sorry." His words were sharp.

I forced myself to remember his reaction from Wednesday night. "It doesn't matter, Jud. Just forget it."

"Maybe I don't want to forget it."

"Why?" I challenged.

Those eyes glinted beneath the hazy lights that hung from above. "Because the last thing I wanted to do was hurt you."

"You can't hurt me." The defense was out before I could stop it, even though it was a lie.

From the banquet room, I could hear the clinking of a wine glass before Eden's voice echoed down the hall.

"I want to thank you all so much for being here to share in one of the most important days of my life. I can't express what it means to see you here. I love you all. Every single one of you."

A round of cheers went up before the clattering stopped again.

"Since everyone we love is here, we have something else we'd like to share with you," I heard her say.

"Jud, you should be in there. With your family." I needed him to walk away. To leave me there like he had Wednesday night.

Only he inclined closer instead, his breath caressing my face, his hand coming up to touch my jaw in that way that slipped like comfort through my veins. Fire streaked through the connection. "Yet, here I am, with you."

"We're having a baby." Emotion wobbled through Eden's distant voice.

Surprise and excitement banged through the space.

Jud's eyes went wide, and I was taking his moment of stupor to duck out from around him because all of this was too much. "We should go back in."

I rushed for the doors like the man wasn't single-handedly wrecking every boundary.

I felt him behind me, meeting me step for step.

Longing slipped from his fingers as he brushed the small of my back as he passed by and edged around the table.

Shivers raced.

What did he want with me? He'd already shown he didn't want anything to do with Juni. My one purpose, and that was never going to change.

Gage jumped to his feet on his chair, shouting around the cupcake he had shoved in his mouth. "I get a new baby and a new mommy?"

"You do," Eden whispered. Adoration poured from her being. Wave upon wave.

I stumbled back to my chair and dropped to the seat. Juni was on her knees. She jerked at my shirt. "Mommy! Gage gets a news baby!"

I chose to focus on the devotion that poured through the room and not the man who was stealing the air from it. "That's wonderful."

Trent scooped up Gage when he scrambled off his chair and went running to them. "It's the best day of my whole life."

"Mine, too, Gage, mine, too, and every single day that I get to spend with you." Eden choked over the words.

A band of devotion wrapped the three of them tight.

Oohs and *awws* filled the room.

It was beautiful.

Real.

I touched Juni's cheek, and she smiled over at me. "I likes it here, Mommy."

"I know, Juni Bee. I know. I like it here, too." Probably too much.

Gage clamored down and went racing for his uncle Jud who had stood and hugged Trent tight, clapped him on his back and uttered something low.

Trent squeezed his shoulder.

Their loyalty fierce and true. There was no mistaking it.

I struggled to breathe.

Jud glanced at me once before he hoisted Gage into his arms. Joy and pain split through his expression.

It pierced me in the chest, and I tried to look away, but my eyes couldn't help but see deeper. To the sorrow, to the grief, to the torment written underneath.

Don't do this, Salem.

Don't fall. Don't fall.

Tenderness took over his ferocity when he tossed Gage onto his back. Gage laced his arms around his thick neck and shouted, "I'll take you down, Uncle!"

"Not a chance, Gage in the Cage." He wrestled around with him.

Before I could stop her, Juni hopped onto her feet and blazed around the table.

"I'll help you, Gage!"

She threw herself at Jud, too.

My heart sank to the pit of my stomach.

But he caught her and tossed her onto his opposite shoulder.

They shrieked and held on tight as Jud playfully roared and spun them. He had both hands on their backs to keep them steady. To ensure they wouldn't fall.

Dread thudded through my veins, taking this stupid hope with it.

"Hurry, Juni Bee, we gotta get him. Chokehold!" Gage shouted.

Juni laughed and wrapped her arms around Jud's neck, too, and Jud dramatically fell to his knees, careful as they all toppled in a pile onto the ground.

They flailed around, *pinning* him.

"Victory!" Juni shouted.

My chest clutched and my head swam.

Torn between the urge to rush for my daughter and steal her away from this place.

Where it wasn't safe.

Where we were treading into unknown territory.

Into territory where our hearts were at stake.

All while every cell in my body clutched in a swell of longing.

I jumped when a warm hand covered mine where I had a death grip on the arm of my chair. I looked to the right to find the sympathy written in Gary's gaze.

"Sometimes the scariest journeys are the ones where the lost finally find the right path to lead them home."

My brow curled, and my head shook.

He squeezed my hand tighter. "It's okay to be afraid. The courageous always are. They just understand taking the chance is worth the fear and the risk."

Emotion locked in my throat, my spirit a disorder, and I was jerking again when Juni and Gage were suddenly jumping at my side.

"Guess whats, Mommy? Gage just asked me if I wanna have a sleeps over at his house, and his mommy said YES! Oh please, oh please, oh please."

Juni weaved her fingers together in a prayer.

"Please, Miss Salem! We're gonna take really good care of her and I got a fort and we can even sleep in it."

"I don't think that's a good idea, Juni."

"Please, Mommy, I'll be soes good, and I never even had a friend before."

My heart seized in a bolt of sorrow, and the word was wheezing out before I gave it permission. "Okay."

What was I saying? What was I thinking? Giving my trust to people I didn't really know?

But my soul?

It promised they were good.

And I knew we had to take a chance if we were ever going to hope for a normal life.

"Yay!" Juni and Gage shouted it at the same time.

Eden edged up behind them with that knowing smile on her face. She set a hand on each of their shoulders. "We'd love to have her. Gage has been asking for a sleepover since the moment he met her."

My mind raced to find an excuse. Why this was a horrible,

horrible idea. "Are you sure it's not too much trouble? Don't you and Trent want to spend the night alone?"

There.

That was a good excuse.

A valid reason when I'd let myself slip into insanity.

Eden giggled. "Um, Trent wore me out last night. This will be a good distraction."

My lips pressed together as I warred.

"How'd you get here?"

I jolted when the low voice hit me from behind, and I shifted to look at Jud who stood there like a fortress. I swallowed the rush of desire that rose in my throat. "We got a Lyft."

His nod was tight. "I'll give you a ride home."

"That's not—"

He leaned in, his hands on the back of my chair, his mouth at my ear. "I'll give you a ride, Salem. I at least owe you that."

Chapter Fifteen

Jud

"ARE YOU READY?" I RUMBLED LOW.

I looked on from where I stood behind her. Chills skated down Salem's arms while she watched Juni drive away with Trent, Eden, and Gage.

The party had wrapped, and Eden's trunk was loaded down with the presents people had brought. Friends and family had drifted off into the night, everyone high on the life Eden and Trent shared.

Slowly, Salem shifted. Felt the ground quake when she did. Energy blistered through the dense night air.

Girl stood there in that skirt and blouse, and fuck, my insides took a tumble into greed.

"I'm sorry." My confession toppled like stones.

Hard and jagged and heavy.

It was the truth.

Salem's gorgeous face blanched, that body flinching like she didn't know what to believe. "Why are you doing this, Jud?"

Confusion thick, my head barely shook. "Don't know. All I know is I can't stop thinking about you. Can't stop going back to the shop. To your fear. Way it felt when I touched you."

The edges of that seductive mouth quivered, and she hugged her arms across her chest like she could block this out. "And we already established it doesn't change things, though, does it?"

"Doesn't it?"

Attraction blurred the lines.

Whipped and lashed and curled, rising around us like a dark, dark storm.

Her tongue darted out to wet her lips. "My daughter is and will always be my first priority, Jud. It's clear you have a problem with that."

Agony staked through my chest. Yeah, it'd hurt like a mother-fucker when I'd first seen that precious thing come flying out the door. When my mind had gone there, taunting me with that penalty I could never fully pay.

But I thought the wall that had gone up between me and Salem might have hurt worse.

I forced the brittle words from my tongue. "I was just surprised."

Her face pinched. "And you are a liar."

Nerves rocked me back, and I rushed an agitated hand through my hair, blinking toward the ground like it would hold an answer.

A reason.

"I've got shit, Salem. Dark, ugly shit."

The fuck did I think I was doing? But the confession had slipped out before I could think better of it. A proclamation I shouldn't offer.

But there it was, hovering in the deep, summer night.

Bare and raw.

Salem's jaw clenched against it, that scar dancing on her gorgeous face. "Isn't that true of us all?"

My throat tightened, the words gravel, "Not like mine."

Guilt clutched and clawed, and still, I stood there, a criminal looking for vindication.

"I don't know what you want from me," she finally said.

Girl so stunning. A mystery. Perfection.

"Want to paint you." It came out on the urging of my fingers.

I'd officially lost it.

Her brow curled, and her voice turned to an accusation. "You want to *paint* me?"

"Think you're the beauty I'm always trying to capture."

That stormy gaze flashed through a million things. Adding up. Like she was back to standing soaking wet in my living room, and she was asking about those paintings.

I'd shut it down then, unable to answer the questions she'd wanted to ask.

But tonight, I didn't know how to stop from inviting her in.

"Jud..."

"Come home with me, Salem."

Reservations sent her skating a step back.

"As friends," I clarified.

Salem all but rolled her eyes. "Seriously?"

"Just...wanna be with you. Don't want to take you home yet." I eased forward, and my voice lowered the closer I got. "Hated the last three days, Salem. Fuckin' hated the way you looked at me. Hated that I hurt you. Hated that things were tense between us. Just fuckin' hated it."

My fingertips brushed her chin.

"Jud..."

"Please."

Thunderbolt eyes struck me hard. "My heart can't take falling in love with you, Jud."

"Who said anything about love, darlin'?" A hint of a smile twitched the corner of my mouth, soft and real and wishing all of it could be different, and Salem smiled, too.

"You're ridiculous."

"Tell me somethin' I don't know."

She blinked up at me, and those tender fingertips found the thrumming at my chest. "That I like you...too much."

My hand covered hers, pressing it close to my chest. "Think I like you too much, too."

Her smile turned somber. "We're a mess, Jud."

"Yeah, a beautiful fucking mess, and I wanna show you what that looks like to me."

Her attention turned to the empty street where her adorable daughter had gone. This little girl who'd stolen a chunk from my soul. Her eyes the color of her mom's and her spirit the drumming of faith.

"She'll be fine with Trent and Eden," I promised. "My brother might look like an asshole, but he's got the best heart there is. Dude would take a bullet to protect the innocent, and I promise you, your daughter is included in that."

Meant that literally.

She set that gaze back on me. "I don't trust easily."

I squeezed her hand in mine, brought her knuckles to my lips.

Tried to ignore the flames and the fire.

Tried to calm the roaring of possession that went sailing through.

The protectiveness that surged at the memory of her fear.

This girl was in trouble.

I knew it. Knew it to my soul.

And I was the fool who wanted to wrap her up and guard her from whatever that was.

"You might not be able to trust me, baby, but you can trust them."

Her voice was wry when she said, "Charmer. And you want me to go home with you?"

"Just sayin' it straight."

She hesitated. "I think what I'm afraid of is I might not be able to trust myself. There's something special about you, Jud."

My chest fisted. "Nah, baby, think it's the other way around."

For a second, we stood there gazing at each other while the world spun on around us. People filtered in and out of the restaurant, cars zipped by on the street, and the heavens twinkled with the lush expanse of stars.

Finally, I stretched out my hand. "Come with me."

She wavered for only a second before she accepted my hand.

Heat streaked up my arm.

Salem made a needy noise, and I knew I wasn't the only one who felt the force.

Gravity.

We should fight it.

Turn our backs.

But I led her down the sidewalk to where I'd parked my bike.

Salem came to stand beside it.

All black hair and tempting curves and unrelenting eyes.

My dick wasn't the only thing that stirred.

Had to fist my hands to keep from reaching out and taking what wasn't mine.

Still, I edged that way and freed the helmet I'd left dangling from the handlebars, my regard unflinching as I placed it on her head and fastened the strap. I had left my Harley facing out, and I climbed on, guiding the girl on behind me, loving the feel of that tight body pressed to my back.

Way her form fit against me like she was molded for my shape.

A tremor rocked through her, and her arms were shaking as she wrapped them around my waist.

My hands squeezed hers, then I started the engine. The roar filled my ears and sent a crash of adrenaline pounding through my veins.

I pulled out onto the main street that ran through downtown Redemption Hills.

The air was warm, but crisp enough up high in these mountains that shivers raced our flesh.

Or maybe it was just this feeling that wrapped us tight.

The sense that the heavens hugged us in an embrace.

That there was a reason for this insistent attraction.

This feeling that I couldn't let go.

Emotion grew with every mile that passed beneath us. As the road blurred and the night deepened and her spirit caught me in a trap.

The truth that I didn't want to be anywhere else than here with her when I eased into the Iron Ride lot.

Blasphemy.

Still, I slowed and tapped the button to open my garage bay.

Easing inside, I spread my feet out to keep us steady then killed the engine. Silence bound the dense, dense atmosphere. The only sound was the panting of her breaths and the thunder of her heart.

Shit.

What was I doing?

Bringing her here like this?

But I couldn't stand the thought of dropping her in front of her house without at least making her understand the way she made me feel.

What I saw.

The beauty she sparked in my heart and mind.

I helped her off, and I climbed to standing, grinning at the way she quickly unwound the strap and handed it to me, girl all nerves while she stood there like a vixen in the middle of my shop.

This enchantress that held me in her sweet, sweet spell.

"Fuckin' fantasy, you standing there."

Her throat tremored when she swallowed, and she fidgeted with her hands. "I have no idea what I'm doing here, Jud."

"Going to show you."

I reached for her hand again, and we crossed the space, her heels clacking along behind me as I led her to the stairs. Shifting, I ushered her ahead of me. "Up you go, darlin'."

Warily, she took the first step, and I couldn't do anything but lean in and breathe near her ear as she passed. "Don't worry, baby. I'll catch you if you fall."

Thunderbolt eyes struck me from over her shoulder. "And what if you're the one who sends me tumbling?"

I quirked a teasing brow. "Now why would a friend go and do something like that?"

Deep laughter rolled up her throat. "Friends, huh?"

I gave her an exaggerated nod.

Pure innocence.

Girl saw right through it.

Fact I needed her here. A hunger had lit, and I wasn't sure I would ever get my fill. How I'd ever be sated. How I'd ever stop wanting more.

That kiss had only evoked a feeding frenzy.

We climbed the stairs to my loft, and I punched in the code on the keypad and opened the door.

Dusky, hazy light echoed back.

I held open the door so she could step inside my home.

A home that normally felt vacant and vast.

Artificial warmth in the dark woods and fabrics, but the only thing I ever really felt were the ghosts howling back. The demons that thrived in the shadows.

Salem stepped inside. Immediately, her attention went to the floor to ceiling paintings hung on the far wall.

An expression of my dreams.

The nightmares that chased me into sleep.

My sins I could never escape.

Could feel the questions rush from her skin, the way she looked back at me, asking me to let her see what lived in the recesses of my mind.

I set my hand on the small of her back. Severity zapped through the connection. "I'll show you."

Salem leaned down and removed her heels the way she'd done the last time she was there.

It dropped her four inches.

This barefooted girl sexy as fuck.

She hooked them in the fingers of her right hand at the same time as she wound the fingers of her left with mine.

Peace.

It whispered beneath my skin.

A slow burn that flooded my veins and threatened to seep all the way to my soul.

A motherfucking fool, but still I led her across the loft, through the open living room and along the far-right side of the kitchen, to my bedroom double doors.

Stalling, Salem swung her attention to me, her tone incredulous. "Your bedroom?"

A low chuckle rumbled out. "Thought you trusted me?"

Her eyes narrowed. "I never said that. Besides, you're the one who just told me I shouldn't."

"I changed my mind." The words were close to a growl.

"Touch me and I stab you." Mischief glinted in those blue eyes.

A bolt of laughter boomed from my chest.

Shit.

This girl was too much.

My little wildcat.

I reached out to open the right side of the double doors.

Salem warily looked through the opening.

Ripples of need.

Waves of unease.

I shifted around to face her, tugging at her hand while I walked backward, luring her in.

Her attention raced across the rambling bedroom. Entire thing was this extravagant show of the wealth I had built. A reminder that I was doing it right for a change.

Had to wonder if that applied right then.

I kept moving across the room to the door on the left wall.

I paused outside it with the girl facing me.

The room dark. Her gaze bright.

"Just what are we doing, Jud?"

Disquiet rattled me to the bones.

"Should I be concerned?" She attempted the tease to break through my apprehension. "Is this where you hide your victims?"

I reached out and brushed back the lock of hair from her face, tucked it behind her ear, my voice close to shaking when I muttered the truth, "No one has been inside here except for Trent."

Not even Logan.

A frown marred her gorgeous face.

I watched as her expression shifted, as she realized I was giving her something I rarely shared with anyone.

A view into my forsaken soul.

I punched in the code that unlocked the door and let Salem into my studio. A studio that took up half the area of the loft.

The soft glow of recessed lights barely illuminated the massive space, just a drizzled white seeping over the shadowy room.

There wasn't any furniture except for the easels that were littered about and the stacks of canvases piled everywhere.

Buckets of paint and supplies were strewn all over. Ladders and scaffolding climbing the walls.

Salem stumbled in, her eyes wide and a gasp leaving her mouth as she took in the scene.

Paint covered every inch of the room.

I didn't only utilize the canvases.

My art spilled onto the floors and the walls. Every surface cloaked in the artifices of my mind.

A kaleidoscope of images—images I'd painted and repainted again. Where the strokes were almost manic, my thoughts and fears and shame imprinted in the scenes.

Place a nightmare.

A mess.

A dream.

Surprise wheezed from her lips, and Salem eased deeper into the studio. In the middle of the room, she slowly turned around, studying it through the dim, hazy light.

"You said you didn't know me." I uttered it low. A morbid confession.

The heels slipped from Salem's fingers, and they clattered to the floor. She all but floated to the far wall, her feet so soft it felt like I was watching a slow dance in the darkness.

She glanced back at me once before she turned and ran her fingertips over the deranged depictions smeared on the wall.

Demons climbing from Hell.

Angels falling from the heavens.

Whispers of dreams.

Half, undefined faces.

Scourges and eternal fire.

So much fire.

Some were rudimentary outlines of my family.

Brushstrokes of hope and joy and desperate devotion.

Indistinct intonations of those that I'd lost and others that I clung to.

They were all haphazardly woven together across every flat surface.

As if she were drawn to it, she moved, her fingers quivering over the crude image of the child that would forever haunt my mind.

Salem's chest heaved and her body shook as she traced the cryptic shape.

The air locked in my lungs as a rush of old agony froze my blood.

"This is me, Salem." I shoved my tatted hands into my pockets. Shame came at me tenfold.

She swiveled back to look at me. Tears soaked her cheeks.

"Jud." My name was a whimper.

"Warned you it was ugly."

Her head shook. "It's the most beautiful thing I've ever seen." She touched her chest. "And the most devastating."

There she was, looking at me in a different light, in the way I should have shown her from the start.

Because what everyone else got was deception.

They didn't get the scars and the tragedy.

But Salem?

Felt compelled to show her this.

A fucking fool.

But there I was, laying it at her feet.

"And you see me like this?" She whispered that, a spec of horror and confusion, her brow pinching in the most gorgeous way.

That frozen blood thudded.

Pulsed harder. A warning that lit in my veins.

Or fuck, maybe it was straight-up liberation. This moment I'd found with an enchantress who floated through my studio.

"No, Salem. Think that's the problem. I see you in an entirely different way. In a way that fucks with my head. Because when I'm looking at you? I see beauty. I see light. I see a treasure and goodness and every fuckin' thing that is right."

She slowly shifted, her gaze soft as she carefully padded in my direction. Waves of energy rippled with each step. She stopped in the middle of the room, the girl warring, though she lifted that chin.

"And I see a man who found me in a storm where I was lost. A man who took the time to rescue me. A man who's a protector. A man who's good and kind. A man who's also broken. I see the pain, Jud. I see it. I feel it because it lives in me, too."

"Enchantress. You've got me transfixed. Don't know what the fuck I'm doing."

Energy crashed from her spirit.

Need fisted my guts, and the words left me on a low demand. "When do you feel the most beautiful, Salem?"

This fierce, unrelenting girl actually blushed. Heat exploded from that delicious flesh.

She lifted that stunning face. "I think I might have forgotten."

I took a step forward. The air trembled and shook. "It's all I see when I look at you. Beauty. You're the definition of it. You don't have to be shy. Don't have to be afraid. You're safe with me, darlin'."

The savage promise stoked the flames. Truth that I wanted to erase that fear from her eyes.

The truth that I was asking her for some of that trust I didn't deserve but wanted right then, anyway.

I should run from the fire.

But I took another step deeper.

Salem swept her tongue across her plump lips as those eyes were doing that thing that slayed me through.

Intense and wild and seductive.

Girl became a vixen in a beat.

Alive under my stare.

"I want to see, Salem, how you feel when I'm looking at you. Show me."

Attraction blazed through the dull, dusky light.

Sparks and flames.

She hesitated—contemplated—then she stared me down as she reached around to loosen the zipper at the back of her skirt.

She let it go and it fell to her ankles.

Motherfuck.

I gulped. Tried to breathe.

She kicked the fabric aside, and the girl stood there in that loose, flowy, knit blouse and a pair of white underwear.

Those legs were bare.

Curvy and luscious and…fuck.

My mouth went dry.

Had to physically restrain myself from going for her.

She adjusted the swoop of the neckline, letting it drape off one delicate shoulder, and she slowly sank to her knees on the floor. She spread them apart, and a pant rasped from her mouth when she did, like the girl was impaled by the same bolt of lust that skewered through me.

"Shit." It curled from my mouth hard and low.

She angled her head just to the side so that scar was exposed, her hair rolling down her shoulders like a river of black.

I felt held.

Compelled.

A spell rippling through the shadows that took me hostage.

Black-fuckin'-magic.

Salem smoothed her hand over her stomach, those eyes piercing as she stared at me from across the space. "This, Jud, this is how I feel when you're looking at me. Like I matter. Like I don't have to hide. Like for the first time in years, I am seen. Like I *exist.*"

Chapter Sixteen

Salem

My throat locked with anticipation as I rested high on my knees.

Held.

Enthralled.

Enraptured.

Caught in a violent storm that had come from out of nowhere. A tsunami that had hit unaware.

Where both of us would drown.

Where I had become a piece of the torment written in the bold strokes of paint that covered every surface of his studio.

A piece of the agony weaved into the canvas.

The thickened air strained in and out of my lungs as I remained as still as I could. A picture for him to see. An element for him to piece together.

To carve and shape and mold me into an abhorrent beauty that matched his walls.

The man stood by the door.

His massive shoulders heaved with each harsh, hot breath that rocked from his wide, wide chest.

A monster.

A wraith.

A tower.

A fortress.

A dark, dark sanctuary where I wanted to disappear.

I was still struck by the images.

By the suggestions that swirled and whispered and screamed from the walls.

As if they were alive and crying out to be heard.

The chaos that littered this bad boy's mind was written in blacks and whites and reds.

But I'd recognized it before, hadn't I? Hell, I'd had the intuition that the paintings out in his living room had been more than personal the first night we'd met.

He was an artist, but I hadn't been quite prepared then for what that really meant.

"You matter, Salem. You matter. Look at you, darlin'."

There was the charm all mixed up with the disorder that was at the heart of this man.

My chest squeezed and the blood thundered through my veins.

"Beauty. The meaning of it." The words fell on a harsh exhale from his lips, and the air that was barely skating up my throat died right there when he slowly toed off the dress shoes he wore.

Obsidian eyes flashed like a rush of the darkest night, rough as they devoured me from across the space.

Without looking away, he leaned down and peeled the socks from his feet.

I gulped, then I was nearly passing out when he ticked through the buttons on his shirt and peeled that off, too.

The man was nothing but wide, wide shoulders. Muscle everywhere, bulky on his arms and chest, his abdomen packed, tapering down and narrow at the waist.

Most all of his skin was covered in ink that seemed to scream the same as the walls, though it remained indistinct in the minimal light cast down from the rafters.

But I could make out enough to get the intonation.

The pure intimidation.

Menace and peril and life.

The mountain of a man stood there for a moment, then he took a step forward.

Energy rushed across the floor.

He approached like a phantom. Like a painting that had come to life.

It covered me whole and caressed me in shadows.

I was right. This man was definitely, definitely dangerous.

There was no question about it then.

And still, I remained there, held in his gaze, feeling the safest I'd ever felt.

I thought he was coming for me, only he slipped by on his bare feet.

Desire rippled through on his wake.

God, that was sexy, too.

Jud Lawson was an anomaly.

Conflict and peace.

Harmony and dissention.

A blinding light in the longest night.

Stealer of heart and sanity and good sense.

Because remaining there on the ground like an offering?

Posing for him?

There was no question I'd lost my mind.

His aura rippled through the room as he moved over to the wall that I faced. He pulled an easel closer, and the canvas he set on it looked like it'd been painted over a thousand times. He knelt to open a few jars of paint.

He picked up a brush and studied me.

I trembled beneath his watch.

"Beauty," he rumbled. "Second I saw you out in the rain. Thought I had to be imagining things. Hallucinating."

"I was terrified," I admitted, our voices dancing through the condensed air.

Louder than they should be.

The thrumming of our hearts was palpable.

Frantic beats that echoed against the other.

A smirk ticked at the corner of his sexy mouth, then it slipped when he glanced at me then to the canvas. He began to paint. Quick, sweeping strokes, as if the images fell from him without thought. "I felt your fear, Salem. I felt your desperation. Wonder if I felt it then, that we were bound to be more than strangers. Wonder if I knew you were supposed to be on the back of my bike that night. Wonder if I knew you were going to become something that mattered in my life."

I struggled to remain still, to swallow, to breathe. But the walls spun and gathered. Jud didn't move, but it felt as if the walls had enclosed and pushed us closer.

He kept sweeping his brush over the canvas in long, frenzied strokes.

"I'm so tired of being afraid." The confession slipped free. "I'm so tired of running."

Those walls shook around me. A warning they might crumble and fall.

I had to remember. Remember to be careful.

Trust no one.

But it was getting harder and harder to do.

Beneath his beard, his jaw clenched. "I want to erase that for you, Salem. Gather up every scar you have and paint it something new."

"Some of the scars cannot be healed, Jud."

It was an admission from my soul. Where the sorrow railed and reigned.

He blinked, caught in his own storm. "And I want to hold that, too. Don't deserve it, but I want it."

"How do you not deserve it?"

And I guessed that's why I'd followed him here after I'd been so angry with him. So disappointed. The truth I'd seen in the well of his eyes—it was grief that had sent him running.

A hard scoff climbed his thick throat. Disgust rolled out with the sound. "Don't you see it yet?"

"I see a man who's in pain and doesn't let anyone around him know."

"Only you."

"Me." I couldn't tell if I was claiming it or if it was a question.

Desire lapped.

I could taste it.

Sweet in the air.

I inhaled it into my lungs, felt it rush my veins and fill my belly.

From where I was perched on my knees, my hips involuntarily bucked, begging for him.

I shouldn't.

But there was a brand-new need burning inside me.

It was only going to hurt.

But my hand was pressing lower on my abdomen, thoughts hitting me so fast, the memory of that kiss, those hands, how good it would feel to just give in.

A growl reverberated the air.

Those black eyes flashed.

Pitch.

Darkened with lust.

His tongue swept across his lips.

"Salem." It was a warning.

"You asked me when I felt the most beautiful. You wanted me to show you how I feel when you look at me. This, Jud. I feel this. I feel desired. I feel wanted. I feel *real*."

No longer mist.

My trembling fingertips barely slipped under the band of my underwear, and the plea rasped from my mouth. "I want you to want me. The way I want you."

There I went, begging for the pain.

But I couldn't stop.

Not when he was watching me that way.

"Enchantress. What do you think you're doin' to me?"

A soft sound of rebuttal stole from between my lips. "It's me who's intoxicated, Jud. Me who doesn't know what hit her."

The brush slipped from his fingers and clinked against the floor.

Slowly, Jud edged my direction.

A dark tower.

A ferocious warrior.

A wicked savior.

I wanted him to be.

To stand for me.

For us.

But I could never ask that of him.

He came forward on those bare feet until he was reaching out and tipping my chin up with the crook of his index finger. "Darlin', I'm no good. Don't you see?"

Shadows played over his hard, rugged face.

"I do see, Jud. I see a man who is kind and good and gentle and fierce. I see a man who's haunted. Haunted like me."

The pad of his thumb traced my lips.

My stomach tightened and my hips bucked again.

He was close enough that I could make out some of the shapes on his torso. They were so much like the images painted on the walls.

Demons and angels. War and life. Grief and destruction. Toiling seas and crumbling mountains.

But there were four bold letters stamped on his left side that I had the urge to touch.

GRIM.

My spirit trembled, as wildly as my fingers when I gave in and reached out to trace the word.

The proclamation.

I closed my eyes as if I were reading it in Braille, and the man shook beneath my touch.

Shame lanced through his being.

"Who I really am, Salem."

My brow pinched. "What does that mean?"

"It means I've done horrible things."

Everything shivered.

My heart and my soul and the night.

This was bad. It was clear in the confession of his eyes that *it* was bad.

The ghosts in his eyes weren't just pretend.

Though, like a fool, I pressed, lifted my gaze to his hard, harsh beauty. "But it's in the past?"

Because I couldn't believe this man was cruel. That he was vile and depraved. Capable of inflicting pain.

"Just because it's in the past doesn't mean it's not who I am. Doesn't mean it doesn't live on inside me."

Jud still held me by the chin, and I took that hand in both of mine and pressed his massive palm to my cheek. Felt the comfort that radiated from his warm skin. The tenderness. The kindness. The care he'd shown. "You're a good man, Jud."

A grunt scraped up his throat, and he slowly climbed down onto his knees in front of me, still towering there as he slipped his hand to the side of my neck where my pulse raged and down over the thunder of my heart.

His palm was splayed wide as he moved farther down to run over my breasts.

A needy gasp raked up my throat.

"Nah, darlin'. I'm not. Because if I was, I wouldn't be doing this."

His mouth followed the path.

My chin.

My neck.

The sensitive skin between my breasts.

Shivers raced, and I all out shook.

He inhaled as he went, but it was me who was inundated with his aura.

It filled my lungs.

Filled my veins.

Citrus and cinnamon and spice.

I got drugged on that late fall night.

He kept angling down until he was kissing over my stomach, and my chest was heaving as my fingers tangled in the long pieces of his hair.

"You should really tell me to stop this, darlin', because I'm about to taste this sweet pussy, and I'm afraid once I do, I'm not ever gonna want to stop."

Lust burned.

Flames licked across my flesh.

I should be afraid of the fire, but my fingers only fisted tighter.

"A friend wouldn't make me wait." The words raked from my mouth on a frantic tease, a bid and a plea.

Because, oh god, I wanted this man's mouth on me.

He rumbled a laugh.

It vibrated me all the way through.

Tingles scattered.

Jud edged back and met my eye, his massive hands holding me around the waist. "You wanna come, baby?"

My nod was rabid.

"Did you touch yourself that night? When I was texting you?"

My tongue stroked my dried lips. "Yes."

"This is what I was imagining, darlin'. Feasting on you. Were you thinking the same?"

"Yes."

From where he knelt, he picked me up like I didn't weigh anything and resituated me so that I was sitting.

Surprise jutted from my lungs, and my hands shot behind me to keep me upright.

My knees parted, my core drenched.

Jud ran two fingers over my underwear. "So wet."

There it was.

The whirlwind.

The push and the pull.

This deep, intense, terrifying man up against the sexy cockiness this boy wore like a brand.

"I need this, Jud."

I didn't think I'd ever needed anything the way I needed *this* right then.

He hooked his fingers in my underwear and slowly dragged them down my legs.

A hiss left his mouth.

"Black-fuckin'-magic."

His big hands gripped me by the outside of the thighs, eyes devouring before he tugged me closer and dove right in.

His tongue parted me.

Licking and sucking and eating me up the way he'd kissed me this week.

It wasn't even in the realm of soft or sweet.

It was an annihilation.

Complete obliteration.

His tongue whipped me into a frenzy.

My hips bucked and my fingers yanked. "Jud. Yes. God. I need you."

"You have me, darlin'. Know what you need." The words vibrated. Shivers raced. He lifted my ass from the floor, and he shifted course and kissed down the backs of my thighs, over my bottom, and licked into my cleft.

A moan ripped from my mouth. "Jud." He chuckled a low sound, and I wiggled in his massive hold. "Please."

The air shifted when those eyes met mine, the intensity something bigger than I could fathom. "Told you, I have you, Salem. I have you."

Then he was slowly setting my bottom back on the floor, and he reached up and pressed two big fingers into my mouth.

I sucked and moaned around them.

"Good girl."

I all out shook when he pulled them away, the man never looking away as he pushed them deep into my center.

A gasp wheezed out.

His fingers were almost more than I could take. There was no question then—this man was going to ruin me. Still, I begged, "Please."

He started to drive them, fucking them in and out. He dipped down and sucked my clit, pulled it between his teeth, but he was lapping and stroking and swirling his tongue.

It took all of a minute, and I split.

Broke apart in his beautiful, menacing hands.

That energy raced, rushed my flesh in a landslide of bliss.

A flashfire.

Combustion.

A charge that shot me to an unknown place. Where I couldn't see. Where I couldn't think. Where it was only me and this contradiction of a man.

A man I wanted, yet some piece of me warned I should fear.

But I didn't.

I succumbed. I gave. I let pleasure win out.

He led me through, his fingers slowing as the orgasm rippled and shivered and gusted through my body.

Wave after wave.

Rapture.

Revelry.

I was sure I'd never felt so good as right then.

He nuzzled his nose into my belly as I slowly came down.

But neither of us touched the ground.

We hovered there, our gazes tangled before Jud curled his hand around the back of my neck and jerked me to the demand of his kiss.

His tongue power.

His mouth truth.

He kissed me until lightheadedness swept over me again.

Until I couldn't breathe, and my fingers were in his hair, his beard, burrowing into his shoulders and raking down his thick, muscled back.

Our chests were mashed together as our teeth and spirits clanged.

Desperate for this connection.

The energy whipped.

A tornado that swept up everything in its path.

My nails scraped down his chest.

Lower.

Desperate.

More.

His muscles flexed and bowed. "Careful, darlin'."

"I'm pretty sure I left careful with my car the night I climbed onto the back of your bike."

A wicked chuckle rumbled deep in his throat. I lapped it, like my tongue could gather the taste of it. I kissed down his pecs and his abdomen as I struggled with his belt.

Jud grunted, and those big hands found the sides of my face. "Salem."

"Let me touch you." It wheezed from my frantic lips, lips that kissed lower as I finally got the buckle free and jerked at the button and zipper.

My hands slipped to his cut waist, and that need was spiraling through me like compulsion.

Necessity.

"I see it, too, Jud, when I look at you. Beauty. The definition of it." At his flesh, I rumbled the same confession he'd given me as I frantically pushed at his pants. "It hurts to look at you, I want you so bad."

He pushed up high on his knees. "Fuck, darlin', what are you trying to do to me?"

"A little of what you've been doing to me."

I finally got his pants down his massive thighs and shoved his underwear down, too, and…whoa…

A shudder ripped through my being.

Jud chuckled again, and he reached out and traced his thumb over my bottom lip since my mouth was hanging open. "You see what you do to me now, Salem? You think it's you who's been lying in want? Been dyin' to get lost in you."

The man was giant. Thick and long and fat. Hot and hard and dripping at the tip.

He also wasn't shy. "Let's see what that hot little mouth can do, yeah?"

A fever ignited in my core, and every part of me clenched in want. A moan got free as I braced my hands on his hips and stretched my mouth around him.

I took in as much as I could as I moved to grip him at the base.

Jud bucked deeper. "Yes, darlin'. Just like that."

I sucked him. Licked him.

He tightened both hands in my hair, and the man began to guide me in a hard, desperate rhythm.

He arched and groaned.

That feeling was in the air.

Shimmering.

Stirring.

"Salem."

A rush of energy captured me, and I relaxed my mouth, let him take me as he wanted me.

His hips jutted, then he was roaring a deep, guttural, "Fuck."

Both hands held me by the sides of the head as he pulsed at the back of my throat. I swallowed around him as he jerked with the waves of pleasure.

He clutched me tightly when he came. "Salem...gorgeous... darlin'."

I could tell when he was coming down, the way the words went from grunts to these sweet little mumblings that fell from his mouth.

I slowly edged back, releasing him from my mouth just as he was brushing his fingertips over mine.

A rough jolt of laughter left him, those dark eyes dancing in the night. "Well, then, darlin'."

That gaze turned adoring.

It panged somewhere in my reckless heart.

I knew better than falling for this man, but I was afraid Mimi might be right—we didn't always get to decide when it was time. Which was why I was a fool for even allowing myself to be in this position.

Where I felt the world falling away and the steady beat of this man taking its place.

Jud tugged up his pants, though he didn't take the time to button and zip them before he slipped his arm around my waist and gently laid us on the floor. He was on his back, and he pulled me on top of him, brought us chest to chest.

"Sorry about those knees." He grinned up at me when he said it, brushing back the hair that fell around my face.

The playful, teasing boy was back in full force.

It pulled a grin from me. "They're going to be scraped up for sure. It seems you need to get carpet in this place."

I let my fingertips glide over the images on his chest.

"Does that guarantee me a repeat performance?" Mischief wound in the words.

I smacked him on the shoulder, though I laughed, fighting the smile as I peered into the depths of his eyes.

"It just might," I admitted.

Every hard edge of him softened, and his gaze sifted over my face, like he was searching for any reservations or regrets. "Didn't bring you back here for that."

"Isn't this the way you treat all your friends?" I tried for a tease, but the question thickened with emotion.

He kept brushing back my hair from my face as I gazed down at him.

The man this stunning creature that I wanted to know.

"Is that what we are, darlin', friends? And here I thought you were going to stab me if I touched you."

"I think I would have stabbed you if you didn't."

"And I think I would've died if I had to keep tiptoeing around you the way we've been doing the last few days. Hated it. The distance."

"I hated it, too."

The truth was, I'd gotten used to his *friendship*, or whatever other lie we wanted to label it.

The muscles in his body flexed. Torment rose to the surface.

"I fucked it up, Salem. Know it. I just…your daughter…"

That grief strobed like a beacon of devastation in the dark chasm of his eyes.

My heart skipped with the secrets I kept locked tight, panged against the ones I knew Jud was hiding, too.

Still, like a fool, I whispered, "What? What is it? You can tell me anything."

Ominous laughter floated from his mouth, and his head shook against the hard floor where he lay. "No, see, that's the problem, Salem. I opened up once and confessed who I was. It didn't turn out so great."

I swore the tattoo imprinted on his side burned against my chest.

Grim.

I swallowed back the disquiet, and I fell into the potency of those eyes. Into the gulf of darkness that waited below the surface.

"My wife—"

I didn't mean for the gasp to get free, but it did, a shock in the air.

Jud's mouth trembled and he curled his arm tighter around my back.

"I tried to be a better man, Salem. I fucking tried to leave the life I was raised in behind."

Dread pounded through my blood.

His.

Mine.

A thunder that roared between us.

He looked up at me, no teasing left in the tone of his voice. "Our father was the president of a violent MC. I was raised in the life, Salem. He taught us to raid. To destroy. To kill."

His teeth ground with the last.

Shame sparked across his flesh.

The air locked in my throat.

Fear and hurt and the rush of his pain.

It was like I could physically feel the ooze of the blood that stained his hands where they burned into my lower back.

I should get up and go.

Run.

Hide.

Pack our things and never look back.

This was the last place I should be. Wrapped up in him.

But I was already there.

Sinking into his being.

The man quicksand.

His tongue stroked over his lips before he continued, "We left that life behind when Gage was born. Got free because there was no chance Trent would raise him that way. We all wanted a second chance. To be something better. To offer something good instead of all the bad."

His voice drifted with regret, then those eyes were pinning me through as he threaded the fingers of his right hand into my hair. "Met this girl…"

His mouth tipped down at the side. I wanted to bury myself in his body. Hold his pain.

"Loved the fuck outta her." A rough chuckle came out with the admission. Shards of gutted sorrow.

"Jud…"

He shook his head to cut me off, and he moved to gather up my hand. He pressed my knuckles to his lips before he took a deep breath and forced out the admission. "Promised myself that I would never go back, Salem. That I was going to live clean. Be right."

Everything quivered around him.

Torment radiating from his body.

The laughter that rolled was spite.

"Got sucked into some old shit, Salem. An old debt the owner had come to collect. My brother Logan…" He trailed off, shaking his head. "I had to do it. I had to protect him."

I couldn't speak, couldn't do anything but watch as the agony pinched every line on his face into horror. "But it was fucked, Salem. They asked me to do something I couldn't. I tried to fix it. Take it back. I tried to stop it, but it was too fuckin' late. I didn't mean…"

He choked on that.

Questions whirled through my mind.

My heart wouldn't let me push him. The only thing I could do was listen. Hold whatever he was willing to give and pray it didn't destroy me in the end.

He swallowed hard, then forced out, "I confessed it, Salem. I came home and confessed it because I couldn't stand keeping secrets from her. Couldn't take any more lies between us. Couldn't sleep next to her while being riddled with that kind of guilt. But she saw who I really was, Salem. She saw the monster and she packed her things."

Sympathy crushed my heart. Because I remembered—remembered the words he'd whispered to Eden.

Thank you for seeing him for who he is and not what he's done.

Grief swam in my spirit.

His wife hadn't seen that in him. And God, I could feel myself slipping into places I couldn't go.

Jud's hand curled over mine, and he ran his palm up and down the back of my hand, as if the motion offered comfort.

Respite.

Reprieve.

I wanted to be that for him.

Then he clamped it down tight as if I could keep him from floating away while the brittle words crumbled from his mouth. "She took our one-year-old daughter with her, Salem. She took her, and I never saw her again."

Air streaked into my lungs.

Hot and thin.

Agony crushed down. A pain I knew all too well. I fought it. Refused it. The rush of tears that wanted to flee. But this wasn't about me.

I hugged him tighter like I could be his rock when I'd never been so certain I could be a stumbling stone.

"That's why I freaked out when I saw Juni. It just...hurt so fuckin' much. Here was this little girl who's so close to the same age as my daughter. My daughter who I don't know. All I know is she's got black hair and the cutest damned laugh, and she left a crater in me so deep and wide that it can't ever be filled. I shouldn't even have you here, Salem. Not for a fuckin' minute should I get the grace of touching you. But I need you to understand *why*. It isn't you or your kid. It's me. It's always me."

"I'm so sorry, Jud."

He kind of shrugged, attempted a smile that didn't land. "And I'm just the fool who keeps trying to be better. Doing what's right. Hoping one day..."

He trailed off at the very second we both realized what he was getting ready to say.

He was waiting for them to come back.

Who said anything about love?

Rejection burned a hole through the middle of me.

God, I was such a fool. So reckless.

But that's the way he made me, and I didn't know how to stop it.

I eased off him, no chance of hiding the way I shook.

I turned my face away as I reached for where my underwear and skirt were pooled on the floor, held back the hysterical laughter that wanted to burst from my throat.

The incredulous disbelief that was fully directed at myself.

Because how could I blame him for that?

I couldn't.

I couldn't.

And still, this stupid want burned. My body alive and my heart invested.

I slipped my clothes on while I felt Jud climb to stand behind me.

His presence powerful.

His pants rustled as he resituated them on his hips and zipped them up. Warily, I peeked at him.

He was standing facing away, and I clipped off a gasp when I saw the expanse of his back for the first time.

It was covered in tattoos, as well, though beneath the designs the skin was gnarled and puckered and pink.

As if the man had been burned alive.

A strangled cry clawed up my throat, and I pushed my hand to my mouth to try to cover it.

Jud stiffened when he heard it. When he realized where I was staring.

Trembling like I'd been zapped by a live current, I pushed to standing. My footsteps were unsure, faint as I slipped that way. With a jittering hand, I reached out and traced the marred flesh.

Jud shivered beneath it.

"You deserve someone to see you for who you are and not what you've done." I whispered the truth of what he'd spoken earlier tonight.

God, I wanted it for him.

I cared.

And maybe that made me the biggest fool of all.

When he looked back at me, I saw the sadness that held his expression. "Tried so hard to be worthy of that."

Jud shifted around, edged in closer. "Thing is, if you saw the ugly parts, you'd go running, too."

He caressed my cheek. "Maybe that's exactly what you should do. Problem is how fuckin' bad I want to keep you."

All of it felt like a warning.

An omen.

A prophecy.

Then he cracked a grin like he hadn't cut himself wide open. "Come on, let's get that sweet ass home. Told you I'd give you a ride. What kind of friend would I be if I didn't come through?"

Right.

Friend.

I kept my focus on my feet as I moved for my shoes while Jud snagged his shirt from the floor and redressed, not sure I could handle anything more.

Worried this gravity would finally consume me.

I needed space, and so did he.

It'd become strikingly clear neither of us were in the position for *this*.

So, we ignored the connection that groaned. Pretended like what we'd shared hadn't meant much to either of us.

We were nothing but feigned, forged smiles as we moved back

through his loft and eased downstairs. But rather than him leading me to his bike where he parked it in his personal bay across the shop, he led me to the pickup parked beside it. He clicked the locks, and we climbed in as the garage door lifted behind us.

The silence between us shouted as loud as the engine.

Jud drove me home.

That energy snapped and boomed and screamed in the cab.

A crackle that called from the depths that we both fought to ignore.

It was near painful by the time he pulled up in front of my house and came to a stop at the curb. He hopped out, ran around the front, and opened the door. He hit me with another one of those deadly grins as I climbed out.

Aloof and carefree.

But I saw the pain written underneath.

I started to walk, only I brushed my hand over his, and I shifted my attention to his rugged, unforgettable face. My voice was haggard as I took a stupid, reckless chance. "Maybe you just need the right person who can see through it."

His expression dimmed and shifted, the smile beneath his beard sad. "Ah, darlin', I'm afraid a love like that might hurt too damned bad."

Warily, I nodded, and I stumbled up the walkway. At the doorway, I paused and looked back at him. He'd shut the passenger door and had leaned against the metal, his hands back in those pockets and a foot kicked over his ankle.

"Friends?" he asked.

"If that's the only way you'll have me." With a soft smile on my face, I tossed back what he'd given me.

Jud chuckled. "Ah, Sweet Enchantress, there is somethin' about you."

A tender smile tweaked at my mouth, and my chest pulsed full, and I had no idea where I stood. How far I would fly or where I would land. If I'd run or if I'd stay, but I knew, without question, I would never regret experiencing tonight with this man.

I gave him a tiny wave before I eased my key into the lock, and I slipped inside.

I jumped when I noticed a dark figure hovering by the kitchen archway, then I heaved out the shock on a long breath when I realized it was Darius. "Shit. You scared me."

Disgust twisted his face. "Told you to stay away from him."

My entire being trembled. "You don't get to tell me that."

Rage vibrated to his bones. He inclined his head as he approached. "When I'm doing this for you? Trying to protect you? Trying to give you and your daughter a chance at a normal life?"

My heart beat hard, a thunder in my chest, and Darius came even closer, grating the words two inches from my face. "Then yes, Salem, I do."

Chapter Seventeen

Salem

Sixteen Years Old

Salem shifted uneasily where she sat with her butt barely hanging onto the edge of the couch cushion. She felt so out of place.

Out of sorts.

Like she didn't belong.

Okay, there was no *like* to it.

It was a simple fact.

She was reminded of it when Darius shot her another glare from across the throbbing room where he was huddled with a group of his friends against the far wall.

The party was packed, the lights cut dim, though colored strobes flashed from where the DJ was set up. The pulsing beat boomed at a deafening level, making it almost impossible to hear.

Forcing her attention from the daggers her brother was shooting her, Salem took an uncomfortable sip from her beer and tried to pay attention to Talia who had some random guy flirting with her.

Talia turned to Salem with a salacious look.

"See, I told you it would be a blast," Talia shouted above the din.

"Total blast." Salem all but rolled her eyes.

Talia reached out and grabbed her by the wrist, shook it around. "Come on, have fun. Why are you the boringest borer ever?"

Salem couldn't help but giggle. "I'm not boring."

Talia looked at her. Deadpan. Nothing but a disbelieving blink.

Salem sighed. "Okay, fine."

But she took life seriously. Her goals. Her dreams. The fact that she was going to make her mimi proud, go to college, have a home of her own.

She was determined to take care of her grandmother the way she'd taken care of Salem and Darius.

It didn't leave a whole lot of time for *this*.

Which was fine because it didn't feel like her scene, anyway. She'd have preferred hiding out in her room watching a movie with her best friend rather than watching a guy who was clearly too old for Talia feeding her a cheesy line that she ate up like candy.

Or maybe it was just that Salem felt like a third wheel.

A spare.

In the way.

Because no one flirted with her.

Ever.

So she tried to hide her unease behind her cup. To fade into the shadows the way she did.

Only Talia nudged her with her elbow hard. "Look who's here."

Salem looked up to find a new crew coming through the front door. Five of them. The air changed when they did. An unsettled charge of unease and intrigue as they walked in.

She wanted to hole up under the weight of it, but she was frozen, locked under the eyes that latched onto her after Carlo had surveyed the crowd.

It was as if he'd sifted through purposefully in search of a wallflower.

Someone clapped him on the shoulder, and Carlo turned to him, and Salem breathed out when she was freed of his piercing gaze.

Her stomach unsure.

Attracted…but…not.

She never could quite put her finger on it.

So, she watched from afar, the interactions that didn't seem so by chance going down across the room.

The low voice in which Carlo spoke to her brother with their heads tipped together, as if giving instruction as Darius nodded along.

A command of the room.

A deal she realized as there was the shaking of hands.

The dirty kind, she realized just as fast, or maybe she'd just caught on to what she already knew.

The way Darius all of a sudden had money.

The way he moved.

The secrets he kept.

Salem blinked and jerked her attention away, realizing she was staring when Carlo leaned back against the wall with his hands stuffed in the pockets of his dress slacks and stared right back.

She peeked again.

His smile was a challenge.

Heat slithered over her flesh. Salem felt like she couldn't breathe.

She tapped Talia's arm. "I'm going to go get some fresh air."

Talia frowned. "Do you want me to go with you?"

"No, it's fine. I'll be out back."

She didn't want to be a downer more than she'd already been.

She stood from the couch and worked her way over people's legs and bodies, angling through the house, pushing through the throng. She heaved out in relief when she made it through the sliding door at the back and onto the patio.

There were just as many people out there, but they were spread out, this crowd not quite shoulder to shoulder the way it was in the house. The volume of the music from inside cut in half.

She crossed the porch and took the two steps down onto the lawn, and she found a close to secluded spot under a tree. She crossed her arms over her chest, contemplated, then decided she'd send Talia a text and leave.

Except the voice whispered over her from behind, "Pupa." It was almost a tsk as his lips scraped across the back of her neck. "I think it's time, don't you?"

She slowly turned, confusion in the knit of her brow as Carlo smiled at her.

Half in affection.

Half condescending.

Her heart hammered. Attraction and fear. "For what?" she managed.

He ran his knuckles along her jaw, cocked his head. "For you to realize you're mine."

Chapter Eighteen

Jud

MONDAY MORNING, I PUSHED THROUGH THE DOOR THAT led from the shop into the lobby.

There was nothing I could do but heave out a stone of relief when I saw Salem sitting behind the reception desk.

So what if I'd been all fucked up over the thought of her not returning this morning.

I'd spent yesterday worrying over what'd gone down between us Saturday night.

The way it'd gotten intense and fast.

Hands and mouths and fuckin' bleeding hearts.

Way the two of us had seemed to cut ourselves wide open.

The confessions I'd made, and the way she'd looked at me like she'd hold part of them if I'd let her.

Like she might see me different.

I scrubbed a palm over my face like it could give me some clarity. Make me remember what I was supposed to be living for, where my loyalty lay, when the only thing I could do right then was edge closer to the girl who was steadily stealing every commitment I'd made.

It was that realization that affirmed I needed to put about fifteen-thousand miles between us, but nah, I treaded toward the desk. "Morning, darlin'."

She was already looking up before I spoke, like she'd gotten hooked by that flashfire of energy, too. Her own relief at seeing me washed through her expression, though those thunderbolt eyes were filled with caution.

This morning, her black hair was this perfect structured mess piled on her head, her lips glossed, her shirt stretched just right over those tits I was really regretting not getting a better look at Saturday night.

"Good morning, Mr. Lawson."

Gruff laughter toppled out. I couldn't help it, not any more than I could help from sauntering the rest of the way in her direction, loving the way her eyes swept over me, flaring at the memories of what we'd done right upstairs.

"Mr. Lawson, huh? Is that how it's gonna be?" I set my arms on the high countertop, shooting her a grin from over the top.

Her tongue licked across her full, plush lips.

My dick jumped at the sight.

"I think that's for the best, don't you?" She whispered that, glancing around to ensure we were alone before she looked up at me from under those full lashes.

Girl so damned pretty.

A punch to the gut.

A shock to the senses.

A fucking fantasy that I wanted to disappear into forever.

There I went, getting greedy when I knew full well I couldn't.

Juni's sweet face invaded my mind. Her little voice. Her excitement for life.

Memories of another little girl that I couldn't quite place. Ones I was clinging to harder and harder the more time that passed, terrified they were going to fade.

All of it was a gutting reminder that getting any closer to Salem was going to turn out bad.

Still, I leaned in, let the confession rumble from my tongue. "Call me whatever you want, gorgeous, I'm just thankful as fuck to find you sitting here this morning."

"You thought I wouldn't be?" Her voice was raspy, the air growing thick, that connection suffocating in a way we couldn't let it.

Didn't matter. I was lost in it, stumbling around in her gravity. "Thought there was a chance you were going to hide from me."

I let the grin take to my mouth even though a fucking riot went down at the thought.

Grim.

Salem knew—knew what it meant.

She might not know the details, but she knew what I'd done.

She saw the blood and the sin and the depravity.

I rubbed at the back of my neck, suddenly conscious of the fact.

Wondering how it was possible she was still sitting there.

"If I were smart, I would." The lilt of a tease filled the words, but her eyes flashed with something that looked a little too close to surrender.

The truth that neither of us understood what the hell we were doing.

Treading on dangerous ground.

"I guess I'm sticking around to make a bigger mess of things," she admitted.

"Nah, baby..." I angled my head at the dwindling stacks on the desk. "A mess is the last thing you're making. Thinking you're the only one who can get this disaster in order. Besides, I'm pretty sure if you decided to hide, I would just have to come find you."

Tried to keep my tone playful, but it shifted to a growl. Possession riding high.

She choked out a disbelieving sound, though she sent me one of those seductive smiles that hit me in the gut.

"You'd come find me, huh?"

"Yup." Like a fool, I kept angling forward.

Drawn.

Had the urge to crawl right over the counter and set this girl on my lap. Get down to an entirely different type of business.

"Told you once I tasted you, I wasn't ever going to want to stop."

Flames lapped. A fucking forest fire that engulfed the entire room.

Thunderbolt eyes struck, and Salem swallowed hard before she edged back, breaking the tether that pulled us together. She cleared her throat, and she glanced at the door again before she looked back at me. "I think we'd better stick to that friends thing, Jud."

"Oh, we're friends, darlin'. *Good, good friends.*"

Couldn't keep the suggestion out.

Her eyes dropped closed, like she couldn't look at me, and my name fell like a plea from her lips. "Jud."

We were held there a minute, in our reservations, in our pasts that seemed to refuse either of us a new path, in the truth of what we both knew she was getting ready to say.

She finally peeked over at me when she started to speak. "I'm not sure either of us can handle this, Jud. Not when the thought of walking away from you already hurts."

Maybe I hadn't allowed myself to admit it, to evaluate it, but I was there, too. The fact I'd go on a hunt if she disappeared.

"I decided a thousand times yesterday that I wasn't coming here," she continued. "I decided I was going to leave well enough alone. And here I am, which is probably the most foolish thing I could do. But you've helped me so much, Jud, and I..." For a beat, the avalanche of words subsided before the admission slipped free. "I want to *help you*, too. And I think the only way we can manage that is if we actually do this thing as friends."

All this goodness came gushing out.

The girl a well of it.

She made me want to drop to my knees.

She was right.

Of course, she was right.

Didn't mean it didn't twist through me like a blade.

"Okay," I said.

Salem blinked like she was shocked I'd agreed.

"Okay," she repeated, like there was a chance of this issue being resolved.

I pushed off the counter and started back toward the door that led into the main shop, but I thought better of it and made a detour. Rounding the counter, I took three steps to erase the space between us.

Salem peeped in surprise, and my hand fisted in her hair, my mouth an inch from hers.

"Okay," I grunted again. "But that doesn't mean I can't still taste you on my tongue. Doesn't mean I don't want to taste you again."

My mouth moved to her ear. "You don't want me to hunt you down, Salem? Get it. But I'm afraid my heart might have already claimed you as my own."

She touched the pounding at my chest. "And I'm afraid this heart is as broken as mine, and we're only going to end up hurting each other. I already warned you I'm in no position to fall in love."

A smirk ticked up at the corner of my mouth, though it was hard to keep the lightness in my voice. "Who said anything about love, dar-lin'? Don't think either of us are searching for forever."

Saying it felt like a goddamn lie.

Not when Salem was the first woman since Kennedy who had my heart tripping that direction.

Only one who could make my mind stray toward the destruc-tion that would be waiting.

Because looking at her? It made me feel like something ugly in my life had gone good, and there was a speck of the dead parts inside that wondered what *forever* might feel like with her.

Thoughts turning to *what if?*

This girl who'd whispered the words to me as if she'd understood them. They were the same ones I'd given Eden because I'd wanted Trent to experience all this world had to offer. Wanted someone to see him as whole and good rather than the vile, piece of trash Kennedy had seen me as once she'd known the truth.

The way Kennedy had fucking shaken, terrified of me, as she'd packed their things.

I'd tried to stop her. Promised it was done. That I'd never step foot in that cesspool again. That the sins were over.

That I'd never kill again.

It'd only made her move faster.

She'd refused to even look at me when she'd gone. She'd parted with a warning that she'd issued toward the floor. *"If you try to find us, I'll go to the police. I'll tell them everything."*

The truth was, what she knew had only scratched the surface of the corruption that had been our lives, and I would have gladly taken any punishment if it wouldn't have implicated my brothers. So, I'd let her leave. Watched her go. Guessed it had been standing there helpless, with nothing to do or say, no defense, no reason to give her to stay, that had hurt the worst.

The worry that maybe she was right.

The slamming of the door behind them the gavel slamming down with a guilty verdict.

From that day on, I'd waited. Kept that promise. Tried to be the man she could one day trust to come home to.

I gazed down at Salem.

My guts tangled, and my heart raced.

Blasphemy.

Traitorous.

Way she made me feel.

"Jud." Salem said my name.

Reverence in the word.

My spirit flailed, not sure what direction it was supposed to be heading.

I reached out and traced her lips. "This sweet, fuckin' mouth. Best thing I ever felt."

Thunderbolt eyes flared, and a heave of air whispered from her lips.

Need gusted in the space.

More than just the lust.

That was the biggest problem of them all.

Had to get it together before I crossed another line that couldn't be uncrossed.

I forced myself to straighten, and I sent her a casual grin. "Your car should be up and running by next week, but until then, there's a car out front with your name on it."

I pulled the keys from my back pocket and tossed them to her desk.

I'd called in a favor to a friend yesterday evening, and he'd dropped it off early this morning.

Salem's brow pinched. "Jud…no. You've already done too much. I can't accept this."

"Sure, you can. That's what friends are for, darlin', don't you know?"

I spun on my boots and stalked back out into the shop, deciding it was high time to throw myself into work and shuck this feeling that demanded I go back to her and confess the rest.

The base wickedness of what I'd done.

I clomped across the shiny black floors, trying to ignore Brock as I passed, except his smart ass was spewing his bullshit the way he always did.

"Ahh, you're looking awful glum for someone who just walked straight outta heaven. Did the girl come to her senses and shoot you down, or did you turn all growly asshole and break her sweet little heart? Maybe I should go in there in case she needs a shoulder to cry on."

Fucker rocked his hips.

I saw red.

Diverted course.

My hands curled into fists, and this rage I kept trying to suppress rose up and threatened to get free.

Proof I needed to keep my ass as far away from Salem as possible because the girl made me crazy.

All twisted up.

"Watch your fuckin' mouth, Brock. Not going to tell you again."

He cracked a grin. "Ahh, come on, boss, what's got you all fired up? Blue balls or you just can't get it up?"

A blur flew across the shop.

In a flash, Brock was pushed against the side of the truck he was working on. Darius had a crowbar pressed to his throat.

What the fuck?

"Whoa, man, I was just joking around." Brock squeaked it.

Darius grunted and pressed harder, pinning him so hard against the metal that Brock kept angling back farther and farther until his feet were barely touching the ground.

Brock wheezed and gasped, his hands frantic where he struggled against the rod.

I edged that way, hands held out in a placating fashion. "Put the rod down, Darius."

His eyes flashed to mine, pure hate, his teeth clenched. It was clear in that glance that his problem didn't have a thing to do with Brock.

I stalked forward another step, until I was at the side of him, cocking my head and gripping the bar in one hand. "Said to let him go. Not going to ask you again."

Another grunt, and Darius jerked back, freeing Brock of his hold. Brock started jumping around, coughing and shaking out his hands.

"What the hell, man?" He screeched it as he flung a hand toward Darius who stood there glowering, a beat from losing his mind. "Are you fuckin' crazy? That shit's not cool. You could have killed me."

"Out," I ordered, not even looking Brock's way, caught in a stare down with Darius who was about to meet the dark side of me.

"Boss—"

"Said to get the fuck out, Brock. Take a break. Come back in an hour and not a minute before."

He warred, pissed that Darius had stepped out, but the asshole needed to learn when to stop running his mouth.

"Fine." He snatched his phone and keys off his workstation and bolted out the side door while I remained in a showdown with Darius. The heavy door slammed behind Brock, and I yanked the rod the rest of the way out of Darius' hands.

"We got a problem?"

There it was. The rage that'd been trying to get loose since the second I'd seen the fear in Salem's eyes last week.

Demon ripping at its chains.

The part of me that had thirsted to come unglued.

The part that had painted in her turmoil, like that look on her face could become my own.

It seemed an issue I wanted to take it out on her brother.

Fucker had an issue, too, though, because he took a step forward. Dude was probably intimidating to a normal person.

"Told you to stay away from her." The words splintered from his mouth.

"She works here. We're bound to run into each other." Couldn't keep the condescension out.

He scoffed an incredulous sound. "Talking about Saturday and you know it."

"She was at my brother's engagement party. She'd taken a Lyft there, thought I'd save her the money by giving her a ride home. Simple as that."

Figured a little lie wouldn't hurt in this case.

"Simple? You think I'm fucking stupid?"

Asshole angled up into my face.

Had to restrain myself from knocking him flat.

Tame the beast that writhed.

One I'd promised all those years ago I'd never again set free.

"Listen, I don't know what your problem is, but I'm about finished with the shade you've been throwing. Your sister has become my friend. I care about her, want the best for her, and if she needs me, I'm going to be there. So, I think it'd be in your best interest if you back the fuck off, yeah? It's going to be your final warning."

I let what I was saying hang in the air.

"Are we clear?" I said it as I tossed the rod he'd been wielding to the top of a tool box. Metal clattered.

He sniffed, stepped back, hatred still boiling in his expression. "Yeah, boss. We're clear."

Chapter Nineteen

Salem

The engine purred as I pulled into the driveway. You know, since Jud had gone and hooked me up with this cute little Mercedes SUV, kind of like the one Eden drove, but silver instead of black.

Putting it in park, I killed the engine then sat in the quiet comfort of luxury and leather.

Jud had to be careful, or I wasn't going to give it back.

My *friend* who was far too good to me.

My bangs whipped when I blew out a sigh. I was the one who needed to be careful. I was getting too comfortable. Too complacent. Settling into a reality that just didn't exist.

Because I didn't exist.

Gloom seized my spirit when the thought hit me unaware.

It tried to seep in and take over.

The truth that the longer we remained in one place, the easier it would be for us to be found.

It warred with that overwhelming sense that kept growing stronger every day.

I wanted to stay. I wanted to stay.

I guessed being here with my family made it seem a possibility.

My stomach twisted.

Jud *made* it feel like a possibility.

But what had really changed?

The fact that Darius had insisted it was time? That enough time had passed, and it no longer mattered?

Sorrow shivered my spirit, grief cutting through the emerging hope.

I knew the lengths Carlo would go.

The sickness he would stoop to.

And that monster was still out there, and as long as he was, Juni and I would never truly be safe.

Before I let myself get too lost in the questions, I grabbed my bag from the passenger seat and opened the door.

Another week had passed with me working at Iron Ride. This week, checks had finally started coming in.

I tossed my bag onto my shoulder that held the stack of one-hundred-dollar bills Jud had paid me with just before I'd left.

Fifteen of them to be exact.

Yeah, a girl could really get used to this.

The truth was, I loved the job. Loved being a part of a team. Loved pouring myself into the work. Loved being a part of something bigger while being able to help my family at the same time.

Pride welled up. A feeling so foreign. One I hadn't felt in so long.

I blinked against the weight of it and forced myself to walk up the sidewalk toward the front door, my heels clacking on the concrete. I slid my key into the lock, turned the knob, and cracked open the door.

The delicious smell of pork carnitas simmering on the stove wafted back.

I inhaled the warmth. The welcome of it. The onslaught of memories that rushed as I stepped into the house, tossed my bag to the floor, and clicked the lock to the door behind me.

"Hello?" I called.

"We're in here, Mommy! You better get your booty in here because it's almost times for dinner and me and Mimi have been in here sweatin' in the kitchen all day." Juni showed at the archway, hands on her hips and full of sass.

A giggle worked its way free. "Is that so?"

She gave a resolute nod. "Yup. Mimi is showin' me hows to make all the dinners from where she growns up, and sometime I want to go to Mexico on an adventure, but only when we decide and we know for sure we gets to come back."

Guilt swelled and obliterated the pride.

I hated the scars that had been etched on my daughter.

Seeing her then, I knew she'd come to feel the same about this place.

Comfortable.

Relaxed.

A part of something bigger, too.

This existence more than just the two of us.

As if she'd found *home*.

And there my child stood, voicing her anxiety that I might have to rip her from the safety of it all over again.

I wanted to drop to my knees and promise her that would never happen.

That we'd found a true refuge.

That we could stay.

But I couldn't tell my daughter a lie that big.

I forced a smile. "I think that would be a wonderful adventure, Juni Bee."

"Me, too, sweet child, me, too." Mimi shouted it from the kitchen.

Love clamored through my chest when I peeked through the archway. Mimi was at the stove, stirring the meat and wearing the same apron I remembered her wearing for my entire childhood.

These tiny pink flowers with a row of three deep pockets in the front.

"How was work?" She arched a knowing brow.

I leaned against the counter. "Busy."

That brow lifted. "And?"

"And what?"

"How was the eye candy?"

"Mimi," I chastised, giving her a stern look.

"You means all the really awesome motorcycles and cars?" Juni screeched. "Did you see 'em, Mimi? Gage said his uncle is gonna make him one for when he's sixteen, and he's gonna give me a ride, I can't even wait, we only gots ten years for that, but that's where my mommy works at the coolest place ever in ever and her boss is a motorcycle man."

Juni started galloping around the kitchen like she was riding a horse though she made revving noises in her throat and held back the throttle on her imaginary handlebars.

Just awesome.

Mimi laughed, pure affection. "Wow, that is something. Just ten years."

Her gaze narrowed when she returned it to me while she dipped a spoon into the pot and took a sip of the broth the pork was simmering in. "Though I was getting the idea that your mommy's boss might be the coolest ever in ever."

"Mimi," I chastised again, though this time it was a whisper, and that heat was lighting up my cheeks again.

Damn it.

"You think I don't notice you waltzing in here night after night with that look on your face? With that light in your eyes? You're different."

A frown pinched my brow as Juni galloped into the other room, and Mimi took the opportunity to edge around the counter to where I stood. Reaching out, she rubbed the pad of her thumb between my eyes before she let her hand slide down to cup my cheek. "That light went dim four years ago, Salem. Wasn't sure I was ever goin' to get to see it again."

Grief billowed through my being.

"I'm not sure I can ever get that piece of myself back." The confession left me on a breath.

"No, sweet child, that part is gone, and that missing piece is going to ache forever. But sometimes someone comes along who can hold that piece with you."

Agony wept in my spirit while my heart panged in my chest.

A tear slipped free.

Mimi wiped it away. "When I lost your momma, I thought I would die, Salem. I thought I would curl up in bed and close my eyes and I'd somehow float away to where she was."

Emotion clogged my throat.

Devastating.

Too much.

My eyes closed against the onslaught, and Mimi pressed her hand tighter to my face in a loving embrace. "But then these two little angels showed up at my door, lost and without their momma...scared and broken...and that part of me that wanted to float away got tethered to that new home. The home I built with you and your brother."

"But you never stopped missing her?" The question croaked from my throat.

"Of course not, and I wouldn't want to. But you and your brother? You held that piece with me. Reshaped it. Reformed it."

"I'm not looking for someone to fix me."

"No, Salem, but do you think I don't know your heart is aching for its home, too? For a tether? For someone to come alongside you and hold that vacant place? One who understands you? Someone who can support you in the times when you feel too weak to carry the burden yourself?"

Jud's pained confession burned through my mind.

Gutting.

Whispering.

Begging.

"She took our one-year-old daughter with her, Salem, and I never saw her again."

And I knew there was a part of him that needed to be held, too.

Loved.

Old misery moaned. I knew better than letting the thought infiltrate my mind. Knew better than to trust.

I lifted my quivering chin, the words hard with the hate that had petrified in my bones. "It's funny how I thought Carlo would be that person for me. That he'd love and cherish and be the one to carry me through all of life's tragedies and stand with me in its victories, and he's the one who destroyed me."

Mimi's expression dimmed with sympathy edged with the old, old anger that had broken her heart. "Did you really believe that? That he would love and cherish you?"

My guts clutched with her truth.

"He was a wicked boy who grew into a wicked man," she continued. "He manipulated you. Lied to you. Made you believe he was someone he was not."

"And I fell for it."

"You were sixteen, Salem. He was older. Powerful and charming and he had his sights on you. I never liked the boy, but none of us could have imagined how deep his evils went."

"I was a fool."

Her head shook. "No, sweet child, not a fool. Just a young girl who believed in the best of people. Believed they could be better. Believed through love, they could be redeemed and restored."

More tears fell, and I gulped. "Can they be?"

A soft smile tipped at the edge of her aged, wrinkled mouth. "Some choose light in this life, Salem, others choose darkness. And some? Some get lost along the way, but inside of them, they burn with the fire of goodness."

"How will I know?"

"I think you already do. Right here, you already know it. Deep down."

She tapped the tip of her index finger against the riot in my heart.

She was right.

I did.

Even though I'd been so young then, there was a piece of me that had known, that had hesitated, my conscience whispering Carlo was wicked and wrong. Just like it was whispering now that Jud was *right*.

Then she stepped back around to the stove and sent me a wink. "Just make sure whenever you *know* it, whoever it is makes your knees knock, too."

"Mimi." I wheezed a breath, laughing low and shaking my head as I edged deeper into the kitchen to help her with dinner.

"What?" She knocked her shoulder into my arm. "Heck, girl, I'm pretty sure this looker makes you shake all over the place. Hopefully in the good bits."

I choked out a laugh while my entire being went down in flames.

Memories of the man between my thighs.

That mouth and those hands.

What he'd done to me.

"Mmhmm…that's what I thought."

"You thought what?" I defended with a smile.

She sent me the most innocent shrug. "That you'd be famished for your most favorite meal."

A giggle slipped free.

Warmth and welcome.

Home.

And I had no idea how to stop the hope of it from taking root inside me.

"Boo!"

Gasping, I whirled around with my hand pressed to my chest like it could stop my heart from jumping free of my ribs.

Tessa cracked up.

She was bent in two, slapping her knee from where she stood behind me on the front lawn of our house.

I'd been watching Juniper do somersaults on the lawn, and I hadn't even noticed she was there.

Complacent.

Reckless.

I blew out a frustrated sigh directed wholly at myself.

"Oh my god, you just jumped like…ten feet in the air. You should have seen it."

She kept trying to catch her breath, like it had been her that'd gotten the crap scared out of her and not me.

Juni cracked up, too. "She jumped all the way to the sky, right, Miss Tessa?" Juni turned her sweet eyes on me. "I saw Ms. Tessa comin' the whole time, Mommy, because we gots you a very good surprise that you are gonna love with all your whole heart!"

My eyes narrowed farther, darting between the two of them.

"That's right. We have a big surprise. We're going out!"

"Umm?"

She grinned, her red ponytail swishing far too excitedly around her shoulders. "The correct response is, hell yes and hallelujah, thank you, Tessa, for dragging me out of my house and showing me a proper night of fun."

"Thank you, but I have Juni…"

I trailed off when Juni giggled like my excuse was absurd, and I shifted toward the house when I felt the disturbance at the screen door. Mimi pushed it open and stepped out, grinning like mad, too.

"Correction, I have Juni, and sweet child, you now have friends, so you're going to have yourself a night of fun. Kind of like you did last Saturday night."

Mimi waggled her brows.

"And just where are we going?"

Tessa shimmied her hips. "Absolution, baby! Time to get your rocker on. There's a band playing tonight that is supposed to be crazy good, and it's my boyfriend's birthday, but he's kinda boring, and I'm afraid he's not going to be any fun, so you have to come with us. I need a wingman."

She jerked at my hand.

My brow furrowed. "Wingman?"

She waved an errant hand in the air. "Okay, okay, you need a wingman because I have a hunch this burly mountain man might show."

She gave me three exaggerated winks.

Great.

When I didn't bite, Tessa hiked an innocent, nonchalant shoulder while her voice twisted with casual manipulation. "I mean, I'm sure he could find someone else to keep him entertained. And I don't know about you, but since Eden and Trent are getting married, I'm thinking that we should really be there to support Trent, anyway, right, you know, since that club is his baby. His heart and soul. His bread and butter. And now they're going to have a baby to support?"

Her voice lowered with the tragedy.

I glared at her. "You're so full of crap."

Trent was clearly loaded.

Hell, all three brothers were rolling in it.

But what didn't sit right was the way my stomach twisted with the idea of Jud being there.

In that club.

Without me.

Doing exactly what Tessa had implied. Finding someone else to keep him *entertained*.

Crap.

This was bad.

Juni Bee tugged at my opposite hand. "It's a party, Mommy! You gotsta. And guess what? Gage is even gonna come to my house to haves a sleepover and Mimi is gonna make us her specialist tacos and we're gonna have popcorn and tell secrets, so you gots to go because you're not allowed to hear."

"Whole thing is set. No bother arguing." Mimi grinned as she passed my purse to Tessa.

Holy wow.

I jerked to look over my shoulder when a screen door banged and Gage's little voice pelted the air.

"Hi, Juni Bee!"

Eden was holding his hand and leading him toward us. A giant backpack bounced on his shoulders as they approached. "Are you ready to have the most fun all the way to the highest mountain?"

"Yes!" Juni bolted that way, skidding to a stop at the curb and jumping in welcome. "This is the best day of my wholes life!"

I sent a death glare at Tessa.

She grinned in triumph. "I know, I'm amazing, right?"

Eden giggled a soft sound as she climbed the curb, and she gave me a tiny, apologetic wave. "I see you've been Tessa'd."

"Clearly, it's a deadly disease."

"It is, and you'll never recover. But don't worry, DD here, we're in this together." Eden's mouth slipped into a tender smile, and she spread her hand over her still-flat stomach.

Affection blossomed, all while fear sprang up in the middle of it.

I shouldn't do this. Shouldn't allow myself to get any deeper.

Because I felt it, spreading through me, sprouting through the cracks.

Love.

Hope.

Home.

It whispered in my ear.

I looked at my grandmother whose expression had turned gentle, and she mouthed, *It's time.*

Juni took Gage's hand, and the two of them went blazing by and scrambling up the steps. She shouted, "Bye, Mommy!" as she went, clearly all broken up about my being gone for the night.

I hesitated, warred, fully unsure.

"Go on then," Mimi urged. "They'll be just fine. I raised you and your brother just fine, didn't I?"

My smile was somber, the words whispered from my mouth, "You raised us the best."

"Eeeps! Let's do this!" Tessa shouted beside me, and she yanked at my hand again, drawing me toward Eden's car across the street.

I tried to skid to a stop. "Wait…I'm not even dressed."

"Um, hello…do you actually think I haven't already thought of this? We're heading to my house to pre-game and get ready. I already have an outfit picked out for you." Tessa opened the door and gestured for me to climb in, dipping low with a flourish of her hand. "Your chariot awaits, madame."

I climbed in, barely able to contain the laughter that bubbled at the base of my throat. "You're insane. Has anyone ever told you that?"

She grinned. "Every single day."

"To tonight!" Tessa lifted her champagne flute and clinked it against mine and Eden's, though Eden's was filled with sparkling cider.

Apparently, Tessa really did think about everything.

My spirit swam with a softness I'd never felt before. Never, in all my life. Because they both did.

Thought about everything.

Truly cared and gave their best to make sure you felt it.

And god, I did.

For the first time in so many years, I felt the true meaning of what *friend* was supposed to be.

My spirit groaned with the loss.

With the treachery and the treason.

Terrified of repeating the same mistakes I'd made then.

But Mimi was right.

There was a part of me that'd known.

Shoving the reservations down, I took a sip of champagne before I glanced in the full-length mirror at the dress Tessa had *found* at the back of her closet, but since it was most definitely not her size, I knew she was full of it, but I didn't bother calling bullshit.

Because I felt beautiful.

Alive.

Excited.

Real.

Emotion crested on my lips.

"You look freaking hot." Tessa clapped her hands wildly. "I can't wait for Jud to see you."

"Jud and I are just friends."

She rolled her eyes. "Um, I think there's a chance Jud might have shit himself when you walked into the restaurant last weekend. Tell me he didn't take you home after the party and ravage you?"

Fire hit my cheeks, and I pressed my lips together as the memories assaulted me.

"Oh my god, he did." She pressed her hands to her face. "I was just messing with you, and he did. Tell me. This girl needs details." She frantically gestured at herself.

"This is true. Only because her lame boyfriend doesn't have a clue how to do her right." Eden said it from behind her glass, taking a sip like she wasn't the one responsible for the words.

"Hey." Tessa pouted and smacked Eden's arm. "It's Karl's birthday, no dogging him tonight." She looked at me and overexaggerated that pout. "Even if it's horribly, terribly, devastatingly true. But I love him," she peeped.

Eden widened her eyes at me in clear disagreement, mouthed, *He's a total douche.*

I choked on my surprise.

Well then, I guess I *had* become a part of their trio.

Tessa pointed at Eden's face. "I heard that."

"Heard what?" Eden giggled.

And there I was, caught up in that whirlwind again. Unsure of where it would take me or where I was going to land. Because Tessa took my arm and jerked me all over like the goof she was. "Well, tell me! I haven't had an orgasm in like…five years. I need to know. Did he do it right? Treat you right? Is he your wild card?"

Confusion dented my brow. "My what?"

She sighed in exasperation. "Your ace? The one you didn't expect?"

Nerves rattled through my being, and my stomach clenched in a bid of want while my mind spun with warnings.

You have to be careful.

Trust no one.

And whatever you do, no matter what, do not fall in love.

I looked at my new friends, that *trust no one* thing kaput, and whispered, "He's definitely the last one I expected."

Tessa squealed. "What are we waiting for? Let's go get your man."

I stumbled out behind her. Wishing it could be that easy. That I could love a man and he could love me in return.

That I could exist in his life.

But the sad, devastating truth was I was afraid that one day, I would disappear.

Chapter Twenty

Jud

I SAT AT THE BOOTH TUCKED IN THE FARTHEST CORNER OF Absolution nursing a beer. Dim lights were strung across the cavernous space, the club two stories of luxury spiked with a dose of dive.

Gave it a dark vibe, like there might be evil lurking in the shadows. Temptation at every corner. Wouldn't be all that far from the truth.

As usual, the place was packed. Line at the door and people vying for the perfect spot to watch the band that was prepping to take to the stage. The DJ was currently blasting a dance beat through the speakers, amping the mood for the main event.

Trent had insisted I come since there was some big band playing tonight. Since Logan and I were part owners, it looked good for us to show our faces. Not that it usually took a whole ton of coercion to get me here, but truth be told, I'd been craving a whole different sort of revelry tonight.

Namely the kind where I got lost in a black-haired beauty with curves for days and thunderbolt eyes that speared me to the spot.

But considering I'd been permanently friend-zoned, and not the good kind with benefits, right here was probably exactly where I should be.

Searching for a distraction. For a way to scratch this itch that was slowly and steadily driving me insane. The way the girl waltzed around my shop like a perfect fantasy, spellbinding me with each step.

More concerning, though? It was the way the demon writhed.

The way it clawed and jerked and howled to go on the hunt when she would constantly look over her shoulder.

My gut told me she was in fear of being watched, and I knew, without a doubt, I'd gladly chase down whatever bastard had written terror on her spirit.

Fuck. She'd gotten under my skin, and in a bad, bad way.

Because there wasn't one face in this entire place that I found more interesting than hers.

Hell, mesmerizing was what it was.

I was taking another gulp of my beer when my brothers came busting through the throng of people who were gathering close to the stage.

They both slipped into the booth opposite me.

"About time," I said, smirking at Trent who grunted at me as he roughed a tatted hand through his hair. "Rough night?"

"If something could go wrong, it went wrong tonight. New barback somehow toppled an entire fuckin' wall of vodka, at least 10k worth, and he denied it and tried to blame it on Leann, so Sage had to fire his ass. Dude threw himself a pissy fit and said he was going to sue. Caused a giant-ass scene. Leann's in tears. Two of the men's toilets clogged. Oh, and the drummer for tonight's band is smashed. Like, straight-up, stumbling into the walls, smashed."

I lifted my beer his direction. "So, you're saying you've been in there lapping that vodka up to ease your pain?"

Logan cracked up and grabbed Trent by the shoulder, rocking him around a bit, dude all grins and easiness. "Now that's what the asshole should have been doing, but he's been storming around here like the devil he used to be. Ruining my night. I mean, come on, look at this place. There are no bad nights. Look at all that deliciousness waiting out there for us to taste."

I think Logan actually whimpered as he gazed out at the women prancing around half naked on the dance floor. Funny how a month ago I would have been game. Find a nice, warm body. Make her feel as good as she made me feel, part ways a few hours later, and leave it at that.

I had always left the door wide open so if my life someday returned to me, there would be no connections.

No obstacles.

I shifted, unsettled by the thought.

Logan turned his smug face back our direction. "Here I was, sacrificing all my nights to watch this guy's son so he could get this place up and running—not that I minded or anything because I love the fuck out of that kid—but now that I'm not playing babysitter any longer, it's my turn to have a little fun. And lo and behold? Who is trying to wreck it for me? It seems our resident funsucker has returned."

Logan's head shook in feigned affliction.

Trent grunted again, then a fucking grin was spreading to his mouth just as I felt the world shift.

My flesh shivered with a rush of intensity, like the crowd had parted and there was only one thing I could see.

Salem.

My stomach dropped to the floor.

She was here.

She was linked elbow-to-elbow with Eden and Tessa, the three of them strutting our way.

She wore this tight black dress that hugged every curve. A slit rode up the side and the neckline dipped low between her perfect tits.

All that devastation wrapped in a black, seductive bow.

Black hair loose and wavy, those eyes taking in the place, jumping all around, but inevitably landing on me. Like neither of us had the choice.

Gravity.

I forced myself to take a gulp of my beer while the expression on Trent's face shifted from glum to glee.

Lovesick fucker.

"Oh, I see how it is," Logan whined, elbowing Trent in the ribs. "Now you're going to fucking smile? And here I thought you loved me?"

"Barely." Trent grinned, all teeth.

Logan pressed his hand over his heart. "I'm hurt."

"I'll show you hurt." Trent could barely contain his laughter.

"So violent, the both of you."

Eden, Tessa, and Salem stumbled up to the edge of the table, giggling and whispering under their breaths.

Fuckin' cute, the three of them.

"We made it! No thanks to this one." Eden sent a scowl at Tessa who waved her off.

"Pssh, don't listen to her. Have you seen us?" Tessa swished a melodramatic hand down her body, then she swept it toward Eden and Salem. "Come now. Tell me all of this wasn't worth that extra time."

Tessa wasn't lying.

No matter how hard I tried to stop it, my gaze devoured Salem where she stood next to the table.

A vixen.

A fantasy.

That sweet, sweet enchantress singing her spell.

My stomach tightened in a fist of lust. Dick shouting *yes, please*.

Salem eyed me like every inch of her was singing the same.

I gave her a jut of my chin, a real easy, "Hey there, darlin.'"

Super casual like seeing her was no big thing, while this girl had me so twisted up, I was pretty sure all it would take was a brush of her hand, and she'd make me forget my name. Forced myself to keep my ass sitting because if I stood, I'd cross the line she'd told me we couldn't cross again.

"Let me up," Trent ordered, nudging at Logan to let him out so he could get to his fiancée.

"Hey." Logan stumbled out of the booth like Trent had shoved him. He popped up onto his feet and straightened out the black button-down he wore. Dude looked like that model again, all grins and charm and…yeah, fucker was slanting all of that at Salem.

My hand curled around my beer bottle, and my knee got to bouncing a million miles a minute.

Didn't mean for the growl to get loose, but it did.

"Nice to see you again, gorgeous." Logan held her by the hands, looking her up and down, voice elevated above the din of the club.

"Nice to see you, too," Salem shouted back at him, though she glanced my way.

The air shivered and shook.

Remaining sitting was brutal. The urge to get up and stake my claim near uncontrollable.

Logan eased over to Eden and gave her a hug. "Big sister, looking mighty fine tonight."

He was lucky Trent didn't snap his neck.

Turning to Tessa, he ruffled her hair. "Tessa."

She tossed a punch to his chest. "Logan! What is wrong with you? You are a total jerk. Do you know how much time I spent on this immaculate design?"

She tried to straighten her hair out.

"And only half a second to muss it up, but I figure this hand is way more pleasure than you're going to get from limp dick tonight, so you're welcome."

He wiggled his fingers in her face.

She smacked them away. "Ewww. And rude. It's Karl's birthday. I expect all of you to be on your best behavior."

She pointed at each of us.

A chuckle rumbled out. No question, Logan was a douche. But not close to bein' the douche that Tessa's boyfriend was. Dude was a grade A dickwad.

Pretty boy type who thought he walked on water but needed his ass drowned in the lake.

"Okay, we're off to get drinks. Can we bring you anything?" Eden asked, glancing at me, then Logan, straight-up joy lighting her smile when Trent finally slid all the way out and came to wrap his arms around her.

He pulled her tight. "You don't need to serve us, baby."

"Maybe I miss working here," she teased.

"And maybe I just want you sitting on my lap…or maybe laid out on my desk." Dude drizzled a row of sloppy kisses along her jaw. If he got her any closer, their embrace was going to turn obscene.

Tessa pushed at his arm. "Ugh, rub it in. I hate you."

Trent smirked at her.

Eden giggled and unwound herself from his hold. "We'll be right back. You wait right there and be a good boy."

Trent sent her a pout.

Sappy asshole, happy as could be.

"Hurry back," Logan sang, full of suggestion as the three women started to wind through the crush.

Irrational anger surged.

Trent and Logan slipped back into the booth. Logan pitched me the most innocent look as he settled into his seat. "Why do you look so…tense, brother?" He angled his head farther, a razzing in his voice. "Hell, if I didn't know better, I'd say you are two seconds from going on a murder spree. Something bothering you?"

Yeah, man, I'm losing my ever lovin' mind.

"Think I made it plenty clear last weekend," I said instead.

The confusion on his face was nothing but a sham. "What ever are you talking about?"

I took a sip of my beer. "You know what."

Couldn't help my eyes from following Salem where she moved through the mob. Girl the only damned thing I could see.

"Oh…that," Logan drew out with a wayward toss of his hand in the air. Like he was just catching up. He scratched at his temple. "You know, I thought I got the message, but then, you see, this hot as hades chick walked up, and I mean scorching, and you just sat your sorry ass over there like she didn't mean a thing, so I figured, like every other dude in the place, that she might be looking for a little fun tonight. I mean, if you're not interested, then I can't think of a better option than me. Well, we all know I'd be the better choice, anyway." He patted Trent on the chest. "Am I right? Tell me I'm right."

Trent chuckled low.

A snarl got free.

Laughing, Logan hit the top of the table. "Look at you, over there about to bust out of your shirt, all Hulk style. Think you should just come out and say it. You want her and what…you're too fucking shy to do something about it?"

"Shy?" I deadpanned. "Look shy to you?"

"Well, I'd say she turned you down like any sane woman would do, but I saw the way she was looking at you, too, so I'm thinking that can't be it."

"Nope. She's going for sane."

While doing it was slowly making me lose my mind. But I guessed I'd been the one who'd fucked up. Laid down those lines. Kept pressing the friend thing because if I was being honest, I was scared shitless. Scared of the way she made me feel.

Girl was making me question what I was living for.

"Fuck." Grumbled it aloud. She really was and that was the most terrifying part of all.

Couldn't let her.

Had to get it together.

To remember my purpose.

"I'm with Logan here." Trent swatted Logan's shoulder. "Two of you both looked like you were about to lose your cool."

On a groan, I scratched at my beard, took a long pull of my beer.

"Think I'm fucked," I finally admitted. Didn't see a point in denying it then. Two of them could see right through me, anyway.

"How's that?" Logan asked, sitting back in his seat.

Disbelieving laughter rumbled out, spite in the words. "Two of us figured we should just be friends."

Logan howled, smacking the table again like it was the most hysterical thing he'd ever heard.

Part of me agreed.

"Friends. Oh my god. That's fuckin' priceless."

I glowered at him. Dude just laughed harder.

"A word to the wise, brother. *Friends* doesn't work. You really think you're going to ignore all of that?" Innuendo lined the question as Logan twirled a finger through the air, like he could stir that energy that raged between us.

"Well, considering she works for me, I'm thinking that's all she can be."

Among five thousand other reasons.

"Uh...hello...Trent over here is *actually* marrying Eden, and you know he had his tiny dick all up in her sweetness the whole time she was working here at Absolution."

Trent grunted. "Watch it."

Logan raised both of his hands. "Hey, man, just telling it like it is. *Tiny* included." He mouthed the last.

"Will knock your ass out," Trent warned, though there was a smile cutting at his mouth.

"Terrified." Logan grinned.

Trent shook his head. "You're a disaster, man. Tell me what the hell I'm supposed to do with you."

Logan hooked his arm on the back of the booth and jostled his index finger of that hand in my direction. "Nah, man, I think it's our brother here who's a disaster." Tone of his voice shifted, filling with a real question, pushing at the marrow. "Are you going to make a move or what?"

Leaning forward, I rested my elbows on the table, rubbed my fingers over my mouth like it could wipe away the truth of the words. "You know I can't."

"Yeah, and why's that?"

"You know why."

Logan scoffed as he came to the realization of what I was getting at. "Are you kidding me? Tell me you aren't still waiting on her?"

I couldn't answer.

Disbelief shook Logan's head. "Kennedy deserted you, man. Took your kid and ran and didn't look back. She doesn't deserve you. I know it sucked balls when she left, but anyone who doesn't see you for who you are isn't worthy to stand at your side, and that's the god-damn truth."

"And who am I really?" Challenge left me on a low punt. "A beast?"

A grin split his face. "Yup. The teddy bear kind."

Fucking Logan. But that was the thing about him. Dude didn't know the half of who we'd been. The half of what we'd done. The sins we'd committed and the atrocities we'd perpetuated.

We'd hid it from him, protected him the best we could, though there was no question some of that bullshit had seeped below the surface.

I shook my head and looked away, into the throbbing mass as if it could offer distraction. "Hardly," I muttered.

"You said it yourself, Jud." Trent leaned forward over the table, tatted finger jabbing into the wood, voice just loud enough to be heard over the roaring beat. "This place? It's our second chance. The whole reason we came here."

Agony clawed through my consciousness, and I looked between my brothers. Two people who meant the most to me. Only ones who could truly get it.

"And I already used up that second chance, didn't I?"

Trent's tongue dipped out to wet his lips. "Fuck that, man. Like Logan said, Kennedy didn't deserve you. Not for a fuckin' second."

Old misery left me on a scoff. "It was me who didn't deserve her or my daughter."

"Bullshit," Logan spat, leaning forward. "You're the best. The fucking best, so don't you dare let any of that get in your way. Yeah, it hurt. I know it, man. I know it." His face blanched. "But we only have this one life, and we're fucking lucky that we do, and it's your duty to live it. Go after what makes you happy. And wallowing around in your misery waiting on someone who didn't take the time to really see you? Fuck, Jud, I know you want to live for what's right, but I think it's time you figure out what that really is."

All the joking was gone from Logan's voice.

Like she'd been summoned from the storm, I glanced to my right at the girl who floated my way.

Eyes the color of a toiling sea. The darkest, deepest blue. Body pure temptation.

A motherfuckin' knockout.

A fantasy.

A dream.

Black-fuckin'-magic.

My conscience screamed with guilt.

Because every second that passed? I only wanted her more.

Music blasted from the speakers from the band that thrashed on the stage while the crowd thrived and toiled.

Place chaos.

Disorder.

Mayhem of the best kind.

People were singing. Shouting. Dancing. Their drinks lifted in the air and their hearts freed in the crashing beat that promised release.

Release.

That was exactly what I needed as I weaved through the throbbing crowd, drawn, compelled, unable to do anything but head in the direction where Eden, Tessa, and Salem danced on the far side of the club.

The three of them had let loose. Their hair whipping around them and heat drenching their bodies as they laughed and danced together like they didn't have a care in the world.

Celebrating life and all it had to give.

Wanted that for Salem. For her to let go. For the fears that haunted her to melt away and surrender to something better.

Something better.

My guts knotted, and my chest stretched tight. This fucked up feeling taking me over that I wanted it, too.

Trent had followed the group over to where they'd moved to carve out their own little bubble.

Dude looked like peril where he'd taken up post on a stool at the bar facing out, watching over his life, ready to strike if any fool became a threat.

My boots thudded on the hard ground, in time with the rhythm, marching straight into destruction.

But I didn't really know how to go anywhere else when this felt like my destination. Where I was supposed to be.

Salem shook her hips, that black dress hugging those curves so right. Had to physically restrain myself from stalking up behind her, wrapping my hands around her waist, and pressing my nose into the hypnotic fall of her hair.

I forced myself to take the stool next to Trent. I dragged it so I could sit facing out, too. He slid a beer he'd ordered for me in my direction. "Looks like you're gonna need that."

A grunt rumbled out as I took a long pull. "Yup."

"Funny what life does, yeah?" Trent mused on a low breath. "Way we think we know the way it's supposed to go—the way we want it to go—then boom, it comes right in and shakes us up."

He glanced my way with a knowing expression on his face. The baby owl tatted on his throat bobbed when he swallowed. "You know it firsthand, man. How terrifying it is, putting your heart on the line and knowing it can be gone in a flash. Logan's right, though."

I grunted. "About what?"

Deflecting with ignorance seemed the way to go.

"Stepping out and letting yourself love someone."

Alarm whipped a storm through my spirit.

"Love? Getting ahead of yourself there, yeah?"

His brow curled. "Am I?"

"Just want to fuck her, man." Let the smirk split my mouth.

Trent laughed an incredulous sound, and he reached out and

gave a condescending pat on my cheek. "If you just wanted to fuck her, you already would have."

Then he snagged his tumbler and pushed to his feet, slanting me a telling glance before he strutted his smug ass out to where Eden was dancing. Girl fluid and hot, ballet in her blood.

Beside her, Tessa was dancing like a total spazz.

Shocker.

And next to her...Salem.

Salem whose rhythm was half time. Driving me out of my mind. Her hips rocking and vibrating in this slow seduction.

She glanced my way.

Thunderbolt eyes struck.

Energy crackled.

I roughed a hand over my face.

Fuck.

Keep it together, man.

Trent edged up behind Eden the way I was dying to do to Salem. Nuzzled his face into the back of her neck. Pulled her flush against his chest.

Salem looked at me as she moved.

Eyes raking, whispering, like she was begging me to do the same.

That connection throbbed.

Booming and shivering.

I attempted to scan the crowd for a good target.

Easy. Quick. No strings.

My gaze traveled right back to the girl.

Her gaze raked me.

My insides shook.

Fuck it.

I drained my beer then pushed to my feet.

I was just going to take this one little thing. I mean, what could dancing with her hurt?

I started that way only to get jostled back by an asshole who suddenly went blazing by. He beelined right for the girls.

Karl, that fucker.

Dressed in a suit with his hair perfectly styled and that douchey-ass expression on his face.

Tessa threw her arms in the air to welcome him.

Poor girl.

"Karl, happy birthday, baby!"

Prick sauntered right in.

He slipped his left arm around Tessa's waist to haul her close, only the creeper did the same to Salem with his right. He tugged them both to him, leaning over and bending them back like he could somehow get more.

Hell no.

Just fucking no.

But that jealousy turned to something else entirely when I saw the way Salem's eyes went wide as they met mine from over his shoulder.

I was already on my way.

I tapped at Karl's shoulder. You know, real friendly-like. "Think you've got your arms around the wrong girl, man."

He cocked a smug grin my direction, a fucking mouthful of too-straight teeth. He curled his arms tighter. "Nah. Think I'm doing just fine. It's my birthday, and I've just decided what I want."

"Get off me." Salem tried to push him off. Asshole didn't even budge.

My hand clamped down on his arm. "Told you to let her the fuck go."

"Fuck off," he tossed out.

"What the hell, Karl?" Tessa shrieked through the mayhem of the bar that just seemed to amplify the greed. Way this fucker thought he could reach out and take whatever he wanted.

Panic radiated from Salem. The same panic I'd glimpsed in my shop that day when she'd thought someone was after her. Like in an instant, she was lost to the past.

She shoved and hit his chest with her fists. "Let me go."

A scream ripped up her throat when he hugged her tighter.

Scumbag got no further warning. My hands were on the back of his suit jacket, and I was tearing him away. The asshole made the mistake of swinging as I dragged him around. He clipped me on the jaw, right about the time both the girls went stumbling back.

Had him by the shirt collar in a flash. My arm cocked back. One jab to his pompous face and his nose was bleeding out. Pussy crashed to the floor when I let him go like the pile of trash he was.

Gasps and shrieks hit the air, and people jumped back to get out of the way, while others gathered closer, clearly thirsting for a fight.

At least this prick Karl seemed to be because he scrambled back to his feet and flew my way.

Trent pitched a grin at me from behind, laughing under his breath that this fucker actually thought he stood a chance. Trent didn't even make a move, just sat back like he was going to enjoy the show, though he edged Eden behind him.

Karl roared as he came my way, and I took him by both hands and gave his scrawny ass a good shake. "Cool the fuck down or I'm going to make this a birthday you don't ever forget."

He spat in my face.

"Oh, motherfucker."

But Tessa was suddenly there, yanking at his jacket. "Stop it, Karl, just stop it."

I let him go, hating to give him a pass, but this was Tessa we were talking about. Girl was sweet as fuck even though she clearly had horrible taste in men. But Karl whirled around and shoved her.

Hard.

Sweet thing flew back, and she knocked into Salem. Both of them toppled, their asses hitting the floor, sending them in a tumble across the stained concrete.

And Karl was dead.

I had the fucker pinned to the ground before he registered that I'd moved.

I set to wailing on his face.

Punch after punch.

Blood splattered. Bone crunched.

Demon laughed and writhed and whispered in my ear.

Calling me back to who I really was.

A monster.

A beast.

Grim.

I cocked my arm back again to render a blow that would flip the switch.

Lights out.

Only a hand caught me around the wrist and jerked my arm back. Trent's low voice hissed in my ear, "Want to end the bastard, too, but how about we do it without an audience, yeah?"

I heaved a stuttered breath while the piece of shit writhed and screamed. He held his mangled face as he pushed up to sitting. Blood seeped through the seams of his fingers. "What the fuck? What the fuck? You're finished, you bastard. Finished. I'm going to own you. All of you."

I lumbered to my feet, trying to rein the violence that screamed through my veins, trying not to look at Salem because I was afraid if I did, it'd send me spiraling all over again.

Some random dude shouted, "Have you on video pushing your girl, pussy. Call the cops, why don't you? Dare you."

That was right as Logan busted through the crowd and came rushing up to my side, eyes darting everywhere. "What the hell? Why do you guys always have all the fun without me?"

Our two head bouncers, Kult and Milo, came barreling in. They shoved back the mob that had gathered around us to ogle the mayhem that always found its way into our house.

Milo and Kult looked around to assess the damage.

Kult yanked Karl up by the collar. Asshole's feet dangled a foot from the ground. Kult was a goddamned mammoth, and he whipped him around like a rag doll.

"Ambulance or the front door, boss?" Kult asked.

Trent looked at me, telling me it was my call.

"Front door," I instructed. Prick could get his own ass to the hospital.

Kult cracked a menacing grin. "My pleasure. Out of the way."

He started to haul a shrieking Karl through the crowd so he could kick the prick to the curb.

Right where the fucker belonged.

One step, and the crush parted, Kult nothing but intimidation and brute strength.

I inhaled a cleansing breath, doing my best to get it together enough to look to where the group was huddled on the floor while my heart raged a riot in my chest.

Eden, Trent, and Logan had already gathered around Tessa and Salem. Eden was frantic, kneeling in front of her friends, her hands shaking out of control as she tried to check if they were hurt.

Milo leaned down, and he gently scooped a sobbing Tessa into his massive, gigantic arms. Dude was basically a mute fortress. Quiet and soft and forbidding as fuck. "You're safe, little dove. Don't cry, you're safe."

He rumbled it like a promise as he started to carry her through the throng.

Trent gave me a quick glance, and I gestured with my chin. "Go."

He dipped his head before he guided Eden to follow behind Milo who cut through the crowd.

My attention shifted to Salem. Salem who had her knees to her chest and was rocking. Rocking and trembling and mumbling incoherently.

Logan stood guard over her, watching me, giving me a fierce look that told me not to be a fool. That he was going to step in if I didn't.

Thing was, it did make me a fool.

A fuckin' fool as I went for her.

Because that girl looked up when she felt me cautiously approach.

Ground rumbled beneath.

The warning of a coming earthquake.

Of devastation.

Destruction.

I leaned down and slipped my arms around her back and under her knees.

Salem yelped.

A shout from her soul.

Mine clutched.

I gathered her closer. "I have you, Salem. I have you, baby."

A sob wrenched from her throat, and she buried her face in my neck, into my beard, against my chest, like she could hide away in the safety of my arms.

"I have you."

And I didn't want to let her go.

Chapter Twenty-One

Salem

I HAVE YOU. *I* HAVE YOU. *I* HAVE YOU.

Jud's promise rained over me as he curled his arms tighter, and he carried me through the swarm of people that undulated around us.

The band continued to play from the stage where half the crowd still seethed below it. Jud stormed right through, carving a path and dipping us into a narrow, dusky hall.

In an instant, it was only the two of us.

His heavy boots thudded on the floor as he peered down at me with that unrelenting obsidian gaze.

A gaze that speared me to the core.

Tears streamed and my shoulders hiccupped with the sobs that wouldn't stop. I couldn't seem to halt the terror that wracked through my body. The panic that had hit me when a stranger had come at us from out of nowhere.

Jud dipped down and pressed the gentlest kiss to my right eye, then the other. "I have you," he rumbled.

My chest squeezed.

Ruined.

I had to close my eyes against the force of it.

His care.

This giant of a man who'd come completely unhinged. Fury and darkness and brutality.

Because of me.

Because of me.

He didn't stop until he was pushing out the massive metal door at the end of the hall. In an instant, the cool air of the summer night surrounded us. The heavens were spun in stars, while fat clouds laden with moisture gathered at the base of the moon.

Jud edged down three steps that dropped us into the employee lot where Eden had parked earlier, and his boots crunched on the loose pavement as he carried me to his bike that was parked in a row of five other motorcycles.

Tumult echoed from within, rippled through the walls and rumbled the ground.

It stirred the dense air into chaos.

I struggled to breathe.

"I have you. What do you need?" he asked, his voice close to cracking.

"Take me away from here." It was the only thing I could manage, but Jud understood.

I wasn't exactly dressed for a motorcycle ride, but right then, it didn't matter. Nothing did except for escaping.

Running.

The way I always did.

Only this time, I wanted to run with him.

For once, I didn't want to stand on my own.

Didn't want to fight this fight that only cost my daughter and me more and more.

One that forever cast us into loneliness.

Jud swung his leg over his bike, and he slipped me around to the back in one smooth movement.

We never lost contact.

As if he knew it was exactly what I needed.

That for once, I needed someone to hold me.

Someone to support me through the fear.

Through the panic.

Through the dread that promised one day, one day, Carlo would find us.

Jud pressed the button that started his bike, and the loud engine growled to life. Power vibrated through the metal, or maybe it was just the power of the man that vibrated through me.

Tremors rushed over my skin and seeped into my bloodstream.

He curled my arms tighter around his waist. "I have you."

My legs were cinched up close to his hips, my chest smashed to his back. Our hearts raced at warp speed.

In sync.

Out of order.

In a perfect, chaotic rhythm.

Anarchy.

This man who had crossed into vengeance for me.

The slit of my dress rode up as I hugged him, and I trembled and shook and clung to him with all my might. A big palm spread out over my bare thigh. "Hold onto me, Salem, and don't fuckin' let go."

Frantically, I nodded against his back, understanding the command for what it was. And I wanted to. For once in my life, I wanted to rely on someone else.

Not to be afraid.

To trust.

But trust was such a precious, precarious thing.

His bike faced out, and he kicked the stand and slowly eased through the lot. He took to the street that ran the front of the club, his movements fluid and confident, as if the man and the bike were one, this massive, fierce, grumbling force that blazed through the night.

I didn't care where he was taking me, just as long as it was away from there.

He made a few turns then he slowed and eased his bike onto the path hidden under the cover of trees just on the outside of town.

My heart sped faster when I realized where we were going.

The bike bounced down the familiar bumpy trail, and I squeezed him tighter as he guided his motorcycle out into the meadow where he'd taken me before. When I'd seen a part of Jud that I didn't want to see.

But tonight, I wanted him to show me everything.

How could I even allow myself to think it? Consider it? But I couldn't seem to keep from slipping into him.

Coming to a stop, Jud stretched out his boots to keep us upright.

Remnants of the panic sent me scrambling off the back and stumbling into the meadow. My heels sank into the soft earth as I took two steps back like I could protect myself from the direction I could feel myself tumbling.

He killed the engine.

In an instant, silence whispered and swam.

The beauty shouted back.

The branches of the high, towering trees swished with the short gusts of wind that blustered through while the babble of the creek murmured its peace.

Wildflowers had sprung up through the soft bed of grasses, the purples and pinks subdued in the murky rays of moonlight that glowed through the clouds that built.

A low roll of thunder quavered in the distance, and the coolness of the approaching storm raced across my heated flesh.

"I'm sorry." The apology fumbled out. The truth that no matter how far I tried to stay away from him, I still dragged him into my disaster.

Into my mess.

Guilt and grief clutched.

Was I putting him in danger?

Overcome, I blinked into the forest.

He rumbled a disbelieving sound. "What the hell are you apologizing for?"

My tongue darted out to wet my dried lips. "I warned you my life has been a mess for a long time. I think tonight is proof that I'm barely holding it together. I should go. Pack my things and leave before something happens that I can't take back."

Jud swung off his bike and rose to his full, towering height.

"No." It was the grumble of a command.

Dull moonlight fell over him, casting his stunning face in shadows. In hard, devastating lines that whispered of goodness.

Of darkness.

Of horror and light.

He took one step in my direction.

The ground shook beneath my feet.

"No," he said again.

"Jud, I have no idea what I'm doing here. My life—"

"You're worried about your life, Salem? About what you're bringing to the table?" He lifted his arms out to his sides. "Did you see me tonight? That's just a glimpse at who I really am. Told you, I've done horrible, horrible things, and I have no fuckin' clue how to contain it when I'm with you. I want to break every rule I've ever made for myself for you."

Visions of his face blinked through my mind.

It was pure savagery.

I gulped for air, trying to find my footing. But I'd stumbled onto dangerous, treacherous ground. Where nothing was solid and the world was slipping away.

Quicksand.

"We're a mess."

Jud chuckled a rough sound. "A beautiful fuckin' mess."

He kept edging forward. Aggression rippled beneath the surface of his flesh, but it'd shifted and found new focus.

A tremor rocked through me when he reached out and set his massive hand on my face. His thumb traced along the scar on my jaw. "Who is he?"

"Jud…" It was a whimper.

"Tell me, Salem. Trust me with this."

"He was my husband. He did this the first time I tried to leave." The admission floated on the breeze.

Every muscle in Jud's body tensed.

"And he forced you to go back to him? Did this to you as a warning?" They weren't really questions. They were vicious razors cutting from his mouth.

My nod was spastic, and another rush of tears bled free. "He said he was letting me off easy. That next time…"

My throat locked. The words held in the torment.

"Salem…baby?" Jud's words were shards, hinged, sure he didn't want my answer.

I blinked through the agony. "But I did it, I got the courage to leave again, but he found us, Jud…he found us and he…"

I couldn't say it. Couldn't let the atrocity free. Still, Jud held my face, like he saw the pain written there. Like he could hold the vacancy that throbbed even when he didn't fully see the details.

"Somehow, Juni and I got away," I continued, "and we've been running ever since. Never truly living. Never truly free. Under the radar, pretending we don't exist."

Rage boiled in the air. A strike of violence. A blister of rage.

His other hand cinched down on my side, and he jerked me toward him.

A gasp ripped up my throat as heat burned through my veins. This man was too much. So much that I was sure he was going to wreck me, though that would fall on Carlo, too, wouldn't it?

The one who would never let me live because I'd survived.

"You exist, Salem. I see you. I feel you. You're alive in my heart and in my eyes. And I won't let him take you from me."

"Jud…"

"Stay with me, Salem. Let me take care of you. Protect you."

My being rocked.

Overcome.

My spirit wanted to cling to his promise while logic reminded me of my truth.

"I have to take care of myself."

Because I would leave. I would leave because this fear promised I could never stay.

Tonight was a horrible reminder of that.

I'd made myself vulnerable.

Exposed.

And still, I was right here, wanting to let him hold that broken part of myself.

Jud brushed away the tears on my face. "It seems to me we're taking care of each other."

My head shook, unable to form a response.

"Magic, sweet enchantress. What you're doing to me. The way you're wrecking me, heart and mind."

His arm curled around my waist. "I have you."

He repeated the promise again as he lifted me from my feet. He held me gently as he sank to his knees on the damp ground. He laid me out on the grass.

The man wavered there, his hands on my shaking knees.

"Look at you. Most beautiful thing I've ever seen."

My trembling fingers reached out to brush over his face. The sharp angle of his eyebrows, his nose, his full, full lips, down through the cover of his beard.

"You stole my breath when I saw you, Jud. I was terrified, but I'm not sure it had a thing to do with you being a stranger finding me in the dark. It was this." I gathered his hand and pressed it to the wild drum of my heart.

"And this." I barely brushed my fingertips over his eyes. "The way you saw me. The way you made me feel seen. The way I felt changed in a beat."

A blanket of lightning flashed through the heavens. It lit him in a stroke of severity. A flare of greed in the night. The man a mountain that towered over me.

Jud groaned a pained sound, and he wedged himself between my trembling thighs. Angling forward, he set one hand on the ground beside my head and the other cupped the side of my face.

Obsidian eyes sparked. "Since the moment I found you, you've been the only thing I could see."

Emotion gathered fast. Welled from the broken parts of me. It crested and overflowed. I could barely force out the words. "Don't make me fall in love with you, Jud."

A sad smile hitched the edge of his mouth, and he traced his thumb at the edge of mine, words tender misery. "Who said anything about love, darlin'?"

He watched down on me. A thousand questions and reservations flashed through his expression, or maybe I was only witnessing what was reflected in mine.

"What do you want, Salem?" Jud asked.

My chin trembled, though I lifted it. "I just want to feel real."

Jud pressed up on both his hands.

Thunder rumbled.

Energy lashed.

Desire burned and blazed.

"What I want to do to this sweet little body." It was a warning. He slipped a hand up my thigh, pressing the bunched fabric of my dress higher.

Without my permission, my hips bucked against the bulge in his jeans. "Please."

The second I said it, Jud snapped and dove in.

Remnants of the aggression that blazed through his blood were dumped into that kiss.

This fierce, unrelenting kiss as Jud devoured my mouth.

It was possession.

A promise of protection.

All the things he couldn't give.

But right then, it didn't matter. Didn't matter that neither of our hearts could stay.

His big hand wrapped around the back of my neck to draw me closer as he pressed harder against me.

Rocking.

Sliding.

Whipping my body into a frenzy of lust.

He dropped to an elbow, and his other hand spread over my shoulder. He drew the fabric of my dress down to expose my left breast.

I heaved a gasp.

The heavens rumbled and flashed.

Need streaked, and Jud kissed me deeper as he kneaded my breast. I whimpered when he pinched my hardened nipple.

Jud moaned as his tongue stroked deep into my mouth, his other hand fisted up in my hair as he demanded my kiss.

He tugged my head back, and he kissed along my jaw, my chin, my throat, right down to the hammer of my heart. Then his mouth was taking the place of his fingers, and he sucked my nipple into his hot mouth before he bit down with his teeth.

A groan bumbled in my throat, mixed with a desperate, "Yes."

"I have you," he grunted at the heated flesh. He eased back to blow on the sensitive skin then he edged back onto his knees and drove his hands under my dress.

It pushed the fabric the rest of the way around my waist.

He ripped my underwear down my legs.

Hot and cold clashed.

The cool of the wind that blustered through and the fire that burned my blood.

Heavy clouds enclosed and veiled the moon.

Darkness eclipsed.

Recklessness obliterated all reason.

The only thing in this moment that mattered was this man.

Jud jerked through the button and zipper on his jeans, and he shoved them around his thighs.

I gulped at the sight.

The man so big.

So massive.

So intimidating.

So right.

He climbed back over me.

I felt delirious.

Fevered.

Frantic, he drove two fingers deep inside me, murmured, "Magic."

Dizziness barreled through, my lungs heaving to find air, but the only thing they found was the sanctuary of the man.

Citrus and spice. A warm fall night.

I lifted my hips, our movements frenzied and rushed as he situated himself between my thighs. Our bodies begged. Heaving and straining to reach the other.

He gathered me up, curled an arm under my back, and pulled my face closer to his.

He brought us nose to nose. "Tell me you want this, Salem."

"If you don't touch me, I'll stab you." I managed the choked, desperate tease.

Jud chuckled a low growl. "There's my girl."

My girl. My girl.

The softest smile curled my mouth as I watched him dig into his pocket then rush to cover himself with a condom.

Quick to come back to me.

While I wished this was more than a fantasy. More than a dream.

I could already feel my heart being crushed, knowing it couldn't last.

I also knew the pain would be worth it to live here for a little while.

He smiled back.

So tender.

So sweet.

Then I whimpered when I felt the blunt head of him pushing at my center. As the man burned between my thighs, as he slowly, slowly, nudged himself deeper.

Thunder cracked.

The sky opened up and began to pour.

Tears filled my eyes again.

Pleasure and pain.

Pleasure and pain.

The man so big I felt him in a way I'd never felt another in my entire life.

As if I were whole. Real. This man a true part of me.

My legs dropped open wide to make room for him, and the air raked from my lungs as he filled me full.

Jud's jaw clenched, and he dropped his forehead to mine and muttered, "Darlin.'"

He mumbled it like praise.

"Take me." I demanded it.

He angled back and greed flashed in those dark, dark eyes.

He pulled out then slammed back home.

A rasp rocked from my lungs, and my shoulders bowed from the earth, every part of me arching to join with him.

"Fuck, baby…my sweet enchantress, what have you done to me?"

One hand fisted in my hair as the other fisted at my hip. He picked up a rough, jagged rhythm.

Deep.

Obliteration.

Jud fucked me hard.

In the way I knew that he would. As if he would own every cell. Every piece. Overtake the places I couldn't let him go.

Too big. Too much.

Never enough.

My hips began to meet him thrust for thrust, and my hands slipped under his shirt, clawing at the muscles of his back, desperate to find a way in, too.

Where his secrets lived and mine wept.

Where there wasn't a day in our pasts that mattered except for the ones we could live together.

Whimpers fell from my mouth, "I need you."

"You have me," he grunted through the pouring rain, through the drive of his body, as he wound us into a frenzy that I was sure neither of us would survive.

Flames.

Friction.

It burned and lapped.

He thrust his big body into mine.

Faster. Harder. Deeper. More.

Pleasure gathered from the ends of the earth, poured down with the rain, sprung up from the ground below, gathered in that broken place.

Then it split.

Broke apart in a thousand glittering lights.

Bliss streaked.

The brittle pieces where I'd held myself together fractured and fell.

Light and darkness blinded my eyes while the man seeped deeper.

Body and spirit and soul.

He rocked and grunted and thrust, met me where I fell apart, a roar coming from his mouth when he came.

Every muscle in his body flexed and bowed and danced with mine, and he clutched me desperately when he burrowed his face in the crook of my neck as our orgasms throbbed through our bodies.

He never let go until we were nothing but a slow buzz of satisfaction.

He edged back and sent me a lopsided grin. "You are something, darlin'."

It was sweet, sweet affection.

A minute passed before I whispered, "Jud."

He pushed back onto his hands and gazed down at me with that tender smile twitching all over his face. I didn't know if he saw the fear written in mine, if he felt it, if he could hold it, but he was brushing back over my scar.

"I will burn the world down for you."

Everything trembled.

The heavens, the earth, and my heart.

"I don't..." I couldn't form the words.

He caressed away the fear, let a slow grin take hold of his mouth, though the words were heavy. "Don't worry, baby. Friends."

A frown curled my brow. He eased in and kissed it before he sat all the way back and resituated my dress.

Then he hopped to his feet and managed to pull his drenched jeans back up his thick thighs.

I tried not to ogle the man, but his cock was still hard. I had no doubt if I asked him, he'd be happy to climb right back over me and make me forget my name.

A tremble rocked me as I lie on the ground and stared up at him.

So gorgeous, my insides burned with the heat of a flashfire.

His hair, face, and beard were soaked.

Shirt stuck to his wide, wide chest.

A force that covered me in the storm.

He stretched out his hand to help me to stand.

I accepted it, arching a brow at him as he eased me to my feet. "Is that what we are, Jud? Friends?"

Dark laughter rumbled out and he pressed his face to the thrumming pulse that raged at my neck. He mumbled at the sensitive flesh, a balm to my soul, "Good, good friends."

Then he curled his arms around me and whisked me back into his hold and carried me to his bike. I looked up at him through the raging storm. "What now?"

"Tonight? I take you back to my place, get you a hot shower to warm you up, then I'm going to fuck you right. Tomorrow? That's up to you."

Chapter Twenty-Two

Jud

There are moments in our lives that we know are going to change everything. That once we take one step deeper, there will be no turning back.

We will be irrevocably changed.

Permanently marked.

A new tattoo that doesn't just cover your skin, but the ink bleeds way down deep, deep enough to imprint your soul.

I had to wonder then which moment had permanently changed me with Salem. When I'd known if I took one more step, it'd be over for me.

Tonight? When I'd wrapped her up and whisked her away? When I'd touched her and taken her? When I'd filled her up and she'd taken me over, branding our bodies in the most magnificent way?

Had it been when I'd crossed the line and kissed her down in the office, overcome with my need to hold her and keep her safe?

When I'd breathed out in relief when she'd shown with that ad to take the job?

Or had it been the second I'd first found her in the rain?

Or maybe...maybe...it had been every single one that had brought me closer to this girl. Each one life-altering, each step warning me if I got any nearer, I was never going to be the same.

And I kept at it, anyway. Unable to stop myself from the lure that called to me in a way that felt unavoidable.

Deeper.

What I did know was she'd scarred me.

Changed me.

Written herself in those places that I'd been sure were already penned. Unable to be edited or redrafted.

Salem had her arms curled around my neck as I carried her up the interior steps of my loft. Her breaths were short and shallow. I got the sense that she knew it, too. That we'd crossed a line that couldn't be erased. That every second of this was different.

It'd felt like a merging out in that meadow. Even more so as she'd ridden on the back of my bike back to the shop, like something had shifted in the passing of the miles.

Like our spirits had managed to spill into the other and there was no way to get them back to their rightful places.

Eyes the color of a toiling sea stared up at me through the whispering shadows that shrouded the shop.

Gauging.

Evaluating.

Seeking.

I punched in the code to let us through the door into my loft. Stepping inside, I let it drop closed behind us. Dim lights warmed the darkness to a dusky glow.

Our clothes were soaked, two of us drenched through.

In unison, we shivered, even though there was a defined heat that surrounded us.

The embers of the fire that singed us still burned beneath the questions that had risen to the surface.

I started in the direction of my bedroom that was on the opposite side of the loft. Halfway there, I felt her pulse speed, the way she cautiously let the words fall from her mouth, the girl asking me to open another door for her. "Did they live here with you?"

Grief streaked through my being, getting loose of the bonds where I tried to keep the memories chained.

"No." Agony raked out with the word.

I kept going, and she watched me like she was terrified I was going to run, when I was pretty sure it was the other way around. It was me who wanted to wrap her up and keep her.

Beg her to stay.

Friends.

What fuckin' bullshit.

I carried her through the kitchen and into the short passageway that led into my room. I passed by my enormous bed and carried her into the bathroom.

I flicked on the light.

We both blinked against the intrusive glare that glinted off the shiny white floors and walls. Once we'd adjusted, I carried her the rest of the way to the shower. Still holding her, I angled in so I could turn on the faucet. Water fell from the rain shower, quick to fill the room with steam.

Carefully, I set her onto her feet like this fierce girl was going to break. Like it was her soul that was going to shatter when I could feel every wound inside me reopening.

I kept peeking at her as I peeled the wet fabric of her dress up her body. Chills raced her flesh as I drew it up and over her head.

Fuck me.

She was a vision.

A straight-up fantasy standing there in nothing but her sky-high heels and her underwear.

A dream wrapped in black ribbons and bows. Her underwear was nothing but a scrap of lace and a satiny string that ran down her ass.

Girl all curves and soft skin and mind-bending appeal.

A grunt slipped from my tongue. "Fuckin' beautiful. Definition of it. Do you have any idea, darlin'?"

I let the question tumble out on the heated air, and Salem looked at me with those eyes that speared me all the way through.

Slayed and pierced and pinned me to the spot.

With trembling hands, she reached out, gripped the hem of my shirt, and pushed it up. I took hold of it when she made it to my chest, and I peeled it the rest of the way over my head.

Her hands spread over my abdomen and rode up to my shoulders.

"And you stagger me, Jud. You make me forget who I am."

Gently, she tapped her fingertips along the designs and innuendo on my skin as if she could tap into their meaning.

As if she wasn't afraid of the horror.

Or maybe she was just strong enough to hold the brutality of what they meant.

She didn't look away from my face when she traced the word branded on my left side.

Grim.

Like she was rewriting that part, too.

But I knew better. Knew better than thinking it could be erased.

Because no matter how much time went by, that demon still lived. Hell, he'd been right there, ready to break loose tonight.

Through the bleary cover of the steam, I knelt to remove her heels.

I was half mad with this lust that wouldn't let me go. The other part just wanted to fall at her fucking feet.

I curled my hand around her right ankle and lifted her foot, and Salem reached down to brace herself on my shoulders. Her question banged through my mind, and somehow this girl was pulling the truth from where I normally kept it sealed.

The hoarse confession grated from my tongue. "We had a place over by where Trent had lived with Gage before he met Eden. It was a little house with a big backyard and a perfect lawn and a pink playhouse that I was building in the back for when Kye got big enough."

"Kye." Salem whispered my daughter's name.

Sorrow wafted through the mist.

Like we were both breathing it.

Were a part of it.

Sharing in the torment.

I slipped off her other shoe and pushed to standing, had to reach out and set my palm on this girl's cheek to keep myself grounded. From falling to pieces. "Sat in that playhouse for weeks, just…waiting for them to come back. For Kye's little laugh to fill the air. For the steps she'd just started taking to patter on the floor. When I realized they wouldn't, I didn't even pack. I just came here. Couldn't take the echo of their voices for a second longer."

Salem touched my chin, brushed her fingers through my beard. "Jud…I'm so sorry."

"Not your fault."

It was mine.

"It doesn't mean I can't hurt for you." She kept peering at me with this expression that sheared through my conscience. Like this girl might be able to get the loss on a level that no one else could.

I swallowed hard, leaned down to work her panties free of those legs. As I went, I pressed a kiss to her thigh. To her knee. To her calf.

I unwound them from her ankles.

She ran her fingers through my hair. "Just like I can feel you hurting for me."

I choked out a breath, pressed my nose to her knee, inhaled. "I'm livid for you, baby. Want to destroy that bastard. Wipe his existence from the earth."

The deranged admission was out before I could stop it.

I knew by the way she shivered that she understood it wasn't a figure of speech. Wasn't an exaggeration.

She had me itching to do what I'd promised I'd never do again.

I turned to work my boots free of my feet. Standing, I kicked them off and shrugged out of my jeans and underwear.

As bare as the girl.

Exposed.

She pressed her palm to the thunder that raged at my chest.

"You're lonely."

Energy thrashed.

"Yes."

My hand went to her jaw, to the scar that made me want to go on a rampage. Hunt down the monster and show him exactly what being a monster meant.

"And you see mine," she whispered so soft. "My loneliness."

"There's no lonelier place than having to hide who we are." My words were out, between the two of us. "You don't have to hide from me."

I wound my arm around her waist and lifted her an inch from the floor so I could step with her into the shower.

The heated spray fell from the ceiling. Icepicks against our chilled flesh. Salem shivered then moaned when I leaned her back and massaged the warm water into the locks of her hair.

"I'm sorry you were scared tonight," I muttered, memory going back to the terror in her eyes.

Old fears flashed across her face.

Grabbing a sponge and coating it with shower gel, I began to wash her.

Carefully the way she deserved to be handled.

Returning the favor, Salem pumped gel into the palm of her hand, rubbed her palms together before she smoothed them over my shoulders and down my arms. She peeked up at me when she admitted, "I think I needed you to see."

She distracted me by running those hands all over my body.

Slowly.

Seductively.

I did the same, somehow knowing this was what she needed. For someone to hold her for a bit. To let her know she was safe.

We washed each other, her hands on me and mine on her.

It was really fuckin' hard to keep my cool with this girl slick and bare and the hottest thing I'd ever seen. It was bad enough when she was clothed. But this? It was mind-altering. Earth-shattering. Being with her this way.

Lost in the shift of this night.

Like maybe we'd both tripped into something better.

Something right.

Our hearts were a thunder that pounded louder than the drone of the shower, louder than the rain on the roof and the thunder in the distance.

We were caught up. Lost in the connection that refused to let us go.

Our hands searched and our mouths roamed.

I kissed her jaw, her cheek, that nose.

Her lips ran over my pecs, my stomach, back up in search of my mouth.

I kissed her long and deep. My hand on her chin to control the desperation.

She sighed and gasped and stroked her tongue over mine. A slow, intoxicating dance.

When the water started to cool, I finally pulled myself out of the trance and turned off the showerhead. I reached out and grabbed a towel and wrapped that lush body in it, grabbed another to wrap around my waist, then I was hoisting her up.

She squealed in surprise.

"I can walk, you know." There was a tease on her sweet mouth as I carried her to the massive vanity against the far wall of the bathroom.

Propping her on the counter, I grabbed another towel to run through her hair. "Now why would you do that when you have me to carry you around?"

Salem giggled. "You'd better watch out…a girl could get used to this, and then you're never going to get rid of me."

I smirked down at her. "Damn it. There you go, foiling my master plan, darlin'."

"Devious." She grinned.

My chest felt light while everything else was tightened in a fist.

Need unending.

Want growing into something it should not.

Love.

I shoved down the stupid, errant thought.

Blasphemy.

Disloyalty.

This black magic that was sinking into my blood and pounding through my body.

Only thing I could do was be here, right now, for her. Show her she didn't have to be alone.

But where did that leave me? Wasn't sure how to stand in front of the beauty of who she was while being me. Worse than that was wondering how the hell I was going to walk when this was over.

Especially when she started running her fingertips over that word again, a clear question in the action.

I blew out a strained sigh then I pressed her hand hard against it like she could feel the vileness pour out. "That's who I really am, Salem."

In question, she looked up at me, waiting.

"Who my father made me." I amended it, not sure if it was true. Because this? It was in my blood. There from the day I was born. Still, I doubted it'd have come to fruition the way it had without the one who'd planted it in me. "But that doesn't make me innocent of it, Salem. I've done the unthinkable."

Salem blanched, and I could feel her heart rate kick up a notch. "I don't know if I can believe that."

I brushed my fingers through her damp hair at the side of her head. "That's because you're seeing who I want to be. Who I'm trying to be."

"Or maybe you haven't ever had anyone see you for the man you really are."

Shame built from the depths where I tried to keep it buried.

Softly, she touched my face, but there was a desperation that lined her voice. "Did you choose that life?"

I gave a harsh shake of my head, the words shards as they popped off with a scoff. "I was forced into it with a literal gun to my head. Told it was my time. That it was my duty, and if I didn't, it would fall on my brothers."

Too bad I didn't fuckin' know our bastard father had already gotten to Trent. Spun him into destruction the same way as he'd done me.

All of us manipulated from the minute we were born.

Those who had tried to stand in the way had been systematically taken out.

Sorrow riddled her gaze. "How old were you?"

I swallowed over the razors in my throat.

My eyes dropped closed, unable to keep looking at her when I made the confession. "Fourteen was my first. My father said it was time to prove my loyalty. He took me with him on a raid, to act as one of his guards. Turned out, I was a good fuckin' shot, and I sealed my fate that day. I rode with the piece of shit until the day Trent found a way out. Asked us to leave with him to find a different life. A better life."

I'd thought I'd found that with Kennedy.

Cupping my cheek, Salem urged me to look at her. "And what if you would have refused? Left before Trent found a way out?"

"My father would have killed anyone I cared about and made me watch."

Those blue eyes were different then. Blazing with an empathy I couldn't fathom when she should be looking at me with the disgust I deserved. "I know evil, Jud. I've seen it. I've lived with it. And I know that's not what's looking back at me right now."

Agony slashed through my conscience, that place that was forever going to wail. "But I went back, Salem. I fuckin' went back thinking I was doing the right thing, and I ended up committing the greatest sin."

The unforgiveable.

Something I could never take back or make right.

I'd given that truth to Kennedy, and she'd left. There was no chance in hell I could offer it to Salem. The girl barely knew me as it was. But somehow, in that moment right then, I didn't think I'd been more in tune with another.

Not with Kennedy.

Not once.

Because she'd never looked at me quite like this.

Like maybe there was a chance that I could be saved.

Like there could be redemption for a man like me.

How the hell could I ask for it, though? When I deserved to suffer with the truth of what I'd done for the rest of my life?

"The only thing you can do is live in the here and now, Jud. The past never has anything to offer but chains…chains and regrets and hard lessons. And yes, we can learn from them, but we can't remain captive to them. You have to live each day for what it has to offer. You don't have to be alone, either, Jud, I'm right here."

Fuck, this girl was sweet.

Fierce and sweet and brave, and the only thing I wanted to do was wrap her up and keep her forever.

"Yeah? But for how long? When are you going to be done running, Salem? When are you going to free yourself of the chains?" Misery crawled out with the grunted hope that kept growing stronger.

Salem itched, fiddled with her fingers as she dropped her gaze. "It's the only thing I want, Jud. To stop the hiding. The running." Warily, she glanced at me. "But I don't know how to make that happen when he's still out there."

I had to focus on continuing to dry her hair rather than coming unhinged.

The only thing I wanted right then was a name. Would handle everything else.

"Who is he?"

Distress hitched in her throat. "He was my brother's friend who'd lived across the street from us growing up. Five years older than me. I started sneaking out to meet him when I was sixteen. My grandmother…Mimi…" Salem peeked up at me with her own shame on her face. "She warned me, Jud, she told me he was no good and that I was only asking for pain. And that's what I got. So much pain. I fell in love with a man who turned out to be wicked—a man who in turn only showed me wickedness—but I didn't realize what that really meant until it was too late."

"How long have you been running?"

"Four years. I don't stay in one place for longer than a few months.

This is the first time I've been anywhere near family. Darius believes that he's given up and moved on, that enough time has passed. That he's no longer after me, and as long as we stay far away and keep quiet, we'll be okay."

Fuck.

"That why you wanted the job off the books?"

Her nod was wary. "Yeah. For years, I've paid cash for everything. Stayed at crummy places that I could pay for by the month."

Her chin trembled. "Juni's medical care..." Her brow pinched in her own shamed horror. "I'd take her to little clinics in small towns, give a false name so she could get a checkup, and then we'd be on our way."

My soul shouted. The truth that this was bad, really fuckin' bad to make her go to such lengths to stay away from him.

I ran my thumb over the scar on her jaw. "What did he do...the last time? When you finally got free?"

Sorrow ripped through her features. "He tried to destroy us, Jud...to take it all."

Rage twitched my fingers, and vengeance ground my teeth. I held her by both sides of the face, forcing her to look at me, to understand. "Won't let him get to you. Promise you that."

Salem leaned forward and placed a kiss right over my heart. "It's not your war to fight, Jud. I shouldn't even be here. But I honestly don't know how to leave."

Had to force some lightness into the mood before I scared her with the rage that pounded through my system. "Now why would you want to go and leave when you get all of this?" With a quirk of my lips, I rocked my hips between her thighs.

Playing.

A taunt and a tease.

Because the only thing I wanted to do right then was steal any trace of sadness from her being.

Figured I'd shore up the rage for later.

Because if that fucker showed his face? He was dead. Fuck the promise I'd made to myself.

That promise that I'd never kill again.

That I'd live on the straight and narrow.

Be ready for when my life came back.

The *one purpose* I'd been living for.

And there it went, fading into the distance.

Blasphemy.

Waiting for him to strike suddenly seemed unwise.

I was going to get the name out of Darius, then I was going to put an end to Salem's pain. Head it off before it found its way to her door.

Salem dug her fingers into my sides and looked up at me with those eyes.

"I don't want to, Jud…I don't want to leave."

Intensity crashed.

A whip in the air.

A fire to my soul.

I dropped the towel I was using to dry her hair and drove my fingers into the locks instead, just as I swooped down to plunder that plush, tempting mouth.

Girl so gorgeous.

So right.

So much better than I should ever ask for.

"Sounds like you should stay then." I rumbled it at her lips, playfully, though I meant it, one hundred percent.

Felt her grin against my mouth, and she edged me back and slipped off the counter and onto her feet.

"In that case," she said, glancing at me from over her shoulder as she sauntered out of my bathroom and toward my bedroom.

Well shit.

There she went.

My vixen.

Nothing but a sweet, tempting enchantress.

And I was fuckin' hypnotized.

Spellbound.

Dropping her towel, she strutted away, nothing but that bare back and perfect round ass, hair falling down her spine, legs curvy and toned.

"Ahh, darlin', now you are just asking for trouble," I rumbled from behind.

"I found you, didn't I?" she teased with a glance back at me.

With a chuckle, I was stalking her way out into the bedroom, catching up to her before she made it to my bed. I hooked an arm around her front, palm coming to her stomach to pull her flush.

Salem laughed and kicked her feet as I pulled her against me. It pulled a rush of laughter out of me, too, and then she was melting into a puddle when I kissed a path down the side of her neck and across her delicious shoulder.

"Fuck, you feel so nice." Rumbled it as I pressed my nose into her hair and inhaled, and she was sighing out.

"You're the best thing I've ever felt, Jud." Her admission wisped on the dense air of my room. "I never expected you…to find someone who would make me dream beyond the hope of only surviving."

I swiveled her around, tipped up her chin. "I'm going to see to it that you have that, Salem. The life that you deserve."

Her beautiful brow bunched, and I let my fingertips trail down her throat. "Turn back around, baby."

She exhaled a needy breath as she slowly shifted, eyes watching mine as she turned.

My breath hitched again. "Bend over, darlin'. Let me get a good look at all that sweetness."

She shivered, whimpered as she pressed her palms onto my bed.

Shit.

So damned sexy.

Her bottom was round, her slit pink and pretty.

I angled in to lick a path down her spine. I palmed her ass as I did. "Every part of you, Salem. Makes me insane, how bad I want you. How I've been dying to get lost in this sweet body, and now that I have, I don't ever want to stop."

I kept kissing down as I muttered the words against her silken flesh.

"Then don't, Jud. Don't stop."

And there she was. That storm that had made landfall. A flash-flood of chaos that lit in my blood and pulsed greed through my veins.

Her aura everywhere. Toasted coconut and sultry sin and a little bit of me.

That set me off, too.

"You mine, darlin'?" I whispered it as I kept heading south, tongue stroking between her cheeks so I could give a nice little lap to her sweet, puckered hole.

Salem gasped then pushed back.

A chuckle rumbled out as I fully pushed back to standing. Dropping my towel from my waist, I reached over to my nightstand and grabbed a condom. I rolled it on quick. I pressed her chest farther against the mattress so she was completely bent over.

Damn, she was a vision.

Perfection.

Complete annihilation.

I let my fingers wander to her drenched pussy, and I pressed two fingers deep inside, grumbled, "Tell me, Salem. Tell me you're mine."

Even if it was just for tonight, I needed to hear it.

Girl writhed and whimpered. "Jud."

"Tell me."

"Yes. I'm yours."

I knew she didn't mean to be. Neither of us had anticipated this.

It didn't matter. She was never going to forget me.

I grabbed the base of my dick and lined myself up with her pussy, nearly passed out all over again when I nudged my head just inside, as I slowly, slowly kept jutting deeper and deeper.

Way the girl squirmed and gasped and sucked for air as I stretched her wide, almost too snug to fit.

My cock filled her up, and her walls throbbed around me.

Swore, the ground started to shake.

I took her by the hips and started to move, driving in and out of her perfect cunt.

View itself had me wanting to come.

"You're perfect, darlin'. So good." Didn't try to keep it from spilling from my mouth. Not when it was the truth. This girl who'd invaded my world and made it feel like something else.

"Don't stop," she demanded incoherently, then she yelped when I picked her up and tossed her onto her back on the bed.

A giggle rolled up her throat before those eyes were sweeping over me as I stood there for a beat, just looking at this girl laid out before me.

That feeling lit in my veins.

Need.

Possession.

Girl was nothing but a siren.

Black-fuckin'-magic.

Because what she had me feeling wasn't possible.

I crawled onto my knees on the bed, and I reached out and dragged her close, put her ankles on my shoulders and drove in deep.

I picked up a rigid, hard pace.

Her hips arched farther from the bed, hair thrashing around her gorgeous face, those tits bouncing with every thrust.

"Think I'm done for, baby." My thumb swirled around her swollen clit. She cursed, shouted my name as her orgasm raced through her body, squeezing me tight, girl heaving for a breath as I slowed to give her a breather.

Then I started to swirl my finger on her swollen clit again.

Surprise filled her face. "I don't think..."

But she was trailing off when I shifted angles and pressed down on her lower belly so I could rub that sweet spot inside her with the head of my dick.

Clearly, she liked it a lot.

Way her head began to thrash as I wound her up all over again.

But the real problem here was how much I liked her, how my chest tightened when another orgasm ripped through her tight, perfect body.

I dropped down to my elbows and gathered her up, moved in and out, my hips thrusting between those lush thighs. My spirit got tangled with the pleasure that burned at the base of my spine and tightened my balls in a fist.

I kissed her when I came, devoured her as bliss went streaking through my veins.

I slumped to my side and pulled her against me after, and my fingers found their way into her hair, and I stared over at her as she stared back at me.

There was a feeling deep in my chest that I was pretty sure I wouldn't ever be rid of.

"Magic," I murmured low.

"Magic," she whispered back.

Peace billowed around us for the longest time, the only sounds our breaths and our hearts and the retreating storm. Finally, I opened my mouth, and I asked something I'd been wanting to ask her all along. "What is it you want, Salem? What in this life do you want most?"

"I want Juni to be safe. I want to stop running. I want a home."

Chapter Twenty-Three

Jud

Jud stumbled in his tracks when he saw Marcello push from the car he was leaned against in the parking lot of Iron Ride. Jud rushed a hand through his hair, half inclined to run, half inclined to grab his gun.

Take out the deviant before he became a threat.

Because Jud would never return to that life.

Because there was the past Jud was afraid would haunt him forever standing out in the snow-covered lot in Redemption Hills. A place this man should never be, should never show his face.

"What the fuck are you doing here?" Jud grunted, hating that he was caught unaware. Being caught unaware in his past life meant you were dead. But considering it was that life he was trying to separate himself from, he'd let down his guard.

Marcello tsked. "You seem surprised to see me."

"I am. Had hoped to never see you again."

Jud had ridden for Marcello and his crew more times than he could count. A guard. A sentry. A deprived warden protecting all the wrong things. How many times had Jud pulled the trigger in the name of the treaty that had been made between their families?

Jud's father had gotten a wide-open corridor to run his drugs through Los Angeles.

Marcello had gotten a killer.

Grim.

The tattoo burned like the scar it was on his side. He could almost hear the blood spilling to the ground. The bodies that'd fallen.

Jud gritted his teeth against the pain of the memories.

Marcello asked, "And why is that?"

Jud lifted his arms out to the sides. "My father is dead, means our deal is done."

Marcello laughed a low sound. "I'm afraid you and I both know it doesn't work like that."

Jud's heart panged in dread, his mind spinning to his wife and daughter who were across the small city of Redemption Hills. Tucked away in the little house where Jud was building a home. In this town where it was supposed to be safe. Where their past lives no longer mattered. Where no one was supposed to know they'd put down roots.

Jud cocked his head, refusing to give any sign that his knees were shaking as fierce as the shitstorm he could feel coming. A hard challenge lined his voice, "Yeah, and exactly how does it work?"

Marcello lifted too casual of a shoulder. "Well, you see, a job was left unfinished." Jud's chest stretched tight as Marcello took a step in his direction and said, "Your baby brother, Logan?"

Marcello phrased his name like a question, like he didn't know full well he might as well have a knife pressed to Jud's jugular.

"You see, he was working our books. He's a smart one, that boy. Things had never been so profitable as when he was sitting behind our desk. And now that he's gone…let's just say things are a bit of a mess."

Dread spiraled and heat flamed.

Jud seethed.

With aggression.

With hatred.

Fuck.

He should have known his father had drawn Logan into the life in some way. Manipulated him. Chained him.

Like he would have left any of them unscathed.

No doubt, their father had made a million threats to Logan to keep it hidden.

Sweat gathered along Jud's brow even though the mountains around him were covered in two feet of snow. "The Iron Owls are dead."

That fucking bike club where their father had led them to Hell.

"The Iron Owls still owe a debt. Your father guaranteed your services," Marcello countered. He glanced around. "And even if he's gone, it seems to me, a few of you are still alive and well. That doesn't have to remain true."

Jud edged forward one step, his voice a slow, controlled threat. "Are you asking for a war?"

Marcello wasn't stupid.

There was a reason they'd wanted Jud.

He was a good fuckin' shot.

And there he stood, itching to take another.

To put this remaining link in the ground.

Marcello smiled too bright. "Nonsense. We're old friends, aren't we? I'm here with a proposition. That is all."

Bullshit.

Any proposition Marcello came to offer wasn't optional.

Still, Jud asked, "Yeah?"

He crossed his arms over his chest.

"You personally do one last job for us. In and out. And your debts are paid. The Lawson brothers will be free to go on with their boring little lives."

Marcello waved a deviant hand in the air.

"And if I don't?"

"Then I'll be having this conversation with Logan, and it won't be as friendly."

Smoke billowed. A heavy darkness that filled the air and choked out hope.

Consuming.

Disorienting.

A black plague that annihilated everything in its path.

Still, he rushed, searched, fumbled through the abyss from one room to the next.

Nothing.

Nothing.

Fear crushed, as suffocating as the smoke that filled his lungs. He pulled his shirt over his face, his eyes wide and unseeing, the world a blur of fire and white-hot pain.

It didn't matter.

He pressed on.

Pushed.

Forever passed.

A second.

A moment.

Misery the time that ticked on the clock.

A roar rose from the depths of him. "Where are you? Please. Fuck. Can you hear me?"

The whooshing of the flames screamed back.

No, this couldn't happen. He wouldn't let it.

He was on his knees. Blind as he searched. A bed. No. A crib.

He felt along the spindles.

He gulped when he felt it. When he knew. When he curled his arms around the limp body.

So light. So small.

He took it into his arms, pushed to his feet, stumbled through the flames.

A window.

He lifted his boot, kicked it, busted through.

Glass shattered and rained and tore his flesh. But he didn't slow. He lumbered out into the night.

Refusing the pain.

Refusing the agony.

The fire raged behind them, and he ran to the edge of the yard hedged by the trees.

Cradling the tiny frame, he dropped to his knees and gently set it on the ground.

His arms shook.

Shook and shook.

While the flames roared and wood crumbled and the structure gave.

No hope for life from within.

Torment wailed.

As loud as the sirens he heard coming in the distance.

Frantic, he breathed against the child's mouth. Breathed and breathed. His hands too big and clumsy against the tiny chest.

I jolted awake. Disoriented. Blinded by the old pain that would forever rage. Sweat drenched my flesh and my body shook out of control as I gasped for air in the darkness of my room.

Hands found me in the night, shocking me out of the stupor.

Tender, sweet hands.

Heart battering at my aching chest, I sat up on the side of the bed.

I felt her crawl onto her knees behind me, and she pressed her face to the scars that burned at my back, her lips soft where they caressed the flesh.

"Jud." Salem whispered it with all the understanding she shouldn't possess. "What's wrong?"

I wanted to tear at my chest. Rip out my heart. Maybe give the mangled thing to the girl before it fully bled out.

"It's okay," she whispered to the charred, marred skin.

My head dropped into my hands. "It's not, Salem. It's not."

She curled her arms around my waist, held me while I struggled to breathe.

"I see you, Jud. I see you for who you are and not what you've done." She uttered the words like they were truth.

My fucking eyes stung while agony ripped through my body.

Ghosts screaming.

Demons wailing.

"Yeah?" It came out on my own spite. She had no idea. No fucking idea. She would run. Turn her back when she knew what I'd done.

Just like Kennedy.

"I was responsible for an entire family dying, Salem. A fucking mom and her two little kids. Me."

Horrified shock rasped from her mouth. But she didn't loosen her hold. She just squeezed tighter.

Agonized comfort coiled in my stomach.

Her lips continued their soft assault.

Sweet encouragement.

Steady annihilation.

Because I couldn't shut the fuck up. Couldn't keep it in. "I tried to stop it, Salem. When I realized what was going down. I tried to. But I was too late."

She tightened her hold, burrowed her face into my back. "I'm sorry, Jud. I—"

"Don't, Salem."

Don't.

Don't make me want something I can't have. Don't make me feel this way.

Like I was grounded. Like in her eyes, I could be better. Like I might stand the chance of being the man I'd wanted to be.

Blasphemy.

"I can't stop, Jud. I can't stop this, either."

Her hands spread out over my front, over the rampage thundering at my chest, this heart that no longer knew what was right.

We were held for a beat.

For a moment.

"I need you," she finally whispered.

It only took those three little words for a frenzy to hit.

I spun and had her pressed to the bed in a flash of greed. Movements were frantic as I yanked my shirt that she was wearing over her head and tore her underwear down her legs.

She was pushing mine down my thighs as I went.

Wild.

Fevered.

Our hands everywhere.

Touching. Gripping. Needing.

"Please," she begged.

In the room pitched in black, I drove into her. No thought. No reason. No sight.

No purpose in this moment other than this girl.

Bare.

Our hearts and bodies and spirits divulged to the other.

My hips snapped and her nails grappled for a place to take hold. To sink in. To get into those places I wasn't sure I could keep her from.

I rolled us, this girl on top, her hair fisted in one hand and the other stroking her clit.

She rode me.

Watched me.

Thunderbolt eyes strikes of lightning in the night.

The need was too much.

Too much.

This frenzy that had lit.

Every move erratic.

Every touch volatile.

I rolled us back.

Drove. Fucked. Pushed. Compelled.

We toppled.

Chaos.

Tumult.

This storm that'd made landfall.

We were on the floor, her back to the rug, her hips jutting from the floor as I slammed into her.

"Jud," she whimpered. "Oh, god, oh god."

I gripped her, took her, devoured her.

She came, and I soared.

My cock pulsed. Poured into this woman who I was terrified was going to steal every bit of me.

Panting, I flopped down, rolled us to our sides, and I stared at her in the darkness.

Fingertips found my face. "I am scared that I need you, Jud. That with you, for the first time in my life, I feel safe."

"I'll kill anyone who even thinks about hurting you, Salem. I will."

It should have scared her.

But this girl? She snuggled into my side.

Grim.

And I guessed for the first time in my life, I was thankful I was him.

Chapter Twenty-Four

Salem

Eighteen Years Old

"PUPA." HE WHISPERED HER NAME LIKE A SECRET. "My wife. My love. My life. You're mine. Forever."

Her stomach twisted as she looked up at her husband's face.

She still couldn't believe it.

She couldn't make sense of how she'd ended up there. As if it'd been destined. Maybe planned.

Her fears had only amplified when she'd voiced reservations, and she'd been silenced. Carlo had attempted to assuage her concerns by telling her she had no need to worry at all. He'd promised to take care of her. Give her a life that she could only dream of. One that she had yet to discover.

But it'd felt rushed. As if she wasn't given time to decide for herself. It'd felt wrong when he'd laughed when she'd asserted she still planned on starting college in the fall.

Mimi had been the only one to try to stop it. She'd warned it was a mistake. Salem had only truly begun to believe it when she'd said she wasn't ready, when she'd begun to believe this wouldn't be the life she'd want at all, and Carlo had shown and taken her to the chapel, anyway.

With a smirk, he'd told her it was cold feet, but Salem was more afraid that her heart didn't warm when he was around.

That there was a piece of her that felt frozen.

"I love you," he said.

"I love you," she said back, unsure if it was a lie.

Because truthfully?

That love she'd once thought she'd felt?

It now came with a heavy dose of fear.

"You do whatever it requires. Am I clear?"

"Yes, Sir."

Salem pressed her back to the wall as she listened to the conversation Carlo was having with Darius. She tried to press her eyes closed even tighter. Like maybe if she did, none of this would be real.

Her life wouldn't be a nightmare.

A sad, cruel joke.

A moment later, Darius ducked out of the room. When he saw her cowering there, he sent her a worried scowl. But he didn't say anything as he headed down the hall. The front door clicked shut behind him when he left.

Chills lifted on her arms when she felt the presence beside her. Carlo traced them with his fingertip. "What are you doing out here, Pupa?"

The tone of his voice was a soft accusation.

Salem gulped. "I was checking to see if you were ready for dinner."

Hooking his thumb under her jaw, he studied her face. "That's all?"

"That's all," she rushed.

He angled his head, pressed his mouth to hers, and muttered, "This mouth…this body…this *mind?* They're all mine, Salem." He angled back, rubbed the pad of his thumb on the middle of her forehead, stared at her when he said, "Be sure not to let it run places it shouldn't. It's dangerous out there."

Salem forced a smile. "I'm happy right here."

His smile was slow. Appraising.

Fear spiraled down Salem's spine.

"Good, my love. Neither of us would want me to have to waste my precious time if I had to come and find you, now, would we?"

"Where would I go?"

He tapped her chin. "Good girl."

Then he turned and strode down the hall toward the kitchen, calling out, "It smells delicious. I'm starving. Let's eat."

She waited until he turned left at the end of the hall then breathed out a pained breath.

She tried not to weep.

Chapter Twenty-Five

Salem

"What's this?" My fingers played along the dress that was sitting on the end of Jud's bed while I held the sheet to my chest with the other.

The palest light floated in through the square windows that ran high along the wall behind his bed. Dawn had barely broken the night, and the barest rays filtered through the darkness to give a token of the coming day.

I'd woken with Jud's massive arms curled around my body, the man holding me tight, his steadying breaths filling my ears and my spirit and my lungs.

It'd taken my all to peel myself away from the sanctuary of his arms, but I needed to get home before Juni woke and Darius and Mimi realized I hadn't come home all night.

Before my heart got any deeper.

Before I fell any farther.

But there I was, careening through the air, no ground below.

Diving into his dark abyss.

My fingers traced over the material. My heart stuttered. This man cared for me in a way no one else had done in my life.

I felt him shift from behind, and I looked back to watch the giant sit up in his bed. The covers slipped down around his waist. He roughed his fingers that worked magical things through his sleep-rumpled hair.

My stomach fisted in a bid of want. In a crash of affection. He was beautiful. In every way.

After last night, I'd never been so sure of anything.

He squinted in the glow of the morning at the things that were laid on his mattress.

"Uh, Logan texted a few hours ago to check how you were after everything went down. He asked if there was anything he could do. I figured you might not want to go slinking back into your house wearing your trashed dress from last night and those heels, so I asked him to pick up a couple things. Not the best selection in the middle of the night, but hell, the man's got shopping skills."

Jud chuckled an uneasy sound. Clearly, he was unsure of his actions.

I glanced back at the dress and noticed there was a box with a pair of sandals tucked inside and some toiletries.

"Hope they fit."

I shifted back to look at him. I couldn't keep the edge of my mouth from tipping up in a slow smile, returning to the day that had changed everything. "I thought I told you if I fucked you there would be no shame to it?"

Jud grinned, though it was soft, his handsome, rugged face kissed by the morning light, hair lit up in the glow where errant pieces were sticking up all over his head.

"No shame at all, darlin', but I figured what happened last night is between you and me."

My heart panged, and my chest squeezed.

Crap.

I was in so much trouble.

I had crossed a line that I was terrified to have crossed.

Trust no one.

But I wasn't sure I could cling to that any longer with him.

With this man who had me crawling back up to him until I was pressing my lips to his wicked, sexy mouth. "Thank you."

A big palm found the side of my face. Obsidian eyes flared as he edged back to meet with the truth in my gaze. "The pleasure is all mine, darlin'."

My teeth clamped down on my bottom lip. What I really wanted to do was curl back into this bed with him.

Let him ravage me all over again.

The way he'd done time and again last night, neither of us sure if it would be the only chance we would have. And those moments? Those hours? They'd belonged to us.

I didn't want them to end.

My chest squeezed with dread, the reality that in a blink, in a second, I might have to leave him behind.

Run, the way I always did.

Because as much as he promised to stand for me, if it came to it, there was no way I'd drag him into the line of fire.

"I really need to get home."

He nodded. "I know. Why don't you go get dressed, and I'll get you there?"

"Thank you," I said again.

I wasn't shy, definitely not after last night, but I felt a blush flushing my body as I slipped off his bed and took the sheet with me. Jud sat there, watching me gather the things he'd had Logan get for me and then shuffle across his floor to the bathroom.

He had this look on his face.

This tenderness that threatened to break up the barriers I had placed inside me.

I dipped my head and ducked into the bathroom before I could let him go any deeper, but I guessed I was the fool who thought that was going to cut the connection.

I could feel it pulse from the other side of the door. A thread that had woven through my heart. A whisper I was sure that no matter where in this world I ran to, it would call to me.

I splashed water on my face, brushed my teeth with the toothbrush that was in the pile, then twisted my hair into a ponytail holder since they'd thought of that, too, before I slipped into the dress and sandals.

The dress landed just above my knees, simple with flowers and cap sleeves, and it fit me perfectly—just like the man.

Before I let myself wane into melancholy, this feeling that one day I was going to lose him, the worry that I couldn't stay hunting me down like the thief that it was, I headed into the bedroom.

Jud had already dressed, and he was lacing up his boots. Still bent over, he cut a glance at me. "Ready?"

"Yeah."

He rose to that hulking, glorious height, his shoulders so wide where he was lit up like a silhouette in the grayed streams of light.

A smirk ticked up at the corner of his mouth.

"What?" I asked as I edged deeper into the room.

"It fits."

I touched the skirt. "It does."

"I like it."

"I like it, too."

It felt as if there was a secret woven in the simple words.

I like you, too, so much, and it scares me more than you can understand.

I was so tired of the hurt. Of the loss and the fear and the veins of joy that always got stripped away.

My spirit shook.

Struck with the realization.

I wanted that vein that I'd found with him to widen and withstand.

Fear clutched my stomach in a grip, rising against the hope that kept bubbling up. It made me feel like I was being tugged in every direction. Questions and worries and these building dreams at odds.

At war.

Before I got lost in them, I grabbed my little purse I'd had from last night, slipped it over my shoulder, and walked toward the door.

Jud cut me off at the pass.

He spun me around and pressed me to the wall. He kissed me hard. Those big hands framed my face while he did. His lips were soft and sweet and enticing.

Emotion rioted.

Want. Fear. Hope.

What was I doing?

Setting myself up for it to hurt worse when this came to an end, that was what.

Pulling back, he canted me a knowing smile. "Don't freak out on me, darlin'. I see those pretty little feet itching to run."

"They run from the pain." The words hitched when I let the admission bleed free.

He brushed the pad of his thumb over the apple of my cheek, his head tipping to the side, his words rough and laden with the promise. "I won't ever hurt you. No one else is going to, either."

Trust.

I wanted to give it to him.

All of it.

Ask him to keep me. Stand by me. Fight with me.

My teeth ground hard when I realized the selfishness of that.

He leaned down and pecked a kiss to my forehead. "Let's get you home."

Home.

The longing hit me full force.

A smack in the face.

Jud touched my scar like he felt it, too, then he stepped back and took me by the hand, leading me out of his loft and downstairs. He bypassed his bike and opted for his truck. He helped me into the passenger's seat and leaned up to buckle me in.

I grinned. "I can do that."

"Now why would you go and do something like that when you can have all of this doin' it for you?"

He ran his lips up the column of my throat and to my jaw when he said it.

My heart thundered in my chest.

The man didn't fight fair.

He chuckled low as he shut the door, and the mammoth of a man rounded the front of his truck.

He hopped in. His presence overpowered the cab.

Citrus and spice.

A warm fall night.

The breaking day.

A whisper of new life.

He pushed the button to open the garage, and he started the truck, backed it out, and took to the road.

He kept grinning over at me as we traveled the quiet, sleeping streets.

Slow and sure.

A little cocky.

Too much of everything I hadn't known I needed.

All while that energy spun and churned and built into a mountain as big as him. A force that couldn't be conquered or subdued.

I didn't think a word had been said between us by the time he made the last turn into my neighborhood. He pulled to a stop at the curb, and he left the truck running when he hopped out and came around to my side.

He opened the door to help me out.

Fire streaked up my arm when he took my hand.

But it was the flames that burned, wasn't it? What left us ash?

I needed to remember.

Remember.

"Thank you." Apparently, those were the only two words I knew since I couldn't come up with anything else to say.

The problem was, I couldn't figure out where we were supposed to go from there. What last night had meant other than…everything.

Maybe that was the most terrifying part of all.

Jud laughed a low sound as he shut the door and leaned back

against the metal, those giant arms crossed over his chest. "Oh, it's my pleasure, darlin'."

My lips tipped up, and I touched the steady pounding at his chest. "I guess I'll see you later then."

He just grinned, and I turned and edged up the walkway. Quietly, I slid the key into the lock. I looked back at him as I did.

"Are we still friends, darlin'?" A playful smile kissed his mouth when he asked it.

My smile his elicited was riddled with affection.

"Is that what you want to be?" Somehow, I pulled it off as a tease.

Jud shook his head, that smile so bright on his face, like he didn't know what to do with me.

Figuring I'd wind up spending the whole day standing there grinning at him like a fool if I didn't stop this madness, I forced myself to turn the knob.

He waited there with all that arrogant tenderness until I disappeared inside the hushed, sleeping house. I had the door locked behind me before he moved back to his side and climbed into his truck.

Yeah, I knew since I was peering at him through the drape that covered the window, and damn it, if the man didn't take a piece of my heart with him when he drove away.

I angled farther to the side so I could watch the tail end of his truck disappear down the road.

"Look any closer, and you're gonna break your neck."

A squeak peeled out of me, and I whirled around to find Mimi smirking at me from the end of the hall, wearing her favorite muumuu and slippers.

"Mimi, you scared the crap out of me." Heavy breaths heaved from my lungs.

She waved me off as she lumbered toward the kitchen. "Figured you'd be sneaking in right about now."

I narrowed my eyes at her. "I'm not sneaking. I just didn't want to wake anyone up."

She eyed me up and down. "And it looks to me like my girl never went to sleep."

"Mimi," I chastised, gaze darting through the empty living room, just in case anyone else could hear.

"Salem," she shot right back as she edged the rest of the way into the kitchen. She flipped on the light and moved directly for the coffee maker.

"Where are the kids?" I asked as I followed behind.

"They built a fort in my bedroom. Felt like I'd better keep an eye on those two before they ended up packing their bags and trying to walk to the moon. Cute as pie, but woo wee, those imaginations are running wild. Could barely keep up with the two of them."

Love pressed full at my chest. "She's a dreamer."

"Mmhmm..." Mimi mused as she filled the carafe with water then poured it into the machine. "Just like her mother used to be."

A huff of air left my nose as I sat on the stool at the tiny bar on the opposite side of the counter. "I used to be, didn't I?"

I'd almost forgotten what that was like.

"You sure did, but you lost those dreams along the way." She paused, glancing over at me. "More like someone snuffed them out."

She reached over the counter and tipped up my chin so she could study my face. "But there they are...the spark of something new lighting in those beautiful eyes."

A frown curled my brow, and I pulled my chin from her fingers and looked down. "I'm not sure I can go there, Mimi."

"And why's that, my girl? Why can't you live? Didn't Darius say it was time? Isn't that why we're here?"

Hope fluttered my heart.

Wings that lapped.

I needed to clip them before they took flight.

"And if I can't stay? What if I love him, and I have to leave?" The true fear flooded out.

What it always came down to.

I didn't exist.

I didn't have a home.

As Mimi stared over at me, belief filled her expression. "And what if you don't take this chance and you miss out on the most wonderful things in this life, Salem?"

Moisture filled my eyes, and she moved to the fridge and started taking ingredients out to make breakfast. Eggs and bacon. Milk and butter.

I got up, rounded the counter, and moved to the pantry to grab the pancake mix from the top shelf, already in tune with her, knowing that's what she'd be after next.

She eyed me as I went, and when I hiked up onto my tiptoes to reach it, she mumbled from behind, "Well, at least he knows how to take care of my girl right. Looks like you can barely walk this mornin'."

On a gasp, I whirled around. "Mimi."

She cracked a smile, though there was something soft about it, too. "What? Don't look so shocked. Every woman should be loved up right. I'm just relieved your looker knows what to do."

"You don't even know what he looks like," I pointed out, like it was going to throw her off course.

"Don't need to. Already can see it in your eyes, right there with those dreams that are flarin' up. Clear as day, sweet girl."

Right. Okay.

She could see right through me.

A second later, a commotion clattered from the hall. "Wakey, wakey! I smells the coffee, so you know whats that means, my mimi is gonna be making the bestest breakfast we ever ate."

Footsteps pounded on the old floors, and a second later, Juni and Gage busted through the archway.

All grins.

Pure sweetness.

Life and beauty and hope.

My chest squeezed.

"Good mornin', Miss Mimi and Miss Salem. Thank you so very much for letting me spend the night." Gage took a seat at the little round table off to the side of the bar. "I am starvin' marvin'. I like my eggs scrambled, please."

The words spilled from his mouth, manners galore.

The smile he created nearly broke my face.

Juni ran my way and threw her arms around my legs. My precious girl beamed up at me. "I hads the bestest time ever in evers, Mommy. I wants to stay livin' next door to my best friend forever and ever. No more adventures, unless we comes right back. Is it a deal?"

She bounced when she begged it.

"I love her all the way to the sky," Gage said, so matter of fact.

My spirit clutched. I touched my daughter's chin. "I'm so happy you had a great time." I deflected from answering her question by asking one of my own. "Were you two good for Mimi?"

Juni looked at me like I was crazy. "Um, yes, of course, we followed every single of all the rules. We don't wants to go gettin' into trouble and have to go to timeout all the way in Antarctica."

"Gotta get all the A's for our whole lives," Gage added.

Wow.

Mimi chuckled. "My, my, those are some goals."

"Well, my new mommy said it's good to get the A's, but the most important is that we always try our hardest, even if we don't get 'em all every time, and she said we have to have the grace, even if we're givin' it to ourselves. She's a teacher and the smartest in ever, you know." The tornado of words whipped from his mouth.

"She sounds like a good mommy," Mimi said as she took out a skillet.

"The best." He gave a resolute nod.

So cute.

For so long, Juni and I had been alone, just the two of us.

Just the two of us.

Enough.

But still, there had always been something missing.

And now…my chest pressed full.

Hope. Hope. Hope.

How easy it'd be to fall into it.

Then I was jerking when I heard the light tapping at the front door.

Worry jumped into my bloodstream, and I frowned at Mimi who looked over at me in question.

"Wait right here," I told the kids, and I edged into the living room and peered through the drape again.

My heart leapt into my throat, confusion and excitement and worry as I twisted the lock and opened the door to the gorgeous man waiting on the other side.

"Jud?"

He stood there with a bunch of flowers in his hands.

So big.

So handsome.

So overwhelming I felt the ground shake, that energy lapping through the cool air. Though this morning, it was different. It caressed and soothed and skimmed.

Soft, slow warmth that wrapped me in comfort.

"Hey there, darlin'. Just thought I'd pop by to make sure you made it home safe last night."

He winked at me.

My belly flipped.

"Uh—"

"Well, look at that." Mimi's voice hit from behind.

Jud smiled. Pure charm. "Ma'am."

I was pretty sure my mimi could see right through him, too, because the man wasn't exactly *polite* last night.

My stomach churned again. Desire and greed. I had the urge to throw my arms around him and hold him tight.

Reckless girl. This was only going to hurt all the more in the end.

But I guessed there was no stopping that destruction because Mimi stepped forward. "Well, what are you waitin' on, my girl? Invite the man in. Coffee is almost ready. He's right on time."

There was no missing the glee in her voice.

"Oh, well, I wouldn't want to impose," Jud said, far too innocent.

"Nonsense, you sly dog, get in here. Breakfast is on the stove," she said.

"Well, if you insist." He stepped into our small house.

Holy shit. What was happening?

Darius was going to lose his mind.

But apparently all pretenses were off when Jud squeezed my hip as he passed.

His head nearly touched the low ceiling.

If he hadn't looked like a giant before, there was no mistaking it then. The way his big boots moved across the floor, eating up the space as he made his way to Mimi.

Mimi grinned wide, and Jud was taking a bough of flowers wrapped in ribbon and offering them to her. "Thought I'd pick up a little something for you on the way."

"Oh my," she said, her hand on her chest and her eyes skating to me.

Sly dog, was right.

He tossed a grin my way.

"Uncle Jud?! What the heck are you doin' here?" Gage was pure excitement from the kitchen when he caught sight of his uncle.

"Well, comin' to see some of my favorite people, of course."

Juni screeched. "It's the motorcycle man!"

Jud chuckled, and I felt myself moving that way.

Drawn.

He knelt down on a single knee and handed her one of the bouquets, this sweet little one with glittery hearts on sticks surrounded by tiny pink roses.

"Is those for me?" I was pretty sure Juni swooned.

"They sure are, Juni Bee."

"Sly dog," Mimi muttered as I came to a stop by her side. "And holy hell, he is a looker. You are done for, girl."

"Mimi." I whispered the warning low.

She laughed and turned her gaze on me. Though it'd gone soft and tender and sure. "Dreams, sweet child, dreams. It's time to reach out and take some of them for yourself."

Chapter Twenty-Six

Jud

I WASN'T SURE IF I WAS PLAYING DIRTY OR PLAYING FOR KEEPS.

The only thing I knew was I'd gotten about halfway back to my place and couldn't do anything but turn around.

I couldn't handle the uncertainty that had taken Salem over since the moment she'd stirred in my arms this morning.

And fuck, I liked her there.

I wanted to keep her wrapped up and tucked away, her heart drumming against mine. I wanted to stay tangled with her sweet, hot body all goddamn day.

Maybe forever.

Because shit, the girl had blown my mind.

Turned me upside down, inside out. I no longer knew if I was coming or going each time I crawled back between those thighs to take a little more.

But it'd been far more than the physical. The way we'd stripped each other bare in every fuckin' way.

Hearts and souls and bodies.

The things I'd confessed to her that I'd sworn I'd never give to another person.

She'd held them like she was strong enough to bear the weight.

I'd become certain I was going to bear hers, too.

But I'd felt it—the shift when she'd come to the realization of where she'd woken.

The veil of night no longer obscuring what we'd done or what we'd shared.

I knew the girl had been panicking. Itching to run and hide.

So, I'd taken a chance, and now I was the one kneeling there in front of her adorable daughter, offering her hearts and flowers.

And fuck me, if my heart wasn't bleeding all over the place.

Panicking.

Feet itching to run while that hidden, ugly place begged to stay. To be good enough to stand in their presence. To take up their side and fight for them. Live for them.

Blasphemy.

Fuck.

What was I thinking?

But I couldn't shuck the compulsion when Juni's precious face stretched in this earth-shattering smile, those eyes the same color as her mom's swimming with awe and joy. "Really? Did you knows I love the pink flowers the most?"

My chest stretched tight. "No, I didn't, but I do now, so I'll be sure to remember for next time."

Felt like an oath sliding off my tongue.

Next time.

"You gots a favorite flower?" she asked, her head angling to the side like the question was of utmost importance to her.

Was Juniper considered a flower?

Yeah.

Was losing my mind.

My cool.

My purpose.

"I think I like these ones right here." I tapped one of the roses she had held tight against her chest.

She giggled.

My spirit thrashed.

In too deep.

Footsteps shuffled in behind us, and Salem's grandmother whisked by. "All right then, Juni Bee, why don't you set the table for our company? Mimi is gonna whip us up some pancakes and eggs."

Juni's eyes widened in exuberance. "Just you waits, Motorcycle Man, my mimi makes the best breakfast in ever in ever. Take a seat and I'lls take care of you."

She grabbed me by the hand and hauled me over to where Gage was sitting on his knees at the table. She patted the chair next to him. "Sits right there."

Like I could refuse.

Not a chance.

"Right next to me!" Gage shouted. "I'm glad you got here, Uncle. I've been missin' you like forever."

Yeah, it'd been *like* yesterday since I'd seen him, but I'd take it.

I leaned in and dropped a kiss to the top of his head. "Me, too, Gage in the Cage. Me, too."

I slid into the spot next to him. Couldn't stop the grin from splitting my mouth. Not when my gaze caught on Salem where she watched us from the archway.

Thunderbolt eyes the softest they'd ever been.

My chest panged.

Mayhem going down right in the middle of me.

This want unlike anything I'd ever felt. This connection greater—bigger—than anything I'd experienced.

It felt like I got knocked in the face when I realized it was true.

Did she feel it?

Salem inhaled a shaky breath while she stared back at me, like she'd gotten swept up by the awareness, too.

Then she straightened and walked the rest of the way into the kitchen. She sidled up to her grandmother and set to work.

"Anything I can do to help?" I asked.

Salem's grandmother waved me off. "You just sit there and look pretty. Coffee will be ready in a minute."

My eyebrow quirked.

Pretty?

Salem hid her smile as she pulled out a bowl and measuring cups, and she peeked at me every few seconds as she started to measure and pour in the ingredients.

When the coffee maker beeped, Salem grabbed a mug, filled it, and picked up the carton of creamer and dumped a small splash in the way I always did at the shop.

And shit, yeah, I liked that, too. Liked that she'd been paying attention. Learning me the way I'd been learning her.

She carried it over to me, her breath turning shallow as she rounded the corner. As that need amplified with each step that brought us closer.

"There you go." Her voice was doing that wispy, throaty thing.

Sexy as fuck.

Sweet, too.

Accepting the mug, I let my fingertips brush over hers.

Warmth raced. Her confusion. Her want.

This *thing* that I was so over pretending didn't exist.

"Thank you, darlin'."

"I think that's the way you take it?" she asked, almost hopefully.

"Couldn't ask for anything better." Let the innuendo slide out with that.

Her grandmother hummed a knowing sound from the kitchen.

Yeah, we were in trouble with that one. Woman watching us like a hawk. Clearly, there was no reason for us to keep up with the charade.

Juni came bundling over with a handful of forks, counting them out as she rounded the table. "One, two, three, four, five." She smiled up at me. "There you go."

I grinned at her. "Thank you."

"You gots it, Motorcycle Man."

And shit, I touched her dimpled chin, couldn't stop it, the affection that rose up and took me under.

A flashflood that came from out of nowhere.

Caught me unaware.

Fifteen minutes later, the five of us were sitting around the table eating what was, in fact, *the best breakfast in ever in ever.*

Straight-up delicious.

But I was pretty sure it was the company that made it unforgettable. My nephew on my right and *my girl* on my left. Salem's grandmother sat next to her, and Juni sat squeezed between Mimi and Gage on a high stool since there weren't enough chairs for all of us.

Juni and Gage prattled nonstop, giggling and stuffing their faces while telling the tallest tales, while I let myself get lost in the feeling.

This sensation that a bad piece of me had gone right.

That maybe...*maybe...*

"That was incredible," I said as I took my last bite. I looked across the table at *Mimi,* like she'd insisted I call her. "I really appreciate you inviting me."

She smirked, all kinds of knowing. "I don't think it was me who did the inviting. Some people just head in the direction they belong."

"Mimi." Horror flew from Salem's mouth.

A rough chuckle scraped from mine. Under the table, I set my hand on Salem's thigh and gently squeezed. Fuckin' loved the way she breathed out a tiny sound that lit a fire in my veins. I glanced at Salem and then at her grandmother. "Well, I'm just glad the door was open when I got here."

"Oh, it wasn't open, young man...it seems you possessed the right key to turn the lock." Suggestion filled her words, and the old woman flashed this scandalous smile, her face weathered and aged, but it was clear the mischief had never faded from her mind.

I choked out a laugh.

Groaning, Salem covered her face with her hands. "Mimi. Oh my god."

Mimi laughed low. "Just tellin' it like it is."

"Well, I wish you wouldn't." Salem widened her eyes at her grandmother when she dropped her hands.

Mimi waved a flippant hand in the air. "Now, what would be the fun in that? Everyone should find the one who can love them up right."

I had to turn my head and press my mouth to my sleeve to keep from cracking up.

"I gots the love for Gage," Juni piped in.

"Oh my lord," Salem muttered, almost sliding under the table in embarrassment.

"Yep," Gage agreed, sitting up high on his knees and chewing a giant bite of pancake. "I love her all the way to the sky which is even higher than the mountains."

"Is that so?" I asked him, the kid so damned cute that sometimes it was hard to look at him.

"Yup. We're gonna get married."

A chuckle rumbled up my throat. "Married, huh?"

"Yes, that's right," Juni said. "We decided last night so I can stay here forever and evers and nots ever go on any new adventures because I don't want to nevers leave. But no kissing. Blech."

Juni curled her face in disgust, all while I felt the turmoil slam into Salem. The grief that struck her out of the blue.

I squeezed her thigh tighter and looked at this woman who bore so much pain, those secrets stark in her eyes, like they were trying to fight their way out to me.

Looking for a safe harbor.

Disquiet blustered through the kitchen, the two children completely unaware, while the rest of us were stuck in the reality of a very complicated situation.

A situation my fingers itched with the urge to *uncomplicate*.

Clearing her throat, Mimi stood and gathered Juni and Gage's plates. "Well, that sounds like a mighty fine plan."

There was pain in her voice, too, though she was hiding it the best she could by pressing her lips to Juni's forehead. Juni grinned like mad under her great grandmother's affection.

I squeezed Salem's thigh harder, my heart shouting like mad.

I have you, Salem. I have you. And I'm not going to let you go.

Salem and I stood side-by-side at the kitchen sink. In silence, I rinsed the dishes while she loaded them into the dishwasher. A casual comfort had taken us over as we worked together like it was something we did every day.

Mimi about had a coronary with the idea of a guest doing the dishes, but I told her since I had the *key*, then I guessed it was my place.

She'd cocked me a grin and gave me a pat to the cheek and whispered, "Sly dog," before she'd sauntered off to see what antics Juni and Gage had gotten up to in the other room.

It was damned impossible not to like the woman.

I angled an eye at the one next to me. Every cell in my body fisted. Yeah, it was impossible not to like her, too.

"What?" Salem asked, redness hinting at her cheek when she caught me staring.

"You're so pretty."

Her lips twitched up along with the faint shyness that I glimpsed every now and again.

This vixen who had so many complex layers. I couldn't wait to peel back each one.

"Pretty, huh?" It was a soft play from her mouth as she gave me a little check of her hip that hit me in the thigh since she was at least a foot shorter than me.

Rinsing the last plate, I handed it to her then grabbed the dishtowel on the counter to dry my hands. Salem placed it into the dishwasher and shut the door, pushing a button to make it spin to life.

Like she felt me staring, which I most definitely was doing, she turned to look at me. This woman who was making me forget every single thing I knew about myself.

I slipped my palm along the contour of her jaw, tipped it up, murmured, "Beautiful. Meaning of it. Every part. This face and this body and this heart."

"Jud." My name was affection. A question. Confusion.

"I'm right here, darlin'," I promised her.

"I see that." Then she narrowed those eyes at me. "I thought it was my decision what happened in the morning?"

There was a lilting tease that infiltrated her voice.

"Well, see, gorgeous, I felt some kind of uncertainty on your part on how that was going to go down, so I thought I might nudge you in the right direction."

Her brow arched. "Right direction?"

"One where the two of us meet."

Reservations slithered across her skin, that gaze dimming with them, though I could feel the rest of her reaching for me. As if she could sink right in.

I hesitated, then asked, "What Juniper said earlier? About the adventures..."

I eyed her as I asked it, already knowing the answer. Moisture filled that gaze, and she blew out a heavy sigh as she nodded. "It's what I started telling her when I'd rush to pack our things and we'd leave in the night...that we were going on an adventure."

My thumb traced her lips, and I tried to keep it together, to rein the stampede that was going to trample my soul. "To keep her from being scared?"

She could barely nod.

"You're amazing."

She started to shake her head, to pull away, but I forced her to remain looking at me.

"Need you to promise me one thing."

Her expression twisted in question. In the trust there was no doubt was hard for her to give.

"Next time you get *scared*? Next time you want to *run*? Promise me you'll run to me."

"I'm scared every single day, Jud." Her confession was out on a pained breath.

I took her by both sides of the face. "I have you, Salem. I have you."

I leaned in, intent on kissing the hell out of her, when the doorbell rang.

Salem pulled back to put three inches between us, though I couldn't find it in me to let her free of my grip.

Juni raced to the window to peer out through the drape. "Oh, no, it's your mom and dad, Gage."

Juni cried it like it was the end of the world.

I couldn't help but grin. "She is something, Salem. The cutest little thing."

Tenderness ridged her lips, though her expression rippled with heartache. "I'm sorry if it hurts you, being around her," she clarified.

My head shook, and I took her hand, kissed her knuckles. "No, baby, she's a part of you."

Fuck.

There I went.

Sinking in.

Deeper and deeper.

Salem froze for a beat before she seemed to shake herself out of it and stepped back far enough to break the connection. She glanced at me once as she turned then eased into the living room. I followed close behind.

Juni freed the lock and opened the door wide.

"Gage can't goes yet, we aren't done playing our game and he gots to stay and finish because Imma about to win. Girls rule, you know." All of it had flooded from Juni's mouth before anyone got the chance to say hello.

Soft affection breezed from Eden's laughter, and she ran her hand over the top of Gage's head as she stepped inside. "Oh, well, I'm sorry to interrupt. How about five more minutes, and then we need to get out of their hair."

"Hair? You aren't in our hair." Juni squished up her nose.

So damned cute.

Eden looked our way. Kindness shined from her being.

"Eden, hi," Salem whispered, going for her friend at the same time Eden moved her way. Eden wrapped her arms around her and hugged her tight.

Trent entered behind, uneasy as usual, eyes darting around like he was assessing for a threat. That unease was shifting into a disbelieving smirk when he saw me hovering in the kitchen like I had the right to be there.

"I was worried about you," Eden whispered to Salem as she pulled back. "Are you okay?"

Salem angled her head. "Why don't you and Trent come into the kitchen for a cup of coffee while we wait for the kids to finish?"

Four of us piled back into the kitchen while the kids went back to their game on the floor.

Salem grabbed two new cups, poured them, while I went to the refrigerator and pulled out the creamer I'd just placed in there.

Trent pitched me a glance, scratching at his temple in speculation.

I grunted at him in response.

Yeah. I was fucked. Already knew it. No need for him to rub it in.

"How is Tessa?" Salem whispered, keeping her voice low.

Distress passed through Eden's expression while rage tweaked every muscle in Trent's body.

"She was more upset than anything. Worried about you," Eden added cautiously. "That's why we both came. To see how you are. If there's anything we can do?"

Anger spiraled through my being.

"I'm fine. I was just…caught off guard," Salem said. "Tessa's not hurt, though?"

"Someone else is about to be." Trent rumbled that below his breath.

Eden pushed out a sigh. "No. Not physically. She is hurt. Hurt that Karl would pull something like that."

"Prick." Another low rumble from Trent.

"Asshole get picked up?" I asked, arms crossing over my chest like it could stop the injection of violence the thought of that fucker pumped into my veins.

"Yup," Trent grunted.

In worry, Eden chewed at the inside of her lip.

"What is it?" Salem asked.

"Tessa bailed him out this morning." Eden rushed it like a disappointed secret.

"The hell?" I spat.

Seriously, what the hell was that girl thinking? I didn't know Tessa all that well, but I sure as fuck knew her well enough to know she deserved better than that pompous dick.

Eden glanced between us. "Between his manipulation and the pressure from her family, I think she feels stuck. Like she doesn't have any other choice but to stay with him."

I stepped forward. "I say we unstick her, then."

Trent chuckled a dark sound. "Second that."

Eden reached out and grabbed Trent by his forearm. "You will do nothing of the sort. Tessa will be leaving him. I'll see to it. But not at the expense of either of you."

She looked directly between the two of us.

Eden knew it all.

The dark. The dirty. The grim.

"Promise me," she demanded.

Frustration huffed from Trent's nose.

Was with him.

Sometimes it was so much easier to manage things when you weren't living on the straight and narrow.

Trent edged around behind Eden, wrapped his arm around her waist, and whispered at the shell of her ear, "Fine. I promise, Kitten."

The look Eden gave me was hard. "No more blood, Jud."

Razors filled my throat as that demon screamed.

All mixed with the promise I'd made myself that night.

I will never kill again.

Salem touched my arm.

So softly.

So right.

I gave Eden a tight nod. "I promise."

A commotion broke out in the other room, and Gage and Juni came bounding our way.

The two of them burst through the archway, nothing but giggles and smiles as they fought to get in front of the other. "We finished ours game and Gage won, he saids it was fair and square, but I'm not so sure, but Mimi said it was a sneaks attack!"

"Boom, bang, kapow." Gage did one of his wrestling moves with an adorable kick, then he went beelining for his dad. He grabbed him by the hand. He started to jump when he asked, "Dad, it's Sunday, and you know what that means. You're gonna teach me to ride my bike without any of the training wheels because I'm so big and ready now, right, Dad, right?"

"It is Sunday, isn't it? Seems like that must be the plan." Tenderness coated the ferocity that was Trent when he looked down at his son.

Squealing, Juni moved to stand in front of her mother. She threaded her fingers together in a prayer. "Mommy, do we gots enough monies that we can get my bike today so I can learns to ride with Gage? I want to learn so bad, right now."

"Juni—" Salem hesitated.

I looked at Salem with a plea of my own, cutting off whatever reason she was going to give that it couldn't happen right then. I took the woman's hand in mine.

Overcome.

Unable to stop it.

Blasphemy.

This magic I couldn't resist.

Let me come alongside you.

A war filled her expression, a line denting her forehead, her eyes full of fear and building belief.

But I saw her yielding.

When her heart gave me the go to say whatever it was I was going to say.

I turned to Juni. "Just so happens your mom said that's what she'd planned for today, and I thought maybe we should go pick it up in my truck."

"Really?" she squealed.

"Yup."

"Can it be pink likes my flowers?"

A low chuckle rippled out, and my fingers were brushing through her hair.

Emotion crested.

Rising high.

Higher than every reservation.

Devotion.

Loyalty.

Affection.

"What other color would there be?"

She grabbed my hand and started to haul me toward the door.

I looked back.

Trent was staring over at me, smug look filling his face.

I had to admit he was right. We never had any idea when life was going to sweep in and shake us up.

"Mimi, we're goin' to get a pinks bike and then we'll be rights back," she said as she blazed through the living room, dragging me along.

Mimi grinned at me. "I approve of this plan."

When we stepped outside, Trent, Eden, and Gage started in the direction of their house.

"Meet us out here in two hours?" I told Trent.

He slapped me on the shoulder as he passed. "Yeah, man, yeah, we'll be here."

I jutted my chin in parting, and Salem slipped out the door and snapped it shut behind her.

I turned when she did.

The breath hitched in my throat.

Fuck me.

Sweet enchantress.

She paused on the top step.

Held like me.

Watching where I'd stopped halfway down the walkway with her little girl's hand in mine.

That energy pulsed.

Though this time, it was different.

Profound.

Dread and hope and dead dreams resurrected.

I saw them twist into a disorder.

While my insides sparked with something I shouldn't feel.

I tightened my hold on her daughter.

Salem finally moved, and I stayed glued to the spot while she made her way down the sidewalk. When she got close enough, I wrapped my arm around her waist and pulled her snug.

I kissed her slow and gentle.

Juni giggled.

"You kissed my mommy. Nows she's your girlfriend."

I looked down at the little thing whose grin was so wide it curled up her entire face.

"That so?"

"Yes. It's the rules. Gage tolds me so."

The hint of a smile tugged at the corners of Salem's lush mouth, and I splayed my hand wide at the small of her back. "Well, then I guess if it's the rules."

I winked at my girl.

"You're ridiculous," Salem whispered back.

"I've been called worse."

Juni tugged at my hand. "Come on, we gotta go rights now."

I followed Salem to the little SUV sitting in the drive.

One I'd called in and finalized the purchase of Friday because I sure as shit wasn't going to put her back in her pile of a car. I just hadn't told her yet.

She grabbed Juni's booster, and I situated it in the backseat of my truck.

Under the arms, I lifted Juni, letting her soar through the air before I tucked her into the seat.

She laughed and giggled and twisted me up in every single one of her little fingers. "Thank you, Motorcycle Man."

I touched her nose. "You're welcome, Juni Bee."

Shutting her door, I moved to help Salem step up into the high cab, then I jogged around to climb in on my side. I started the engine and began to pull from the curb, though I stopped when I saw the black truck slow as it approached from the opposite direction.

Salem tensed, and Darius glared as he passed, that barely constrained rage burning in his eyes.

"Crap," she mumbled when he disappeared behind us.

I reached out and squeezed Salem's hand. "Baby, it doesn't matter what he thinks. It's you and me now, and he's gonna have to get used to it."

Chapter Twenty-Seven

Salem

"ARE YOU SURE YOU DON'T WANT TO PUT THESE ON?" Nervously, I held up the training wheels that had come with Juniper's pink bike. "I think we might want to start there since your bike is brand new," I encouraged.

It was futile.

Juni had already shot the idea down about five million times since we'd returned, and Jud had spread a work blanket out on the driveway and gotten straight to work.

He chuckled low.

Dark and deep and sweet.

"Worrier." He grinned up at me.

"Obviously." I was happy to take the title. It's what I did.

Juni had of course picked the frilliest bike there was at the store. Pink with flower accents and ribbons coming off the handlebars.

From where she was kneeling next to Jud on a work blanket *helping*, Juni looked up at me like I was clueless. "Um, Mommy, doncha know I'm alreadys so big and I has to go fast so I can keep up with my best friend? Otherwise, he's gonna leave me rights in the dust."

Doncha already know? Jud mouthed it from behind her as he worked a ratchet to place a screw.

My stomach tilted.

Apparently, I knew nothing.

I was clueless.

Foolish.

Reckless.

Letting myself get absolutely swept away by this bearded, mountain of a man. He fought a grin where he knelt in front of the bike with a wrench in his hand, almost finished piecing it together.

He had a tool bag that he'd pulled from the back of his truck, and he continually rummaged through it to find what he needed, the man focused and intent and still patient, answering the gazillion questions Juni lobbed at him as he worked.

So gorgeous in his jeans and tee. The material stretching over the lines and planes of his back. The muscles in his arms flexing as he cranked and screwed, and damn…

I had to bite my lip when he glanced up at me again. In an instant, a smirk took to his face.

Crap. He totally knew I was enjoying the show.

Sure, I'd seen him working over plenty of *bikes* at the shop.

But this? This was different.

It was personal.

Intimate.

As if he were building something from the rubble.

Breathing it back to life.

With it? I didn't know how to stand there without letting my mind wander to the places I shouldn't let it.

Into a fantasy where this was normal.

Where it was right.

Where I didn't have the urge to look over my shoulder to make sure it was safe.

That my daughter could play outside without an ounce of fear.

Where loving this man wouldn't put him in danger.

It was that hope that bloomed and blossomed and became something terrifying.

Because *forever* whispered in my ear.

Taunting me with what the rational side of myself knew I could never keep but I wanted, anyway.

For him to touch me the way he had last night.

Ruin me.

Keep me.

This man who'd wormed his way in so thoroughly, I could literally feel his heart beating through my being, as if he'd become the blood in my veins.

This fierce, hard, intimidating man who was so incredibly sweet.

One who was broken and carried a guilt so dark and ugly I could almost physically feel the outline of the scars on his spirit.

And I wanted to heal it—heal it the way he was healing me. Like Mimi had said, the scars and the vacancies would never fully fill, but there was someone out there who could help hold them so they didn't hurt quite so bad.

Jud eyed me like he'd felt the crash of reservations as he angled up to secure the basket on the handlebars. "You good, darlin'?"

"Yep."

A smirk slanted at the edge of his mouth.

So sexy.

My stomach twisted.

"Huh, you look like you're itching to take a run." He said it like a tease, though there was no missing the current that ran through it. "And here I would have thought you'd have had plenty of exercise last night."

"Nope, still plenty of energy," I tossed out, popping up on my toes.

"Good thing," he grated, so low, the words a promise that slicked across my flesh.

Shivers flashed.

He chuckled a dark sound.

Damn him.

He knew exactly what he was doing to me.

"And why's that?" I cocked my head, mock innocence in my voice. "Did you have something in mind?"

Yeah, I should probably keep my mouth shut.

Balancing the bike upright, he reached over and tipped up my chin. "Sweet Enchantress…but now you're not playin' so sweet."

"I like sweets, you wants some cookies?" Juni piped in, scrambling to her feet.

Jud laughed and dipped in and kissed my temple. "We'll revisit this later, baby."

He turned to Juni. "How about we save the cookies for later and we take this thing for a spin first?"

"Oh, yes!" She clasped her hands together. "I gotta gets my helmet and my pads and my best friend, then I'll be all ready."

"I'll let them know."

Jud thumbed into his phone and sent Trent a text.

A minute later, their front door flew open.

Gage came blazing out, hopping the whole way down to the edge of the street. "My dad said your bike is done. Are you ready, Juni Bee? We gotta race."

"Ah, I think we aren't quite ready for racing yet, buddy," Trent told him as he went to wheel Gage's bike from the carport and down the driveway, a helmet hanging from the handlebars.

Eden came out behind them, a soft smile on her face.

"But Dad, that's what the wheels are for. The racin'." Gage lowered his voice like it was a secret.

Clearly, Lawson blood beat fast in his veins.

"It's okay, we can do the races. I'll beat you so bad, you ain't never gonna knows what hit you! Bet you five dollars," Juni shouted.

Apparently, my daughter was secretly competitive. "Um, you don't have five dollars, Juni Bee."

She took Jud's hand. "Who needs money when you gots a motorcycle man."

My heart panged, and my attention whipped up to Jud's face. Jud who looked like he was stricken.

He pressed his free hand to his chest, then he grinned at me, so soft, so tender, riddled with affection. "Seems I got stung by a little bee."

Lightheadedness swept through my head.

A wave of joy and hope.

Needing to distract myself from the impact of it, so unexpected, so right, I rushed to help Juni into her helmet and the set of pads Jud had gotten for her knees and elbows.

I had to remind myself I couldn't rely on anyone but myself. I was just begging for the pain. Because this man was carving out a place for himself inside me, and I was terrified of it becoming a vacancy.

Another hole that throbbed and moaned for all of eternity. I knew it, knew it too well, the way it felt when you lost something so important you no longer could remember how to breathe.

How to walk.

How to move on.

Jud touched my hand that I didn't realize was shaking, that my movements had turned jittery as I'd ensured all of Juni's protective gear was tight and secure.

"Darlin', it's okay."

The words were a hard scrape.

A score in the air.

I swallowed hard.

He looked at me like I was a treasure.

What was I doing? But I couldn't do anything but watch when Jud patted the seat of the pink bicycle. "Hop on, Juni Bee."

She squealed, and he helped her get settled, showed her how to work the brakes and the pedals, all while keeping her upright.

Gage went jetting by with Trent running behind him to hold him up so he could learn how to pedal and balance.

"I'm flying, Juni! You better hurry up! I'm gonna ride up the highest mountain and then shoot all the way to the stars."

"Don't leaves me!" she shouted, pushing her feet hard at the pedals. Jud started to jog behind her, keeping her straight.

Emotion gathered in my chest.

A fist.

A crush.

A caress.

Tears blurred my eyes as I stepped out onto the street behind them to watch two brothers who I knew had suffered so much pain, take up the simple, ordinary task of teaching these two children how to ride their bikes.

So much patience.

So much care.

And I wondered if Trent thanked God that he had his son, safe and secure, and if it was killing Jud that his daughter was out there somewhere. That he didn't know her. If his own vacancy was shouting out inside of him.

Condemning.

Reminding him of what he'd done.

I jumped when the hand took mine. I glanced to the left at Eden who had come up beside me. She squeezed my hand as we both gazed out at the men racing and laughing with the children.

Juni was screaming, her movements a little erratic as she jerked at the handlebars.

"Just relax, Juni, and go with the flow. I have you. I have you," Jud repeated.

I have you.

My heart throbbed and my spirit moaned.

"I see so much of my fiancé in you," she whispered out into the distance. "He was so scared of it…scared of loving someone. That he would be wrong to accept it."

My throat suddenly felt tight, burning as the old wounds writhed.

I could feel her glance at me, though I couldn't look away from where Jud laughed as he ran along holding Juni up.

A shield.

Fierce, unrelenting armor.

A cushion that would catch her, waiting beneath.

They guided the bikes in circles, raced the straightaways, crisscrossed as Juni and Gage chased each other.

Giggles and joy floated on the summer air, all while Trent and Jud jumped in on the taunts.

"You're going down."

"Ha, you don't even know what's coming for you."

Everyone teasing and playing.

Easy.

Right.

"Different, of course," Eden added, "but in the end, it's always the tragedies, the mistakes, our scars, and our regrets that hold us back from the goodness—the gifts—that are waiting for us to receive them."

"Me and Jud? Oh, we're just having fun." The lie felt like a thousand-pound weight. "We both agreed that neither of us are in a position to fall in love."

Eden let go of a soft scoff, one made of gentle disbelief. "You think that man doesn't love you? I doubt I've ever seen anything so blatant as what he feels for you."

Fear bottled tight. It constricted my throat.

"He can't..."

I trailed off.

Because the truth was, I couldn't...I couldn't let myself fall.

Be so reckless.

I was just worried I was already there.

"Let go, Dad!" Gage shouted. "Faster! I gotta go faster!"

"You're sure you're ready?"

"Yep!"

"Remember how to brake."

"I know, Dad, I know!"

Trent let Gage go.

Gage wobbled for a second before he took off by himself.

He screeched when he realized he was unassisted. "I'm doing it! I'm doing it! Look it, Mommy! Look it, Juni! I bet you can't catch me! You see that mountain over there? That's where I'm going all the way to the top."

His entire face was full of a grin.

Juni followed behind, Jud right behind her.

Her rock.

Her fortress.

"You ready to try, Juni Bee?" he asked her.

"I don't knows!" she shouted at him, terror in her eyes as they whizzed back by on the other side.

He chuckled. "I'll be right here beside you. You need me, I have you."

My heart rattled.

"Okay, I can do it! I wants to be like you, Motorcycle Man!"

He let her go.

My daughter soared.

Rode and played and *lived*.

My chest stretched. Pressed full. Overflowed.

I thought there was a chance it might burst.

Jud ran along beside her. "You're doing it, Juni. Look at you, big girl."

"I's doing it!"

Trent jogged beside Gage, and the four of them headed up the road.

"Come on, let's go." Eden giggled and tugged at my hand, and we jogged after them, laughing, too.

Juni was singing, "I'm riding, all by myself."

"You can't catch me," Gage shouted at her.

Juni pedaled faster in a bid to catch up. She pedaled up and over the little hump in the road, pulling away from Jud who ran behind her.

She was cracking up when she passed by Gage. "I'm winning!"

I wondered if Jud saw it at the exact same time as I did. The car sitting at the curb that radiated evil.

The way a bolt of rage struck in the air when Jud recognized it.

The way fear spiked through the heavens like a fiery, poisoned arrow.

Jud was no longer laughing but sprinting behind her. He grabbed Juni from the bike and yanked her against his chest in a bid of protection. Her bike kept going, flying forward, tumbling and skidding across the ground.

The driver of the same black car that had been outside Jud's shop suddenly tore from the curb and sped away.

Jud held Juniper like he was a shield. His giant shoulders heaved with aggression.

Trent grabbed hold of Gage and stilled him as the squeal of tires at the end of the road echoed through the neighborhood, as the engine accelerated before it disappeared in the distance and a bated silence took over.

Nothing but panted, shocked breaths, clanging, horrified hearts, and the frantic clattering of my footfalls as I ran for Juni.

The second I had her in my arms, my legs gave, knees going weak.

I dropped to them on the hard pavement, hugging my daughter to my chest.

"Salem." Jud's deep voice rolled through the tense, bottled air.

A sob of torment—the truth that this would never end—tore from my lungs.

Strength and hope gone. The truth that he would always, always catch up to me.

Chapter Twenty-Eight

Salem

Twenty Years Old

Salem edged down the hall of Carlo's office. She didn't know what stalled her feet. Why she slowed. Why the hairs at her nape lifted in dread or why sickness churned in her belly.

She'd dropped by his realty office on her way back from the store. She'd thought she'd stop to offer her help since she was bored out of her mind. Maybe fiddle around at the front desk. Organize something. Make calls. Find leads.

Whatever.

The only thing she knew was she ached to go to school. To work. To create something with her mind and hands.

To do something other than flit her days away at the ostentatious house Carlo had built for them where they now lived on the opposite side of the city.

Miles away from her mimi.

An eternity away from her heart.

She'd thought she'd at least try to do something that mattered.

Give it a shot.

Make Carlo see she was more than a *pretty face meant to be waiting for him at home.*

His words, not hers.

She was second guessing that decision right then.

Chills scattered when she heard the voices coming from his office at the back.

She edged that way, quietly…so quietly.

Not because of the way the voices were lifted. But because of the way they were controlled.

She made it to Carlo's office door that was cracked open an inch. Her heart battered at her ribs as she heard his words curl through the air, "You had a second chance. You were warned, were you not?"

His tone was casual and cruel.

Condescending.

She peeked through the slit left in the door.

Her entire being stuttered. Coiled and locked.

A man was on his knees in front of Carlo's desk. His hands were bound behind his back and a gun was to his head.

Carlo sat behind the desk, an elbow propped on the arm of the chair and the side of his head rested against his fingers. As if he were more annoyed than anything else.

As if this were common.

An everyday problem to be dealt with.

"Carlo, please," the man begged.

Carlo shook his head. "You know the rules. You had your second chance. You failed."

Salem jolted when the shot rang out. Her hand flew to her mouth to stop the scream that raced her throat and fought to make its way out.

Tears blinded her eyes.

Heavy and horrified.

Her heart screamed.

Her stomach soured.

Her still flat stomach that she clutched like she could keep the child safe.

She had to.

She had to.

"Clean this mess up," Carlo ordered, and footsteps began to thud.

She pressed herself behind the partition. Hid. Stifled her cries.

And when it was clear, Salem ran.

A scream tore up Salem's throat as she was tossed to the floor of Talia's apartment where she'd sought refuge until she knew where she was going to go. She tumbled then scrambled around to sitting, holding her knees to her chest.

Violently, she shook.

Shook and shook.

Carlo treaded forward on his shiny dress shoes.

He knelt in front of her, tilted her chin up with the tip of the knife.

The blade gleamed in the slivers of light that burned through the room.

"Salem." He tsked. "Why so foolish?"

"I…I—" She couldn't find the words.

A reason to give.

A *purpose* other than the one that she had to get away from there.

Whatever the cost.

"Did you see what you made me do?"

He gestured to Talia's body slumped in the middle of the room where her best friend had bled out. Agony clutched Salem's spirit. Horror and guilt and hate.

How could he?

She squeezed her eyes closed as if she could block it.

"Such a shame." He tipped her chin up higher. The tip pierced her skin the barest fraction.

She suppressed a scream, though her body still shuddered.

"I thought you were smarter than that, no?"

A whimper got free.

He clicked his tongue, and she shrieked when he suddenly took her by the hair and yanked her to standing. He hauled her to the middle of the room and forced her to look down where Talia lay. He was behind her when he hauled her back against his chest, the knife at her throat. "I warned you not to waste my time with ridiculous antics. I was worried…searching everywhere for you…for two days, Salem. How could you put me through that?"

"I'm sorry." It rocked from her throat.

"You're lucky I believe in second chances, Salem. You get one," he warned in her ear.

Then he gripped her by the chin and dragged the knife up her jaw.

Blinding pain seared through her being as he cut deep into her flesh.

Her head spun and the world canted to the side.

Blackness flickered at the edges of her sight.

Still, she heard the warning before passing out on the floor. "It's the last one you get. I suggest you don't forget it."

Chapter Twenty-Nine

Jud

I'D OFTEN WONDERED THE DAY THE DEMON WAS BORN.

If who I'd become had purely been a circumstance of my upbringing. If it was due to my mother's fear when we'd been little boys, the way she'd tried to shield and protect, all while her cries would seep through the walls at night, fill my ears, and make me be the one who wanted to shield and protect *her*. The way she'd promised she'd find a way out, that everything would be better, until the day all four of us had to stand and watch as she'd been brutally mowed down.

If it'd manifested that day into abounding rage and eternal hate.

Possibly it'd bloomed in my blood the day I was conceived, and the wickedness of my father had been passed on to me.

Or maybe it had already been a piece of my soul, grabbing a free ride when I'd been plucked from Hell to walk this Earth.

I was betting on the latter right then.

Because fury had taken up residence at the base of my throat. Wrath was the only thing I could taste. Bitter venom on my tongue because God knew, the vengeance itching at my hands was sharp as a blade.

I didn't think I'd ever felt more helpless than I had yesterday afternoon.

That straight-up fear that had hit me so hard I might as well have run flat into a brick wall when I'd seen the blacked-out BMW about six houses down from Salem's.

In an instant, my spirit had seized as awareness smacked me in the face. A swell of depravity in the atmosphere, a crash of evil blistering through the rays of late afternoon light.

I'd grabbed Juni. Held her tight.

I'd known, right then, that I'd do whatever it took to protect her.

That I wouldn't let go.

The car had been gone in a split, fucker taking off before I could get a chance to catch a glimpse of who was inside, my focus all wrapped up in making sure that Juni was okay.

But right now, it was Salem I was dying to wrap up and hold. Promise her it would be okay. Honestly, I was shocked she'd shown at work today. Hell, if I were being honest, I was shocked she'd *stayed*.

The entire day today, I'd watched her riding a razor-sharp edge, wearing those heels and a modest black floral dress, girl so apprehensive it was alive in every step she took.

Anxious.

Agitated.

Afraid.

Nah.

She wasn't okay.

Could feel it.

The energy that whipped and thrashed and howled.

Bashing against the walls and trembling along the floors.

A warning that shook me to the core.

My girl was getting ready to run.

It had taken forever to get her calmed down yesterday afternoon. With the commotion out front, Darius had come running, demanding to know what the hell I'd done.

Had wanted to clock the asshole in the face.

I knew it only came from worry, though. Knew the same fears that lived inside Salem lived inside him. He'd uprooted his life and moved here to a place where Salem would be safe. Even if he hated me, he wanted the same thing for her that I did.

Her freedom.

Her joy.

Her peace.

So, I'd sucked it up and allowed him to help us get her back to the house. I'd hovered and worried, sharing glances with Trent, both of us on edge.

All while poor Juni kept touching her mother's hand and telling her it was going to be fine. When she'd said, "See, Mommy, the bad man is gone. We don't gots to worry. We can stays right here. We don't need to goes on a new adventures."

It'd ripped out my fuckin' heart.

Like the adorable smile she pinned on her mouth would make everything better, and just claiming it would make it true.

This little thing who wanted to *stay*.

Darius had knelt in front of where we'd seated Salem on the couch, brushing her hair back and insisting it was a random car. He'd done his best to coax her into peace. He said it was probably someone who lived in the neighborhood or maybe a friend who stopped by often, which would be a good explanation for it showing twice.

He'd told her time and again it was her paranoia getting the best of her.

Personally, I'd known his suggestions were bullshit, especially considering I was certain it was the same car that had been lurking outside my shop.

I hadn't argued, though, since it'd been the only thing that had gotten Salem to settle. What bought me the time I was gonna need to weed this fucker out and put him in the ground.

Darius had taken her by the face, said, "You're fine. You're not going anywhere. Promise me you won't just leave."

She'd sniffled and taken a deep breath, whispered, "I promise."

All while the demon inside me had raged.

Because even when I'd finally stepped out of her house after nine last night, I didn't get far. I'd sat in my truck, standing guard.

Even once the sun had cracked the sky, I'd still been buzzing. On alert as I'd followed Salem to the shop.

She'd been here for three hours without saying a word to me. Lost in her worry.

I tried to focus on work, but the only thing I could feel was her anxiety winding tight, and I couldn't do anything but edge into the reception area again, needing to check on the one who'd upended my world.

My skin prickled the second I stepped inside.

A storm on the horizon. One that made landfall the second I felt her spirit thrash through the room.

It beat the fuck out of my insides. Destroying me in the best and worst of ways.

She wasn't behind the desk, and in an instant, I looked to the farthest wall of the lobby where a counter ran the length. She stood away from me and facing the counter, slowly stirring a cup of coffee, those long locks of black cascading down her back, that dress hugging her curves, wearing those heels she was killing me with day after day.

But her head was drooped between her sagging shoulders, this fierce, brave girl curling in on herself, turmoil radiating from her being.

I knew she felt me.

That energy zapped.

Vibrations pulsed from her body, skidding through the air and trembling across my flesh.

A flashfire of greed staked through my chest.

Possession.

Didn't have the first clue which of us was compelling the other, just knew there was no destination other than the one where we met.

Slowly, I edged closer. My boots thudded the floor with each measured step, and my heart climbed into my throat, cutting off the flow of oxygen.

Chills rippled down her arms as I inched up behind her.

Girl withdrew and withheld.

Wavering.

Wanting to run and hide, all while desperate to sink back into my hold at the same damned time.

"Baby." The word was a ragged grunt.

All those barriers hardened, and she gritted the defense, "I'm not your baby, Jud."

My mouth moved to her ear. "Aren't you?"

My hands found the caps of her shoulders, and I ran my palms down her trembling arms until I threaded the fingers of both our hands together.

A shiver rocked down her spine.

"I don't know if I can do this, Jud." Her voice slipped into grief.

"What's that?"

"Stay."

Every cell in my body revolted. I tightened my hands around hers. "I know you're afraid, darlin'."

It would have been a scoff coming from her mouth if the sound hadn't have held so much pain. "Afraid? I'm *terrified,* Jud. Every day of my life is this. Trying to stay one step ahead of him, petrified of the day he catches up to me."

"Give me a name."

Salem's head shook. "You can't fix this."

"Let me try."

"It's not your burden."

My spirit roared and the demon writhed. I swallowed it down and slowly turned her in my hold.

Blue eyes speared me, but where they normally flamed and struck and stormed with determination, they'd dimmed with defeat.

I touched her jaw, running my thumb over the scar that represented everything that she was.

A fighter.

A survivor.

Beautiful, inside and out.

"Not sure how it could be a burden, Salem. Not when you've become my everything."

Anguish lanced through her expression. I tipped her chin up farther. "Is this when it normally happens? When you pack up and go?"

Salem blinked and her head barely shook. "No, Jud, normally it's just instinct. The feeling that I've stayed too long. That I've become complacent, exposed. I leave long before I get the feeling someone might be watching me. That's the moment I turn to vapor all over again. If I were anywhere else? I'd have left the first day I noticed that car lurking around. But because of Darius? Because of Mimi? Because I want to give my daughter a home? Because of *you*...?"

She trailed off, unable to say it aloud.

We had kept her here. Given her a reason to stay. Given her hope.

I wanted to give her more of them.

A thousand of them. All of it. All of me.

Purpose.

Ferocity fired through the dimness of Salem's eyes. "If he had found us before, Jud? If he'd caught up to us any time in all these years I've been running? You need to understand...we wouldn't be here. And if that car..."

Alarm bled through her aura, pulsed like the blare of a warning.

Barbs of fury spiked in my insides, demon clawing for a way out. Still, my touch was soft as I took her gorgeous face in my hands. I begged her, "I asked one thing of you, Salem. Asked the next time you felt the urge to run, that you would run to me. Run to me, baby."

"And what if I crash right into you? What if the weight causes you to fall?"

I cocked a grin I could barely afford. "Nonsense, darlin'. Have you seen me?"

She choked a soggy laugh, and tears got loose of her eyes. They streaked down her cheeks and into my hands.

"Run to me," I murmured again.

"Jud." My name was a whimper.

Hope and fear and ecstasy.

"You're real, Salem. You aren't vapor. You exist. You're real and whole and mine. *Exist with me.*"

She was in my arms before another denial could fall from her lips.

I lifted her off her feet and slanted my mouth over hers. I had one hand in her hair and the other arm looped around her back.

Her hands were frantic as she tried to find a place to take hold. Fingers in my hair. On my face. Sinking into my shoulders. She curled her arms around my neck while I held her close. Her heart beat wild, an insurgence that overtook mine.

My tongue stroked into the sweet well of that delicious mouth.

Lapping.

Licking.

Salem moaned a tiny, needy sound, and I was carrying her toward the bathroom that was just to the left of the counter. I flipped on the light switch and was quick to turn the lock. I moved another step inside and propped her on the counter. I wedged myself between those thighs, tugged her closer, kissed her deeper.

"Jud." It was a breath. Throaty and seductive, and fuck…

"I have you," I promised, letting my hands wander her back, sliding over her hips and to the outside of her thighs. I tugged her so she was barely hanging onto the edge and rocked her pussy against my jean-covered cock.

She whimpered, "More. I need you. I need you. I need it all."

"You have me, darlin'."

It was the goddamn truth.

I was done for. Done for.

This girl possession.

A fantasy.

A dream.

I was straight-up spellbound.

"Enchantress," I rumbled at that mouth as I rushed to shove the skirt of her dress up around her waist. Her legs exposed and those thighs lush. My fingers sank right in.

Every movement between us was wild.

Desperate for more when it wasn't ever going to be enough.

"Please," she uttered low as she jerked at the button of my jeans. As she kissed a feverish path over my shirt. The sound of my zipper being ripped wide open echoed against the walls. It mixed with our haggard breaths, with the pants that jutted from our lungs.

In a second flat, she had her greedy little hands on my dick.

She stroked me hard. I grunted, edged back far enough that I could grab hold of her underwear and rip them down her legs. And she was right there, angled back on the counter, her legs spread wide.

Bare, her cunt glistening with her need.

"Always so wet, darlin'. So fuckin' sweet," I rumbled.

I had the aching head of my cock pressed to her center.

A firestorm whipped through the tiny room.

I ground out a hiss at the contact, and I took her by the outside of the thighs.

Wasn't breathing as I watched myself stretch her wide. As I rocked and jutted and pushed my way into her tight little body.

Bliss clawed its way along my spine.

Girl too much.

Perfect and right and everything.

Salem was gasping, shaking as I filled her, hands under my shirt and pushing it up before her nails were raking down my skin, like she was searching for a way in.

I groaned out when I was fully seated. "Fuck, yes, darlin'."

Then I was crushing my mouth back over hers.

Fever reheating.

I took her hard. Every stroke of my hips possession as I slipped my arms under her legs and took her by the waist to angle her just right.

Thrusts deep and desperate.

She held onto my shoulders.

Stifled moans wheezed from her mouth as I scored myself into her body.

As I marked her.

Every fuckin' dive of my dick was a claim.

A proclamation.

Could feel her winding up.

Every nerve ending in her body came alive.

Like all of them were arching toward me.

Pleasure radiated from her being like a shimmery, blinding light.

And I couldn't get close enough.

Wanted to fall in and sink under and disappear in her storm.

Get lost there forever.

"Forever." I didn't mean for it to slip out as I picked her up off the counter and pressed her to the door.

I needed her closer.

I pinned her against the metal.

Felt the coolness echo through the heat.

The flames.

The fire.

I bucked into her as she rode over me.

Hard.

Explosive.

Wild.

Her gasps were mine and my grunts became hers.

The air crackled.

A picture fell from the trembling wall and crashed to the floor as I pounded into her. Chasing down the sensation that burned around us like one of those dreams.

Tangible but unattainable.

It only spun us farther. Wound us into this disorder that only belonged to us.

Our bodies melding.

Molding.

Melting into bliss.

Felt it when she split.

When her walls clamped down around my cock and every molecule of her body blew.

A total eruption.

Her nails sank into my shoulders, and she burrowed her open

mouth against my throat in a silent scream as the orgasm streaked through her body.

Salem tremored and throbbed and shot me into paradise.

Where it was just me and her.

I surged and jerked as my sight blurred at the edges.

I finally tripped.

Every promise I'd ever made myself no longer existed.

Because every part of me belonged to this girl.

Salem sucked for a breath while I held her tight where she was pressed to the door.

I edged back an inch, my arms a fortress around her body. "I have you, Salem, I have you."

Emotion crested through her features, and slowly, I set her onto her feet. I pecked a kiss to her jaw, then pulled my jeans over my hips, left the fly hanging open as I grabbed a washcloth from under the sink and ran it under the faucet.

I knelt in front of her and dragged it between her thighs, cleaning her up, caring for her in a way I wondered if anyone ever had.

I kept peeking up at her, at the way she watched me like I was *real*, too, even though there was no missing the tumult that still spun through her spirit.

I tossed the washcloth to the hamper in the corner, then I grabbed her underwear and slowly eased them back up her legs. My words were a grumble when I met her gaze, "I want you and Juni to move in with me."

Shocked panic filled her expression. "What?"

Standing, I slipped my hands up under her dress, adjusting her underwear over her gorgeous ass, doing my best not to cop another feel but unable to do anything but glide my hands back down her thighs, anyway. I pulled her against me. "At least until we know it's safe. I'm not going to be able to sleep if you aren't by my side."

"Jud." It was a defense.

I shook my head. "Run to me, Salem. Let me be there for you. You know it's where you belong. Where you're going to be safest. You know I'll fight for you. Fight for your daughter."

A war blistered through her expression, and her eyes dropped closed for a beat. Felt my own shock when she gave, when she nodded and said, "Okay."

Thank fuck.

Hugging her to me, I ran my fingers through her mussed hair, pressed my lips to her temple before I angled back and met her with a little more of the truth. "No better place than being in you."

She sent me a wry smile then she looked around like she'd just noticed where we were. "We really should probably keep our hands to ourselves during work."

I nudged her chin, shot her a grin. "Perks of the job."

"Jud." Exasperation filled her tone. "I'm serious."

I set my hands on the door on either side of her head, leaned down, and murmured, "Now why would you want to make that kind of rule when you can have all of this?"

I was serious, too.

I let my fingertips slide back under her dress, pressing to the fabric between her thighs.

Salem curled her hands in my shirt. "You don't fight fair."

A rough chuckle scraped up my throat. "Never said I did."

She fought the smile that twitched at her mouth, lightness filling her eyes but unease still lingering under the surface. "You're ridiculous."

That time I laughed, dipped in to peck a kiss to her lips.

Then my tone went serious. "I'm going to put an end to your fear, Salem. I promise you that."

Her nails scratched into my beard, and her voice became a plea. "I can't stand the idea of you getting hurt because of me."

The grin I cracked was *grim*. "Hate to break it to you, darlin', but I've been in far more precarious situations than this."

Her throat tremored when she swallowed, and then she warily gave me a nod. "I need to get back to work."

She turned and undid the lock.

I grabbed the picture and slipped it back onto its hook before I zipped my fly and buttoned my jeans as I followed her out.

As soon as I stepped out into the lobby, I felt it.

A heatwave of hate that blistered through the air.

Salem stumbled a step before she lifted her chin and breezed by her brother who was lurking by the window.

No doubt about it, he'd heard me banging the fuck out of her two minutes ago. Not that it was any of his business, but the asshole looked like he was about to explode, fucking red in the face, hands curled into fists, like he thought he had a say.

"Salem," he grated.

"Don't," she said, lifting a hand and moving behind the counter. "Just don't."

Shooting me a look that could slay a lesser man, Darius gritted his jaw, looked at Salem once more, before he turned on his heel and stormed out through the door that led into the shop.

I followed.

"Darius." My voice was low when I called after him.

He didn't slow or turn. The only reaction he gave to me shouting at him was the flinch of his shoulders. He stalked for the bay where he'd been working.

I kept right up. "Want to talk to you, Darius."

He spun on me, hands flying out to push me against the chest. "Told you to stay the fuck away from her."

"You might not have noticed, but your sister is a big girl, she can make her own decisions."

"Decisions that are going to get her killed," he spat.

The assertion skewered through me, making me stumble a step before I got in his face, hissing back, "Bullshit. I have her. All I need is a name."

He rattled a sarcastic, horrified sound. "You have her? You don't have her. You have no fuckin' clue."

I took him by the collar. "Give me the bastard's name."

Darius writhed in an attempt to get free of my hold. "Fuck you."

He shoved me again, and I stumbled back a step, just as he flew at me. Dude actually thought he was gonna start something in my shop.

I was getting ready to take him by the wrist when a bustle came from the side.

Brock was there, his scrawny arms pushed between us to keep us apart. "Hey, now, hey. Break it up. As much as I love me a good fight, last thing we need around here is blood spilled all over this floor. More work to do when we already have plenty. Play nice, boys. Clearly, you both love the same girl, for different reasons. Least I fuckin' hope so." Brock cocked a salacious smirk at Darius. "I mean, it must be hard to have a sister that looks like Salem. I feel your pain, man. But take it down a notch or two, sound good, sweetie pie?"

Darius edged back. Hatred boiled in his blood, and he glared at me with vicious eyes. "I warned you, Jud. Warned you to stay the fuck away from my sister."

With a harsh shake of his head, he swung around, charged across the shop, and bashed through the side door. It swung all the way open, and the metal smashed against the exterior wall. It let in a bright glow of light that he disappeared through before the door clattered shut behind him.

I stood there.

Dumbstruck.

Cracking up, Brock clapped me on the shoulder.

"You did it now, boss. Looks like you got a little too *friendly* with someone's sister." He tsked. "Couldn't keep your hands off all that deliciousness, could you? Not that I blame you. Salem is fine as hell."

I grunted at him.

Backing away, he lifted his hands in surrender and grinned. "Don't sweat it, man. Obviously, she's worth it."

Without saying anything else, he turned and went back to work.

I glanced at Salem who stood horrified in the doorway.

That feeling squeezed my chest.

Yeah.

She was fucking worth it.

Whatever the cost.

Chapter Thirty

Jud

"WHERE ARE YOU GOING?" KENNEDY FROWNED FROM their bedroom doorway as Jud tossed a change of clothes into his duffle bag.

"Consult on a custom bike." The lie burned as it fell from his tongue.

A dagger.

A blade.

He felt as if he were slicing right through the vows he had made even though a whole ton of them had been silent. The ones Kennedy had no clue he'd needed to make.

His wife's frown deepened. "I thought you were booked out?"

Jud zipped the bag and strode across their bedroom. He pecked a kiss to her temple, trying to keep himself together, to act normal, like this was no big deal. Fought not to be so stupid to lose his cool and blurt where he was actually going.

Kennedy wouldn't get it. Wouldn't understand. Wouldn't accept he had no other choice but to do one last job.

For Logan.

For his family.

The truth was, he'd protected Kennedy from the world he'd come from. Protected her with every fiber of his loyalty. He couldn't burden her with who he'd been. With the inhumanities he'd witnessed and the atrocities he'd committed.

He'd turned a corner and planted a new life.

But the roots of that old, wicked life drew him. He was caught in the snare of the ghosts that dragged him back to the past.

Grim.

He gritted his teeth and forced a smile. "It's an important client. I'd be a fool to say no. I'll be back in a couple days."

She pressed her hand to his chest. "Okay." Then she tipped her head. "Be careful?"

"Always," he promised, then he kissed her long and slow before he crept into his daughter's nursery. She was in her crib, fast asleep, the tiny, sweet thing lost to her dreams.

Love exploded. Beat at his chest.

He splayed his hand over her belly, made the silent promise, ***"Just this once."***

Then he left the little house and climbed onto the back of his bike, and he rode through the night.

A monster. A wraith. A demon.

Grim.

And he swore this would be the last time he would be ***him.***

Marcello waited at the meeting point, in the seedy part of the city that felt like Jud's old stomping grounds.

Ground covered in blood.

He killed the rumbling engine of his bike, swung off, and approached him slowly, like he might be walking into an ambush, which knowing this prick, that's probably exactly what it was.

Marcello quirked a satisfied grin. "You made it."

"Told you I'd be here."

His grin widened. "Always so amenable."

Jud grunted. "Not always."

It was a testament. This was the end. The last thing he would subject himself to.

Jud stared at the man he all but detested. Marcello and his family had been pulling Jud's strings for years, and he was finished being anyone's puppet. "Let's roll. I want to get this finished, and then it's done. Do you understand?"

Marcello smiled. "A deal's a deal, my friend. We stand by our commitments."

"What's the score?" Jud asked.

"We just need to send a warning to an associate who's gone off the rails. Remind him where his loyalties stand."

"A warning?"

That wasn't what he was expecting.

He'd thought he'd be getting his hands dirty. Forcing out information or maybe silencing a threat.

Marcello tsked, laughed a light sound. "You act like we're horrible, unreasonable people."

Hot air puffed from Jud's nose.

Horrible didn't even cut it.

They were wicked. Vile. Cruel.

Just like Jud had been.

His stomach twisted.

Something after tonight, he refused to ever be again.

I jolted from the memory when Salem touched my elbow.

I kept getting swept up in those old memories. I guessed it was because I never wanted to go there again. They were a reminder of the spiral I'd slipped into, of what I'd lost, of all the mistakes I'd made—and standing there, I felt this astounding internal declaration that I'd never repeat it.

I was going to live for these two.

Live whole and right.

"Are you having second thoughts?" Salem tilted her head, like she'd thought I might have changed my mind about wanting them there rather than the truth swimming out to the horizon of where hope waited.

That I wanted her here. In every way.

"Not even close, darlin'. I asked you here, didn't I?"

"More like demanded it." It was a tease, even though there clearly wasn't a whole lot of easiness as she remained just inside the door to my place.

Like she was unsure of where she fit or belonged.

Looking around like she'd never stepped inside before.

Juni actually hadn't been there before, and the little bee was buzzing around the living space with a pink backpack strapped on her shoulders. Her black hair was in pigtails, those blue eyes gleaming in excitement as she explored the main room of the loft.

She touched about everything, not slowing as she went.

She skipped into the kitchen. "Wow, Motorcycle Man, you gots the biggest kitchen I ever seen." She pulled open the refrigerator and poked her head inside, no shyness to it. "My mimi is gonna be the most jealous so we better nots tell her 'cause we only got a butt bumper over at our house."

I eased deeper into my loft, a smile pulling at my mouth. Was impossible for it not to be there with this wild little thing filling up the vacancy.

"Butt bumper?" I hedged.

"Means we're bumping our butts all the time we gotta go in and do the cooks."

Amusement hummed in my chest.

Energy crackled, but it was different this time.

It was slow and sure.

A rumble of satisfaction as my chest pressed full.

My spirit singing that this was right.

Old guilt made a bid to drown it out. Ancient devotion that no longer quite fit.

That purpose fading at the horizon of my mind.

Grinning back at Salem who still wavered at the doorway, I carried the overnight bag she'd packed thirty minutes before. "Come on, let's get you two settled."

She'd refused to bring any more of her things. She'd insisted it was temporary, and she'd be back at Darius' house soon.

Too bad every bone in my body shouted *hell no*.

Doubted there was a chance I would be able to let her go considering every part of me raced toward something I'd chalked up to loss.

A type of devotion pumping through my veins that I'd never thought I'd feel again.

But I guessed we'd cross that bridge when we got there. Think I was lucky enough to convince her to come here tonight for a *sleepover*, which was how she'd explained this little trip to Juni.

After what'd happened with Darius this afternoon, she was the one who'd started to have second thoughts. She'd tried to give me a thousand reasons why it was a bad idea.

I'd only had to give her one to change her mind: *I have you*.

I'd followed Salem to their house this evening to get their things. I had been wary of having another altercation with Darius, but he'd been nowhere to be found, so I assumed he was somewhere blowing off steam.

Mimi—that sweet thing—she'd been more than keen on the idea, even after Salem had flitted around, worried about leaving her alone.

"The heart knows when it's time," Mimi had whispered to her.

Emotion panged at the thought of it.

A void filling in the middle of my chest.

These walls no longer felt so lonely with Salem and Juni there.

I had to believe it was true.

That my heart was whispering it, too.

Juni was hot on my heels as I moved toward the bedrooms on the far-right side of the loft. I tossed open the guest bedroom door. "Here we go."

Juni blazed around me. "What? You mean I even gets my own room? I loves it here." She jumped onto the enormous bed, bouncing on her knees on the mattress. "I think I wants to stay for all the forevers. I thinks it's a good idea because my best friend Gage only lives a little bit away and he can come here and play. Is that okay, Motorcycle Man?"

Warm laughter tumbled free as I edged in. "Well, since Gage is my nephew, and he likes to come over here and hang out with me every once in a while, that sounds like a pretty dang good plan to me."

There I went, racing toward a destination I never thought I'd go.

"Jud." My name was a plea coming from Salem where she'd edged up behind us. A warning filled her tone. Reservations she didn't quite know where to place.

Be careful.

Don't make promises we can't keep.

I'm in no position to fall in love.

Turning around, I set my hand on her gorgeous face. "I have you, Salem."

Thunderbolt eyes speared me.

Deep.

Intense.

Penetrating.

I brushed the pad of my thumb along her jaw, then I forced an easy smile. "Come on, let's get you two fed."

"Yes! I'm starvin' like a martian, all the way up in the planets."

I grinned back at Juni. "Seems like you've been spending too much time with Gage in the Cage."

"No such thing, Motorcycle Man." She hopped to her butt then slid off the side of the bed. "He's my favorite friend, and we're gettin' married, and if you get married, you gotta spend always together."

Right.

I cut an eye at Salem.

Joy washed through her expression.

Hope and belief.

Fuck.

I wanted to put that look on her face every day of her life.

"We're gonna have to keep an eye on those two," I said with a tease, angling down to drop a kiss to the side of Salem's cheek as I passed.

"That's your jobs, doncha know? You're the adults." Juni tossed it out, so pragmatic as she blazed back out to the kitchen.

A laugh tore free.

"I'll be sure to remind you of that when you're about fourteen." I shouted it behind her as I turned in the direction of the master bedroom.

At my assertion, the breath hitched in Salem's throat.

I turned to look at her from over my shoulder.

Salem had frozen outside Juni's door.

She stood in my apartment like she'd become a part of the makeup.

A fixture on the floors.

A stroke of the paintings.

Permanent.

So goddamn pretty she knocked the air right outta my lungs.

A fantasy wrapped in a black, decadent bow.

"Could look at you all day." The praise rumbled free.

Warily, Salem glanced around, fidgeting and letting her nerves get the best of her.

I let go of a casual laugh to put her at ease.

"Come on, Wildcat. I see you getting ready to strike." I strode the rest of the way into my room, set her things on the floor. Her presence was nothing but a stir that hedged me from behind.

Chaos and light.

When she still didn't say anything, I turned around and took her by the face.

Kissed her deep.

A bolt of need punched through my body.

I pulled back to stare down at that stunning face. "Do you trust me?"

She chewed at her bottom lip before she admitted, "I'm scared of how much I do."

"You think I'm not scared, too, Salem? That all of this isn't fuckin' with my mind? But that's the thing about trust—it's always a little scary to give. To rely on someone when we've only been relying on ourselves. And fuck yeah, baby, you are a fighter, a survivor. Fierce and determined. So goddamn beautiful you make my knees shake. But it doesn't matter how strong we are, every one of us needs someone who is willing to fight for us, too."

She reached out and scratched her nails through my beard, those eyes on me when she whispered, "What I'm really scared of is losing you."

"Then stay."

I said it like it was simple.

Like nothing else mattered.

"Are you two done kissin' or what?" Juni's little voice filtered from the kitchen and into my room.

On a chuckle, I took Salem's hand and threaded our fingers together.

She looked at the knitting of our beings, feeling it, too.

The merging.

The meeting.

The way it was supposed to be.

I led her out the double doors and into the big main room. Juni had already made herself at home, digging through the pantry. "You ain't gots much, Motorcycle Man."

She said it with a disappointed sigh.

"How about we order pizza for tonight and we'll get some more groceries in here tomorrow?"

"Don't teases me." Juni stared at me with her mother's eyes.

My chest stretched tight.

Fuck.

I was done for.

I pulled out my phone. "No teasin' to it."

"Hallelujahs," she sang.

"What's everyone's favorite?"

"Cheese!" Juni popped up at the countertop where I was resting on my elbows so I could scroll to my favorite pizza place.

I touched her nose. She giggled.

The hole Kennedy and Kye had left inside me felt fuzzy. An old haunting that I'd never quite shake. A blur that had begun to form into something else.

I slanted a questioning gaze at Salem. "How about you, darlin'?"

"Cheese is great, as long as we order a salad on the side." She looked at her daughter when she said that.

Juni shrugged, so grown-up. "I gots no problems with the vegetables. Sheesh, Mommy, do you even know me?"

So much sass.

My head shook in amusement, and I punched in the number, set on taking care of these two the best that I could.

Only the blaring that suddenly screamed through the loft froze my fingers on the screen. The alarm was so loud, it was disorienting.

Deafening.

I heard it like a crash of lawlessness. A shearing of peace.

Everything seized for one shocked second.

Salem's spirit frozen—frozen in terror—my heart frozen in the same.

Then she started to mumble, "No. No, no, no, my baby."

Torment clouded her expression.

I shot into action when I realized it was the fire alarm from downstairs in the shop going off.

On instinct, I grabbed Juni.

The little girl curled her arms around my neck and buried her face in my beard. My attention shifted to Salem the second I had the child in my arms.

Salem.

Salem who was nothing but panic. Her face was a sheet of white. Like she'd run headfirst into a ghost that'd come to claim.

Her eyes filled with what I knew deep down she believed was inevitable—she thought she'd been discovered.

My own wounds throbbed. Curdled my senses into a wad of old disgust.

Bile rose in my throat, and I wanted to succumb.

But I had way more important things to protect than my past mistakes.

I grabbed Salem by the hand. "Follow me," I shouted over the alarm.

The siren blared. Banging off the walls and amplifying. Blasting so loud it twisted the air into a daze.

The world in confusion.

Salem clamored along behind me toward the set of emergency steps that ran out the backside of the laundry room. I flung the door open and bounded down the stairwell that crisscrossed three times.

Juni curled her arms tighter and burrowed her face deep into my neck, like she trusted me to silence it, keeping her harsh, hard breaths silent, like she'd been taught how to hide.

All while I could feel the crush of Salem's heart. The desperation in her steps.

I held them tighter, shouting, "I have you. I have you," over the clatter.

We busted out at the bottom and into the waning day. Twilight hung over the earth, slipping behind the trees and casting the world in a kaleidoscope of golds and purples and deepening blues.

Salem heaved a breath as soon as we were outside, and I tightened my hold on her as I raced us around the side of the building toward the woods that separated Iron Ride and Absolution.

Where it was secluded.

Where neither of them would be seen.

Salem was gasping, choking over her fear.

Wanted to wrap her up. Promise she was safe. That I would never let anything happen to her. Instead, I spun her, passed her daughter into the well of her shaking arms.

"Do not move!" I told her. I grabbed her by the outside of her upper arms to emphasize it. "Wait right here. It's going to be fine. I promise you."

Her nod was jerky, Salem in shock as she clung to her daughter.

I warred, not wanting to move, but the alarm was still screeching through the coming night.

I ran back that way, hitting the button on my phone that controlled the garage bay doors.

All five of them began to lift.

A small strain of smoke billowed out of the one closest to the lobby.

I ran along the front of the building. My heart seized when I realized where it was coming from.

Salem's piece of shit car that was still on the riser smoldered, the barest smoke wafting out from the driver's-side window that had been left down.

Dipping inside the shop, I grabbed the fire extinguisher from the wall, fighting a war of my own fear, my own regrets.

Felt like the ugliest, dirtiest parts of me had found their way free and were taunting me.

The small fire a jeer that threatened to erupt to an all-out inferno from Salem's car.

I hit the button to the riser to lower it, and I jerked out the pin on the extinguisher and sprayed the foam over the flames.

It was out as fast as it'd started.

Strain heaved and shock clutched my chest, this crazy-ass billow of relief mixed with the disorder.

Sweat dripped from my forehead, my blood a boil of aggression and adrenaline.

I swallowed it down and looked inside the window of the old car.

The remnants of a charred, oily rag were on the seat.

My gaze whipped around, searching for a reason.

An explanation.

Dread curled and trembled the ground beneath my feet.

The extinguisher slipped from my hands and clattered to the concrete. It rolled under the car while bile throbbed in my throat.

A warning.

A hiss.

Nothing added up.

I moved through the shop, hitting the stop button on the alarm as I passed. The silence roared. A ringing in my ears as I began to search every nook.

Every cranny.

Any possible spot someone could hide.

I came up short, nothing else out of place.

I scrubbed both hands over my face before I dropped them to peer through the empty shop.

My stomach was in knots. Nausea burned through the middle. I swallowed around the ball of razors in my throat.

It had to be an accident.

A slip up.

A misstep.

That rag left in the wrong place.

But what would have sparked it?

"Fuck," I spat then I inhaled, trying to get my head on straight as I barreled out of the bay and toward the only destination I knew.

To where Salem and Juni were hidden in the cover of the dense thicket of trees.

My heart battered and crashed, and every single muscle in my body bowed in possession.

Salem was there. Her daughter in her arms, hiding her face but still peeking out as I approached.

"It was just a small fire caused by an oily rag. Alarm is super sensitive to protect the shop."

It was true, but it still felt like bullshit.

Salem knew it, too.

She was shaking. Shaking and shaking.

She spun a circle, her black hair whipping around her shoulders like a darkened, chaotic storm. "No."

Panic built, and her fear compounded.

"No," she said again before she darted around me and took off running. With Juni held in her arms, she headed back toward the side stairway.

I kept up behind her. "Salem. Wait. Let me check it out to make sure it's safe before we go back inside."

I might as well not have said a thing because my words didn't penetrate the wall of her panic.

She never put Juni down the entire way up to the loft, her feet banging the stairs and her distress clawing the white bricks.

She burst through the laundry room door, ignoring me as I tried to stop her.

"Salem, please. Calm down. Let's take a deep breath. A minute to think this through."

The distress radiating back was her only answer.

Seeping from her pores and burning from her flesh.

"Salem."

She was already in the guest bedroom, snatching up Juni's bag, then she blew out and into my bedroom. The only thing she took the time to grab was her purse.

She didn't look at me as she rushed back out the door and across the loft.

"Salem. Fuck, please. Stop. Look at me." I fumbled behind her. Trying to break through. To climb over the barriers and find my way to her. To where it was me and this girl who'd changed everything. One who'd rearranged every loyalty.

I didn't make a dent.

Without slowing, she darted back through the laundry room and into the stairwell, her footfalls frenzied as she careened down the steps.

"Salem…please. Listen to me. I have you. I have you."

"Please, Jud, don't." It was the first thing that came out of her mouth, and she tossed it out without looking back as she banged through the bottom door and out into the deepening night.

She ran for the SUV she'd left parked right outside.

"Salem. Don't."

I tried to grab her arm. To hold her. To let her know it was going to be okay.

Shaking me off, she pushed the button on the lock and set Juni into the backseat. Her movements were frantic as she strapped the little girl into place.

She slammed Juni's door and slipped by me while my heart lodged in my shredded throat.

"I'm sorry," was all she said as she jerked open the driver's door, refusing to look at me as she did. She started to climb inside.

I took her by the shoulders and spun her around to face me. "I know you're scared, but I need you to remember right now what you promised—if you get scared, you run to me. Remember, darlin'. Run to me. I'm right here. Right here."

She squeezed her eyes closed like she couldn't look at me when she said it, the words ragged when she forced them out. "I'm sorry, I can't stay, Jud. I can't. I need to go before it's too late."

Agony whipped through the atmosphere.

My guts screamed. But it was my heart shouting louder.

Taking her by the face, I forced her to look at me. Begging her to see. To hear. "I'm in this with you, Salem. You're not alone any longer. Don't you see? I have you, darlin'. I have you."

Her eyes just pressed tighter, girl closing herself off, regressing back to the place where she couldn't trust. Where her fear reigned, and her hopes didn't matter. "You have to let me go, Jud. I can't do this. I'm sorry. I'm sorry."

Desperate, the confession I'd been trying to deny to myself came blundering out. "I can't let you go. I can't. I love you. I fuckin' love you, Salem."

It was true.

So fucking true the verity of it nearly dropped me to my knees.

But I had to remain standing.

Hold up this girl.

Because she choked on the agony, and Salem nearly bent in two, falling apart as she surged forward and pressed her face to my chest and curled those hands in my shirt. Clinging to me as if I were a buoy in the raging, toiling sea, she frantically kissed over my heart. I felt the grief and lost dreams leave her on a sob.

She inhaled, breathed me in, then she pushed her hands against my chest to push me away. "Who said anything about love?"

I staggered back.

Salem swayed. Caught in a torrent of sorrow. Her arm shot out to catch herself on the door before she fell, then she swallowed, built a fortress around herself, and jumped into the driver's seat.

"I'll figure out a way to repay you for the car. Both of them." She was facing forward when she said it, cool and robotic and like she wasn't tearing me apart. Reaching out, she grabbed the door handle and slammed it shut.

My palms pressed to the window. "Salem. Baby, don't go. You don't have to do this."

Could see her frenzied movements as she fumbled to start the car. I banged at the window. "Salem. Don't. Don't run away. Run to me."

My pleas didn't penetrate, or maybe they made her fight this harder, the way she refused to look at me as she threw the car in reverse. She peeled out as I flew back and stumbled out of the way.

The SUV jolted forward when she put it in drive, tires squealing as she gunned it on the loose gravel.

Like a fuckin' fool, I ran behind her. "Salem! Salem! Please."

Salem.

My entire being writhed.

Writhed in fucking agony because my entire world was fleeing.

Running, the way she did. The way she'd promised she would do.

I was a fool.

I had known it in an instant.

The way this girl'd had me tangled in a beat.

Need.

Possession.

Black. Fuckin'. Magic.

Nothing but pure, utter devastation.

And my sweet enchantress's spell? It finally brought me to my knees.

Chapter Thirty-One

Salem

Tears streamed down my face, blurring my sight until it was impossible to see. A fog of torment blinded and obscured, while white-hot blades of heartache cut and slayed, slicing through the middle of me.

It left that vacancy gaping wide.

I felt like I was bleeding out.

"Salem!" I could hear Jud shouting, his pull yanking at my spirit and rending me in two. "Don't do this."

I squeezed my hands around the steering wheel like it could keep me on the right path. Make me remember who I was and what I had to protect my daughter from.

To keep from giving myself in a way I never should have in the first place.

Salem.

It banged through my mind and shredded my heart.

I love you. I fuckin' love you.

Tears blurred my eyes and soaked my face.

He wasn't supposed to. This wasn't supposed to happen.

Juni whimpered from the backseat. Quiet and afraid. "Mommy."

"I know," I mumbled. "I know."

And I hated that I did. Hated what I was putting her through.

But I had no other choice, did I?

Not while the terror continued to rip through my consciousness. A foreboding that warned of what was to come. Of what would always be lurking, ready to consume when I allowed myself to get sloppy.

To get comfortable.

Reckless.

If Carlo had found us? If he was responsible?

That thought had me ramming the accelerator to the floor. The tires peeled out on the loose gravel.

I had to get away. Put a lifetime between us and this place. Become someone else. The way I always did.

You exist.

Through the rearview mirror, I saw the hulking, beast of a man lumbering behind us.

As if he were chasing down something real.

I could feel the reverberation of his footfalls as he chased us across the lot.

I pinched my eyes closed like it could stop me from feeling the impact of who he was.

From hearing the shout of his soul.

Shield my heart from the call that screamed every bit as loud as the sirens that had blared through the building. As loud as the instinct that told me I had to go.

That I could never stay.

That for me, there was no such thing as *home*.

But my spirit?

It thrashed.

A riot that gripped my insides.

It ravaged the hollow space that could never be filled.

"Go," I whimpered, to him, to myself, to this feeling that welled up.

But it only grew.

Clouding judgement.

Obliterating reason.

"Please," I cried to myself, like it could sever the pull. That severity that had been there from the moment Jud had found me in the storm.

The SUV bounced across the gravel drive, the tail end skidding as I erratically whipped around the side of the building to the front parking lot.

Reckless.

I headed across the lot toward the exit, trying to force myself through the sludge of agony. I tried to press harder at the accelerator, but a tremor rocked through my leg and shocked through my body.

Salem.

I could still hear him calling my name.

In the middle of the lot, I rammed on the brakes.

Closed my eyes.

Prayed.

Salem.

His voice curled around my being and wrapped me in comfort.

A sob ripped up my throat. I held tighter to the steering wheel and pressed my forehead to the leather as another cry lacerated through my insides.

Fumbling, I put the SUV in park, and my foot was floundering around to engage the emergency brake, my fingers on the door latch and cracked it open.

I couldn't feel my feet, but I knew the ground wobbled below me.

Jud was there, sweeping me into his arms a second before I crumbled.

My arms curled desperately around his neck. "I didn't mean to, Jud. I didn't mean to fall in love with you."

It spilled out.

The confession of my soul.

I didn't mean to, but I did.

I did.

"I know, darlin'. I know," he murmured at my ear as he held me against his chest.

Massive arms surrounded me.

His heart thundered, a pound, pound, pounding of peace. Of safety. Of saving grace.

He exhaled the heaviest breath into my hair.

He reached inside the car and shut off the engine.

He didn't let me go, he just moved to Juni's door, opened it, unbuckled her, and helped her down.

He held me with one arm, his other hand securely wrapped around Juni's.

"I have you," was all he said as he started to walk back around the building.

Warmth skated across my skin, sank below, embedded itself in my marrow.

I burrowed my face into his beard. Inhaled his aura. Drew it into my lungs.

Relished the sanctuary of this man.

Citrus and spice. A warm fall night.

A protector.

While every muscle in his body vibrated with the truth of the length he'd be willing to go for us. The ferocity that sped and churned.

A grim, wicked savior.

I clung to him.

Gave.

Trusted.

Loved.

Reckless.

A sob curled up my throat, and I pressed my mouth to his shoulder and released it.

In it was surrender.

Concession.

A yielding to his sacrifice.

"I have you."

It penetrated, bled into my cells, and became a part of my heartbeat.

"I have you."

He somehow managed to get the heavy metal door open without setting me down, and he held it so Juni could slip inside. He took her hand again as he carried me upstairs.

His footsteps echoed.

Heavy and firm.

Juni scrambled along at his side, her little spirit quieted and held, yet somehow calmed.

As if she had fallen into the same peace.

At the top landing, Juni moved ahead to hold the door open for us to pass.

"Thank you, Little Bee," Jud said so quietly, with so much care and adoration. He carried me directly into his bedroom, and he set me on the edge of the bed and knelt in front of me.

He brushed back my hair and searched me with those obsidian eyes. "I know you're scared of it. Hell, I know this is terrifying for us both. Neither of us expected it. But I love you, Salem. I love you with all of me. With the good parts and the bad parts. With the ones that are whole and the ones that are broken. All of them—they belong to you."

Emotion filled every cell in my body. Spirit and soul.

"Say it's forever." The plea left me on a whimper.

"It's forever, baby. Today, tomorrow, and always."

I touched his face as emotion overwhelmed. Possessed. "I love you, Jud. I love you in a way that should be impossible. With a love so big and massive it hurts."

He cocked me a tender smile. "I understand that feeling well, darlin'. Think I've been feeling it since the second you walked into my life."

He gathered my hand and pressed it to his lips. "I will do whatever it takes to protect you and Juni. You have to trust that."

For a second, his eyes dropped closed. When he opened them, I was sure I could see all the way down into his soul.

He was laying himself bare.

There was no secret, no shame, no hurt that we wouldn't hold for the other.

"You've been fighting for so long, Salem. Let me fight for you."

I touched the lines of his rugged, handsome face. "*With me*," I corrected. "Because I'll never stop, not until she's safe."

Old wounds curled and gutted.

Jud held me by the face. As if he held those, too. Shared them with me. "I understand, darlin'. Neither will I."

"Forever." It left me on a promise.

The pad of his thumb traced along the gnarled scar at my jaw. "Forever."

Energy whispered, a soft whirring in the air, stirring through the disorder.

My words were soggy. "We're a mess."

A smile twitched beneath his beard as he slipped his palm up to rest on my cheek.

Adoring.

Emphatic.

Whole.

"A beautiful fuckin' mess."

"You gonna have a kid around, you're gonna have to learn to watch the bad words, Motorcycle Man, or else you're gonna have to go to timeout all the ways in Antarctica with my mimi because she gots the bad words, too."

Our little bubble popped, and Jud's surprised laugh split through the severity.

"That so?" Jud's entire face spread into a grin.

"Yup," Juni said from the doorway.

My light. My hope. My joy.

Those were the things I wanted to give her, too.

A tremble of realization rocked through me.

And I knew, I couldn't—couldn't truly do that if I kept running. If I packed up and left every time I felt a shiver lift the hairs at the back of my neck.

It was time I truly *fought*.

Found a way to find true peace. I didn't know how to do that, but I knew, right then, that Jud would be there beside me as I did.

"Then I guess I better watch it," Jud replied.

"Because you wanna keep me?" She screeched it, pure delight.

Jud looked at me, his thumb tracing along my jaw before he looked back at my daughter. "Yeah, Juni, I wanna keep you."

My heart pulsed.

"Why don't you take a shower?" he suggested when he turned back to me. "I'm going to make some calls and get someone over here to keep watch tonight, and then I'm gonna get our Little Bee fed. I want you to relax and know you're safe. Okay?"

My nod was soft.

"Good."

Jud edged up and pressed his mouth to mine.

Soft and sure.

A promise.

He stood, those eyes raking over me, a glint lighting from the depths.

My chest tightened and a bubbling of desire sprang from within.

With a soft touch of my jaw, Jud turned and strode for my little girl, his big boots eating up the floor.

So intimidating and fierce.

So tender and sweet.

This destructive charm that had ruined me. Crushed up the places inside me that had hardened to stone when he took Juni's hand in his and led her into the main room.

I went into the master bathroom and turned on the shower. As soon as it was warm, I stepped into the spray.

I closed my eyes beneath it and lifted my face to the pelting water.

And I believed.

Believed there was something better for my daughter.

Believed there was something better for me.

I let the rivulets whisk over my body and soothe away the storm. Let the warmth settle into my bones.

And I knew I needed to trust Jud with it all. I had to give him every truth and every sorrow. He needed to know the whole of it so he could understand what we were up against.

The fracture cleaved inside me throbbed. That chunk of my soul that would always remain missing. One that could never be filled or healed or restored. But one I could no longer allow to be made in vain.

Resolved, I washed with Jud's soap, pressed it to my nose, cherished what we'd found, then I rinsed, feeling brand-new when I stepped out and wrapped a towel around my body.

A faint smile pulled at my mouth.

One that felt permanent.

I dried and changed into the sleep pants and tee I'd packed in my overnight bag, then I slipped out of Jud's bedroom, coming to a stop right outside the door.

The television was on and *Finding Nemo* played on the screen. Juni was on her knees at the coffee table, enraptured by the show while she ate a slice of pizza.

But it was the voices in the kitchen that stalled my feet and piqued my ear.

I edged to the end and peered out. Jud and Trent stood at the island, their conversation hushed and heated and hard.

But they weren't at war with each other.

They were at war with my enemy.

One they didn't even know.

"Doesn't sit right," Jud muttered. "Oily rag was in the seat. Sure, it could have been forgotten, but then what? It's not just going to catch fire."

Jud shook his head before he continued, "And the amount of time that alarm was going off until I got down there? Car should've been completely engulfed in flames."

"You think the alarm was a warning?" Trent said it like he was already right there, a partner to Jud's speculations, seeing it for what it was, too.

A token.

A premonition.

My spirit dampened and swam. I tried to remain steady. To keep the dizziness from whirring through my head. Still, apprehension clutched my chest in a fist.

"Yeah. I think someone set the alarm. Salem freaked out that it might be Juni's father who she's been dodging for years." He roughed an agitated hand through his hair before he met Trent face on. "I think it was her brother, though. He's the one who has access, and whoever it was knew exactly how to stay out of line of the security cameras. The dude was pissed this afternoon when he realized things were getting real between me and Salem, and if someone actually wanted to set fire to the place, they would have. He knew I'd find it quick and put it out."

My spirit shivered with the impact of what Jud implied.

Darius?

Would he do that to me?

I blinked against the staggering pain the thought evoked. I didn't even want to process or contemplate it.

Trent sighed. Somehow it sounded of relief. "Reckless, but understandable. I mean, I'd want to burn your shit down, too, if you got your dirty paws on my little sister."

He cracked a grin at that.

I wasn't smiling. I couldn't fathom that Darius would do something so awful. So hurtful.

Gulping, I forced myself to listen.

Jud chuckled and threw a targetless punch at his brother. "Fuck you, man."

Trent laughed then sobered as he shifted gears. "But that black car..."

"Yup. That's what is tripping me up. I have to figure out what's going on there, but this? Tonight? The fire? My gut tells me it's Darius."

"Thinking you're probably right. Dude's most likely pissed and making his feelings known. Thinks he'll scare you off. He'll get over it. I'm going to post Milo out front, though, just as a precaution."

"Thank you. Just...have to keep them safe, Trent. Whatever that means." Savagery quivered through Jud's words, steel lining his voice.

Trent tucked his hands into his pockets. "You accept it yet?"

Jud's big chest widened on a heavy exhale. "What? That I love her?"

But it was my lungs that locked up. Locked in a hope that I'd never expected. One I had never dared dreaming of since I'd started this fight.

And I guessed he must have known I was there the entire time because those eyes found mine where I was eavesdropping off to the side.

Obsidian flashed with desire.

With greed and goodness.

With everything I'd had no idea I'd needed.

He stretched out his hand in my direction. "Yeah. I did."

Intensity flickered through the glare of the lights.

I felt seen.

Adored.

Understood.

I edged out from behind the wall and shuffled that way, my head lowered in a bit of embarrassment since I'd been caught unabashedly listening to their conversation.

Jud didn't seem to mind. He just wrapped an arm around me and tugged me close. He dropped a kiss to the top of my head and spun my heart up all over again.

"Yeah," he murmured. The sound vibrated through me like a warm caress.

Trent smiled at me from where I peered out.

"Good." He returned his attention to Jud. "I'm going to get back to the club. Give me a call if you need anything at all."

"Will do."

"Thank you," I said.

Trent's expression shifted. Firm affection. "It's what this family does, Salem. We stand for each other, until the very end." His eyes snapped to Jud for a beat before they were back on me. "Seems you're a part of that now."

A lump lodged itself in my throat.

Home. Home. Home.

The promise of it swam and sang.

I barely managed a nod.

Trent and Jud bumped fists and then Trent was gone.

Jud pressed his mouth to my temple. "Let's eat. I'm starving."

I stood at the doorway while Jud took his turn tucking my daughter into bed. He knelt at her bedside, his low, gravelly voice rolling through the dense air.

Filling her ears with a tease and a play.

Sweet, sweet comfort.

Little giggles lifted from her mouth, and he tickled her softly as he kissed her forehead, while I felt his spirit winding through the room.

There was a vehemence scored into the middle of him.

His strength, his power, his loyalty, given to her.

I felt it tremble the floorboards when he stood, when he pulled the covers up higher over her shoulders, when he whispered, "Goodnight, Juni Bee."

"Night, Motorcycle Man." Juni's voice was sleepy, lulled into the peace of the evening we'd spent together.

For hours, the three of us had been curled on the couch like a family.

A depiction of what I'd once thought an impossibility.

Affection rode on those waves of intensity. It softly batted against the walls and radiated from our spirits.

It wound around us with each pass.

Knitting.

Weaving.

A slow, steady binding that threaded us together.

I felt the tether of it yank when Jud turned in my direction.

The man hulked my way through the shadows of the room that Juni had claimed as her own.

Eyes as dark as the night flashed in the bare light that glinted from the hall.

My heart panged as he stalked my way.

This man who was so obscenely gorgeous.

Forbidding.

Intimidating and raw.

A ruthless fortress.

A wicked savior.

One I'd never believed could be mine.

Then the beast of a man had to flash me that sexy, devilish smile. His voice was a low scrape when he uttered, "Darlin'."

My stomach fisted in want.

He backed me the rest of the way out of the bedroom, and he pulled the door shut halfway, leaving it mostly open as he edged me the rest of the way to his room.

There, he shut the door and locked it. He set his phone on the high table just inside, the security system alight on the screen. "I have all the monitors on. Milo is posted outside. She's safe. You're safe. You don't have to be afraid. Not anymore."

I guessed he read it in my eyes. That I couldn't fully accept his claim. As long as Carlo still roamed, I knew we'd never truly be safe.

"Who is he?" Jud demanded, his voice a growl.

"A monster."

Dark shame dimmed his features for the barest second before rage rushed in to burn a path through his expression. He edged me deeper into his room. His hands slid up and down my arms in a soothing fashion.

It didn't matter.

I could feel the violence skate through his veins.

Palpable.

Volatile.

"Don't want you to be afraid of me." Grief struck through his features.

"I'm not."

He kept coming closer, encroaching, forcing me back with each towering step he took.

"When Kennedy left me, I locked it all down, Salem. Swore I'd never hurt another. Swore I'd never bear the weight of new blood on my hands. Swore I would never kill again. Thought I could be good enough, and one day she would come back to me and see me as someone else, and I was going to be ready for when she did."

He inhaled a shaky breath. "So, I stuffed the demon down deep. Chained him. I kept him hidden from everyone except for my brothers who've always known. But he's right here, and I've let him loose. For you, Salem. For you and your daughter. He's going to fight for you. I just need a name and this ends."

I should be terrified of his admission.

Grim.

But I was only terrified of what it might mean for him. Of what he was asking. Of the direction I could feel him aching to go.

From where I stood at the edge of his bed, my hands curled into his plain white tee. I clung to the fabric like it would forever tie him to us. "No. Not like this, Jud. He's already stolen too much from me. I won't let him take you, too. You can't just go rushing in there."

I knew if I gave Jud a name, he'd disappear into the night. Right then. No hesitation.

Lines of hatred dented Jud's face. "I can't stand to see you in fear any longer."

My throat constricted, sorrow racing the length. "I know, Jud, I know. But we have to be smart about this. He's..." I blinked, tried to suppress the memories, the things Carlo had done. The hole he'd carved out in the middle of me. The vacancy that would always wail.

Excruciating.

I set my hand on Jud's face, my thumb brushing the defined cut of his cheek, this beautiful man who had no idea of just how good he was. What I saw when I looked into his eyes. When he let me see way down deep into his kind, giving soul.

"I know you want to put yourself on the same level as him, that you somehow think you're wicked. You're not. *You're not.* I see you, Jud, like you've seen me, and the two of us are so much greater than our circumstances. So much greater than the wickedness that those who should have loved us and protected us shaped us to be."

It was a wickedness I'd run from. The kind of wickedness to which Jud had believed he'd succumbed.

My hand tightened in emphasis on his face. "He's the *demon,* Jud. Cruel and callus. Without thought and without care. He is *nothing* like you, and you are *nothing* like him. And he will destroy anyone who gets in his way."

Anyone.

And despite Darius' reassurances, I knew Carlo still believed that job was incomplete.

Jud pulled me closer. Torment radiated off him in waves.

His face was pressed to my neck as he breathed me in. As if I had become his rock. His anchor. Juni and I the reason for this life. "I need you to tell me, baby."

My arms wound tight around his neck, my head rocking back as he began to kiss a desirous path down my throat. "And right now? Tonight? I need you to love me. Because I've never truly been."

"Salem." It was a grunt. A plea. A confession.

"Jud," I murmured back. "Love me. Love me the way I love you. In a way that can't be broken."

"Forever," he said. He kissed my eyes. My cheeks. My soggy lips. "I love you, darlin'. Love you with every piece of me. Every hole and every scar and every hope. Everything belongs to you. To you and Juni. Do you understand what that means?"

His tongue stroked over my lips.

A moan echoed in my throat.

Edging back an inch, he watched me while those big hands peeled my shirt over my head. Then he knelt to drag my sleep pants and underwear down my legs.

Cool air brushed my flesh. Need spread out to touch every cell in my body.

Jud straightened to his full, massive height, and the man stood before me as he wound himself out of his clothes.

Nothing was said.

The room was silent except for the heated whisper of our breaths and the thunder of our hearts.

He lifted me onto the mattress and came to hover over me. He gazed down at me through the lapping shadows, one arm rested above my head, the other on my face.

"Do you understand what that means?" he reiterated, his voice low and deep.

His thumb traced my scar. Energy crashed as he rumbled the words, "It means I have you, darlin'. I have you."

His promise rained down.

It seeped through my skin and became one with my blood.

He pushed himself inside me.

Stealing my breath. My body.

But my heart?

It was already long gone.

For a moment, we just stayed there. Joined as one.

Then I nudged him and urged him to roll to his back.

He took me with him, and I straddled this man who'd changed everything. The man who'd taken a broken, shattered life, the pieces strewn all over this country, and held the rest in the palms of his beautiful hands.

I stared down at my wicked savior as I moved over him.

As our bodies connected so perfectly.

As he touched me.

My stomach. My hips. My breasts.

Our breaths synced. Our spirits joined.

And for the first time in my life, I felt a part of someone.

Physically.

Spiritually.

Like I was not just tied with his soul, but I was a part of his existence.

"Salem." His big hands circled my waist as he guided me in a slow, desperate rhythm.

I splayed my hands over his wide chest. "Jud."

He rolled us again, until I was pinned, those massive arms around me. The longer pieces of his black hair fell across his face, his eyes feral, gleaming and bright, his beautiful body thrusting into mine.

"It's you and Juni now. You're mine. I'll fight for you, live for you, die for you, whatever it takes." The words grunted from his mouth. "Do you understand?"

And I lost myself to it.

To this surrender.

To his belief.

His love.

His life.

"I love you, Jud. I love you." And I gave him the one thing that was the hardest part. "I trust you with it all."

Chapter Thirty-Two

Salem

Twenty-One Years Old

THE LIGHTS WERE DIMMED, AND THE TINY ROOM WAS quiet. The only sound was the steady whooshing that pulsed at a quickened beat as the technician held the probe to Salem's swollen belly.

Salem was sure her heart was just as big as her protruding stomach, pressing at the confines of her ribs as love overwhelmed.

As it overcame.

As her purpose became clear.

With that clarity came the devastating fear she'd waded through for the last year. A dark, ugly current that lapped at her ankles. Rose higher and higher. She knew if she didn't learn to swim, she would drown.

Salem gulped as the technician sent an encouraging smile back at them. "Everything sounds perfect. Would you like to know the sex?"

"Yes," Carlo insisted as he hovered over the side of where Salem lay.

"A girl…and a boy."

His pride ballooned bigger than the rest. He turned to take Salem's face in his hands, and he looked at her as if he adored her. "You did it. I knew you would give me an heir. A man to carry on my family name. A son to follow my path."

Salem forced a trembling smile, tears blurring her sight and running down the sides of her face.

Carlo leaned in and kissed them. "Good girl," he whispered before he turned and left.

They were parked at the curb on the quiet neighborhood street, and Salem struggled to breathe as she peered out at the unassuming single-story house that sat behind a white-picket fence.

Oaks grew proud and tall, their thick, full leaves dappling the ground in shadows as rays of sunlight shimmered through the branches. Birds flitted through, and the sound of children laughing and playing in the distance echoed in her ears.

The peace felt at complete odds with the barrage of fear and second guesses that filled her mind.

Was she really going to do this?

Was she brave enough?

Strong enough to see it through?

Was it a mistake?

She curled her hand tighter on the door handle as if it could keep her grounded.

Centered.

Reminding her of her purpose. The truth that she had no other choice.

Salem shifted to look at the detective who sat behind the wheel of the gray sedan. "You're sure we will be safe here? That we will be protected?"

Salem's mangled jaw was lifted in a challenge, desperate for the woman to give her reassurance. It didn't matter they'd gone over the plan a thousand times. She needed to hear it again.

Detective Whitacre reached out and squeezed Salem's hand. "I know you're scared right now, but you've done the right thing. And I promise you, you are under our protection. No one will get close to you, not before the trial or after. You and your children will be safe."

Salem spread a hand over her stomach that was so large she could hardly sit. Their time to come into this world was only four weeks away.

Love and hope blossomed. Bloomed against the dread that felt like a millstone that threatened to drag her to the bottom of the sea.

She knew…she knew the detective was right.

Putting Carlo behind bars for the rest of his life was her responsibility.

She needed to rid this world of his depravity. Of his viciousness. To get justice for her best friend. Justice for the rest he had hurt. For the families that had been destroyed.

But most of all, she had to protect her children. Shelter them from that life. Keep them from being molded in his design.

But once she went into protective custody, there would be no turning back. She wouldn't be able to check on her brother or grandmother.

This morning when Salem had gone to say goodbye, to confess what she was doing, she'd almost changed her mind. But Mimi had hugged her tight as she cried, as she'd whispered in her ear, "I'm willing, sweet child, to face whatever is to come. I have no regrets. But you must go. I have already lived my life. Now it is time for you to live yours."

Salem had to walk away.

Forever.

But for her children? To give them a good life?

She had no other choice than to leave this life behind.

Chapter Thirty-Three

Jud

Guiding his bike along the deserted path, Jud eased up behind the car that stopped along the backside of an abandoned warehouse. It was well beyond midnight, and a thick, murky darkness hung low on the city.

A dull glow pushed against it, rising up from the eternal lights that glinted from this place that was nothing but a festering cesspool.

He hated it there—hated it because he'd sworn he would never return to walk these cursed streets, and there he was, doing the bidding of the perverted.

Jud killed the rumbling engine of his motorcycle and kicked the stand.

His nerves rattled. An unsettled feeling that wafted through the cool night air as he swung off his bike at the same moment Marcello and two of his men, Tony and Kolin, climbed from the car.

They were quiet.

Too quiet. Too guarded.

Intuition lifted the hairs at the back of Jud's neck. His fingers twitched as he was hit with the uneasy awareness that had kept him alive for years. A sense of foreboding that told him he had walked into an ambush.

Something was off.

Tony and Kolin went to the trunk where they pulled out four cans of gasoline, their seedy guilt clear as they scanned the area.

That feeling writhed, tendrils climbing through Jud's nerves and winding around his neck.

His heavy boots barely made a sound as he edged forward. The short-barrel rifle strapped to his back burned like a brand as he strode their way. Every step ensured he was walking straight into a trap.

This was bad.

Really fuckin' bad.

He could feel it.

Marcello angled his head in silent communication for them to follow. The four of them slinked along the dense foliage that broke open to the edges of a park. They kept low as they prowled along the short fence that ran the backside of a neighborhood.

Alarm swept through his bloodstream, a pound, pound, pound that drummed as he followed Marcello and his men farther along the backside of the sleeping houses. Marcello looked at them, his eyes dim as he indicated for them to ease up the side of the cover of trees. They paused about five yards beyond the back fence line of a small house.

Anxiety wound through Jud. Those tendrils of alarm closed off his throat as they all knelt within the cover of night beneath the shelter of those trees.

"Just who are we pressin', Marcello?" Jud's teeth gritted as he hissed the question below his breath.

Marcello cracked a smug smile. "There's been a small change of plans. We are now on a retrieval mission. We are here to return a boy child to his rightful place."

Confusion stormed while rage spiked. That disquieted anger pumped through his veins and sizzled across his flesh.

He'd anticipated bullshit.

But this?

What exactly did that mean?

A recovery mission of a child?

Whatever it was, it didn't sit right.

It was all off.

All wrong.

Marcello knelt lower, dropped his voice quieter. "There will be two officers standing guard. One inside and one out. Jud, you are here to ensure clear passage into the house. Do it quiet and quick. I will get the child. Kolin and Tony, you ensure no one else gets out."

They nodded as if they had already been prepped for their roles.

While venom burned on Jud's tongue, the world starting to spin, the truth that he'd indeed walked straight into a trap.

Coerced into deviance.

"Why am I here? Why would you come all the way to Redemption Hills to drag me back here?" he demanded, attention flicking around, trying to figure the score. What the fuck this was about.

Marcello had hundreds of men at his disposal.

"This mission is of the utmost importance. One in which failure will not be tolerated. Under the dire circumstances, I was charged to find the best. You are the best, no?"

It was pure provocation.

"Who is the target?" Jud demanded, angst lining his bones.

Marcello knew the charge.

Jud only killed if the killing was earned.

"That is none of your concern."

"You know I don't do jobs blind."

"You do now. I'd not question that, if I were you."

Marcello gestured for them to proceed.

Jud warred. Unsettled. A rattled sensation climbed through his conscience. A warning that called out low at the back of his head. Marcello was manipulating him. It was all bullshit.

The men remained angled down as they crossed the fence line and into the house's yard. Jud followed, prepared to bolt.

Ready to turn his back and walk.

Shun this life the way he'd promised he would do.

Fuck Marcello and his family.

He had a choice. They didn't get to control him.

He was prepared for a fight. For this to go south when he walked. He would most likely have to battle it out, but it would be a war worth fighting.

Only he stilled when he caught sight of a silhouette through the window.

A woman.

She paced, back and forth, back and forth. His insides clenched when he saw the clear outline of a child swaddled in the well of her arms as she paced.

His guts twisted and curled.

Nausea swam.

Marcello gestured to move, and the reality of his instructions warbled through Jud's mind.

Ensure no one else gets out.

"Are you fuckin' crazy?" Jud spat, his voice still held quiet. "There's a woman in there."

A mother.

"Do your job, Lawson," Marcello stated low. "Ensure my passage and do it now. Five minutes and this is to be done."

Tony and Kolin started to douse the backside of the house in gasoline while Marcello crept along behind them, looking for the best way to enter.

Disgust burned a hole through Jud's middle. Conscience screaming. World shouting. His gun was out and cocked.

Marcello grinned back like the bastard thought Jud was doing his bidding. Only Jud pointed the barrel at him. "Not gonna happen."

Fury burst in Marcello's expression. "You dare point a gun at me?"

"It's an honor, actually."

Marcello's men dropped the cans and rushed to pull out their guns. The cans clattered against the dry earth, ringing out like an alarm for the guards inside.

A voice echoed from the front. "Possible breach at the rear. Securing perimeter."

A split second later, it was a blur of disorder. A man dressed in a suit who had been posted out front came around the side of the house. A gunshot rang out from Kolin, hitting the officer in the head.

He went down.

Pandemonium.

Inside and out.

Shouting.

Jud fired.

Kolin froze then fell flat on his face.

Gone.

Jud had hit Tony in the thigh. He cried out in misery as he dropped to the ground.

Jud ran for Marcello who crawled along the ground on his belly like the serpent that he was.

"Don't move, asshole."

Marcello flopped around, leaning up on his hands as Jud stood over him. The barrel of Jud's gun was pointed down at the monster who was there to enact the unthinkable.

The unforgiveable.

Surprise knocked Jud off balance when Tony suddenly rammed into him from the side. He fumbled, fell to the lawn, his gun sliding just out of reach.

With his gun in one hand, Marcello scrambled to get on top of Jud.

Jud fought him for it, squeezing his wrist to knock it loose.

Tony was back on his feet, and he kicked Jud in the ribs. Pain splintered through his side. He gasped out but managed to knock the handgun from Marcello's hand while Tony continued his assault.

Kick after kick.

Pain lanced through Jud's body, but he refused to give. To let either of them see this through.

He tossed Marcello off, and he grabbed Tony's ankle and twisted it hard when Tony went to kick him again. The man screamed in agony, falling back at the same time Marcello managed to get to his feet to scramble for his gun that Jud had tossed aside.

Jud kicked out, sweeping Marcello at the ankles and dropping him flat to his back.

Jud jumped up, darting for his gun and sweeping it off the lawn.

He fired a shot at Tony who was lumbering to his feet.

Blood splatted as the impact flew him back, another monster in the ground.

Both Marcello's soldiers were slain, and it was just Jud and this piece of shit.

A piece of shit Jud was going to be all too happy to rid the world of.

Marcello was on his ass, and he pressed back on his heels, scooting himself backward. "You've made a grave mistake."

Jud sneered as he encroached, his aim clear. "Pretty sure that's you."

A shout and cry echoed from inside.

It distracted Jud for the barest second—a second that allowed Marcello to flick a lighter and get to his feet.

"He'll assume it was you." The words were vile. Cruel and careless and without mercy. "You won't walk away from this."

Marcello went to toss it, and Jud rushed. He knocked Marcello back to the ground, had his foot on his throat with the barrel aimed at his face. "Don't."

Marcello cracked a grin. Tossed the lighter behind him.

The demon writhed.

There was no remorse when he pulled the trigger.

When blood splattered and his body slumped and Marcello no longer existed.

But it was too late.

The cans caught.

A whoosh.

A flame.

An explosion.

Heat blasted across Jud's face as the inferno sparked to life in an instant.

"No!" he shouted.

He dropped his gun beside Marcello's lifeless body and ran for the flames.

They had already consumed the back wall, eating up the wood and lapping at the ceiling.

Smoke billowed. A heavy darkness that filled the air and choked out hope.

Consuming.

Disorienting.

A black plague that annihilated everything in its path.

Still, he broke through the back door, searched, fumbled through the abyss from one room to the next.

Nothing.

Nothing.

Fear crushed, as suffocating as the smoke that filled his lungs. He pulled his shirt over his face, his eyes wide and unseeing, the world a blur of fire and white-hot pain.

It didn't matter.

He pressed on.

Pushed.

Forever passed.

A second.

A moment.

Misery the time that ticked on the clock.

A roar rose from the depths of him. "Where are you? Please. Fuck. Can you hear me?"

The whooshing of the flames screamed back.

No, this couldn't happen. He wouldn't let it.

He pressed deeper into the smoke-filled house.

He was on his knees. Blind as he searched.

A bed.

No.

A crib.

He felt along the spindles.

He gulped when he felt it. When he knew. When he curled his arms around the limp body.

So light. So small.

He took it into his arms, pushed to his feet, and stumbled through the flames.

Searching for a way out.

A window.

He lifted his boot, kicked it, busted through.

Glass shattered and rained and tore his flesh. But he didn't slow. He lumbered out into the night.

Refusing the pain.

Refusing the agony.

The fire raged behind them, and he ran to the edge of the yard.

Cradling the tiny frame, he dropped to his knees and gently set it on the ground.

The boy child.

His arms shook.

Shook and shook.

While the flames roared and wood crumbled and the structure gave.

No hope for life from within.

Torment wailed.

As loud as the sirens he heard coming in the distance.

Frantic, he breathed against the child's mouth. Breathed and breathed. His hands too big and clumsy against his tiny chest.

Tears blurred, burning down his ash-covered face.

No. Please. No.

Heavy engines roared up the street, sirens blaring, flashes of light in the night.

"This way! Help! Please!" He shouted it when he saw a paramedic round the side, when the man came up short at the bodies strewn across the ground.

The man's eyes widened when he saw Jud wailing over the child.

The man jogged across the yard.

One second later, Jud was gone.

Just another monster that disappeared into the night.

I jolted awake to the dream, flying upright. Sweat drenched my skin, and my heart ravaged my chest.

I squinted, disoriented, waking up to the barest light filtering in through the windows.

For years, I'd woken up alone, lost in a nightmare that would forever haunt my life. It tortured me with what I'd been partner to. With what I'd had no power to stop.

Her hands found me in the pinked rays of morning light.

That energy crawled and clashed.

Comfort and torment.

I swung my legs off the side of the bed while Salem crawled to curl herself around me from behind.

The way she'd done before.

This girl with so much understanding.

Way she saw me in a different light. Like maybe she could hold this burden with me the way I was going to hold hers.

"You're in so much pain," she whispered, pressing her lips to the marred flesh of my back. Where I'd sustained the burns that had marked me for what I'd done. Scars that reminded me each day of the senseless loss, the kind born of a wicked life.

"She left me when I told her." Yeah, I'd told Salem this before, but I thought maybe she got it then. My shame. How I was going to ask her to bear some of it. How I needed her to.

She curled her arms tighter around my body. "I see who you are, Jud."

I could feel her spirit.

Her compassion. Her love. Her worry.

"I hate that she left you over something that hurts you so much." Her voice was a whisper of compassion. Of strength and belief.

The confession clawed at my throat, though fear tried to snuff it out, to hold it back.

"I'm right here," Salem promised. "It's okay. You can talk to me."

I guessed it was the love in her voice that opened the gates for the words to get free. "Even though Kennedy didn't know the full details of my past, she'd known there was something." I huffed out a self-deprecating sound. "Guess it's written on me. Fact I'm wicked."

Immorality carved into my spirit.

"You know I don't believe that." Salem murmured it. Giving me more of that belief.

I gathered up the hands she had on my stomach and brought them up to press over the uproar going down in my chest. I held them there tight. To the thunder that now belonged to her.

I swallowed around the ball of barbed wire embedded in my throat. "Thought I was doing the right thing—protecting my brother from that life. But it was bullshit..." My voice grew thin as the visions flashed through my mind.

She held on tighter.

"They'd told me I was just supposed to shake someone down. Give them a warning. Get someone back in line who was going off the rails. I swear it. I didn't know. I didn't know. When I got there, it was all wrong, Salem. All wrong. They were asking me to do something there was no chance I could do."

Dread curled through her body, but still, she held onto me, girl wrapping me in this silent support. In this feeling of wholeness that I'd never thought I'd experience again.

"There was a family in a house...they wanted...this boy." I could barely force the words out. "I was supposed to take out the officers there to protect the family so they could get in and take the baby."

Shame carved through the confession. Grief and agony that I couldn't contain. It bounded out into the room from my spirit and echoed back, amplified in the swimming rays of muted light.

I choked on a breath as I forced myself to continue. "Turned out the plan was to set the house on fire to trap the mother inside. Get rid of her. I didn't know it at the time, until the news reported it the next day, but there were two children in there, Salem. A baby boy and girl. A mom and her children."

Grief constricted the words, a guttural cry lanced in the middle of them.

"They wanted the boy...but they didn't want the woman or the girl child to leave that house."

Her arms stiffened, and she inhaled a sharp, biting breath.

I held her hands tighter to me as I let the confession free. "I tried to stop it. Tried to stop them from taking the boy. From hurting the rest. But no one made it out of there alive. Not one of them survived because I tried to intervene, and I made it even worse."

She started to jerk away, but I held her closer as the words scraped like fire from my tongue, rushed and pleading, like I could rearrange them into something else even when I knew there was no chance of ever erasing this truth.

"I tried, Salem. When they realized I was going to fight them, it became a battle. I managed to take out all the men who came to end them, but not before the house was set on fire. I tried to get them out—to find them—to help them."

It left me on a haggard moan.

Or maybe it was just Salem's.

"Where?" she demanded.

"Los Angeles. Four years ago."

A choked sob ripped up her throat as she struggled to break free of my hold.

I let her go as realization slammed me.

When I realized she saw me then.

The real me.

And she was going to leave me, too.

I didn't want to even look at her, to see the fear and loathing that would no doubt be written on her face. But I couldn't stop myself. Not when she scrambled away like she was the one being burned, choking and gasping and heaving out for the breaths that wheezed from her lungs.

"No," she begged.

"I told you, Salem. Told you it was bad." I forced myself to look back at her.

I nearly died right there when I saw her expression.

The horror.

The terror.

Tears streamed hot down her gorgeous face, and her mouth was trembling everywhere.

She slipped off the opposite edge of the bed. "No. No, Jud, no."

Torment clotted my throat. "Would never hurt you."

She backed away, her hands clutched to her chest, clawing at her heart like she was going to rip it out.

"Darlin'?" I was such a fuckin' fool because I pushed to my feet and started around the bed like I could be worthy of holding some of her fear when I was the one who'd caused it.

"He...he...f-f-found us." The words tripped from her tongue.

A frown curled my brow. "What?"

"He found us. No. He found us." Frantic, she spun in a circle. She suddenly lurched forward, scrambling around on the floor until she found her shoes.

She jerked them on, hopping around to try to keep her balance.

I rounded the end of the bed, approaching her like she was a wild animal that'd been backed into a corner. "What are you saying? Who found you?"

A distressed sob raked from her throat and ricocheted against the walls. "He found us, Jud. Carlo. He found us."

She may as well have bashed me with a sledgehammer. The way pain splintered through my head. I stumbled and my knees locked.

Sickness, hatred, and dread coiled through the room. A vortex that would suck us in and consume.

"Did you say *Carlo*? What are you saying, Salem? Tell me you're not saying what I think you are." The demand cracked through the heated air.

Carlo.

Marcello's piece of shit older brother.

He was the family head. The one who'd called the shots. Gave the orders. He was the one I'd thought I'd have to spend the rest of my life looking over my shoulder for, sure he'd be back for revenge. Thinking one day he'd come for me. Instead, the coward had up and disappeared after it'd all gone down.

The bastard who'd had his wife and babies killed. The one who was responsible for the deaths of the two officers posted to guard them. Not to mention his brother and two of his men who had been found on the scene—only those three had been compliments of me.

Carlo was one of LA's most wanted. As far as I knew, he'd become dust. Vapor. There had been no sign of him for the last four years.

She backed away. "Did you do this? Oh my god, did you do this? Trap us?"

A disorder blustered through her words, and my brow pinched in pained confusion. "What the fuck are you talking about, Salem? Tell me what the hell you are saying. I would never hurt you. I love you. I fucking love you. Please, tell me what is happening."

She gasped against my words then rushed for her purse, and she tossed out the words like they made perfect sense. "Not everyone died in that house, Jud."

"What? Fuck, Salem, tell me what the fuck you're talking about."

She flew around to look at me, her face soaked. "The news reported that we all died, Jud. My son...Lucas...he was in his crib. I lost him. Oh god. I lost him." Her knees nearly buckled when she said it, and her hand darted to the table to steady herself. Her grief was so thick I could taste it. "But Juni and I...we got out."

Sorrow trapped her in that dark, dark storm.

She squeezed her eyes shut before a rush of words tumbled from her mouth. "I was rocking Juni in the other room. We heard noises, and I went to go for him...I begged to go for him, Jud, but the officer...she forced us out the side door and said she would get him. *She promised she would get him.*"

The words broke on the last because she hadn't.

She hadn't.

Dread sank through my spirit.

Because I had.

I had found him.

Had found him too late.

And there was nothing I could do. Nothing I could do.

The walls spun.

It had been Salem in that house.

Salem and Juni.

And her son. Her son.

Gripping my head, I bent in two.

"Oh, fuck. Salem. No." Agony clawed through my being. Enough to drop me to my knees.

I managed to stay standing so I could move for her. The only thing I wanted was to wrap her in my arms. Hold her and protect her.

On a yelp, she put her hands out in front of her. "Stay away from me, Jud. Don't you understand? If you didn't do this? It was him. It's a set up. He found us. He's going to kill us both."

"No. Won't let that happen."

"You killed his brother, Jud." The plea spilled from her mouth. The truth of what all this really meant.

"I did."

Terror filled the void between us.

Rippling and shivering.

"I was a fool for coming here. For losing sight of my purpose. I have to go. We have to get out of here before it's too late."

"Let me—"

She shrieked when I reached for her, and I felt it then. The blame. The hate. The truth of what I'd caused. What I should've stopped but had been too blind to see.

She backed out of the doorway. "Stay away from me."

"Salem, please."

"Stay away. I mean it."

Chapter Thirty-Four

Salem

PANIC FLOODED MY BLOODSTREAM.

A surge of terror that rose high and swept me under, but it was the heartbreak that would do me in.

Jud.

It seared me in two.

Cleaved me in half.

Jud had been there that night. He'd been there, and he'd tried to stop it.

As soon as I'd accused him of working with Carlo, of tricking me into falling for him, I'd known it was wrong. I felt Jud's agony just as sure as I felt my own.

Those aching pieces of myself that were barely held together were obliterated in his pain.

In this torment that I couldn't fathom.

Couldn't process.

It was gutting.

Shattering.

It only spiked the anxiety farther. The rush of adrenaline—of awareness—that promised I had to get out of there.

Leave it behind.

That for me and Juni, there was no such thing as *home*.

Jud couldn't fix this. It was only going to destroy us all.

My mind spun with every horrible possibility. There had to be a bigger reason I was there in Redemption Hills. A bigger reason I had found Jud. A reason we had come together.

It spiraled with every gut-wrenching scenario of how Carlo had found us.

I knew it. I knew he had. I knew he was there.

Watching.

Waiting.

Sickness clawed and crept and seeped all the way to my bones.

A cold dread that shivered and froze.

This time when I pressed down on the accelerator, I forced myself to ignore everything else around me.

Every call and every claim.

I couldn't give thought or reason or purpose to Jud's pleas as he chased behind us. As he tried to break through the disorder the same way as he'd done last night, although right then, I knew we'd already ended before we'd ever really begun.

Our destinies had already been carved in stone.

"Salem…just listen…you can't leave like this. Fuck, please, don't do this."

Juni whimpered from the backseat, more afraid than I thought she'd ever been, while I mashed the accelerator to the floor. The SUV fishtailed as I skidded out of the Iron Ride parking lot and onto the street.

My hands cinched around the steering wheel as I prayed. As I prayed for a moment. For a break in time. For a fighting chance.

For escape.

Tears blurred my eyes as I sped down the street, barely slowing as I took a sharp right.

I flew past Absolution then took a left at the next intersection.

Prayed these wings would give us flight.

I barreled down the roads of the small town, spinning it into chaos, the brightening sky ominous as the sun lifted on the mountain.

As the glimmering rays gave way to a new day that I was terrified would be our end.

How could this happen? How could I let this happen? I'd known not to come here. Not to become complacent. Not to fall.

I took the few quick turns before I made the last left onto the sleeping neighborhood street. My aching heart was lodged in my throat, and my stomach was twisted in knots of terror as I quickly approached the narrow driveway of the small house that had come to mean so much.

I knew Darius and Mimi had wanted to give us this home, while *home* had begun to feel like it was in the arms of a man who I'd left behind on the other side of this city.

This sweet, hopeful town that now felt like a trap.

An ambush.

I rammed on the brakes and came to a jarring stop.

Juni cried out through the bottled fear. "Mommy."

"I know, sweetheart, I know."

My entire being shook uncontrollably as I rushed out of my seat and yanked open the back-passenger door. I fumbled to remove my daughter from the straps—my reason, my purpose, my life—knowing I'd only have to put her right back in them.

I hated it.

Hated it.

I guarded myself against the pain, against the coming hurt and loneliness, and focused on what I had to do.

Run.

With my daughter in my arms, I jogged up the sidewalk. I was barely able to get the key into the lock. When I finally managed it, I tossed it open. The wood slammed against the interior wall, shaking the little house like an earthquake had come to toss it from its foundation.

I wondered if it had.

The door banged shut behind us, and I bolted toward the suitcase I'd shoved in the corner. One I had believed I would never have to use again.

A fool.

A fool.

I set Juni onto her feet and began to stuff our necessities inside.

"Mommy, no, I don't wants to go on another adventures. We like it rights here, remember? We gotta stay here forever, and the bads man can never come here because it's the bestest place we ever gots."

For a beat, my eyes squeezed shut, wishing it were true. That I could offer it to my daughter.

Give her the life that she deserved.

"We're going to go someplace extra fun, Juni. I promise. Don't cry. Please, don't cry."

"Mommy, no." She pressed her little fists to her eyes.

God.

How could I keep doing this?

But I had no other choice.

We'd left that night under the cover of darkness. Amid the agony of leaving half myself behind. The cutting away of life that had scourged me to the soul.

My son lost to a battle he never should have had to fight.

I'd been helpless to change it.

Helpless to do anything but fight for my daughter.

I'd been running ever since. Unsure if Carlo was one step behind me. My gut had told me he'd never believed the reports that we'd all perished that night, even while I'd prayed that he was gone himself. That when he'd disappeared, he'd disappeared from this earth.

He'd never stood trial.

Had never been held accountable.

Had never paid for the sins that he'd perpetuated because the only choice I'd had left was to run. To protect my daughter.

Trust no one.

I grabbed Juni's shot records and the few documents that I had, my sight blurring over as the hope dimmed from my sight.

The hope of her going to school.

Of living a normal life.

Of having a home.

A family.

For the joy I could feel fading away.

"What are you doing?"

A tiny scream got free when the voice caught me unaware, and I was on my feet and swinging my attention toward the hall.

Darius stood at the end of it. His arms were stretched across the length, and he hung onto either side, like he was holding himself back, like he'd been caught up in the turmoil, too.

"Leaving," I told him.

I hated that it was true.

"What? No. You don't have to be afraid, Salem. Told you that you were safe. That you don't have to run anymore."

My head shook as grief fell down my face in hot streams of despair. "He found us."

Darius' brow curled and he roughed a hand over the top of his hair. "What?

What are you talking about? You're fine, Salem. Just calm down."

"I..." I trailed off, unable to form the words. The trust Jud had given me, the truth he'd confided in me.

I'd had to stomp all of it under my feet.

"Tell me what the fuck is goin' on, Salem."

"Jud...he knows Carlo."

Darius blanched before awareness raced in to take over his expression. Groaning, he scrubbed both palms over his face. "Shit. Knew this was gonna happen."

Ice froze me to the spot, and I blinked through the stupor. "What?"

Darius let go of a harsh sigh. "Warned you to stay away from him. Told you he was trouble."

There was something in the way he said it.

As if he were annoyed rather than panicked.

Dread slithered down my spine, a slow awareness that I didn't want to take hold. "What do you mean? Tell me what you're talking about, Darius."

Darius shook his head and took a lumbering step forward. "I told you I was gonna make it right for you."

My brow twisted, and I took a step back. "I don't understand. You're scaring me."

Darius slowly approached. The words dropping from his tongue were daggers that pierced me through. "Carlo found me, Salem. He promised he wasn't after you. He only wanted the man who killed his brother. The one responsible for him losing his son."

"No." I stumbled a step back farther. Dull blades sliced through my middle. Pierced me to the core.

Darius wouldn't. He wouldn't.

"It was time, Salem. I had to do it for you. For Juni."

"Oh my god." Horror gusted from my lungs, and I pressed my hands against the cavern carved in my chest like I could hold myself together as the panic multiplied tenfold.

There was no question then.

Carlo was there.

He'd been watching.

The car.

It was him.

It was him.

Darius kept coming my way. "All I had to do was get in with Jud. Find his weaknesses, Salem. See what was gonna hurt Jud most, and you'd be free. But first, I had to prove my loyalty. That's why I brought you here. To convince Carlo that you and Juni were still alive but no longer a threat to him. In exchange, you and Juni are free to live your lives in safety."

"You're lying. You're lying. You wouldn't do that to me. To us." I begged it.

"Do it to you? I did it *for* you."

"No, Darius."

"You were supposed to stay away from him, Salem. I'd hoped last night…that the fire would remind you of what was important. That you'd realize you didn't belong there. That you'd come to your senses."

"I can't believe you'd—"

The words clipped off when I felt the commotion at the end of the hall, and my attention whipped to the right to find Mimi shuffling into the living room. Confusion was written on her face, her aged eyes darting between us, though hurt was written there as she caught up to Darius' confession.

She hadn't known.

Darius had done it.

He had set us up, and I wasn't sure we would be able to get out.

I grabbed Juni's hand. "We have to go, sweetheart."

"No, Mommy, no more adventures. Please." She tried to yank her hand free.

Agony lanced while the betrayal whipped.

How could he do this to us? When we'd finally had a chance?

"I can't believe you'd do this to us. I can't believe it."

My gaze jumped to Mimi, and I felt my heart breaking all over again. "We have to go, Mimi. I'm so sorry. I'm so sorry."

Old sorrow spun through her eyes, but it was pained disbelief when it shifted to Darius. She looked back at Juni and me. "I understand, sweet girl. Don't be sad. I've cherished these months with you two. Months I never thought I'd be given."

Tears streamed, and I tried to hold back a sob, but it was so big it busted through and banged against the walls.

"Come on, sweetheart," I begged.

Darius hustled behind me as I dragged the suitcase and tried to coax my daughter into following.

She cried and whimpered and tried to dig in her heels. "But this is our specialist place, Mommy. We gots to stay with Mimi and Gage and the Motorcycle Man."

My teeth gritted, and I forced out, "We have to go."

Darius moved forward and grabbed me by the wrist. "No, you don't, Salem. You're safe. Carlo gave me his word. You're safe. He just wanted the details of Jud's family, how to hurt him most, in exchange for your safety."

"And you're a fool if you believe that's true."

Dismay pulsed through my being, the thought of Jud or his beautiful family being harmed in any way. The people who'd accepted me and my daughter as if we were one of them.

Good, kind people.

I had to warn them.

Darius tightened his hold. "No. You were the fool for falling in love with a man you don't belong to. A fool for leaving Carlo to begin with."

Shock cleaved through my being. The treason my brother had meted nearly dropped me to my knees.

"How could you say that?"

Pain curled his face and a strained breath wheezed from his lungs. He flung a frustrated hand out into the room. "Because you and I both knew what would happen if you left him. The lengths he would go to get you back, and you agreed to testify against him, Salem. Took his children and went into hiding."

He swallowed hard. "I've been terrified for years, searching for a way to make this right. To take back what never should have happened in the first place. But I couldn't do a fucking thing. Carlo had claimed you as his and there was nothing I could do. Nothing I could say. It didn't matter you were my sister. He was the boss. So now, all these years later? If I had a way to finally give you the life you deserved, to set you and Juni free? I had to do it."

I tried to yank free of his hold. "No, you didn't have to do it," I shouted. "You didn't. You lied to me. You *lied* to me."

I rushed toward the door. He grabbed me again. "What did you expect me to do, Salem? Let you keep running forever? What kind of life would that be? For you and for your daughter? How was Juni ever going to feel secure? Grow up? Go to school? How? I had to do something."

Disbelief coiled in my spirit. "And what you did was destroy our chance."

I whipped the door back open and rushed out, hauling Juni behind me. Darius followed, coming around to my side, trying to get in my face. "Listen to me, you're safe. He gave me his word."

The vile, cruel laughter that echoed from the end of the walk had me freezing in place.

Ice slipped down my spine.

My hand curled tighter on my daughter's hand.

"It's been such a long time, Pupa. Look at you…as beautiful as ever." Carlo's voice was close to casual from where he leaned on the driver's side door of my SUV, wearing a suit, his hands mindlessly stuffed in his pockets as if he weren't there to destroy.

I knew better.

Terror seized me.

Rocketed through the air in fiery bolts.

I tried to breathe, to think, to plan.

Because I wasn't going out without a fight.

I screamed when Darius was suddenly yanked back and forced to his knees with his hands behind his back. A gun was pressed to the back of his head by one of Carlo's men.

Another man lurked behind them.

"What are you doing?" Darius seethed. I could feel his fear rush through his muscles, the way they bunched and sweat dripped down the side of his face.

Carlo laughed a condescending sound. "It seems I've had a change of heart."

Darius thrashed. "No. You promised. I gave you the information you wanted on Jud. You have him. Now let Salem go."

"I've learned there's something he wants more." Cocking his head, Carlo grinned at me.

Without another warning, a gunshot rang out. Darius slumped to the sidewalk, blood pooling around him.

A scream ripped from my soul.

A scream of agony.

Of disbelief.

Of horror.

Of fear.

"No," I whimpered as I grabbed my daughter and hid her face against my body, desperate to protect her from the cruelty that had found us.

My eyes darted everywhere as I looked for a path. For a direction to run. For a way out of this place.

I would fight.

I would fight.

"Come here, Pupa," Carlo quietly coaxed, as if I were precious. "Bring my daughter to me. I'd like to meet her." His head cocked to the side and his mouth twisted in an annoyed sneer. "As for you…it's a shame you already used your second chance. We could have been so good together."

"No." My head shook, my veins filling with a frenzy as I searched for a way out.

He tsked.

In a flash, I scooped up Juni and took the chance.

I ran, my feet frantic as I raced across the lawn in the opposite direction of Carlo and toward the street with my daughter in my arms.

Mimi shouted, and out of my periphery, I could see she was running for Carlo with her arms waving above her head.

Oh god, no.

"Mimi, no!" I shouted into the air, still running, praying for her to come to her senses.

Another shot rang out.

A grunt and a crash and her voice was silenced.

Agony ripped through me.

Staggering.

Unimaginable.

But I kept running.

I had to. I had to.

Another shot. This one from the other side of the street. Then shots began to fire from every side.

What was happening? What was happening?

A disorder engulfed. Chaos.

I curled down and kept rushing away, my arms around Juni's head as if I could protect her from the hail of bullets.

Through it, I somehow saw as both of Carlo's men fell.

It was one second before Carlo's arms wrapped around me from behind.

He yanked me against him. Hard and vicious.

A scream yelped from my throat.

We toppled to the ground in a heap, the vicious man's arms chains around my body.

But not before I let Juni go.

Not before I screamed, "Run, Juni, run! Run and don't look back."

Chapter Thirty-Five

Jud

HELPLESSLY, I WATCHED HER PEEL OUT OF THE LOT, THE SUV accelerating quickly before it disappeared at the end of the street.

"Fuck! Salem!"

I sucked for a breath I couldn't find.

I felt like I'd gotten torn right in two.

By the memories of what I'd done, but more so, by hers.

The truth coming to light. I couldn't process the magnitude of her loss. Of what she'd been through.

And I'd been there that night.

I wanted to claw my fucking heart out of my chest.

But that urge? It only came in as a close second to the burning need I felt to hop on my bike.

To hunt Carlo down.

Like I'd said, all I needed was a name. And now that I had one? I wouldn't stop until it was finished.

Wondered if it was fate that name was already written in vengeance.

Retribution itched at my fingers, the thirst to go on a rampage so strong I could taste it on my tongue.

Need to give this girl the life she deserved.

One without me in it.

Right after I wiped the stain from her life.

The monster from this earth.

The demon inside raged. Jerked and thrashed against its bindings. Chains that pulled taut, links stretching to the brink of breaking.

In turmoil, I stormed back toward the building on my bare feet, wearing nothing but my underwear, my ears ringing with the promise of blood.

Probably looked like a psychopath. Wasn't far from the truth.

I ran back around the side of Iron Ride to the set of stairs that led to my loft. I jerked open the heavy door and pounded upstairs, flinging open the upper door and going straight for my room where I'd left my phone on the nightstand.

I ripped it free of the cord, frantically jabbing at the contact.

It rang three times before Trent's recorded voice came on the line.

"Fuck," I spat, then started to rattle off the message when it beeped. "There's trouble, Trent. Carlo is here and the bastard is after Salem. Think Darius is somehow involved. I don't know…fuck…I just…"

Could barely get it out, words breaking as I tried to explain. "There's a bunch of shit I don't have time to explain, but I think she's in danger. She left here panicked. Need you to keep a lookout for her at her place. I know she's set on leaving town, but I'm not sure if she will go there first. I'm gonna…"

My eyes pinched closed.

Because I didn't fuckin' know…didn't know what I was going to do. I just knew I couldn't sit there idle. Couldn't wait. "Just keep an eye out."

Ending the call, I grabbed my jeans from the ground and yanked them on, pulled my tee over my head before I was shoving my feet into my boots. I tucked my phone into my back pocket, then I made a beeline to my closet where I kept my safe. I punched in the code and cranked it open.

I tossed on my holster, loaded it up, and I was blazing out the main door and running downstairs.

Ready to go on a hunt.

Hitting the ground floor, I jogged for my bike.

I stalled out when I saw the dark figure curled up on the floor near the middle bay. My eyes narrowed, and my heart hammered.

Shock slammed me when I realized there was a person bound on the floor.

I streaked that direction, pulling my handgun from the holster as I went.

Dread nearly dropped me to my knees when I saw it was Logan. Tied up and beat to hell. A thick piece of tape covered his mouth.

Blood pooled around his sagging, limp form. Felt bad that I took comfort in the moan that vibrated from him where he lay on his side.

"Fuck, Logan, I've got you, man. Hold on."

I tried to get the tape off without ripping it, without hurting him more, but he was shouting something behind it.

"I'm sorry, man." I issued it before I gave up and tore it free because I didn't see any other way around it.

Except, in an instant, he was screaming, "Go, Jud, go. It's a distraction. I'm a fucking distraction. Go!"

"What—"

He cut me off. "I'm just a warning, Jud. A distraction. Pulled me from my bed in the middle of the night and planted me here. It's clear it's not me he wants. It's you and Salem. They would have put a bullet in me rather than kicking the shit out of me otherwise, and you know it. Go. Find her."

I warred for the barest fraction of a second before I pulled my switchblade from my pocket, flicked it open, dragged it through the thin rope to free him.

Second he was, he shouted, "Go, man. Go!"

I was on my feet, racing for my bike, pushing the button to the garage door as I passed. It opened, and I dialed 9-1-1, shouting the address to the shop, saying I needed a paramedic at Iron Ride, then shouting I needed an officer at Salem's house, that a mother and child were in danger.

The operator tried to ask for more details, but I ended it and hopped on my bike, and I was on the road, flying through town. Traveling so fast that the streets blurred beneath me. Lines becoming one. The sky a quickened haze above.

I only had one thing I could see.

One destination.

One purpose.

I would set this one thing right.

Give a new life to this girl who'd become everything. One who I wanted to live. To find joy. For her sweet Juni Bee to fly free.

In a daze of fury, I made the last turn into their neighborhood. I pinned the throttle, flying up the short hill where the houses rested back in the cover of trees.

Then the air heaved from my lungs, and I thought my ribs were gonna cave. A gush of horror shocking free as I squinted into the distance.

Juni.

Juni was running up the sidewalk.

Alone.

A cyclone of terror rippled around her.

I skidded to a stop beside her and was off faster than I could make sense of it.

She ran for me, her precious little face soaked with fear. I had her in my arms in a flash of desperation.

Relief slammed me. A punch to the gut. A riot in my soul.

"Motorcycle Man. You cames to save us. The bad man is here." She cried it where she'd burrowed her face in the side of my neck, words distorted in my beard.

But I felt them ricochet through my spirit.

And every promise I'd made to myself fell away.

The commitment to be better.

To live clean.

That I'd never again have a man's blood on my hands.

The devil screamed, and I heard the strain of the chains when they finally snapped.

There was a car parked on the curb, and I ran for it, took a fist and put it through the glass on the side that was hidden from the street. Pain barely even registered as the shards fell free.

I swiped them away, pulled open the lock and opened the door, and placed this little girl who owned me heart and soul into the backseat. I took her by the face. "Lay on the floor. Do not get up or show your face until either me or Trent come to get you. Do you understand? I need you to be the best hider in the world right now."

Furiously, she nodded. "Okay."

"Good girl."

Then I shut the door, gave a furtive glance around to make sure no one saw where she was before I was back on my bike and speeding over the hump in the road that gave way to the plateau where Salem's house sat on top of the hill.

Ahead, I saw it, the blacked-out BMW sitting in the same spot where it'd been the day Trent and I had been teaching the kids to ride their bikes.

Then my mind spun with dread when I saw the carnage spread out up ahead.

Bodies were strewn all over the front lawn.

Trent was across the road in front of Eden's house with his gun drawn.

And Salem…Salem was angled to face him, Carlo behind her with a gun to her head, the piece of shit using her as a shield.

And me?

I pulled the gun from where it was strapped to my back, and I let the demon go.

Chapter Thirty-Six

Salem

THE AIR WHEEZED DOWN MY CONSTRICTED THROAT.

Pain fractured through my being.

Mental.

Emotional.

Physical.

The dread and the fear so intense I couldn't see.

A cold sweat clogged my pores and saturated my soul as I mourned for what I could only process as loss.

Darius.

Mimi.

Jud.

Juni.

Juni. Juni. Juni.

Silently, I prayed that her little feet had carried her someplace safe. That she'd escaped this Hell. That someone good and kind and right had found her and come to her rescue.

Carlo rammed the barrel of his gun into the back of my head. He pressed it hard to my skull, the metal a painful threat.

I tried not to cry out.

Not to give him the satisfaction as he curled his fingers deep into my skin.

He faced me toward Trent who was across the street with his gun aimed our direction, fierce and hard and dark.

It was a stand-off.

Carlo was using my beating heart as a shield because if he killed me then, there was no question Trent would take him out.

Trent who'd slain the two men as if he were simply checking off a to-do list. The men caught unaware before they were on the ground.

"Let her go," Trent ordered, "and I'll make this easy."

The threat curled through the atmosphere.

Carlo laughed an incredulous sound. "I think you've forgotten who I am."

"Didn't care then. Don't care now." Trent said it offhanded, though I could hear the venom that lined his voice.

The way his words were calculated. Meant to distract Carlo's anger from me and place it on himself.

As if he were buying time. Precious moments for Juni to escape.

My spirit flooded with gratitude. With a small hope that after all of this, my daughter would be okay.

Then my ear tipped into the distance. To the savage roar of an engine that approached from somewhere beyond this trauma.

Out of place.

In perfect time.

A wicked savior I'd wanted to spare.

Behind the grumbling prowl of the motorcycle, I heard the whirring of sirens.

I immediately knew how Trent had shown at the precise moment we'd needed him.

Jud.

My pulse sped as a shred of hope pushed through the fissures of dried ground.

Sprouting.

Swelling.

While the fear and torment spun.

As if Carlo sensed the coming disorder, he held me tighter against his body. "Move and she's gone."

Trent scoffed. "And you and I both know what happens then."

Trent moved to the right, and Carlo matched him, step for step.

The two circling.

A stalemate.

The motorcycle engine howled, carried on the wind, that hope springing higher while fear battered against it. The need to protect this man. The man I loved wholly. Trusted wholly. One who'd also been caught in the snare of my brother's foolishness.

Then the sound of the motorcycle slowed and stopped.

No.

I wanted to weep when I realized I'd only conjured it. Imagined something that wasn't there.

When I had to accept it wasn't Jud.

That I'd stumbled deeper into the fantasy where I could be his and he could be mine. Where two broken souls could come together. Where they'd find a home.

Agony crushed.

Carlo and Trent continued the writhing, malignant circle.

"I guess I'll have to take my chance then." Carlo snarled it as he rammed the gun harder against my skull.

Pain fractured and the world started to tip to the side when I felt his finger tremble on the trigger.

This was it.

It was it.

Then a flurry hit.

The roll of the engine and a moment later the fury of the bike.

It all happened so fast I could barely digest it.

The blur of sound and glinting metal.

But I guessed it was my heart that recognized it. Processed what was happening as if it played out in slow motion.

Jud blew by.

A rifle drawn.

My mouth dropped open, and the gun trembled at my head.

A millisecond later, there was a deafening crack.

A scream tore from my soul as everything shook.

Carlo flew back, his arms no longer bound around me.

I slowly turned to see his lifeless body bleeding out on the ground.

Shock dropped me to my hands and knees. I gasped as I tried to see through the disorder.

To the motorcycle that skidded on the pavement, to the way Jud never fully stopped before he jumped off. The bike tumbled and rolled, while the mountain of a man stalked my way.

His boots a thunder on the pavement.

A pound, pound, pound that filled me to overflowing.

I wheezed and cried, "Juni."

Jud knelt in front of me. "She's safe, Salem, she is safe."

"Oh, god." I crumbled, no longer able to keep myself upright.

But it was his arms that supported me.

His arms that curled around me as he took me into the safety of his hold. He sank onto his butt on the road and pulled me into the well of his lap.

He hugged me and murmured and whispered, "I have you, I have you."

I'd known there was something about the man that whispered of his darkness.

Of danger.

Of bloodshed and barbarity.

But I'd never been so sure of the goodness, of the righteous ferocity that burned inside of him—not until right then.

My wicked, wicked savior.

"I have you, Salem. I have you."

A sob tore free. I released it at the warmth of his neck where I clung to him, my face pressed into his beard, into the disorder of his pulse that drummed so hard I could feel it become one with my being.

Massive arms encircled me.

Held me in their warmth.

Sirens screamed as three police cars arrived on the scene. An ambulance and a firetruck came to a stop behind them.

"Mimi," I cried. My sobs were uncontrollable as my fingernails sank into Jud's shoulders.

The loss.

The loss.

"Mimi."

I felt the movement of him gesturing wildly.

Footsteps stampeded around us.

Curses and shock.

The horror of the massacre that had unfolded on our lawn.

An officer loomed over us.

Jud pressed his mouth to the top of my head. "I'm so sorry, Salem. I am so fuckin' sorry."

My head shook beneath his chin, lost beneath the cover of his beard and his giant heart. "You saved us."

He'd saved us.

His shame had been mine and Juni's saving grace.

That horrible night four years ago and again today.

Our wicked, beautiful savior.

And I prayed, he'd let me save him from the horror of the past I finally understood.

One that I shared with him.

Our hearts knitted and forever bound.

Chapter Thirty-Seven

Jud

I HOVERED OUTSIDE THE INTENSIVE CARE ROOM WHERE THE lights were cut dim and a slew of machines quietly hummed and beeped.

My goddamn heart pressed at my ribs and climbed to form a lump in my throat.

It was funny how Salem had said when she'd first come here that she'd felt like an outsider, like she didn't belong, when I'd never been so sure of it for myself than right then.

But I didn't know how to walk. How to turn and go.

Not when this enchantress of a woman had caught me up.

Got me spellbound.

Black-fuckin'-magic.

My feet moved of their own accord, unable to resist the lure.

Still, the shame slowed my steps. Hung my head. Ripped my already mangled heart to shreds.

I slipped through the door that remained open a crack and edged up behind the chair that was pulled close to the hospital bed.

Salem held her grandmother's hand. Held it firm but soft.

I set mine on the caps of Salem's shoulders, needing to be there for her, to hold her up when I knew she was close to faltering. My voice was haggard when I said, "She's going to make it. She's strong. Crazy strong. A survivor. A fighter. Just like her granddaughter."

Salem's chest shook in tiny quivers, like the girl was trying to keep her cries subdued. "I always wanted to make her proud. To grow up and be something. To take care of her. Support her and provide for her the way she'd provided for us."

A slow chuckle of affection rumbled out. "I might not know all the details of your lives, Salem, but I know the way Mimi looks at you. With pride. With joy. With love. You don't have to question that."

"I hate it," she choked. "I hate that it came to this. Hate that the choices I made when I was young caused so much pain and loss. I hate what Darius did. Hate that he's gone. Hate that I'm so thankful that because he did, Juni can finally experience the life I always dreamed she might have."

Salem reached up and took my left hand, clasped it tight.

I tried not to weep. "And I hate what I cost you."

Visions flashed.

A fire. The child. The misery.

Salem squeezed tighter. "No, Jud."

Unable to stop myself, I leaned down and wrapped myself around her. I hugged her to me like I didn't have to let her go. My mouth came to her ear. "It's okay, darlin'. I know. I know."

Then I forced myself to straighten and walk away from this woman before I caused her any more pain. Told myself it was all an illusion. That what we'd felt was just a horrible twist of fate.

Most of all, I tried to convince myself the door closing between us wasn't the biggest blasphemy of them all.

"Fuck!" I shoved the stack of papers off the desk. They scattered onto the barren lobby floor. Where the vacancy shouted and the loneliness throbbed.

All wrong.

All fuckin' wrong.

I gritted my teeth and jerked open a drawer, digging around the perfectly organized files on a mission to find what I was searching for.

But stepping inside the lobby only reminded me of what was missing.

My motherfuckin' heart, that was what.

A week had gone by since the shitstorm had gone down.

Darius was gone, along with the monsters he'd sold his soul to. But I had to believe he'd sold it to save Salem and Juni.

Logan had been badly bruised and battered, but I'd known he was going to be just fine when he'd started running his mouth the way he always did while being checked out at the emergency room.

Rubbing it in that I owed him.

Truth was, I'd give the punk everything. Never had I done anything as hard as leave him there that way.

A choice made.

One he'd ended up patting me on the back for and telling me he would have kicked *my ass* if I'd done it any other way.

Didn't mean that guilt hadn't eaten at me.

Found out through Trent that Mimi was home. She'd lost use of her left arm, possibly permanently, but she was alive and breathing. And Juni and Salem?

They were free.

Free.

And in the end, that was the only thing that mattered.

Not the gaping hole carved in my chest where my heart had gone missing.

Not the twisted ache in my gut.

At least that's what I was trying to convince myself of as I stomped around the office like a beast unchained.

Grunting and groaning and drowning in my own misery.

It was worth it. It was worth it.

Every second of pain, it was worth it.

No, the debt couldn't be paid, but I was going to count it an honor that I'd gotten to be there to help them through to the other side.

To safety.

To peace.

To life.

When I couldn't find what I was looking for, I slammed the drawer shut and leaned lower to tug out the bottom one. I started to rummage around when I stilled.

When I felt the shift in the air when the lobby door opened.

A crackle of energy.

A spark of life.

I squeezed my eyes shut, sure I was only dreaming, fantasizing about a girl who'd done me in.

Only I heard the clicking of heels on the hard floor.

Felt the way the earth spun and the ground shook.

Warily, I straightened to look over the high counter.

The breath knocked out of me at the sight of her stepping into the lobby.

The girl was nothing but devastation wrapped in a black, seductive bow.

Black hair and eyes the color of a toiling sea. The darkest, deepest blue.

Thunderbolts that struck straight through me.

Salem was there.

Wearing those fitted black pants and a silky blouse that hugged her in all the right ways, those sky-high heels waltzing across the floor like she owned the place.

A motherfuckin' knockout.

A fantasy.

A dream.

Every cell in my body clutched, and my fingers itched with the urge to paint.

To mark this beauty that would forever live on inside my memories.

Salem angled her head.

All fierce confidence.

Purpose in her step.

"I hear you're looking for some help around here."

I choked out a surprised laugh.

This girl.

I shook my head and planted my palms on the top of the desk because the only thing I wanted to do right then was reach out and take what my spirit screamed was mine.

"You did, huh?"

She nodded, so nonchalant. "Yeah. I heard it was kind of a mess in here, and this burly, giant, oaf of a man was in desperate need of help."

Disbelief left me on a chuckle, and I arched a brow. "Oaf?"

Another emphatic nod, though there was a tease lighting at the edge of her delicious mouth, and this feeling was gathering quick in my stomach. Something far too light.

"Yeah. It seems the owner of this place is really great at what he does, but not so good at seeing what is right in front of him, at knowing what he needs, at understanding what he deserves, so I'm here to help him out."

My mouth trembled. Didn't mean for it to, but there was no controlling the way every nerve in my body came alive.

I edged around the end of the counter.

The girl was five feet away.

Salem's aura hit me in these overpowering waves that threatened to knock me from my feet.

Toasted coconut and sultry sin.

"Yeah, and what's that?"

Thunderbolt eyes flamed when she lifted her scarred chin. "Me."

That single word pierced me.

A confession.

A plea.

All the lightness fled from the room, and I swore I could feel her heart batter and thunder.

"Don't know how you're even standing there right now." The words scraped from my mouth.

"On my own two feet." She answered it without thought.

"But..."

"But what, Jud? But what? Can you honestly stand there and tell me you don't love me? That you don't want me?"

Shaking out a pained laugh, I averted my gaze. "Now that would be an impossibility."

"Then what? Do you blame me for losing Kennedy and Kye?" Her voice hitched at that, a clasp of remorse and sympathy.

I surged forward a step, the words grunted from my mouth. "What? Are you kidding me, Salem? No. Baby, no."

She crossed her arms over her flailing chest. "Then what?"

My head hung in shame. "I'm afraid you won't ever be able to look at me without seeing *him*."

Didn't need to say his name.

It already shouted and banged from the walls.

Lucas.

Lucas.

I hadn't known it before. I'd only known his weight and his shape and the piece of my soul he'd taken with him when he'd gone.

It'd only required one single moment for the child to leave forever written on me.

Emotion slicked across my flesh when Salem stole forward, when she scratched her fingertips into my beard, into my jaw, when she forced me to look up and meet her eyes. "You're right, Jud. I will never be able to look at you without seeing him. Without thinking of him. Without recognizing the scars on your back when you tried to save him. Without remembering it was you who gave me the time to get Juni out. Without seeing the man who saved us. The man who saved us twice."

Torment clutched my spirit. "I was there."

Said it like a confession.

Salem smiled and ran the pad of her thumb over my lips, her voice so soft when she whispered, "You were there."

My eyes dropped closed. "Salem."

Her fingers slipped into my hair. There was no stopping it, nothing I could do to keep my arms from linking around her waist.

From tugging her against me.

From breathing out in relief.

In hope.

My head dropped farther, and my forehead rocked against hers. "We're a mess," I murmured.

Salem eased back an inch so she could gaze up at me. She touched my cheek. "A beautiful, fucking mess."

I grunted a laugh and pulled her tight, burrowed my face in the sweet spot of her neck.

"Darlin'."

She sighed.

I cocked her a grin, let the tease rain free. "So, you're looking for a job?"

She bit her lip. "Mmhmm…I'm looking for a job. I'm looking for my home. I'm looking for my purpose. Most of all, I'm looking for my man, the one who promised me *forever*."

Then she fisted both hands in my shirt, a gleam in those eyes. "And if he doesn't kiss me soon, I'll stab him."

Rough laughter bolted out, and I had her off her feet and in my arms.

And I kissed her as my heart found its rightful place.

Kissed her hard.

Kissed her fierce.

Kissed her until she was the only thing I could see.

Black. Fuckin'. Magic.

Epilogues

Salem

He'd asked me once what I dreamed of most. My answer had come so easy yet had seemed impossible—a home.

A place where my daughter was free. Where we could put down roots so she could grow and flourish. Where we'd know we'd be safe and secure.

A place we could always return to because we knew that's where we belonged.

I gazed out over the little backyard at the group of people who had become that.

A safe place.

A refuge.

A family.

Our home.

Affection pulled tight across my chest.

There was my mountain of a man angling back to throw the football to Logan who had broken around Trent and was in the makeshift end zone.

My wicked savior.

My rugged, sweet Jud.

So big.

So handsome.

His love so fierce and overwhelming I felt the ground shake.

Like he felt the crack of energy in the air, he stopped to shoot me a grin from where he played on the lawn with his brothers.

Gage and Juni were, of course, in the mix.

He winked at me.

"Well, look at that." Mimi's voice hit me from where she sat in the chair next to me on the porch. "That sly dog sure knows how to love a woman up right, doesn't he? There you are, sitting all the way over here, and he's still got my girl's legs shaking."

"Mimi," I chastised quick.

Eden giggled from the chair on the other side of her. "Mmhmm… those Lawson Brothers have some tricks up their sleeves."

"They sure do. Nothing but a swoon fest," Mimi stated.

"Mimi," I said again, holding back laughter and shaking my head.

"What? You know it's true."

I rolled my eyes and huffed. "Fine."

It was true.

So true that I still didn't know what'd hit me.

My life upturned. Upended. Set to right.

So unprepared for the joy we had found.

Tessa laughed from the other side of me. "Fine? Girl, you are legit on fire right now. About to go boom." She made an exploding motion with her hands. "Like, your mad love has become some crazed love. It's a little obscene, if I'm being honest. I think I got pregnant just sitting beside you. Get it together, why don't you?"

I swatted at her arm. "Shush it."

Grinning, she widened her eyes. "Never."

Laughter floated, and my head shook as I sank back into the

warmth and relished the way love poured through the summer day. The sky bright and blue and stuffed with plumes of white clouds.

Trent handed the football off to Juni.

"Go, Juni, go!" he shouted.

She started to dart up the lawn in the wrong direction. He was cracking up when he picked her up midstride and spun her around so she was facing the other way. "That way!"

"Oops!" She giggled and laughed and floundered her way down the lawn.

Jud was right behind her, lumbering slow, taunting her in his sweet way. "I'm gonna get you, Juni Bee."

"No way, nots a chance. I'm ways too fast for you."

He kept up behind her, staying a step away, and Juni screamed, "Touchdown!" when she crossed the imaginary line. Jud waited until then to tackle her. To wrap his massive arms around her tiny body and carefully topple them to the ground.

Juni giggled as he spun her so he was on his back and she was pinning him to the ground. "No way, too late, I already gots the points. Girls rules, remember?"

Gage flew their way. "I'll save you, Juni Bee! We gotta hold him down."

Gage dove on top of them, quick to change strategies as he pinned Juni between him and Jud. "Doggie pile!"

They both flopped over the top of Jud, squirming to hold him down while he playfully flailed.

"I'm going to take you out! One…two…three…tap it out. You're done for, Uncle Jud!" Gage scrambled around to pin his shoulders to the ground while Jud continued to struggle, his laughter booming, his support and care so clear.

"Two against one, no fair! Gage in the Cage is getting too rowdy and strong for me. I'm done for!"

Then Juni edged Gage out and flattened herself over the top of Jud, clinging to his neck. "Don'ts you worry, Motorcycle Dad. I gots you, and I'll protects you and loves you forever."

Everything stilled.

Jud's spirit and my heart and this love that had risen from the ashes to become the most beautiful thing.

Jud curled his arms around her and sat up, hugging her to his chest. "Forever."

Jud

It was dark by the time we got back to the loft. Juni was fast asleep in the backseat of my truck, and her mother was resting in the seat next to me. Her head lolled back, that river of black cascading around her gorgeous face, toppling over her shoulders and caressing her cheek.

When I pulled into my spot in the farthest bay of the shop, I couldn't help but do the same.

Reach out.

Trace the scar on her jaw.

Whisper, "We're home, darlin'."

A soft smile pulled at her mouth, and those eyes fluttered open.

Thunderbolts that were never going to lose their power when it came to me.

I was a goner.

Done for.

Hers until the end of my days.

I put my truck in park and shut off the engine, sent her a grin. "Wait right there."

Hopping out, I rounded the front of the truck and opened her door, angling up so I could unbuckle her and help her out.

Salem sent me a playful smirk. "I can do that myself, you know?"

I touched her chin. "Now why would you want to go and do that when you have all of this to do it for you?"

I gestured at myself.

She giggled as I helped her out onto her feet. "Cocky, much?"

A rough chuckle came sliding out. "You have no idea."

Her fingertips fluttered over my chest. "Oh, I think I might."

I laughed, swung in for a quick kiss, gave a little swat to that delicious ass. "Let's get you inside."

"Bossy."

My eyes narrowed.

Salem laughed, and my heart went to stampeding.

Every moment.

Every day.

Had no clue it could be like this.

I opened the door to the backseat and unbuckled my Juni Bee, pulled her sleeping frame into my arms, cherished what I'd been given.

Would never for a second take advantage of it. Forget the magnitude of this gift.

We crossed the shop, and I started up the steps behind Salem where she ascended in front of me.

It sent me back to that night close to a year ago, when she'd been soaking wet, and I had been wholly unprepared for what was getting ready to crash into my life.

The chaotic storm that was getting ready to make landfall.

But sometimes it's the storms that breathe new life.

Salem punched in the code and opened the door, and I carried Juni to her room and tucked her into bed.

Our new house was being built across town, right next to the one Trent and Eden were building for their family.

We had a guest house going up in the back so Mimi would have her own space, but where she could be near, and Salem could stand up and care for her the way she'd always wanted to do. The main house would have five bedrooms, one I hoped one day would belong to Kye.

At Salem's urging and encouragement, I'd taken a chance, bit back the fear, and reached out to Kennedy last month. She'd finally replied two days ago. Her response had been cautious but promising.

Kennedy was living on the east coast. She had remarried and had two more children. Our interactions back and forth over the last two days had been a bit strained, but somehow over the years, it seemed her distrust had lessened, and she'd agreed to allow me to at least write to Kye.

To slowly become a part of my daughter's life.

I would cherish anything I could get.

I leaned in and kissed Juni's forehead, pulled her covers up tight, gave into the squeezing of my chest when she whispered in her sleep, "Night, Daddy."

"Goodnight, Juni Bee."

She might not have been born of my blood, but to me, she was my daughter in every way.

Wholly.

Truly.

Soft hands slipped up my back, and Salem pressed her face to the middle of my spine.

"Love her so much," I rumbled as I turned. I took my wife's face in my hands. "And I love you."

"Forever," she said.

I took her hand and led her out, shifting to walk backward as we went into our room. Only I didn't head for the bed, I led her to the door to the left.

Salem let go of a seductive laugh. "What's this?"

"Wanna paint you." I tapped the code into the pad next to the studio door and opened it to a haze of darkness, pulled my girl into the kaleidoscope of images held in the muted light.

Images that had once represented my shame.

My nightmares.

My dreams.

But it'd taken this woman to help me see that sometimes the mess was beautiful.

Salem kicked off her sandals and padded into the studio. Her breaths were soft and awed. It seemed like each time she went in there, she discovered something new.

Still, she was drawn to the crudely cut image of the boy child.

Her son.

The one I was sure her spirit had recognized the first time I'd brought her into my studio.

She fluttered her fingers over the frantic strokes of paint.

She'd said once she didn't know me. But now, she knew everything.

Every fiber.

Every thread.

All my shame and all my hope.

My wife slowly turned around, wearing the long summer dress she'd worn for the family barbeque this afternoon.

So pretty.

So right.

A fantasy.

My redemption.

I kicked my shoes from my feet and pulled my tee over my head. I dropped it to the floor and moved toward the cans of paint stacked across the room, watching her as I went.

"When is it you feel most beautiful, Salem?"

I repeated the same question I'd asked her all that time ago. Before I'd understood what we meant.

Salem padded forward to the middle of the room.

She got to the floor. A little awkwardly, so fucking cute that it made me lightheaded. Giddy with this joy I never thought I could feel.

She pulled the fabric of her dress tight over her massive, swollen belly where our baby boy grew, and she tipped her head to the side so her jaw was exposed.

Those thunderbolt eyes were open and free.

"When do I feel most beautiful, Jud? Every single time you look at me."

the end

Thank you for reading *Say It's Forever*!
I fell so hard for Jud & Salem, and I hope you loved them every bit as much as I do. If you're hungry for more, head to my website, www.aljacksonauthor.com, for your free bonus scene!

Logan's story is coming soon in *Never Look Back*.

Have you fallen for Jud's brother, Trent?
His story is available now!

Give Me a Reason

Looking for more swoony words to hold you over until then?
I recommend hopping over to read my Bad Boys of Sunder, Bleeding Stars! Start with

A Stone in the Sea

Or if you love another single-dad romance, I recommend hanging out with my small-town alphas!

Start with *Show Me the Way*

Text "aljackson" to 33222 to get your LIVE release mobile alert
(US Only)

Join the A.L. Jackson Book Club
(delivered via newsletter!)
https://geni.us/ALJacksonBookClub

About the Author

A.L. Jackson is the *New York Times* & *USA Today* Bestselling author of contemporary romance. She writes emotional, sexy, heart-filled stories about boys who usually like to be a little bit bad.

Her bestselling series include THE REGRET SERIES, CLOSER TO YOU, BLEEDING STARS, FIGHT FOR ME, CONFESSIONS OF THE HEART, and FALLING STARS.

If she's not writing, you can find her hanging out by the pool with her family, sipping cocktails with her friends, or of course with her nose buried in a book.

Be sure not to miss new releases and sales from A.L. Jackson - Sign up to receive her newsletter http://smarturl.it/NewsFromALJackson or text "aljackson" to 33222 to receive short but sweet updates on all the important news.

Connect with A.L. Jackson online:

FB Page https://geni.us/ALJacksonFB
A.L. Jackson Bookclub https://geni.us/ALJacksonBookClub
Angels https://geni.us/AmysAngels
Amazon https://geni.us/ALJacksonAmzn
Book Bub https://geni.us/ALJacksonBookbub

Text "aljackson" to 33222 to receive short but sweet updates on all the important news.

Printed in Great Britain
by Amazon